Ladies of the Dance

May Mansoor Munn

Ladies of the Dance

Anemone Press
Houston
2013

Anemone Press
Houston, Texas

Copyright © 2013 by May Mansoor Munn
All rights reserved
Printed and bound in United States of America

First Edition
Cover illustration by Jeff Mansoor
Book design by Ann Walton Sieber

Library of Congress
Cataloguing-in-Publication Data

ISBN:978-0-9857832-1-1

Munn, May Mansoor
Ladies of the Dance

16 15 14 13   4 3 2 1

For my mother, Ellen, who raised five daughters, and survived war and occupation with dignity and humor. And for Aunt Aida, whose life inspired both story and setting.

I hope my novel reflects my gratitude, and my belief in the universality of our human longings — regardless of ethnicity, religion, or politics.

Contents

AUTHOR'S PROLOGUE

T HE RELENTLESS RAIN on that January night in 1948 seemed oddly foreboding for a girl recently turned thirteen. Thirteen: a miracle grown-up age, I told myself as I drifted back to sleep.

I was jarred into wakefulness when the window casings in our Jerusalem house came crashing to the floor. The bewildered wails of my younger sisters followed as they sought refuge in our parents' bedroom. But I remained anchored to my bed, listening, wondering. Surely with the coming of morning light I could discover for myself what had occurred?

Early the next day, I stood with our neighbors in silent vigil, and faced the rubble of what, a few hours before, had been the Semiramis Hotel. The hotel, in the Katamon Quarter of west Jerusalem, was only a few blocks from our house. We watched as British soldiers dug through the debris, retrieving what they could of lost humanity. Yet they could not raise the dead, those unfortunate Brits. They could barely wait for their service to the British Mandate over Palestine to end so they could finally go home to a world which was, they hoped, much more sane than this.

And although we, the Palestinian residents of Jerusalem, did not want to abandon our homes and neighborhoods, there were ways to make us leave. Terror in the night was one effective way:

whether in Jerusalem, in Deir Yaseen or places in between.

Soon after the Semiramis bombing by the Haganah, my father, a physician, gathered our family together and shared his apprehensions. Placing guards in our neighborhoods was, obviously, no guarantee for our physical safety. Our family, along with many other Palestinian families, would have to leave Jerusalem. And since my dad still had a medical job with the British Mandate, and was lucky enough to own a car, he would continue to drive to Jerusalem from the relative safety of Ramallah—where we would live for now. His only defense: the medical emblem on the windshield of his car.

In a world of turmoil and uncertainty, fear can be a great motivator. And so our Palestinian exodus would continue: by car, by foot, even by bus—offered by those eager to see us leave. Palestinian families often carried with them whatever savings they had, hidden in pouches in their clothes or belts. Many brought with them the old iron keys to their houses—to prove ownership. Sometimes they buried their dowry jewelry in secret places in their gardens—with the hope of return after violence subsided and peace became a reality in Palestine.

I missed my friends and missed our house in Jerusalem. I missed the *saru* tree that I climbed to the roof—disappearing from the sight of my younger sisters, pretending I'd gone to "heaven." I missed the small ice cream shop my aunt Nabi took me to, just past the checkpoint where she assured English soldiers standing guard that, like me, she was under age and did not need a special pass to go through.

Here in Ramallah, huddled in the shadow of an old stone wall, I took to writing. Nothing spectacular, just small rhymed poems or verses in Arabic and English of sorrow, loss, and heartbreak. At thirteen, I still failed to comprehend the violence of the world around me, and adult answers to my questions remained murky, evasive. Palestinian refugees continued to stream into Ramallah, looking for temporary shelter. Men, women, and children, frightened by violence and war, had abandoned homes in Lydda, Ramleh, and Jaffa, and had sought refuge here. Many camped in UNRWA-donated tents in open spaces around Ramallah—including the empty lot behind our house. They would later leave for more permanent refugee camps where countries like Jordan and Lebanon took them in.

When I stopped at our one-room Quaker meetinghouse, I discovered that nine refugee families had taken shelter there. A cacophony of sound had replaced the disciplined silence. Rags, gunny sacks, and cardboard across the backs of benches formed privacy walls. Families huddled together, babies suckled at their mothers' breasts unaware of older siblings adjusting to benches, to the faces of strangers. As I stood in the doorway frozen in place, parents and children stared back at me—an intruder into their lives.

It was everything, all that happened, that caused the loss of my innocence at age thirteen. I rebelled against the specter of violence, hatred, and fear—the tsunami of human existence. In the written word I discovered my special balm. My ardent hope was that words, both spoken and written, would help ease the burden of our lives and transform our yearnings for a better, kinder world. Over the years, I've written personal essays, poems, short stories, and this novel, in an effort to understand—and explain—this complex land of my youth. It was only after Israel defeated Jordan in the Six-Day War of 1967, and occupied the West Bank (including Gaza from Egypt, and the Golan Heights from Syria), that our family was finally allowed to cross the border and see what had become of our former home in Katamon, west Jerusalem.

We discovered a building transformed into a two-story house where two Israeli families now lived. We introduced ourselves, and explained that we were the former Palestinian owners of the house. One family invited us inside and offered us hospitality; the other family would not talk to us, and quickly closed the door. We were later told that Israel now owned the house; that if we wanted to claim it, we should have paid taxes all the years between 1948 to 1967, when we lived under Jordanian rule.

Ladies of the Dance is a novel, a work of historical fiction, set in a town more like Ramallah than Beit Nuba. I decided to resurrect the name of Beit Nuba, a border town razed by Israel soon after the 1967 war, where my father, with nurse, driver, and medical supplies (lent to him by the Lutheran World Organization), would park the mobile clinic under a shade tree where villagers waited in line for treatment. The Semiramis Hotel, the destroyed Jerusalem hotel that I had witnessed as a girl of thirteen, has also been brought back to life and transported to another setting. This is what fiction has allowed me to do: to bring back to life what has been destroyed, what is still alive and well in my imagination, and in my heart.— M.M.M.

What set things on edge was [Egyptian] President Gamal Abdel Nasser's startling decision to demand withdrawal of the 34,000-man United Nations peacekeeping force that for 10 years patrolled the [117-mile] armistice line between Egypt and Israel....

Israel had never consented to let the U.N. forces patrol her side of the frontier, and for that reason they had been restricted to the Egyptian side....

The New York Times, May 21, 1967

"I do not wish to be alarmist... but in my view, the current situation... is more menacing than at any time since the fall of 1956."

U Thant, Secretary-General of the United Nations, May 1967

CHAPTER ONE

The Letter

HER SANDALS FLAPPING against the pavement, the old woman, *Um* Amin, trudges toward *Abu* Mahmoud's coffee house with the bravado of one who has little to lose. Despite her faded and patched long *thobe* with its sparse embroidery, she moves with an air of careless dignity, her hennaed hair braided and tucked under a black scarf. Her eyes are still sharp, but her bones feel brittle, her legs creak with every step. Nearby, two men at a table on the sidewalk play a backgammon game, the clatter of their dice punctuating the early morning stillness. Her glance moves furtively toward the lone man seated a few meters away, now fingering his prayer beads, his eyes half-closed. Her son, Amin— miracle birth of her later years—has planned this clandestine meeting with Lutfi Abdul Kader.

As she approaches the table, her hooded green eyes slant toward Lutfi's face. She notes the wild disarray of Lutfi's beard in contrast to his pale, chiseled features.

She clears her throat. "What is it you want from me?"

With some flourish, he hands her a sealed envelope. "Hide it in your dress... for safety."

Note: see Glossary p. 320 for translation of Arabic words and phrases.

She snatches the letter from his hand, tucks it into the secret neck opening of her long *thobe*, pats it into place.

"The boy's hearing is impaired," Lutfi begins. "And he's rather slow. But, every morning, just before ten, his grandmother sends him to *Abu* Tarek's bakery to buy fresh bread. Go to the bakery. Then follow him home...."

"Beit Nuba has many hills. My legs may not survive...."

"He lives at his grandmother's house, near the Hotel Semiramis."

"Ah. The Semiramis." *Um* Amin blinks. "I did the washing there years ago. I recall a boy, Omar, a loner, and his younger sister, Alya. She would bring her doll clothes for me to wash...." She smiles at the memory.

"Omar Habeeb now manages the hotel; Alya teaches school." Lutfi's fingers pause over his prayer beads. "Omar tells me the boy likes marbles...."

"Marbles. Yes. I bought some already." She blinks against the early morning sun. "Better I take the bus... or a *service* taxi?"

"The *service* taxi will stop near the bakery."

From his wallet, Lutfi takes out two *dinars* and several *piasters*, places them on the table's edge.

"The price of marbles, and a *service* taxi."

She scoops up the money, tucks it into the slit in her wide *thobe* belt. "You want change back?" she asks, sarcasm in her voice.

Lutfi shakes his head. "Do what you want with the rest."

"Buy a house maybe?" Her laughter comes in spurts, drowns out the clatter of backgammon dice nearby.

A street sweeper pushing his cart beyond the curb comes into view. The old woman's laughter ends abruptly as she waits for the crunch of cart-wheels on pavement to subside.

"Who should get the letter, then?"

"Omar, of course. But, in case he's not there, talk to the boy's grandmother. Ask about the hotel receptionist, Nawal."

"Is she to be trusted?"

"Nawal, yes." A pause. "But Omar's sister, Alya, must not

know of it."

"Ah. Alya. Always getting into things."

He nods. "Alya Habeeb is too frivolous for my taste. Many of her friends are suspect... foreigners among them." He reaches for his coffee cup, drains it dry. "Leave as soon as you can. Be back before dark."

"*Insha'Allah*—God willing."

"This will be a small test for my friend Omar. Also, for you and your son, Amin." Lutfi fingers his beads absently. "For all of us."

She squints against the sun, sighs, a mother's uneasy sigh. Why would Lutfi doubt Amin's loyalty to the Cause? A Cause that sears his waking hours, has become his food and drink?

Dice clatter sharply against the wooden board; the game-box closes with a bang. Loud voices raised in argument cut into her musings.

The backgammon game has been won.

And lost.

"You forgot to tell me the boy's name," she says, impatience in her voice. "What he looks like...?"

"Badri. Eleven years old, but small for his age." Lutfi gives her a quick smile. "With reddish curls... and freckles, like lentils, on his face."

"Badri," she repeats. "Not a bad name for a boy with lentils on his face."

Plaisir d'Amour
Saturday evening, May 1967

THE GUESTS of the Semiramis this evening huddle around the dance floor like moths drawn to a single light bulb. They savor the *arak* liquor and the *mezza* hors d'oeuvres, and allow the music to absorb the ominous voices. But, beyond the frenzy of light and color and the gyrating bodies of dancers, beyond the clustered tables are the black and somber pines.

A privacy of sorts, this table that lies at the edge of the courtyard under the pines where Alya Habeeb and Majed Alami can see and not be seen. A grid of light and shadow through the trellis encases their table, the yellow *turmus* beans, and the Liebfraumilch wine bottle with its blue-clad nun.

Alya glances across the flickering, glassed-in candle at Majed, notes the preoccupation in his amber eyes. His fingers drum on the edge of the table to the tango he has refused to dance with her.

"Can't make fools of ourselves," he'd said earlier as he led her back from the dance floor, his hand on the small of her back—smiling, as if to reassure her that his was a feigned vanity, a mere yielding to decorum imposed on him against his will.

Alya's foot taps restlessly to the rhythms of Hagas's band as she listens, imprisoned, in her chair. In the dance she loses her inhibitions, her secret fears, blots out the questions she dare not ask of Majed—or of herself.

In his brightly lit enclave, Hagas bends over his mandolin, strums a sprightly tune Alya hasn't heard before. Members of the band with 'oud, drum and tambourine play their rhythmic backup to the melody Hagas now plays with special fervor. But on most afternoons, Hagas prefers to play his music for customers at his own Ali Baba Café. There, despite the clicking of dice on backgammon boards and the cacophony of voices, he plays the old tunes, he told Alya once, in memory of his Armenian grandfather, a captain in the Ottoman army—before the massacre.

As she refills her wine glass, Alya wonders what epithet her mother might fling at the image of this "woman in blue" now gracing the "work of the devil."

Alya's glance scans the men and women in the alcoves around the dance floor, settles on Dick Brandon, the British journalist, seated with two other men. If she dared flaunt her will, she'd ask Dick to dance. Dick is fairly nimble on the dance floor—and not afraid to make a fool of himself.

Majed's voice strains above the music. "Sorry I missed you

Thursday. But I wish you had...." He hesitates.

"...warned you I was coming?"

"Not wasted your time." He gives her a level look. "For the last few days I've stayed late recording my programs—in case an emergency comes up." A shrug. "Like a roadblock at the Kalandia airport when the king comes to call."

"Abed was solicitous." Alya reaches for a salty *turmus* bean, and with thumb and forefinger she loosens its skin, pops its kernel into her mouth. "And your sound engineer even offered me coffee."

"I love surprises," Majed had told her six months before, holding her face to absorb her proximity, the reality of her devotion. "And you? Don't you like surprises too?"

"Yes, of course," she had answered—the reply of a woman who, like a sliver of moonstone, is dependent on the sun. For she liked what Majed would have her like, and would become what he wished she were—small price to pay for love's security.

Alya would marry him in an instant—if he'd only ask.

"Whenever I call your house," she says now, "the maid tells me your mother is either in 'crisis'... or too busy to come to the phone. And when I call to the station, Abed either forgets to give you my messages...."

"...Or else ignores the telephone during prayers?" Majed leans back in his chair, gives her a rueful smile. "For Abed, the lifeline to God during prayer takes precedence over telephone lines."

The swell of Alya's irritation is not aimed at poor Abed, but at the elusive *djinn* spirits who conspire against her, keeping her and Majed apart.

"It's been several weeks," Alya says after a while, "since we last met in Jerusalem."

Majed reaches for her hand, caresses its outer shell as if it were an entity all its own. Instead of passion, decorum is the order of the evening, here in this place where all is exposed to the sky.

After days, even weeks, of the celibate life, a craving had taken hold—a yearning for Majed's touch to erase the wilderness of herself. Impulse had propelled her that afternoon, had taken her all the way to Jerusalem.

"My time wasn't completely wasted on Thursday," Alya says now. "On my way there, I dropped by Sari Pappas, and his sister, Julia...."

"Sari knew you were coming to see me?"

"I asked him to give Omar the usual alibi—in case he called looking for me."

Julia was busy painting an exotic bird on a pottery plate when Alya stopped by. But, when paint accidentally splattered on the bird's head, Julia, in a fit of rage, smashed the plate against the wall.

"Broken pottery," Sari told Alya before she left, "is symbolic of my life."

With little time to console Sari, or listen to his woes with Julia, Alya hurried on, arriving at the radio station promptly at 7 p.m.—only to find Majed gone.

Majed now smiles at Alya across the table, but his smile is one he bestows on countless women who come up to him in restaurants and other public places, begging for a special song, or the scribble of his name on paper.

Loving a man like Majed Alami, Alya decides, can erode a woman's confidence and wreak havoc on her life. In her mother's eyes she is *habla*, a dimwit rejecting eligible suitors who offer marriage and security, all that a sensible woman of twenty-seven—and past her prime—could ever hope for, even want. Yet she remains content with eating lentils, a poor woman's dish—barely sufficient to fill her belly, but enough to whet her appetite for more.

❀   ❀   ❀

"In history class," Alya tells Majed, "I give students facts about other people's lives... but am never quite sure of my own. And when I try to clarify the world's past, the thought of you intrudes, and clouds my thinking. And yesterday... in mid-sentence about Danton's trial, I felt like weeping."

Majed moves the plate of *turmus* to the side, leans across the table. He speaks slowly, deliberately, as if Alya is hard of hearing. "Here in Beit Nuba, it's not easy... living in my mother's house, trying to keep my sanity intact."

Only in Room 17, on the second floor of Pensione Al-Ahram in the Old City of Jerusalem, does Majed peel away the layers of decorum he has built around himself. Only then will he admit his need, even his love for her. In their rented room, with its balcony overlooking *Abu* Zaid's Bible Souvenir Shoppe, Majed caresses the birthmark on her right breast and runs his fingers through the untamed hair she loosens from clips and barrettes to please him.

And even after love-making, he does not turn to face the wall, or fall asleep, but talks to her of life and politics.

That last time in Jerusalem, as she lay beside him wrapped in lilac sheets, staring up at a water stain on the ceiling, Majed's voice seeped through her languor, and surprised her with its intensity.

"We've become a shadow people, and our dreams of Palestine have lost their substance...."

The water mark on the ceiling winks down at Alya from its giant cyclops eye.

"...we can't afford to wallow in the past. We must learn to adjust our identities, accept what we've become... and go on from there."

The eye in the ceiling disintegrates, becomes a complex of water veins set in plaster. If the roof isn't fixed soon, Alya thinks in sudden panic, it may collapse and bury us, lying here, wrapped in lilac sheets.

"All we have left are a few stale crusts of bread. Crumbs, even." Majed holds his face close to hers. "We might have to settle for crumbs...."

Her mind refuses the logic Majed offers, rebels against the realities he speaks of. She can't bear to look at the faces of the children in the refugee camps outside Beit Nuba—faces that remind her of her own good fortune—of her own helplessness.

Alya refills her glass, takes a quick swallow. Perhaps enough wine in her blood might dull the sharp edge of her impatience with life's incongruities.

With settling for crumbs.

As Majed shakes a cigarette loose from his Players pack, the diamond on his index finger glints like a signal. His mother's gift to Majed on his thirty-first birthday—with the pledge that he marry within the year.

"Only if I'm pushed into it," he assured Alya not long ago. "And only with good reason."

Alya is not one to "push" Majed Alami into anything—even *with* good reason. She gives love freely, without preconditions, and hopes for love freely given in return.

Majed asks suddenly, "Was your father one to face Mecca five times a day?"

She stares beyond the darkness and the swirls of smoke at the man she's loved these many months—to whom her mother has never been formally introduced. He holds onto his cigarette, careful not to drop ashes into the wine glass as he waits for an answer. Majed's question triggers a long-ago image of her father in his crocheted skull cap facing some corner of the room he considered East.

"When we lived in Jerusalem," Alya says softly, "my father and his brother, 'Ammi Musa, went to *Al-Haram* every Friday for communal prayer. Omar often tagged along."

During those early years in Katamon, the small tiled kitchen was the center of her mother's mornings, where she wrapped grape and cabbage leaves, cored and stuffed green squash, sau-téed the garlic, and browned the vermicelli. And in between the smells of nutmeg and sautéed garlic, her mother sang the old hymns or recited Psalms and Bible verses she knew by heart.

"Soon after we were forced to leave Katamon and came to Beit Nuba," Alya says now, "the ritual of my father's prayers ended, even as my mother's began in earnest."

Alya glances down at the back of her right hand resting on the edge of the table, the delicate veins, almost blue in color, that map out her existence.

Does he love me? Alya wonders now, a yearning in her bones—for certainty.

She says, instead, "My mother wears her orthodoxy like a gi-ant cross around her neck." Alya smiles ruefully. "God, I'd think, would like a reprieve from the prayers my mother hurls at him... day in, day out."

"Prayer, then, means nothing to you?"

Alya meets the perplexity in Majed's eyes and wonders at this interrogation—this sudden interest in her beliefs.

"Prayer, my mother told me," Alya says now, "can soothe the mind, can sometimes ease the pain. But it does *me* little good."

Memories of her childhood, like Petra sand compressed in a bottle, shift, create their own design. Her parents had worked out an uneasy truce in the matter of their "mixed" religion. Omar would be his Muslim father's, to mold, to convince; and her Or-thodox Christian mother would raise Alya as she saw fit.

And almost every Sunday in Beit Nuba, while her mother knelt in her choir pew and chanted prayers of adulation, Alya, age eight or ten or even thirteen, sat wedged between the black-clad thighs of the women who had staked out places on the front row in the church. She listened to the "Kyrie Eleison," breathed in the aromatic incense, and waited for the service to end.

Majed flicks cigarette ashes into the ceramic ashtray, meets Alya's glance. "My mother is also convinced that next to *her* brand of Christianity, all other faiths are heresies perpetrated on mankind by impostors."

Alya braces herself for what she must ask. "I wonder why I'm *persona non grata* at your mother's parties these days."

Majed shrugs. "Her guests are a motley group—you know the kind." He takes his time, blows out smoke rings that disintegrate above his head. "Last week even Clara turned her down. These days, no one discusses the antics in Amman anymore... or tells a decent joke. The topic is politics. Always politics."

Her eyes are intent on his. "So... how do *you* fit in?"

"It's the Beit Nuba code: An unmarried son's first duty is to the woman who gave him birth." He laughs. "Besides, I *live* there...."

Butrus, their waiter, suddenly appears through the trellis archway, his tray poised for service.

"A Chablis this time," Majed says. "And some *tabbouleh* salad would be nice."

"The English reporter..." Butrus hesitates. "He wants to know where Miss Alya is hiding."

"Why should you tell him anything?" A note of resentment in Majed's voice.

"Your Majed-friend thinks I'm a bloody spy," Dick Brandon told Alya after he'd met Majed by chance at the American library in East Jerusalem. "But, in my line of work, I make friends wherever I go—both in Beit Nuba and in Tel Aviv. It gives one's writing an authentic ring, and impresses the chaps back home."

The music eases to a stop, and in its place Hagas's voice fills in with his usual meandering commentary and a few jokes thrown in. He mentions the humble folk who come to his café to savor the *hummus* and *foolyeh* dips, to sip the coffee, and sometimes even to listen—if he's lucky—to his music.

But here at the Semiramis, Hagas says, people come all dressed up in their Western clothes and bring their spouses or friends to drink *arak* or wine, to nibble at *mezza*, to listen to the

Western music and to dance—to show the world that we, too, are created equal, and our women can surpass their own in beauty and in grace—not merely in belly-dancing.

Scattered, self-conscious laughter greets that one.

"The West judges our world by its *own* terms," Hagas says and flutters his pudgy hand to emphasize his point. "We must be *Western* à la mode, it seems, to deserve serious attention." He wags his finger, points it to the floor. "But don't forget, my friends, *this* is the spot that gave the world monotheism... along with advanced medicine, algebra, and the science of the stars. This land is the bridge of civilization, and...," a pause, "...the source of convoluted politics."

Laughter comes in spurts, dies out as Hagas launches into a story about a Turk, an Englishman, a Palestinian, and the American captain of their lifeboat.

"We'll play a game," the captain tells the other three. "It'll be fair and square. But the loser will have to jump overboard—the only way the rest of us can survive."

The American captain turns to the Englishman. "Can you name the British liner sunk by Germany off the Irish coast in 1915?" "The *Lusitania*," answers the Englishman correctly. The captain turns to the Turk. "How many people died?" The Turk thinks long and hard, finally makes a guess. "Over a thousand," he says. "Good enough," the American captain replies. Finally, he turns to the Palestinian, looks him in the eye and says, "Name them."

In the end, of course, the Palestinian is forced to jump.

Even Majed laughs at this one.

Hagas eases himself back on his stool, closes his eyes, waits as the rest of the musicians file back to their places. He bows, then lifts an arm above his head as if to pull down a shade. The band begins to play "Mack the Knife" with gusto.

Alya's extended hand toward Majed is a plea. "Let's dance this one...."

Majed shakes his head, gazes at Alya through wisps of cigarette smoke. "Right now, I've got other things on my mind."

"Then why did we meet here," Alya asks irritably, "instead of Jerusalem...?"

"I needed a little background music to cheer me up." Majed's eyes focus on Alya's face. "And I did want to talk to you about...."

Majed's voice splatters in her head as his words rearrange themselves into tiny glass cups, await her scrutiny. But the music distracts, blocks out their secret meaning. Alya stares at her empty glass as if it held the puzzle of Majed's mind, begins a tattoo on the table in time to the music's beat.

And when Butrus finally returns with the *tabbouleh* (but why did he forget the forks?) and the bottle of Chablis, she pours herself a glass and gulps it down—to ease the throbbing in her head.

"You must give up the frivolities of your life," her mother pleads. "Stop wasting your days and mine. Get married to a decent man and give my heart peace."

Majed brings his chair over to Alya's side; sets it down, rattan sides touching. He drapes an arm across the curve of her shoulders, allows it to rest heavily on the nape of her neck. As the spice of his cologne merges with the odor of cigarette smoke, Alya restrains an urge to reach out and trace the outline of his jaw with her fingertips and feel the familiar indentations beneath the taut skin.

He takes her hand in his and begins to talk to her of duty and tradition and love's insecurity. After a while his cigarette smoke absorbs her thoughts, clings to her face, gives her little room to breathe. Gently, almost imperceptibly, she withdraws her hand from his, and allows it to sink free in her lap.

She drains her glass of wine and feels it scorch her throat. But with the next glass the burning subsides, turns into a glow that courses through her veins, intensifying hunger. The mound of *tabbouleh*—*sans* forks—lies temptingly within reach. Yielding, she dips the romaine lettuce into the dish, scoops up the cracked wheat and parsley, then hungrily licks her lemony, oiled fingers, smacking her lips, avoiding Majed's gaze.

Majed shifts his arm to the back of Alya's chair, takes a drag on the stub of his cigarette before he grinds it down into the ashtray.

This time, as Alya reaches for the wine bottle, Majed's hand clamps down on the bottle's neck. Her right hand forms a fist and slams against the table top, rattling bottle and wine glasses. The candle flares up, wavers. Snuffed out, it trails a streak of gray.

A fly buzzes overhead, black with iridescent green eyes, a darker shade than the dress she wears—worn once to impress Professor Antone in Beirut six years ago. Too risqué for Beit Nuba without a shawl, its lacy back scooped low and the spaghetti straps forming bows above each shoulder blade.

Alya smiles to herself (for who else would understand *this* joke?), picks up the bottle and pours herself more wine in one continuous gurgle that spills onto the tablecloth. She sets the bottle down, tilts her head back and drains her glass. She begins to laugh then, a skeleton rattling inside her woman's skin. Her shawl slides from her shoulders, falls to the ground in a fluffy heap.

A plan begins to form in the recesses of her mind. But the malagueña the band is playing now hammers at her brain, interrupts intricate plotting. She centers her glass over the damp tarantula stain and tries once more to concentrate, to plan her strategy. But what terrible revenge would erase the hammering in her head and bring her back from stupor? She presses her knuckles against her cheeks to ease their burning. If the wine were a little sweeter, she would drain the bottle dry.

But why does Majed look at her so oddly, his eyes narrowed, his lips pressed together like a bit of uneven twine?

She smiles to set his mind at ease, but has no confession of her own to bring them into alliance. She blurts out a timid, unimportant question to fill the spaces of their silence.

"So... who's that lucky girl of your dreams?"

Majed looks up warily. "A history student of yours—at least seventeen. We plan a long engagement, until she graduates next year." His head turns, spins toward hers, like a scarecrow's. "My mother and hers are from the same clan. Third cousins, I think."

"My *student*, then?" Hers, a disembodied voice, floating on ice.

"Her name is Nahida Salim."

Ah... little Nahida, with thick braids the color of ripe wheat—and full of questions. Not about past events and men secure in their graves, but about modern-day politics.

"Does Nahida know and *approve* your mother's plans for her life?"

Majed gives Alya an uneasy smile. "*Her* mother knows. And approves. That's enough for now...."

Enough for what? For whom?

Words shift, retreat behind the rhythm of music from the courtyard. What was Alya's place, then, in the pattern of Majed's life... she who was convinced that to love was *not* to manipulate or coerce into bondage....

She asks, a dimwit, understanding little, if anything, "But how can a grown man be forced to do anything against his will?"

When he finally begins to answer her, Alya recalls the dragon lamp in Majed's room—the black of its ceramic tail, the flame of its tongue wrapped around the lamp's base. She listens now to Majed's voice, seduced by dragon-eyes flashing yellow.

Alya has pondered family character in the portraits in his mother's house. Above the mantelpiece—next to a Madonna statue with baby Jesus in her arms—Majed's eyes, imprisoned in his father's face, stare moodily at the world.

And in the *liwan* front room, a large family portrait of little Majed lined up with other young relatives on both sides of solemn grandparents. Behind them, adult children stand at attention—with Majed's mother leaning forward in a dress with ruffled sleeves.

Weeks before—during a lull in one of his mother's parties—Majed took Alya by the hand down the corridor to his room. "We won't be missed," he said, and kissed her lightly on the neck.

The odor of stale cigarettes and lemon oil had permeated his well-ordered room. On the dresser, next to the dragon lamp, sat a photograph of a two-year-old Majed in monk's habit, clinging to his mother's hand.

He'd nearly died of pneumonia, he explained. But after a "miracle cure" took place, Majed was ordained "monk for a year"—his mother's vow to her priest. To God.

The neatness of his room, Alya suspected, was imposed—like a monk's habit on a small boy. But in their borrowed hotel room in Jerusalem, Majed throws his clothes helter-skelter on the rug, and even tilts pictures on the wall—his own rebellion against the perfect order of his mother's house.

Alya says now, "You must have known all along that nothing would come of it?"

Yet she had hoped, in secret, that something might.

"Love doesn't always mesh with marriage plans," Majed says in his public, well-modulated voice. "As lovers, we were caught up in our own private fantasies."

The music pulsates in Alya's head, tugs, like a kite string, at a dozen questions. She sips her wine, then turns her beggar's face toward his. "What *is* your mother's hold on you?"

He begins to tell her what she already knows: bits of stories grafted onto a war that gouged their lives. In 1946, a sniper's bullet had cut down his father's life. Two years later, when war planes roared overhead, Majed, twelve, ran out to touch the sky.

His frantic mother ran after him, shielding him with her arms as shrapnel ripped into her flesh. Later in the bathroom—with his mother's blood staining his face—Majed heaved his fear and wept tears of guilt.

After the war, refugees swarmed over his mother's yard, trampled petunia and carnation beds, pulled at near-ripe white mulberries. By the time the refugees left for the UNRWA camps, they'd stripped the mulberry tree bare.

"Ever since you came to my room that day," Majed tells her, "my mother's impulse was to fling herself at me, to protect me against...."

"Shrapnel?"

"And you."

Wine, working its way into her blood, dulls the edge of this latest revelation. But her teacher's mind demands logic, demands clear cause and effect. She shivers, holds her shawl against her breasts.

"I suppose," he says finally, "you don't quite fit the image of the future mother of her grandchildren."

And when she asks why, he hesitates, before trying to explain.

She takes a quick swallow of wine, stands up shakily. "You and I need one last dance to celebrate our 'private fantasies,' don't you think...?" She smiles at him without rancor, readjusts her shawl. "I think I'll go ask Hagas to play 'Plaisir d'Amour'...."

But why is Majed's mouth clamped shut, his head tilted to one side, the dragon-eyes staring?

"I won't be long, my love." She gives Majed a quick wave before she makes her way uncertainly through the opening in the trellised wall, past the bougainvillea vine and the vaguely familiar faces. She pauses near Dick Brandon's alcove, smiles at him as he stands up to greet her.

The other two men at Dick Brandon's table push back chairs, and stand, waiting—for what? "Newsmen all," he says in introduction. The one from Amman in opaque glasses momentarily traps Alya's hand in his. The other, with round pink cheeks, bows low. "A genuine pleasure, Fräulein."

"Stay a while?" Dick asks. "Or does Majed lurk in the shadows, counting the moments until your return?"

"Majed can't count," she says. "He prefers..." Readjusting her thoughts, Alya settles down in the chair Dick has pushed her way, fumbles with the drooping strap of her dress.

Her eyes meet Dick Brandon's behind their gold-rimmed glasses, skim over the other faces. She asks, "Any excitement, by chance?"

"Nothing by chance in *this* part of the world," Dick Brandon says. "Uli and I plan to fly to El Arish in the Sinai in a day or two—to view the changing of the guard...."

"Guard?" she asks. Nothing is making sense anymore.

"Surely you've heard? Egyptian troops are taking over from

U.N. troops on the Egyptian–Israeli border...."

She blinks against the bright lights. Why is she expected to absorb everything she hears? First Majed. Now this.

"And we've been invited for lunch with an Egyptian major general on the Mediterranean."

"Why not swim the ocean blue?" Alya sings in her head. "To float, by chance to drown? With waters washing over you...."

"What do Egyptian major generals serve for lunch?" she asks, instead.

Dick, frowning, realigns his glasses. "He wants to show off his Egyptian troops—the ones replacing the UNEF...."

"I'm afraid," the German says, "Nasser's actions do not bode well for your part of the world."

The newsman from Amman turns the angle of his dark glasses toward her. "Nasser's playing a dangerous game. A ploy to regain the leadership he's lost. He told Syria not to worry—that *he* would protect her against Israeli attack. And yet, his troops are tied up in Yemen. Talk is cheap with Nasser. A braggart... that's all he is."

Alya's thoughts race leadenly in place, grind to a halt. She stares into the dark lenses, uneasy with this form of camouflage. Yemen? Syria? Israel? Is it important that she sort it all out?

"It's rather volatile." Dick Brandon's voice parallels Hagas's melody in her head. "U Thant, I'm afraid, should have...."

Is Majed still waiting—thinking, "I've waited long enough?"

"Nasser is trapped in his own rhetoric," the German says. "But what choice did U Thant have? After all, Egypt is a sovereign state and can *demand*...."

"The Israelis won't let it pass...."

"Newsmen must be wily," Dick once told her. "Like gypsies reading palms, they must predict what will happen next. But even gypsies, like me, can make mistakes."

"And naturally Dayan waits in the wings, looking for any excuse," the German says.

"As an Israeli hawk, Dayan...."

The Jordanian's dark disguise holds Alya captive. Their voices mesh above the music, drift in and out of Alya's wavering concentration. This talk of politics has made her forget what she came for, where she needs to go.

Once more to retrieve her shoes and move on. She glances over at Dick Brandon's hand poised over his beer mug in an effort to emphasize a point. What point? She listens distractedly to the brittle English accent with its faint Irish lilt, but after a while the accent disintegrates, replaced by other voices, other accents.

"Breakfast tomorrow then?" The English eyes are slightly blurred behind their lenses. "If you like, I'll even bring you a sample of my aunt's Darjeeling tea."

"Not too early, please." The men rise, nod their heads, and she nods in return. Safer than smiles or waves. Now to make her away toward Hagas.

She waits until the piece ends. Hagas looks up, his wide brow glistening with perspiration.

"Ah, my dear Alya! What can I do for you?"

Nothing in her head except a tune the band played only a week before. She begins to hum the first few bars, straining to recapture the melody.

Hagas beams, claps fleshy hands. "'Plaisir d'Amour?'"

She nods, relieved. "When we come back to dance, I'll give you the cue to begin...."

Hagas reaches for her hand, brings it to his lips. "A celebration, then, for you and Majed?"

"It could be...." A celebration, certainly, for fools.

She turns on her heel and weaves a path between tables, smiling brightly as she makes her way back toward the trellis opening. She stands there, eyes adjusting, as she scans the shadowed area under the pines. Where is Majed hiding? She sees Butrus, the waiter, then, gliding toward her, barely touching earth.

"*Sayyid* Majed asked me to give you this...."

She takes the scrap of paper from his hand, leans against the pine tree to catch her breath.

"Are you all right, Miss Alya?" Butrus asks.

"Why wouldn't I be?" Alya laughs, her laughter brittle on the misty night air. She turns and carefully makes her way toward their deserted table. Majed's chair becomes her own as she extends her legs and lifts her arms above her head, stretching. She breathes in the heady, pine-scented air, fills her lungs with it.

The Chablis remains near the *tabbouleh* dish to keep her company. Two flowered plates, and forks at last. And the glassed candle, its orange flame gasping at air.

A dog-shadow bobs along the pine trunks a few meters away. It stops, angles a leg, then melts into the dark.

As she begins to read the loops and flourishes of Majed's words, Alya pours herself a glass of wine, drinks hungrily, and drinks again. After a while Majed's words fuse with the wine she drinks, are absorbed into her blood.

Rearranging the shawl around her shoulders, she holds onto its fringes for support, and begins to make her way back, past the zigzag of tables toward the still-empty dance floor. Terror dissipates, and in its place a gypsy song revives, begins to work its miracle.

She turns her face toward Hagas and the waiting band. Raising her hand, she gives the signal for "Plaisir d'Amour" to begin.

Poised over his mandolin, Hagas studies her through mournful eyes. She tries once more. The downward and emphatic thrust of her right arm. The music, maestro! If you *please*....

The ragged notes slam haphazardly into each other, scraping at the melody. Once more the signal, this time an imperial command.

The music surges forward, lifting her up and holding her safe. It fills the blank spaces of her mind, propels her effortlessly around the dance floor. She flings her shawl to the floor and, tilting her head, looks up at the pinpoints of a trillion stars. The waltz swirls around her ankles, wraps her in sequins, warms her ice-cold blood.

She is the envy of all those women who gape at her from nearby tables; she turns the heads of their men. No longer the gangly elf with untamed hair, she is transformed into a ballerina—a fairy princess. Light as air, she floats over pine trees and

the red-*karmeed* tile of older houses into the secret places beyond
Beit Nuba.

A hand grasps her arm, disrupts the rhythm of her dance.
Through the shimmer of music and wine she hears a familiar
English accent.

"Better stop, my dear Alya. Omar's on his way."

She wrenches her arm free and holds it stiffly, defiantly,
against her waist. Why should she stop now when the music has
barely begun? She closes her eyes, glides across the dance floor,
grinning secretly to herself.

But the music suddenly dissolves, leaving her stranded on the
dance floor. Humming to herself, she tries to move leaden feet,
but her foot stumbles, a shoe slips off.

This time another hand clamps down on her wrist, fingers
dig into her flesh. As a stab of pain shoots up her arm, she leans
against his shoulder, and holds him up—lest he fall.

She smiles into the scowling darkness of Omar's face. "I was
good, wasn't I? Wasn't I?"

Why won't he answer her?

Badri

BADRI WATCHES furtively as the old woman in *Abu* Tarek's
bakery tugs at her *thobe*. As she readjusts the opening of her dress,
an envelope flutters to the floor. She picks it up and tucks it back
inside her bosom. Badri's glance takes in the outline of sagging
breasts, moves toward her leathery face. Her hands flutter like
trapped pigeons, her lips form words he can barely hear.

The aromas of freshly baked bread mix with the acrid smells
of smoke and burnt wood, enfold Badri like a blanket; smoke
stings his eyes. He blinks at the circles of dough now inside the
oven's belly. Sweat drips from *Abu* Tarek's brow as he maneu-
vers his giant wooden spatula and rescues new, risen bread from
the flames. He pauses as the old woman approaches, leans his
spatula on the oven's ledge, and wipes the sweat from his face

with a corner of his apron. Badri can guess from their gestures and grimaces that *he* is the subject of their talk. "The boy's not too bright," *Abu* Tarek is probably saying, "can barely decipher words and meanings."

But many times he, Badri, can interpret sounds—especially when he focuses on someone's lips. Besides, *Abu* Tarek has never seen Badri flick a marble or throw a stone on target. And only Nawal knows that, in an abandoned shed on the Semiramis grounds, Badri plays his secret marble games and makes kites that soar high above the *saru* trees and tall pines of Beit Nuba.

Badri turns away from the old woman, and extends his coins to *Abu* Tarek in exchange for warm bread. But *Abu* Tarek holds up the palm of his hand. Wait, his hand says. Loaves of bread need my attention before anything else.

Finally, with the bread secure in his cloth bag, Badri slings it across his shoulder, and begins his trek back through the narrow streets of Beit Nuba's old town, toward his house. Near Jad's grocery, a small dog begins to trail after him, sniffing at his heels. He stamps his feet to shoo it away. When he looks back at the dog, he spies the old woman near the welder's shop, trailing after him, tracking him down.

But how can he run away from the old woman when his *Sitti* has etched on his brain: "Walk—never run on sidewalks. And if you run in the street and a car drives up behind you, you may not hear it honk...."

Badri quickens his footsteps, begins his climb past the line of *saru* trees of the Girls' Mission School—the school where Miss Alya, and Clara, the married American woman, teach. Not long ago he caught a glimpse of Clara at dusk in a car with Omar Habeeb. But when he tried to tell his *Sitti* what he had seen, she wagged an angry finger in his face, covered his eyes.

A passion-flower vine drapes the low stone wall of Clara's house on the school grounds. Clara, standing in her yard smoking a cigarette, looks up into the large mulberry tree. Does she hope for ripe mulberries in May? Badri has never seen her husband in their yard, staring up into trees. He's only caught a glimpse of him now and then.

And, although Clara now gives him a friendly smile, Badri skulks by—fearful of the woman's American ways.

Miss Alya and her brother, Omar, live in the Hotel Semiramis, a few meters from his grandmother's small house, where he and his mother, Miriam, live. Every afternoon, Badri climbs the fig tree in his front yard and waves at Miss Alya as she walks by. Often, she waves back. Sometimes, *Sitti*, his grandmother, comes out to sweep, to pull weeds from the garden, to air out her lungs.

But, last week, when Miss Alya passed by and did not look their way, his *Sitti* told him later, in their secret sign language: "Poor Alya Habeeb. Twenty-seven—and still unmarried...."

Badri absorbs his *Sitti*'s comments on other people's lives: small puzzles he mulls over but can't quite figure out.

He glances quickly behind him, and notes that the old woman is inching up the rise in the road, trailing after him like a serpent.

Dodging a speeding car, Badri crosses the street and turns right at *Abu* Abdo's coffee shop onto the main street. Men huddle at their sidewalk tables, their faces intent on the noisy brown box near the open door. With magic power in hidden wires, his *Sitti* has explained, the box can broadcast the voices of Egyptian singers like *Um* Kalthoum or Abdul Wahhab, or it can even give the latest news.

But no one tells Badri the news these days—not even his *Sitti*. "No need to muddle your head with it," she says.

If only he, at eleven, could decipher the headlines that newspaper boys of eight or nine thrust in his face.

The smells of spit-roasted *shawarma* lamb trail after Badri as he makes his way toward Cinema Dunya on the corner. At Hatimi's bookshop, he pauses to stare at the atlas in the display case—open to the map of Africa.

Not long ago, Nawal gave him a book about Africa with pictures of serpents curled around tree trunks; of lions, like kittens, playing in the grass; of fierce-looking men with spears.

Someday, Badri plans to visit Africa and see for himself.

Shifting his bag of bread to the other hand, Badri makes his way uphill past the taxi stand and the flower shop toward the Hotel Semiramis.

Before he takes a right turn toward his *Sitti's* house, he darts a backward glance. But all he sees is a taxi in a swirl of smoke, and children playing tag in the street. He sighs with relief. The old woman is lost, gone astray, turned to dust....

His tall, eagle-eyed grandmother, *Sitti*, with her crinkled gray hair, is waiting for him by the fig tree in their front yard.

On most summer nights, when the dance band in the Semiramis courtyard plays its lively music, *Sitti* mutters curses at those who disturb her sleep. But, with his mother, Miriam, still at work in the hotel kitchen, and his *Sitti* asleep, Badri, restless, steals onto the hotel grounds and, camouflaged by the bougainvillea vine, watches the gyrations of men and women on the dance floor.

Last summer, when Butrus, the waiter, discovered Badri's hiding place, he threatened to tell both *Sitti* and his mother, Miriam—but nothing ever came of it.

Sitti takes the sack of bread from Badri's hand, counts the loaves, then counts the change. She smiles, revealing missing teeth.

Once more he has passed the test.

Scurrying up the fig tree, Badri squints back at the road, but instead of Alya, he spots the old woman moving slowly, deliberately, her *thobe* a black smudge in the road. Somehow, she's managed to track him down, has followed his scent all the way home.

Still as a cat, Badri stretches out on an upper branch, rests his cheek on the back of his hand, and watches as the old woman lowers herself onto the stoop, takes off her shoes and begins to rub her feet. *Sitti* sits next to her, their heads coming together in conspiracy. Badri's cat-form rearranges itself, his eyes focus on the small cloth bag the old woman now takes out from some hidden place of her *thobe*.

Sitti's radar eyes search out Badri in his lair, but this time, the language of her hands entices, becomes a plea.

"A gift," her fingers say. "A nice surprise. Come down and

see for yourself."

Badri jumps, lands in a heap on the ground. He scurries closer to his *Sitti*, watches, wide-eyed, as she pulls open the drawstring bag.

A treasure of marbles, he thinks, and claps his hands with glee. Gurgling noises strain against his throat as he bounds around his *Sitti*, his legs folded like a frog's. When Badri plays his marble games in the Semiramis shed, marbles turn into soldiers and tanks, are transformed into ships. Marbles—better even than ice cream cones.

Sitti's hand clamps his shoulder down, demands restraint. His eyes focus on her face, her hands as they point toward the Hotel Semiramis. "Take the letter to Nawal at the hotel," she tells him. "No one else must know—or see."

The marbles bag sways in front of Badri's eyes. "All this will be yours when you return."

A wordless song forms in Badri's throat. Men and women spin to the drumming in his head; Nawal, who sits at her hotel desk all day, begins to dance. Thoughts clink, like marbles, reluctantly settle in the bottom of the bag.

"It's a good thing Nawal has patience with you," *Sitti* says now, and shakes her head.

When she has time, Nawal shows Badri the shape of letters and words on paper. Badri knows how *his* own name can look, with dots and flourishes. But when he tries to imitate her writing, his words clump together like worms.

Sometimes, he tries to teach Nawal the secret signing words that *Sitti* and his mother know. Nawal has learned, now understands, most of what he tries to say.

Badri crosses the Semiramis parking lot, the letter safe inside his Africa book. Near the bougainvillea vine, he looks over at Omar's dog asleep in the middle of the dance floor.

Sitti's word-gestures echo in his head. "Tell no one about the letter... except Nawal."

Badri plans to return later to the hotel, to show Nawal the marbles the old serpent-woman will give him as a bribe.

The Foreign Affairs and Defense Committee of the [Israeli] Knesset received a briefing Wednesday from the [Israeli] Premier Levi Eshkol, who is also defense minister, and from the military chief of staff, Major General Yitzhak Rabin.... Official circles described Egypt's moves as "predominantly demonstrative acts of political and psychological warfare."

The Christian Science Monitor, May 19, 1967

CHAPTER TWO

Omar and Lutfi

OMAR HABEEB carefully opens the sealed envelope Nawal hands him.

"Meet me in Nablus not later than 10 o'clock Saturday morning," Lutfi has written. "A matter of some urgency...." The scribble of his name is intertwined with the symbol of *Al-Assifa*, The Storm—Fatah's *nom de guerre*.

"Badri brought the letter a little while ago," Nawal says. Her eyes, lined with kohl, bulge slightly in her narrow face. Omar nods, gives her a quick smile.

"Thank you," he says.

And even though he trusts Nawal completely, Saturday morning, when Omar stops at her desk, he mentions his trip to Nablus only in relationship to the luncheon for their Amman guests.

"Much better, I think, to order the special *knafeh* dessert face to face. Our Amman guests look forward to the best Nablus *knafeh.*" Omar adds, as a safeguard, "I might even spend the day. But I plan to be back before dark, *insha'Allah...* God willing. And should Mrs. Brown call...."

"Yes?" Nawal's eyes downcast, an odd quiver in her voice.

"Tell her..." He hesitates. "Just take a message."

Instead of driving his own car, Omar decides to take a seat

in a *service* taxi. These days he drives absentmindedly, his mind preoccupied with politics... and with thoughts of Clara Appleby. Clara, alias "Mrs. Brown," wife of the biblical scholar George Appleby—the American woman he loves with illicit fervor.

In Nablus, the taxi deposits Omar near a spice and *za'atar* shop in the old part of town. The pungent smells trail after him as he makes his way to *Abu* Mahmoud's coffee shop, half a kilometer away.

Lutfi Abdul Kader strides toward Omar with a rolling gait, his beard unkempt, hair in disarray, his head tilted to one side. Thin to the point of boniness, he has the intense, wide-eyed look of a man with a vision—and a Cause. The prophets of old may have burned with the same zeal that now flows through Lutfi's veins, but while they claimed a vision from God, the fire of Lutfi's own inspiration sprang from that early dawn raid at Es Samu, a town ten miles south of Hebron, when Israeli troops in jeeps, personnel carriers and Patton tanks, and with bullhorns blaring, ordered the villagers of Es Samu to evacuate their homes.

While Lutfi, his wife, Amal, and their relatives and friends waited with the rest of the town in the fields and caves beyond Es Samu, demolition teams dynamited their homes—including Lutfi's newly built house—not much of a house by Western standards, with only two rooms, one a living and eating area, the other a bedroom. Two goats roamed the yard during the day, tied to the carob tree at night.

The raid, apparently, took place in retaliation for "terrorist" acts that Palestinians had committed on the Syrian–Israeli border. But the Syrian border was a long distance from Es Samu, and Lutfi, his wife and relatives had never committed terrorist acts against anyone.

The soldiers in this "retaliatory operation" may not have meant to harm Lutfi's goats, or even the Jordanian soldiers who came roaring down from Hebron in trucks and jeeps, too late to defend the villagers of Es Samu.

In the ambush, thirty-seven Jordanian soldiers were wounded, twenty-one killed—the Circassian Ali Baha'uddeen among the dead. Ali was a friend of Lutfi's—an even better friend than Omar Habeeb.

"I knew you'd come, my friend," Lutfi tells Omar now. They embrace, then stand back to survey what the years have wrought.

Twenty-five years ago, in Katamon, Jerusalem, Lutfi and Omar were boys playing games in the street, chasing *Sitt* Hala's cat—chased, in turn, by *Sitt* Hala's broom. Since then, they had gotten together during special holidays, written newsy letters about the changes in their lives.

Until the raid on Es Samu.

Inside the glass front of *Abu* Mahmoud's coffee shop, a platter of *knafeh* with bright orange, syrup-drenched top glistens in the mid-morning sun. Men sip their coffees or *arkeelahs*, play backgammon, their voices drowned by the hubbub of traffic. Omar and Lutfi settle down at a secluded table on the sidewalk *Abu* Mahmoud claims for his own.

"So... how's life treating you these days?" Lutfi asks.

Omar leans back in his chair. "Managing the Semiramis takes a steady hand. But keeping up with my sister takes agility." He heaves a sigh. "Alya is stubborn, and too independent for her own good."

Lutfi gives him a consoling smile. "Some experts tell us we live in the age of women's liberation...."

"Liberation...from what?"

"From the world of men, I suppose."

For Omar, Alya's attitude rankles—her intellect lurking around corners to catch him off guard. Her ingenious twist of argument sometimes defies his own male logic—as if, God forbid, *she* could be right after all.

Omar even sees it in Nawal's thin face turned toward his in deference, a precision of mind that nitpicks at the larger, more obvious truths.

An unshaven waiter, his apron stained, shuffles toward their table, sets before them two demitasse cups and a steaming brass pot of coffee.

Lutfi pours himself a cup, takes a long slow sip. "I hear you're entertaining distinguished guests at the Semiramis on Tuesday," he says.

"An informal luncheon... with a small conference afterwards."

"And *Abu* Mazen will be there?"

"How did you know?"

"I... hear things."

A boy approaches, waves a newspaper at them. "*Addifaa?*" he asks, in a voice made hoarse with calling. "*Defender* paper?"

Omar drops a *piaster* in the boy's hand, then scans the headlines, meets Lutfi's steady gaze. "Our U.N. Secretary-General is off to Egypt to meet with Nasser..." He shrugs. "Does U Thant actually believe he can change things?"

Lutfi gives Omar a rueful look. "Nasser's order to replace U.N. troops with his own is not just meant to impress the Arab world."

Omar sets his cup down, leans across the table. "If war comes, do you know what it'll mean to win? To reclaim Palestine? To return to Haifa and Jaffa and Lydda and Beir-Es-Sabi'... even Katamon?"

Omar's vision hovers between them—iridescent, light as air. Scraps, by way of miracle, might turn feast and fill the empty spaces of his belly.

If only he could make Clara understand. But when he tries to explain, she becomes the reluctant student, wriggling in her seat.

"Nasser's sound and fury signifies very little...." Lutfi says. "The decision for war, my friend, lies in *Israeli* hands."

"But with the latest of Russian arms, and—as champion of Palestinian rights—Nasser can surely win this one...."

Lutfi's fist hits the table's edge, rattling coffee cups. "But why should we depend on the Egyptian president's whims? As Palestinians, we must take charge of our *own* destiny—follow our own leaders...."

"You mean like *Abu* Ammar?"

"And Fatah...."

"Most Arab governments will not tolerate a guerilla group

like Fatah inside their borders," Omar says with fervor. "But at least Syria welcomed Fatah with open arms...."

"But always with strings attached," Lutfi says bitterly. He runs his hand through his disheveled hair, looks intently at Omar. "Do you recall the assassination plot in '66?"

"Last year? I heard rumors...."

"More than rumors, my friend. Some in the Syrian government meant it to be a trap. But through a fortunate error in timing, *Abu* Ammar escaped with his life. And yet...."

"And yet?" Omar repeats impatiently.

"Syria then accused *Abu* Ammar himself of that plot...."

Fragments of what Omar had heard last year ease into place. Syria had imprisoned both *Abu* Ammar and *Abu* Jihad—depicting them as conspirators and traitors.

Then suddenly set them free.

Lutfi now trains his radar gaze on Omar's face. "I have a favor to ask, my friend. We'd like you to deliver a message to Fahd Abdul Nabi—*Abu* Mazen, if you prefer. As assistant to the Minister of Education, he moves in the highest circles in Amman."

"You obviously answer to *Abu* Ammar...."

"I answer to our freedom fighters," Lutfi says quietly, "the *fedayeen* who risk their lives for our Cause."

Envy, like vapor, spreads through Omar's veins, warms him with a steady heat. For the Cause is Omar's as well—branded on his heart since birth. But how could he, as manager of the Semiramis, afford the luxury of a life lived on the edge, a life of sacrifice?

Lutfi smiles a reassuring smile. "We won't ask you to sully your hands, Omar, or endanger your life. The *fedayeen* will do that at a moment's notice. Only if King Hussein refuses our offer...." Lutfi pours himself another cup of coffee, sips meditatively. "I hear you have a storage shed behind the north wing of the hotel...?"

A two-room shed with a broken lock where the boy Badri plays his games. Nineteen years before—for two short weeks—it became home to Omar's family seeking refuge from the fighting in Katamon.

"Your spies," Omar says, "seem to be everywhere."

Lutfi moves his head, his eyes squinting in the sun. "Fatah belongs to the Palestinian people... unlike the PLO—spawned by Nasser in '64—and now under his thumb. Our people work in Syria, in Amman, in Nablus—even in Beit Nuba." He taps soundlessly on the table's edge as if in rhythm with his thoughts. "Injustice can haunt a man beyond the grave," he continues. "For how could I ever forget the pile of rubble—once my home in Es Samu?"

For a moment, the hard, glazed look in Lutfi's eyes turns to mush.

After the raid on Es Samu, Omar did not hear from Lutfi—until now. Had Lutfi gone to Syria for training with Fatah... and *Abu* Ammar?

"Ask Nawal to be on the lookout... since our courier will deliver the letter Monday." A flicker of a smile akin to a smirk appears on Lutfi's face. "You're a lucky man, Omar. A woman like Nawal will do almost anything for the man she loves—if he but ask."

Omar forces a smile. "Your spies are misinformed... where Nawal Abdo is concerned."

"Have it your way." Lutfi drinks his coffee in one final gulp, sets his cup down. He glances at his watch. "It's past noon, and my wife, Amal, expects us at the house for lunch."

Before they leave, Omar orders a fresh *knafeh* dessert tray for special delivery to the Semiramis on Tuesday morning. As they drive in silence in Lutfi's dented Fiat, Omar considers Nawal's mixed assets. Conscientious to a fault, she reports in detail what Omar would sometimes prefer not to hear. Yet, whenever Clara calls, Nawal relays her cryptic messages with guarded discretion. A good thing.

Lutfi's wife, Amal, greets them at the door of their small house, her hand resting lightly on the dome of her stomach. She aims a radiant smile at her husband, then turns a more formal gaze toward Omar.

"Please, come in. Lunch is ready," she says with a nod. Her pink face reminds Omar of Alya's childhood doll that, in a fit of temper, he once flung in the yard, that his mother had forced him to retrieve.

Amal brings a platter of rice, and Lutfi carries aromatic lamb and green-bean stew to the table. As they pass food around, Amal inquires about his mother's health, about his sister, Alya.

"Have you read *Al-Ahram*'s latest headline?" She turns a worried face toward Lutfi, "that 'war is inevitable'?"

Lutfi shifts uneasily in his chair. "Why worry about headlines meant to sell papers, and nothing else...?"

"I worry for our child... for the children of the world." She turns her troubled glance toward Omar. "But why didn't U Thant stall for time before he ordered U.N. troops removed?"

"U Thant had little choice," Omar says. "Sinai, after all, is Egyptian land."

"As a girl of eleven in '56," Amal begins reflectively, "I heard men talk. President Eisenhower, my father said, stood firm against the invasion of the Suez." Amal's small, ringed fingers draw diagrams in the air. "I only hope President Johnson will keep war bottled up in its genie bottle...."

"Both East and West have trained their generals and armed their clients to the hilt," Lutfi says, cynicism in his voice. "So, if war *does* come, the common man—along with women and children—will bear the brunt of it...."

Color drains from Amal's cheeks. "Let's not think of it...."

In the tiny living room, they sip *hale*-scented coffee, nibble at *baklava* sweets, and banish politics and war from their conversation. Talk drifts, instead, to the dreaded topic of marriage in Beit Nuba.

"A real marriage," Lutfi says, "takes into account traditions and family, and lasts a lifetime—unlike marriages in the West."

Talk of marriage depresses Omar, puts him on guard. In Beit Nuba—as well as Nablus—"personal" life is in the public domain—to be analyzed and dissected at will. Omar smiles warily, spins out an excuse about work and busy-ness and the lack of suitable mates. As Amal sips her coffee, her skeptical glance weighs Omar's evasive comments.

But how can he speak freely, even to good friends, of love's passion—of Clara Appleby?

Although, at age thirty-four, Omar prides himself on logic, his other self wallows in a world of miracles, where dreams take on the smooth, crisp lines of reason. For love, his mother has told him often enough, is a delusion reserved for the very young. For fools. But marriage, pragmatic and independent of love's passions, is a duty that gives shape and stability to one's life.

Amal shifts her gaze to her husband's face; sighing, she pats the flowered apron over the bulge of her stomach. "Why not spend less time on politics... and taking risks?"

Lutfi reaches for his wife's hand. "That day will come. *Insha'Allah.*"

When Lutfi offers Omar a ride to the Nablus taxis, Omar says, "I need to walk, to clear my head of cobwebs."

In parting, he thanks Amal for the meal, and in reply to her remark about the "*positive* aspects of marriage," he answers, "It's all in God's hands....," the ultimate answer for all well-meaning suggestions.

Omar walks away, his compact frame thrust forward, his Roman nose raised slightly as if to test the air. Restlessness, like splinters in the flesh, eggs him on past the shops and humanity in the crowded *souk* toward *Abu* Mahmoud's coffee shop, two kilometers from Lutfi's house.

A donkey's braying drowns out the honking of passing cars. Car fumes mix with the aroma of fresh-baked goods as Omar makes his way to a secluded table on the sidewalk. He orders hot minted tea from a tall and skinny waiter, then settles back to absorb smells and sound—to block out thinking.

But thoughts continue to intrude as he reviews what he's promised Lutfi to do: to deliver a clandestine letter, and, if need be, to allow Lutfi the use of a storage shed on the Semiramis premises. But no one expects him to be a *fedayee*—ready to sacrifice his life for Palestine. He doesn't expect it of himself.

As afternoon melts into dusk, Omar sips the sweet minted tea, and watches cars weave their noisy paths through a humanity taking risks.

An intense longing for Clara propels him back to the last *service* taxi leaving for Beit Nuba that evening. One of seven passengers, he wedges himself into the back seat of an old Mercedes taxi, between the car door and a rotund man in a business suit.

As the taxi winds its way outside Nablus toward the Beit Nuba road, the rotund man to his left—oblivious of government spies—launches a tirade against the Jordanian monarchy. And despite a cacophony of arguments, Omar drifts off to sleep, wakes up when the taxi driver announces their arrival at the Beit Nuba Manarah Circle.

After the other passengers disperse, Omar pays the extra *piasters* for the private drive to the Hotel Semiramis. His dog, Asmar, waits at the gate, and Omar squats down to pet his fur, to look into the mournful eyes. Hagas's band is playing the last stanza of a Fairuz song of love gone astray. As guilt washes over him, he breaks off a red silken flower from the cactus nearby—a peace offering for Nawal.

When Omar walks into the front *liwan*, he finds Nawal on the telephone, her voice straining against the music. "Yes sir. You say you'll come with Miss Madding to lunch Tuesday?" Color seeps under her gold-rimmed glasses. "One room, or two? I *must* know by early Monday."

Her navy dress, with its lace collar, gives Nawal an air of fragility, as well as decorum. She takes the cactus flower Omar offers, gives him a quick, grateful smile.

"Both Jaleel Hawa and Miss Madding confirm they'll be coming to the Tuesday luncheon." An ominous pause. "They might even spend the night."

The television producer from Amman, Jaleel Hawa—once a classmate of Alya's—has visited the Semiramis many times before—but never on business, and rarely alone. His love life is fodder for gossip in Amman. And even here, in Beit Nuba.

"Have you heard from either *Abu* Mazen or Madam Jaber?"

"Yes. They send greetings. They will also come."

Omar asks abruptly, "Anything else...?"

"The couple in Room 24 left in a huff—furious that the dancing began early this year. Since the music had kept them awake half the night, they had overslept and missed the early bus tour to the Dead Sea and Hisham's Palace in Jericho.

"In a fit of rage, he flung his room keys against the window pane, breaking the glass, and losing the keys." Nawal adds under her breath, "Such a beast of a man..."

Omar flinches. Men throwing tantrums, breaking things, fill women like Nawal with dread. On a few occasions, Nawal has even witnessed Omar's *own* anger on display.

Nawal's eyes lift modestly to Omar's. "Mrs. Brown called."

"Yes?"

She fingers the lace on her collar. "She left no message."

"A courier will deliver an important letter Monday," Omar says abruptly. "Let me know the moment it arrives."

"Yes," Nawal says under her breath.

As the band begins to play a lively Spanish melody, Nawal's face takes on the look of a mystic at prayers. Keys and broken windows and calls from "Mrs. Brown" seem erased from her memory.

And how can he think of the alleged "Mrs. Brown," in this public place, with Nawal looking on? Only in his room sealed from the world can he grasp the covert reality of Clara in his life.

Before Omar turns away, Nawal says, almost as an after-thought. "Your monthly letter from Brazil came today. I slipped it under your door."

Omar's second-floor room with its small balcony overlooks the courtyard where the band often plays. Sometimes, after revelry ends, Omar steps out on his balcony and gazes beyond the lemon tree and the misted hills of Beit Nuba toward Jerusalem in the south, and the faint thread of light he's convinced is Katamon.

But now, in his room, Omar picks up the lilac envelope and contemplates the words *República Federativa do Brasil* stamped crookedly above his name. The writer: Milady, his uncle's widow, and owner of the Hotel Semiramis.

Milady's sentences form erratic patterns on lilac paper. "I often think of your Uncle Tawfeek," she writes in curves and flourishes, "how he used to be, how he became—his mind glazed over, holding onto that deck of cards—as if to life itself. But El Asfouriyeh hospital in Beirut was not too bad a place for a senile old man...."

He reads the letter as he would a news report, skimming words and sentences, looking for clues. Old ghosts revive, seep through unguarded cracks—"refugee" burnt deep into skin and bone.

"...Surely you recall how your uncle took you in—out of Christian charity. You, a ragged boy of fourteen, and Alya, only eight. You were his sister's family, after all, even if the faith of your poor father was..."

The word "Muslim" erased—like an unwanted blemish on his skin?

"Have you begun the outdoor dancing yet?" Anxiety in her scribbles. "The dancing certainly draws the crowds. And helps pay your uncle's debts."

And in the end, profuse regards to his mother, *Um* Ramzi, and to Alya from Milady, her sister and her nephew, Usama....

And a plethora of gratitude to Omar, who mails his uncle's wife in Maceió, Brazil, several checks a year, and a careful accounting of the Semiramis business.

If Omar could recreate the past, what words would he choose to march, like toy soldiers, on the edge of the precipice? He gets up, moves restlessly around his room, pausing to contemplate the parchment on the wall above his desk, to read the black-scripted words.

"Allah is the Light of the Heavens and the Earth. Allah is....

Sadaka Allah ul-'atheem.... God, the Great, speaks only truth...."

Each day at dawn, Omar chants the words with fervor, as if in hearing his own voice, he will become convinced.

"*Hayyou 'ala-assalaah...*" "Wake up for prayer..."

At the break of dawn the *muezzin*'s voice calls all Believers to prayer in Holy Jerusalem. Through the keyhole of his father's bedroom, Omar, the boy, watched his father mouth the sacred words as he held his hands against his waist, then to his knees, touching forehead to prayer rug, standing, bending low, and kneeling again. Facing Mecca.

On Friday, their holy day, father and son visited *Masjid Al-Aqsa*, where the faithful listen to the sermon and perform the rites of prayer. And there, a young Omar, crouching near *Mihrab Ali Pasha*, would look up in awe at the Golden Dome of the Rock.

But somewhere during their forced move to Beit Nuba, Omar's father lost his faith in a merciful and compassionate God. And as he became a man, Omar came to know little of God, less of himself.

Life, Omar thinks now with a pang of envy, is simpler for men of faith or for those who accept as kismet whatever comes their way.

He turns on the radio for the latest news from Cairo and hears, instead, the husky voice of *Um* Kalthoum, the Egyptian singer, fill his room with "Ya-Lail...," her song of the night, drowning out Brazil and politics.

"Ya-Lail..." seeps into his blood, revives his yearning for Clara.

Last week, Clara gave him a silver tie clip he now keeps in the olive-wood box on his dresser. He picks it up, tests its weight in his palm, savors the gleam of polished silver. Squinting, he rereads the English lettering—meant only for his eyes.

"For the fun times, Clara."

Clara. A name that conjures up a secret part of his being. When away from her, Omar reminds himself that Clara Appleby is neither *djinn* nor *afreet* from the nether world, but flesh and blood. He thinks of her now: teal-blue eyes, hooped earrings against the plump line of her jaw, her warm talcum smell, her laughter that unravels, at least for a little while, the tangle of himself.

He turns off the lamp. Slivers of light through the shutters lance the darkness of his room. He holds open the slats, and looks out beyond the lemon tree at the dancers in the courtyard below. In the eddy of color and motion he catches a glimpse of Alya in a blur of green. But he can't quite make out the man with her. Is it the Englishman, Dick Brandon? Or Majed Alami, the man from the Jerusalem radio station? But with the kaleidoscope of whirling bodies, it is impossible to tell. An arranged marriage in her teens, Omar decides, would have given him a break from worry over Alya's antics.

As Hagas's band changes tempo and begins to play a popular tune by the singer Sabah, Omar's heart lifts and despite his earlier resistance, he gives in to the strains of the melody.

Last Wednesday in their hideaway above Hagas's café, Clara offered to teach Omar to dance.

"When I was growing up," she confided, "we couldn't dance, or drink, or chase after boys. They tried to convince us those were 'lustful workings of the devil.' But this gal got liberated just in time...."

Omar was yet to be liberated from the terror of the night when, pressed against the sky, he cried out and no one heard his voice.

He begins a pantomime of the waltz, his arms sculpted into a parody of an embrace, and moves with measured steps between bed and bureau and the narrow desk where the bird clock casts an elongated shadow on the wall. He thinks of Clara in his arms and tries to believe that grace and elegance do not matter in the spirit of the dance.

His mother's voice reverberates with her knocking at his door. She knows he's in there, hiding from the world. From her.

When he unlocks the door, her watery eyes blink up at him from a pale and sagging face.

"How do you expect me to sleep with that... that noise?"

She points toward the balcony, spits out the word as if it were an olive pit. "And where's your sister at this hour when respectable young women are safe at home, sleeping in their own beds?"

Using well-worn phrases he's used before, Omar tries to soothe his mother's fears. He drapes an arm around her shoulders and steers her back through their joint parlor, past the caged canary and the supine body of Bisseh the cat, back to her room.

At her door, she shrugs his arm away, wheels around to face him. "My brother, Tawfeek, would have never allowed this... this debauchery from the West." A tremor courses through her frame, her voice becomes a fierce whisper. "Ever since she went to study in Beirut, Alya has made a mockery of tradition. Life, for her, is a farce... a comic Juha tale...." She heaves a sigh. "God forgive your father for sending her to college in Beirut. But this, he insisted, is a modern age where educated women can better fend for themselves." A cynical laugh. "As if marriage—a woman's security—means nothing. Nothing at all."

Retreating into her room, she gazes reverently at the wooden cross on the facing wall. Essa, or Jesu the Christ, in agony on the cross; the same golden Christ that hangs from a chain around her neck, to ward off the evil of the world, to give her strength.

She adds, bitterness in her voice, "Men are unimpressed with a woman whose head is filled with book-knowledge and radical ideas. But, what good is art and history to a man who wants a good meal, a clean home—and children?" She looks down dejectedly. "If only she'd married Usama, Milady's nephew from Brazil... But your sister," she adds scornfully, "insists on a man of her *own* choice."

Her glance moves furtively past the Bible and the pillboxes on the stand next to her bed, toward the faded photograph of a smiling, tow-headed boy: Omar's older brother, Ramzi—who died soon after his third birthday.

She picks up Ramzi's photograph and holds it against her sagging breasts. Her old grief, tightly coiled inside her, breaks loose once more.

Her hand grips Omar's arm. "God's punishment. To take my

beautiful firstborn, my Ramzi. To break a mother's heart."

A year after Ramzi's death from pneumonia, Omar burst into his mother's world: small and dark with sinister eyes and a restlessness, she claimed, that drove her to distraction. And in Beit Nuba today, over thirty years after his brother's death, his mother is still called by his dead brother's name: *Um* Ramzi, Mother of Ramzi.

His mother's voice once more pries him back from his musings.

"Look at you, thirty-four, and still unmarried." She shakes her head as if the thought is too much to bear. "Isn't there a woman good enough for you?"

"But why not Nawal?" she continues. "At 26, she may be past her prime and too skinny for my taste, but we know her background, her origin, and her mother is a good woman. And what about grandchildren to hold, to play with—to watch over me in my waning years?"

Um Ramzi's voice, a spider's web, closes in on him. Omar has little energy left to answer her, and even if he tried, she would understand little, if anything.

Back in his room, Omar finds the loud *dabkeh* folk music a relief from the pleadings of his mother's voice. The music vibrates against the closed window panes, reminding him he has yet to make his usual rounds among hotel guests—as he does each evening.

Omar steps out onto his balcony, and camouflaged by the lemon tree, he looks down at the courtyard, his hands clenching and unclenching, deep in his pockets. A lively tango has replaced the *dabkeh* music, thinning out the crowd on the dance floor. He catches a clear glimpse of Majed Alami holding Alya a little too snugly, his face buried in the dark flame of her hair.

His chest tightens. How long will Majed Alami court his sister without commitment? How long will she allow it?

Omar's protective instinct ejects a buried image of his youth. In shoes frayed and thick with dust, he runs ahead of his parents, sister, and hordes of other refugees, toward a remnant of a

Roman arch that will shelter them for the night. Snug under his arm, the game of kings and queens, gift from his uncle, *'Ammi Musa*, on Omar's birthday.

Alya, eight, scrambles after him, trips and falls, bloodies her knee.

His father's voice cuts short his momentum. "Hold onto your sister's hand, you hear? You're a man now. You have no time for games."

At thirty-four, Omar plays his games in secret. His public image—affable, coolly rational—belies the passionate contradiction of himself.

Only Clara can respond to the beggar who comes knocking at her gate. If only he could give her something, besides himself, that she wouldn't throw away. Or lose.

Earrings would please her, he thought once. Vermicelli-layered golden hoops, twisted and held together by a rosebud clasp.

"What do you take me for? Your harem girl?" Clara said. She faced him, one leg tucked under, the other swinging toward him like a pendulum, unshod, toenails bright pink. "If hubby only knew where these came from!"

In the courtyard, musicians announce a break. In his room, Omar studies the faded photograph of a teenage girl standing primly by a white picket gate, a ribboned poodle in her arms. In those long-ago days, that younger Clara did not smoke cigarettes or wear earrings or paint her toenails pink. She had not yet travelled to distant lands or learned to break the rules. *That* Clara once sang "Amazing Grace" at a revival meeting, bringing the town atheist to his knees.

That's what she told him not long ago.

Except for the tie clip, Omar keeps Clara's other presents in the upper drawer of his dresser—along with his father's old shotgun.

The gun, relic of an earlier age, lies cradled among the assortment of Clara's gifts—ties, scarves, a cowboy shirt—as harmless as a toy. On their forced trek to Beit Nuba, his father took aim at a bird in flight, barely nicked its tail, yet brought it down intact. The pigeon, roasted on an open flame, became their meal that day.

Omar holds up a clip-on tie against his shirt, grimaces at his image in the dresser mirror.

Even in his childhood pictures, Omar's eyes, deep-set, brooding, focus on a hostile world. No wonder his mother could not bear his taking the place of Ramzi, her other, bright-eyed son.

When the music resumes, Omar returns to the balcony. In the pool of light a lone figure glides across the dance floor in an elliptical curve, one arm extended, the other dangling at her side. Adjusting the jalousie, Omar scrutinizes the figure in green, in her solitary dervish dance.

Like mechanical monkeys in their suits and frilly shirts, Hagas and his band continue to play their music—as if to egg Alya on.

For a moment the branch of the lemon tree blocks his vision. But the sprightly music lubricates Alya's movements, conjures her back into view, her green dress a blur, her hair a tangle across her face.

Rage sweeps over Omar like a sudden fever. What demon goads Alya into making a spectacle of herself?

He takes in the flare of lights, the huddle of men and women at its periphery. But a crescendo of melody pulls him back into the vacuum of light, revives his boyish dread. He stares at the barrel of his father's gun aimed at the bird; watches as bird spins against an azure sky, trailing a curlicue of light to earth.

He thinks now: a blast of gunfire into the lemon tree would stop the ritual of Alya's dance. Would bring her back to earth.

Washington, noting continuing Syria–Israel and Egyptian–Saudi tensions, has reminded the nations concerned that if aggression occurs the United States will go straight to the UN—and that it also reserves the right to use force to keep the peace.

The Christian Science Monitor, May 19, 1967

Egyptian Major General Sa'ad Shazly, trained at Fort Benning, invites Western reporters to luncheon at the terrace overlooking the Mediterranean. Egypt flies Western newsmen up into Sinai to show them the armed array at El Arish....

The New York Times, May 20, 1967

CHAPTER THREE

To Crash a Party

BEHIND ALYA stands the guillotine etched against the sky. A man kneels, grinds his face into hers, and Alya, unclothed, is pinned to the ground. Burning eyes test the amalgam of what she is; pass judgment on her life. Children weep for her shame.

Her mother's voice inserts itself into her dream. "If you and Omar *must* quarrel, why choose the middle of the night when decent people are asleep?" The muffled voice repeats the familiar refrain. "Only prayer gives me strength to bear my cross, to be purified from sin...."

But the early morning sun balks at purity as opaque light filters through the Indian silk curtains, displays its patterns on the rug. The useless clicking of Alya's doorknob punctuates her mother's wails.

Alya huddles under bedcovers, tries to erase dream-images pressed against her skull. Shivering, she holds the satin edging of her blanket to her wounded cheek, leans back against the damask pillows, slowly opens her eyes.

On the facing wall hangs her sketch of a man and woman in profile, nose to nose; the man's eyes fiercely burning, the woman's glance downcast, weighted by love.

When her mother's footsteps finally retreat, Alya throws off her bedcovers, stretches like a cat. She gets up, and, holding onto the dresser for support, she leans toward her stranger's face in the mirror. The tie clip's sharp edge in Omar's hand had certainly left its mark.

Averting her face, she unzips the dress she still wears, tosses her clothes in a heap near the bathroom door. As she steps into the shower, a blast of cold water turns her skin to ice. When warmer water finally comes, she stands, chastised, her arms folded across her breasts, and waits for heat to wash away the residue of pain.

Afterwards, wrapped in terrycloth, she sits at her desk and decides to reactivate her plan, and as the melody of "Plaisir d'Amour" begins to unravel in her head, her slippered foot, revived, begins to dance. And even when Jamila's voice interrupts her thoughts, the melody, though fainter now, persists.

"Your Englishman, he waits at the veranda," Jamila says through the bedroom door. "Your tea, he says, is getting cold."

"Please. Give me a few more minutes...."

From her armoire, Alya chooses a navy skirt with a flowered gypsy blouse. She brushes wet, unruly hair, secures it with a mother-of-pearl clasp and touches coral to her wounded cheek, for camouflage.

When she finally makes her entrance, Dick Brandon smiles broadly, drops his newspaper to the floor, and reaches for her hand.

"Behold! A new woman," he says. "Sedate, even." He winks. "Looks as if you've recovered from last night."

"Last night seems like a blur," Alya says as she takes a facing seat. She looks past teacups, and thick pita bread and olives and Syrian white cheese, at pink African violets in earthenware pots on the veranda ledge.

"I've read the paper twice. The second time—between the lines," Dick says. "You came just in the nick of time." His longish hair and the glow of his morning face belie his middle age—

as if in the night an outer skin was shed.

"If I were you," she says, "I'd give up journalism and settle for an uneventful life in the English countryside."

He shrugs. "The English countryside might begin to interest me only when I'm 95...." His eyes behind their gold-rimmed glasses scrutinize Alya's face, her cheek. "Did your brother shoot to kill or was it just a warning shot?"

She smiles wanly. "I did the unforgivable in his eyes. I made a spectacle of myself."

"And in revenge, he slashed your face?"

Alya smears marmalade on bread, looks back into the perplexity of Dick's face. "It was an accident. I'm sure he didn't mean to...."

The screen door swings open and Jamila appears, teapot in hand. Short and rotund, with a creased elfin face, she shuffles toward them, sets the steaming teapot on the rattan table. As Miriam's junior aide-de-camp, Jamila takes orders with skepticism, moves at her own pace.

Dick pours tea for both of them, offers Alya the flowered cup with the fluted edge. She takes a long, slow sip. "I'm sure you did your best last night to keep Omar at bay...."

"All I said was 'Go easy on her, old chap.' No heroics, I'm afraid."

"Poor Omar." Alya's thoughts ratchet slowly into place. "So what plans do you have for today?"

"To visit a good friend in Tel Aviv. But since that's impossible, I'll stay on *this* side of No Man's Land and get ready for my Sinai trip tomorrow."

"I didn't know you had friends in Tel Aviv?"

"Also in Rome and Istanbul. And even here, in Beit Nuba."

"Nawal thinks you're a British spy," Alya says with a smile. "So does my mother."

"And what do *you* think?"

She reaches over, pats his wrist. "How about a secret agent of some sort?"

"Why not? I've always coveted a little intrigue in my life."

"Lucky for you... intrigue and excitement lurk right here in Beit Nuba." Alya reaches for a black olive, for another sip of tea. "This evening, Madam Alami is giving her monthly bash... and I haven't been invited."

"Majed's mum?"

"One and the same. Her Serene Highness 'Let them eat crumbs' Marie."

"You've had a falling-out?"

"So it seems...."

Dick Brandon readjusts his glasses, as if to clarify his vision. "A falling-out... with both mother and son?"

"I'm afraid so...."

"Ah!" He sits up in his chair, eyes her skeptically. "You plan to crash her party tonight, I presume?"

She grins at him. "But only with a little help from an English friend."

"Does Majed suspect your plans?"

"You're the first to know." She grins. "In college, I once played a convincing Nora Helmer in Ibsen's 'A Doll's House.' The reviewers were quite impressed."

"Aha! A woman of many talents." He meets her gaze. "And you want me along?"

"...as friend and witness...?"

Alya begins to laugh; as if laughter rattling teacups could dissolve humiliation, even despair. But this woman scorned is a woman to be reckoned with, and pressed against the wall, she's likely to stick out her foot and trip the culprit as he passes her by.

Mischief flickers from Dick's eyes. "I've crashed other parties before—for political, even personal reasons. So, for tonight, I'm all yours...."

"But tomorrow, you're off to other adventures?"

"I'm flying from the airport in Kalandia to Cairo, and on to Sinai and El Arish." He adds reflectively, "After Sinai, I'd like to stop in Gaza to interview Shukairy of the Palestine Liberation Army." He leans back in his chair, rubs his palms together. "And if I'm lucky, I might try to wangle a tête-à-tête with Nasser—especially now, with Egyptian troops at the Straits of Tiran."

"Never a dull moment...."

His facial lines deepen. "Haven't you heard? Israel has called up its reserves and is beginning to mobilize."

Alya props her chin in the palm of her hand, asks solemnly, "Do newsmen have their own prejudices, and do they secretly take sides?"

He hesitates. "We try to tunnel through the mire toward what *seems* to be the truth. And we try not to be distracted by rhetoric—from *either* side."

When they last studied the unification of Germany, Alya's student, a bewildered Nahida Salim, had asked, "But how could a state like France fall so easily into Bismarck's trap?"

"Rhetoric, I'm afraid, can galvanize a nation," Alya says now. "Can cause a war or two."

Dick Brandon's voice sounds like an echo from the past. "War is an infection in the blood," he says, cynicism in his voice, "a kind of disease that must run its course..."

The meshed sunlight no longer drenches violets, has moved stealthily toward the table's rim. Alya sips her tea, grown cold, and ponders incongruities.

The Party

THE SHUTTERED FACADE of the old Barclays Bank stands guard over the town center, known as the Manarah Circle—and the old lamp clock, always twenty minutes late. Alya and Dick Brandon walk toward the road veering south from the circle's hub, make their way past a line of *saru* trees. They pass an alley where a cat, crouched on a garbage can, swivels its head and stares at them from chatoyant eyes; and as they approach, it scurries into the shadowed dark.

Alya tries to keep pace with Dick Brandon's long-legged stride, her heels clicking on the flagstone sidewalk. A heady bravado—the fatalism of a bullfighter in the ring—triggers a six-year-old memory of a Sunday afternoon, of the stench of sewers from the Sabra and Chatilla refugee camps outside Beirut.

A lover's quarrel had brought her there from the American University, to walk, to sort out the tangle of her life. She'd watched a boy of twelve dance before a goat with horns in the makeshift arena of an empty lot. Teasing it with the skinned point of a stick, he had egged it on with the flag of a lost homeland. Men, women and children gathered to watch, oblivious of the oppressive heat, of the stench that hung like a murky vapor overhead—grateful for entertainment on a Sunday afternoon.

"You look smashing, my dear," Dick says now. "That wrap, and your hair in a chignon—give you a positively *regal* look."

"'Smashing' is good enough," she says, smiling.

Would Majed recognize the wrap and the linen dress he gave her almost a year ago?

Would he even be there?

An impressive line of parked cars winds its way from the Alami house past the *saru* trees down the sidewalk. In the brightly lit patio of the Alami home, men and women cluster amid ferns and potted flowers, laughter occasionally perforating the hum of voices. A dog barks, and Alya recognizes the nervous yap of Madam Alami's dog, Shushu.

"Not too late to change your mind," Dick says, at Alya's elbow.

Alya laughs. "And risk turning into a pillar of salt?" Unlatching the gate, she steps into the garden, inhales the scent of the lavender bush, waits for fear to subside.

They walk up the steps leading to the glassed-in patio. An older couple interrupt their animated talk to look their way, to nod before turning back to their conversation. Two men sipping the alcoholic *arak* drink stalk each other in their rattan chairs, their voices raised in argument.

"Jordan's king," the older man says, "lacks backbone. Why is he afraid to declare solidarity with Nasser?"

"Be careful of what you say," the younger one warns. "Or you might end up like the known *Baathists*—in a prison cell."

He leans forward, whispers something in the older man's ear. The other heaves his shoulders in a massive shrug, drains his *arak* dry.

Near the door, a lanky young man in glasses says, loud enough for Alya to hear, "Would you believe eighty-two consonants and only three vowels in the Ubykh language?"

"It *deserves* to be extinct," his companion replies.

Inside the *liwan*, a pall of cigarette smoke, like fog, hangs over men and women standing in clusters around the *mezza* hors d'oeuvres tray. Loud voices spill out from the formal living room, beyond the *liwan*, absorb quieter conversations. Heads turn, eyebrows lift, as Alya and Dick Brandon make their way toward the round brass tray laden with food, balanced on an accordion-like stand—bought years before in Damascus. In the middle of the tray, the dragon lamp sheds light over the small *sfeeha* pizzas and the dwindling supply of shish kebabs and the lamb-stuffed *kibbehs*, and the exotic array of salads, dips and fruit.

Fused into both boy and goat, Alya stands in Madam Alami's arena, prepared to entertain on a Sunday eve. As she savors the *kibbeh*, inner turmoil begins to abate, gives way to a defiance of the heart. She smiles her approval as Dick Brandon loads his plate with food and disappears behind a large tropical plant. Blinking against the dazzle of light, Alya pinpoints familiar faces, searches out an absent Majed. On the wall, the familiar portrait of Majed, six, and his sister, eight, flanking seated grandparents. Behind them, a handful of relatives, with Majed's mother leaning forward in a dress with ruffled sleeves.

"Some actors—even actresses—take to politics quite well." Madam Alami's high-pitched voice drifts toward Alya from the living room. "Take Madame Mao, of China. And what about your governor Reagan of California? A former actor, your magazines say." A shrill laugh. "Acting and politics, I'm afraid, can be one and the same...."

"Madame Mao is power-mad," a male American voice with a Midwestern accent interrupts. "In some *foreign* countries, when a woman loses youth and beauty, she goes after power. Just like

Madame Mao."

A softer woman's voice remarks, "Isn't that also true of women in America?"

A woman's laugh muffles the American's response.

"...even in our culture," Madam Alami continues, "our women must learn the politics of power. But one must admit, their chance to practice it is very slim...."

"In *your* neck of the woods..." The American voice, though polite, is unrelenting. "Women wield power in a roundabout way... through husbands, even sons."

"Speaking of sons," Madam Alami says. "My own son is late, as usual... " An uneasy laugh, a wave of a plump, bejeweled hand.

Alya stands in the doorway and scans the faces of the men and women gathered around Madam Alami's chaise longue. The American, tall, with a trimmed blond mustache, is an assistant at the American consulate in Jerusalem—a Mr. Warner, who speaks Arabic with an Egyptian accent. He's dropped by the Semiramis once or twice with Muna, the intense-looking woman at his side, who works in the consul's office as secretary.

Muna, with her ironic smile and caustic remarks, nibbles at a cucumber stick, looks up at Mr. Warner. "And what, pray tell, does an *unmarried* woman do? Or a widowed mother with daughters? What kind of power do you suppose....?"

He smiles down at Muna. "Sorry, my dear. I should have mentioned fathers. Fathers are the key."

Slightly stooped—perhaps with the social weight of offering deference over the years—Mr. Warner speaks with the authority of a diplomat who, despite making his point, does not *mean* to offend, but who believes his opinions are of consequence and should be heard.

His deference tonight is directed toward Madam Alami, his hostess, who leans back against the brocaded cushions of the chaise longue, and moves her hand in rhythm with her speech. The arch of her dark penciled eyebrows gives her an expression of continual surprise; but it's her voice that commands attention, adds drama to lackluster words.

Although Madam Alami's power may have come from her father, long-time mayor of Beit Nuba; or her martyred husband; or even, in small part, from Majed, her son—this power is now hers alone. Alya secretly envies her status in Beit Nuba, misses the parties that, once a month, bring guests together to savor eclectic gossip or parry with politics.

It was during one of those early parties about a year ago that Alya first introduced her brother to Clara Appleby.

Straddling a leather hassock, Dick Brandon is wedged between the sideboard and a rubber plant, a plate of food precariously balanced on his knees. He holds up his champagne glass to Alya, mouths the word "Cheers!"

The maid, Su'ad, in a white uniform, enters the *liwan* with a steaming platter of *knafeh* dessert.

Madam Alami reaches for Mr. Warner's hand, pulls herself up, teetering for a moment on high plastic heels. Regaining her balance, she moves toward the tray of *knafeh* and in a ringing voice invites guests to taste "the best *knafeh* Nablus has to offer."

Alya moves covertly next to Mr. Warner, who takes a bite of *knafeh* and mutters something about "native food being a bit messy."

When her turn comes, Alya takes the *knafeh* plate from Madam Alami's hand, murmurs, "So glad I could make it this time...."

The older woman's eyes widen as she stares at Alya, her lips working themselves around cryptic, unintelligible sounds.

"Sorry to have missed your last few parties," Alya says. "But I've been quite busy—helping Omar at the Semiramis, and teaching school." Alya's smile extends toward the American diplomat and Muna. "Besides, my poor mother considers attending parties—where liquor is served—a *sin*." A shrug. "And almost as bad as our own dance parties at the Hotel Semiramis."

"But surely, you have your *own* opinions on what constitutes sin?" the American diplomat says with a wink.

Alya gives a short laugh. "Or even on 'women and power'—your previous topic." Her eyes hold Madam Alami's with confidence. "As women, I'm afraid, our very survival depends on the *men* in our lives: our grocers, our garbagemen, our generals..." A titter of laughter ripples around the room.

Madam Alami stares at Alya, her mouth slightly open.

"I predict," Alya continues, "that this month of May of 1967 will bring changes—a revolution, even—in the status of women."

"I see little sign of your so-called 'revolution,'" Muna says, as if she were on the verge of tears. "Nothing seems to change. Not here, at least."

"In the States," Mr. Warner says, smiling, "the birth-control pill has caused our own women's revolution. And as much as some of us male chauvinists would *like* to—we can no longer keep our women barefoot and pregnant... and down on the farm."

A rotund man with thinning hair says expansively, "We appreciate our women for their modesty, their devotion... and their ability to be good wives and mothers. This, after all, is what God has intended their role to be...."

The woman at his side directs her gaze at Mr. Warner, "Think of the divorce rates in *your* country! Surely...."

The semicircle has widened to include other listeners. Madam Alami takes a step or two backward, as if for a better view. Or for escape?

"Madam Alami is a fine example of motherhood," Alya says. "And her son Majed is proof of her devotion and sacrifice." Male heads nod in approval; women whisper among themselves, glance surreptitiously at Alya. "And although Majed is working late tonight," she pauses, looks around the room, "he wanted me to share the news with you that we're engaged to be married...."

Madam Alami's mouth begins to twitch, emits a garble of sounds. The plate of *knafeh* in her hand tilts; syrup runs to the edge, drips onto the dark velvet of her dress. Muna moves swiftly to her side, takes the plate away, begins to dab uselessly at the stained dress.

Pity for Madam Alami dilutes Alya's giddy mood of triumph. She slips back to the *liwan* and Dick's corner. "The first volley of shots has been fired," she whispers.

Dick Brandon looks up. "Now that you've made your point, can we leave?"

"But Majed has a part to play in this unrehearsed skit. So, I'll have to wait till he shows up."

"Ah, yes. Majed, our prime suspect...."

Madam Alami's frantic voice strains against other soothing voices. Alya turns toward the *mezza* tray, scoops up *baba ghannug* eggplant dip onto her plate.

"The poor lady," Mr. Warner says at her elbow, "obviously did not expect *that* sort of news."

"Some mothers," Alya says, "have a hard time giving up their only sons... to other women."

His eyes are coldly appraising. "Hard to believe that a son wouldn't tell his own mother news like that. Only a coward...."

Alya reaches for a cucumber stick, says cheerily, "Cowards are bred in the best of families."

"So I've heard...."

Muna and a woman with mauve-dyed hair drift back into the *liwan*, huddle on one side of the *mezza* tray. A sudden thirst propels Alya into the clutter of Madam Alami's kitchen. She finds Su'ad there, scrubbing the *knafeh* tray in the sink.

Su'ad trains her chipmunk eyes on Alya's face. "Madam Alami almost fainted at the news of your engagement to Majed." An awkward pause, a clearing of the throat. "But you're a lady— whatever she says...."

"But yet, this is not a done deal," Alya says. She lowers her voice. "For how could I marry a man whose mother manipulates his life?"

Their eyes lock briefly, disengage as loud voices from the *liwan* break into their moment of conspiracy. Alya recognizes Majed's voice raised in argument, hears a woman's unfamiliar voice. Through the partially open kitchen door, Alya catches a glimpse of Majed in a dark suit and red tie, his chiseled features burnished in the light of the dragon lamp. His gaze focuses on the woman at his side. But Alya can't see her face, notices only the flutter of her hands against her sleek black dress.

"He's brought another woman with him," Alya murmurs.

"Don't worry. You'll invent something," Su'ad says and begins to load pita sandwiches onto a platter.

Have they begun to suspect Alya's deception? After all, she is an intruder into their shiny world, where invitees are selected from a thousand applicants and screened for defects in background and character before becoming members of the club.

As Alya walks back into the *liwan*, Majed's startled eyes fix themselves on her face. She considers the dark misery of his face, extends her hand toward the woman at his side. "I'm Alya Habeeb, Majed's fiancée," she says amiably. "I don't think we've met...?"

The woman offers her cool, white hand.

"...Samia Baha', producer of 'Spotlight on Music' at the Jerusalem radio station." A clearing of the throat, as if gritty sand has been trapped there.

Alya says with alacrity, "But before a woman gives up her freedom for marriage, she must consider all her options." A short, ironic laugh. "And I've already considered mine."

She looks into Majed's somber eyes, sees her distorted image in their lens. Does he believe that, if he stares hard enough, she may dissolve, or sink back to earth?

His fingers dig into her upper arm; his voice comes to her like the soft scraping of dried leaves. "What is it you want from me?"

She pulls her arm free. "It may be too late to ask now...."

Madam Alami advances on high heels, a tank intent on demolishing obstacles in its way.

"You're quite mistaken, my dear," Madam Alami says tersely. "My son never promised you anything. Never even considered...." Her voice disintegrates into the warm smoky air.

"But you won't have to worry...." Alya gazes across the barrier of the *mezza* tray at Madam Alami. "Despite all the promises in the world, how could I bring myself to marry a self-centered man who... who has no will of his own?"

Madam Alami's eyes widen, her mouth trembles. "You'll never set foot in this house again. You... you..." Her hand massages her throat as if to coax the flow of words.

"Refugee?" Alya prompts. "Half-breed?"

Madam Alami's voice sputters the ultimate insult.

"*Bint sharmouta!*"

Alya and Dick Brandon have already made their way outside onto the patio when they hear the crash. Alya turns just in time to see Majed's mother sprawled on the floor in the middle of fragments of the dragon lamp, wedges of sandwich bread, and black and green olives. Hands reach out, pull Madam Alami to her feet and guide her gingerly toward the couch.

With Shushu nipping at their heels, Alya and Dick Brandon make their way through the garden gate and out into the street.

"Unforgettable performance, old girl—better even than last night," Dick says cheerfully. "And a bang-up ending, I must say."

"Not quite a Nora Helmer exit. But then, Ibsen was more creative than I could ever hope to be...."

"It took longer than one evening to write 'A Doll's House.'" He smiles at her. "But yours was creativity on the wing."

Despite Dick Brandon's assurance, a fierce sense of loss overwhelms Alya. As they pass the street lamp by the apartment house, Alya tries but fails to catch a glimpse of the alley cat she had seen earlier. She thinks of the scavenger cat, scrapping for bits of meat and bone, for life itself.

Her self turned alley cat.

The White House said that President Johnson considered the tense Middle East situation to be "a matter of deep concern," and that he was following the situation closely....

The New York Times, May 20, 1967

Nancy Reagan's principal regret about being "a governor's wife is that the hectic social schedule gives her little time to dress as casually as she likes...."

Life, May 19, 1967

CHAPTER FOUR

George and Clara Appleby

GEORGE APPLEBY takes off his glasses, inspects them for blemishes, then readjusts them behind the slight hump of his nose. He glances with patient deliberation at Clara, braces himself for confrontation. So difficult to explain to her the essence of his work: the lectures he has to prepare—and attend; the book he plans to write. Several years ago, as a student in his Philosophy of Religion class, Clara listened with rapt attention to his analysis of Will Herberg's "leap of faith," and argued about Saint Augustine's "just war" theory with a passion that caught him off guard. In those days she reminded him of a woman researching possibilities for her life. But it was her paper "Destiny vs. Fate" that won him over, that finally brought her into focus as a woman to be reckoned with, a woman to invite out for coffee and blueberry pie. And later—despite her youth—even to marry.

God, Clara told him, had "spoken" to her only once; when, at seventeen, she confessed her sins and was saved at Brother Daniel's makeshift altar back home near Dalton, Georgia.

George's present research into the book he plans to write— "Birth and Death Symbolism in the Religious Rituals of the

Ancient Amorites of the Holy Land"—is meant to impress his colleagues at his college in Memphis, to win him tenure. And, in a small way, to impress Clara.

"That title is a bit heavy, don't you think?" Clara said, "so why not B.S. for short?" She had doubled over with laughter, tears running down her cheeks.

He finds it difficult to understand Clara's moods these days. Even now, as she fingers the beaded flowers in the yellow vase near her elbow, her flippant look challenges the serious things in his life. She wiggles her toes above the Da Vinci horse on the cover of the *Life* magazine, teasing him, hoping he'll change his mind.

He says, "Archaeology, my dear Clara, is the backbone of biblical history. And the conference at the Y this evening will be about...."

"...You've told me, haven't you? Something about 'the layers of history at Herodian...'" She reaches behind the cushion, retrieves a crumpled pack of Pall Malls, shakes a cigarette loose. "But it's been so long since we've gotten to 'know' one another—in the 'biblical' sense, I mean." She looks up from teal-blue eyes.... "As man and wife, damn it."

She arches her neck and laughs—corrosive laughter grating on his nerves. Then lights up her cigarette, exhales white, nebulous smoke through her mouth. In the past, he's begged her to stop smoking—at least when he's around. She picked up the habit three years ago—"instead of having babies," she said. Her excuse these days is "to fill in her time between teaching Home Ec and surviving the 'wild outpost' of Beit Nuba...."

When he first got to know her ten years ago, Clara had no bad habits to speak of—except, perhaps, to interrupt his thoughts or writing with the insignificant details of her life.

George Appleby frowns, studies the formation of his slender, bony hands. "You know it hurts me to see you smoke— to see you expose your life to danger." He sighs, glances at his watch. "And if you're doing it for spite...."

Clara stubs her cigarette into the ashtray, her finger rocking against the flattened cylinder. "I suppose," she says, as if in conversation with herself, "I should try to keep my bad habits undercover, shouldn't I?" A simpleton, that's what George was. She's married a simpleton, married him for his mind, for his spirituality—for punishment.

Nine months ago, George walked into their Memphis kitchen while she was measuring flour for her banana bread. "Pack your bags, my dear," he announced. "We're off to the Holy Land for a year."

He wanted to surprise her, he said. Besides, he knew in his heart she'd approve. "This is my one chance to take my sabbatical; to do my research for the book I've been meaning to write."

As she stood, her back to him, pretending sudden deafness, he wrapped his arms around her waist, brushed his lips against her neck. And just as she was about to reach for the baking soda, he spun her around and kissed her with the fervor of a man who like a boy wanted instant approval from the woman in his life.

Love-making that afternoon eased Clara's resistance and underlined her hope that leaving Memphis for a year might help relieve boredom, might even solidify a marriage gone astray.

George described Beit Nuba as a "fairly modern Palestinian town—ten miles north of Jerusalem—with a solid mixture of East and West." It also had a Mission School where they "welcomed teachers from America. *You* could apply, my dear...."

A week before their scheduled flight to Kalandia, the Jerusalem airport, a man in a pin-striped suit appeared at Clara's door.

"Jeremy Bernard Hutchins," he said, and flashed a U.S. government ID card at her. "I'm here for a friendly chat. I thought, perhaps—."

A slow panic began to work itself into her blood, like yeast. "My husband is at a faculty meeting and can't be disturbed." She took a deep breath, smiled brightly in his face. "What's George been up to now?" she asked.

"Not to worry, ma'am. Dr. Appleby's just fine." Impersonal, yellow-flecked eyes glinted at her from a clean-cut face. A small, conspiratorial smile. "I promise you... he hasn't made our ten-most-wanted list yet."

"Or, am I the guilty one?" Her voice on guard, impatience giving way to resentment for this disruption of her Friday afternoon.

"I'm here to ask for your help, ma'am." A pause. "May I come in?"

He follows her through the clutter of boxes on the living room floor, takes a seat on one end of the leather couch. Clara excuses herself and disappears—returning with steaming coffee mugs and day-old macaroons, which she sets down on the glass table between them.

"Thank you, ma'am," Jeremy says, his glance taking in her attempt at hospitality.

His hands rest lightly on his knees—large basketball player's hands, used to dribbling balls. Mid-thirties, she guesses—an older version of the earnest young men on bicycles who came to her house in Georgia or Memphis, and tried to prove to her that their faith was worthy of her consideration.

But nothing ever came of it.

Clara settles into the wicker chair facing him, crosses her legs, and reaches for a Pall Mall. "So what is it you really want from me?"

He begins to talk somberly of "world conflicts that could seriously undermine the safety of America, and democracy, and our good friend in the Middle East—Israel."

His missionary voice pauses, before gathering momentum. "Beit Nuba—where you and your husband plan to go—is an interesting Palestinian town, a summer resort where people come from all over the Middle East to visit, sometimes to live for a month or two. And one of its finest hotels—the Semiramis—has outdoor modern dancing during the summer months."

Clara listens, hypnotized by yellow-flecked eyes and a voice rattling lessons by heart. "Many Beit Nuba folk are fairly affluent—with relatives in the States. Yet, the refugees who've lived there since the war of '48—Israel's War of Liberation—are still considered 'foreigners.'"

"Just like in any small town in the States," Clara says. "If your granny wasn't born there, then you're considered a foreigner...."

Jeremy acknowledges her comment with a nod, but continues without a pause. "The educated ones speak good English—better than you and I. But, since Arabic is the native tongue, it might help to pick up a few useful words or phrases...."

Clara sips her coffee grown lukewarm, looks up, meets his appraising gaze. "Are you, by chance, recruiting me as a spy?"

"An informant, a source, would be more like it." He grins, leans back against the cushions of the couch. "I bet you've read a lot of spy novels. I've even read them myself. But real espionage is a complicated business—reserved for pros. What we're doing here is asking a bright American woman—one we can trust—to keep her eyes and ears open, to mingle with the natives... and, if anything interesting comes up, to please let us know... that's all."

Clara moves her hand carefully over the coffee table, flicks ashes onto a ceramic dish. Her glance hovers over coffee mugs, moves precariously to Jeremy's face.

"And what, dear sir, am I supposed to keep my eyes and ears open... for?"

"Trouble-makers, mostly. People who blame all their political miseries on the American government—or on Israel." He smiles a friendly smile. "The Jordanians are mostly all right—despite the pro-Syrian *Baathists* among them. But watch out for some of the radical Palestinians—those super-patriots with a subversive agenda. Those who resent Israeli and Jordanian rule over their so-called 'Palestine.' The Jordanian government tries to keep track of them, has some of them locked up in prison on some charge or other."

He gives her a confidential look. "And be on the lookout for words like 'PLO' or 'Fatah'... and people who profess their membership in either group. Confusing, I know. But after a few weeks, things will sort themselves out. You'll learn what could be subversive, and what has to be reported...."

Clara has read le Carré novels with convoluted plots where men and women were not what they seemed, and nothing was made clear until the very end. But it was the beginning and middle of things that made life precarious, even dangerous.

She nibbles at a macaroon, then asks, "What role will George play in all this?"

A pained expression appears on Jeremy's face. "Your husband's a little too... academic, we think." He clears his throat. "Not enough flexibility to meet the criteria..."

"...of a spy?"

Jeremy stands up, loose and confident in his pin-striped suit, basketball hands dangling at his sides. "We're appealing to your loyalty, ma'am, to your patriotism. We're convinced you're smart enough to handle this on your own—without your husband's help."

Flattery, Clara thinks, is a nice little touch....

"Still, as a free American citizen, I have the right to say no...?"

"You certainly have that choice." A short pause. "But most good citizens would consider it an honor to be asked." He smiles his amiable smile, then takes out a card from an inner pocket. "Let me know before you leave what you decide. I've written my own number in pencil on the back of the card."

"I'll make every effort to remember..."

He adds as an afterthought, "And don't forget, once you're there, you should register at the American consulate in East Jerusalem. It's important—in case of an emergency—to know you're under the protection of the U.S. government."

At the door, her hand is swallowed up in his, and for a moment, Clara wonders how it would feel to make love to an agent with basketball hands, wonders if he talks in his sleep. She could find out all sorts of secrets if he did.

Then what?

He'd ignored the coffee she'd set before him, had not tasted the coconut macaroons. People in his line of work, Clara speculates, are trained to be suspicious of coffee and coconut macaroons—and even those who offer them.

And yet, hadn't he stated earlier that she was a "bright American woman"—to be trusted completely?

The day before their flight to the Middle East, Clara called Jeremy's penciled number on the back of the card. "I need more time," she said. "I'm still thinking it over."

"Have a very good trip, Mrs. Appleby," Jeremy said, his voice respectful, calm. "I'm sure you'll do the right thing."

But here, in Beit Nuba, with her soul in tatters, Clara is still in the middle of things, still unclear what is the "right thing to do." But George, who figures things out logically, deliberately, seems to know—even when he isn't quite sure. But her own life shifted with the wind, bumped into cross-currents, occasionally crashed to earth.

Like now.

The ticking of the clock above the doll cabinet imposes its own pattern on her mind's disarray. Why not take an hour or two to amuse herself, and—as Jeremy suggested—"mingle with a native?"

When Clara calls the Semiramis to ask about Omar, Nawal's voice sounds tired. "Tell him Mrs. Brown called," Clara says. "It's a question about lunch…."

Clara surveys the room, wiggles her coral-painted toes above the *Life* magazine cover. A funnel cloud has dipped into her living room, to test the ground, has strewn beaded flowers on the floor. She drops to her knees on the rug and crawls toward the scattered flowers, her bell-like earrings clinking against their hoops like a signal. This moving around in circles, on hands and knees, is a game she played with her brother Kevin when she was eight, and he almost twelve. But she was faster then, more agile, and he, older, moved deliberately, not knowing the purpose of the game: "Escape from your Enemy!" she'd call out, and he would hide behind a chair, and cover up his head.

Stop taunting your poor brother, her mother would call from the kitchen. Wait till your father gets home; he'll thrash your hide.

Clara's father was gone for weeks on end. But when he finally came home—that muscular and well-tanned man who was her dad—he bounced her on his knee and laughed at her giggling.

He reprimanded her only when her mother demanded it.

The child Clara never knew what sin her father had committed to make her mother mad, knew only that she hated his work, which took him away from her. Something to do with lead sheets lining chemical tanks, burning in seams, wrapping pipes.... He tried to explain it all to Clara the week he left for good.

"Lead-burning is a real man's job," he bragged. "I belong to an elite club. Only a few of us left...."

It was also dangerous work—like real spying, Clara learned later. Before he left that Thursday, her dad gave her the lead horse he'd kept on the shelf in their one-car garage. "I made it just for you," he said, allowing it to nestle in the palm of her hand. Then added, "Take care of yourself," and walked out of her life.

Clara picks up the yellow vase, examines it, discovers the hairline crack. Life was cracked, with beaded flowers strewn on the floor. Her father gone forever from her life at twelve, and she left alone with her mother's tongue-lashings.

At sixteen, Clara fell for Jake Wilbur with his baby-blue eyes and his "born to lose" tattoo on his wrist. And when she finally gave in to him, his hard muscles holding her down in the grass behind the girl's gym, it was like drinking hard liquor, burning her insides with it. No decent girls allowed boys like Jake Wilbur to do nasty things to them, her mother said. You could get some disease.

Babies, even.

But Clara wasn't ready for babies then, did not want Jake's legacy. If it was a boy, he would have grown up tall and pimply, with a scattering of amber chest hairs, like Jake's. If a girl... Clara tried not to think of it.

Omar

THE RITUAL OF SUNDAY evening meals with Mustapha—the handyman and night clerk at the Semiramis—and his
family was a welcome reprieve from the daily grind of Omar's
life. That evening Omar shared their meal of *malfoof* rolled cabbage, with Mustapha, his wife, Haleema—and seven of their nine
children. During those evenings, no one ever asked Omar why he
remained unmarried, or heaped praise on the lawyer's pretty sister
down the street, or extolled the home-making skills of the third
cousin of a good friend. And no one ever suggested that Nawal
would make the ideal wife—as his mother repeats more often
than he cares to hear. Omar was also grateful for children's questions or noisy games that disrupted all attempts at conversation.

If he could ever convince Clara to divorce George and marry him instead, he might be blessed with a son like Mustapha's
tousle-headed boy, Nabil, who turns Omar into a willing donkey
with his "dy-oh! dy-oh!"—his chubby bare heels aiming rhythmi-
cally at Omar's ribs.

But instead of a visit to Mustapha, Omar walks briskly past
shuttered shops and silent coffee houses toward the hotel. Jasmine fragrance trails after him as he enters the Semiramis lobby.
Nawal looks up demurely from her desk.

He props an elbow on the counter, asks, "Any mail?"

"No mail or letters," Nawal says. "But Mrs. Brown called.
Something about a lunch…."

To Omar's relief, Nawal rarely asks prying questions. Yet, despite her discretion, did she ever wonder or suspect…?

"Where's Alya tonight?" he asks abruptly.

Her eyes meet his, waver. "At Madam Alami's party, I think."

"Ah!"

He asks if she would do him a favor and remain at the desk
for another hour or two. She glances at her watch. "Before midnight, then?" she asks.

"Certainly," he says. "Before midnight."

He dials Clara's number from the privacy of their upstairs

sitting room.

"It's about time," Clara says.

"How are you?"

"Misery wants company." He hears the faint tinkle of her earrings. "George's gone to Jerusalem for what he tells me is an 'important lecture' on Herodian." A shudder of a sigh. "The nerve of him! Leaving me all alone on a Sunday evening."

Omar's heart aches for Clara—tied to George because of imagined obligations. It happens in Beit Nuba, where divorce is as rare as an eclipse. And of course, in America, the land of divorce and alimony.

He hesitates. "Do you want me to come?"

"Come. As soon as you can."

Euphoria, like simmering water, becomes steady heat in his veins. "I'll call Hagas. Make sure Sylvia isn't back from her travels, that her room is still available...." A pause. "If only we were married... all our problems would be solved...."

Clara's voice is crisp with skepticism. "The way I hear it, my sweet, marriage laws here are stacked up against us females. All a man has to say is 'I divorce you' three times, and the ever-loving wife is thrown into the trash bin." A brittle laugh. "No thanks. That's not for me."

In his nineteen years of living in Beit Nuba, Omar can recall only two men who had invoked that "right." One, the ex-owner of Hagas's café, lived in Kuwait with his second wife, sent money to his first. Last summer, when Omar saw him in the streets of Beit Nuba, the man confessed his misery and his longing for the "old uncomplicated days," when he had only one wife. The other man, *Abu* Masri, lost his mind soon after his second marriage to Sabha, the baker's daughter.

Omar says into the receiver, "Only men in the sandiest deserts are fools enough to discard their wives so easily. And not many of those live in Beit Nuba anymore." His chuckle is intended to reassure her and to remind her that, in this modern year of 1967, progress has been made.

"I threw a vase at George just as he was leaving." Clara's

voice is light—without rancor. "The darn thing missed him by a silly millimeter...."

Omar says, "I'll meet you under the *askadinya* tree in twenty minutes. Please don't be late."

In a town where older women keep an eye on the escapades of the young, and where men dissect politics over food and aromatic coffee, the second floor of the Ali Baba Café has become an oasis of sorts, a refuge from the demands of Omar's work at the Hotel Semiramis.

Privacy—it's a small gift I give you, Hagas said. A way of repaying your father's friendship and the kindness he had shown.

During the day, customers wander into Hagas's Ali Baba Café to eat the homemade *sambusik* and meatless, lemony grape leaves, and the small, pizza-like *sfeehas*. They sip the coffee and the *arak* liquor, and linger over their *arkeelahs*, hubbly-bubblies, make jokes about politicians, or lament the passing of their youth. Sometimes they even argue about Hagas's chickens running loose in the street.

Hagas usually closes his café at sunset to get ready, with his band, to play for the dancing at the Semiramis. On Friday and Sunday evenings when the Italian band plays instead, he locks up his café for the night, and in the privacy of his kitchen, plays his mournful tunes on his mandolin. Occasionally, he wanders over to *Um* Nuri down the street to play a game of cards.

Before she died, Hagas's wife, Olga, entrusted him with her treasured chickens. A year after Olga died, their daughter, Sylvia, abandoned her room and moved to England. "I'll be back someday," she promised. Now, while Hagas waits for her return, he allows Omar the use of her room. "Just treat her stuffed animals with care," he asked, averting his eyes from Clara's cigarette. "And don't drop ashes on the rug."

He does not judge them as others would, does not snicker or raise his eyebrows at their illicit meetings. The earth turns and turns and brings you tribulation, Hagas said. So why not a little pleasure for a change?

Sylvia sends postcards to Hagas of places he has never seen, never knew existed. They arrive just in the nick of time when he's almost given up hope of ever hearing from her again.

Sylvia's latest postcard is of Stonehenge.

Hagas shrugged. "Large, bulky stones," he told Omar. "She should visit the Egyptian pyramids instead—or come home to see stones embedded in rock. Beit Nuba hills are kneaded with them...." He laughed, a rueful laugh, his thick hairy wrists slumped over the table's edge. He and Olga went to the pyramids on their honeymoon. Now those were stones to be reckoned with.

When no one answers the phone at the café, Omar decides Hagas must be at *Um* Nuri's. He dismisses Clara's worry that Sylvia may be back from England; and he still has the keys to gain them entrance.

Last night, an eon away, still clings like a sticky web to Omar's mind. Alya had pranced before the mirror, brushing back unruly hair, laughing in his face. But he didn't mean to lose control, to strike her face. It was only when she picked up the tie clip Clara gave him that anger broke barriers of restraint.

Omar envies men like Dick Brandon, schooled in English ways. He envies his cold reporter's mind—narrating with unruffled formality the excesses of mankind. If only he, Omar, could train his thoughts to set up hurdles against the world's discrepancies.

He flips open the wooden box on his dresser, picks up the broken tie clip, holds it at the hinge. Even Clara's message seems distorted now: "For the fun times..."

Clara and Omar

BEFORE CLARA leaves the house, she chooses cloisonné earrings to match the turquoise of her dress. Muted twilight offers camouflage as she crunches gravel underfoot and makes her way toward the gate. A boy is rolling a wire hoop in the street, guiding it deftly with a stick. She passes him by and blends into the wall, her heels clicking against the sidewalk.

She finds Omar waiting in his car under the *askadinya* tree.

"You're on time," he says happily, and pushes open the car door.

"Why wouldn't I be?" she asks, irritation in her voice.

She slides into the car-seat, and wrapped in silence, they ferret their way into the Old Town of Beit Nuba, past the voices of children playing *takka wigri* near the frayed edges of squat buildings. Beyond the walled Christian Orthodox church, a tall minaret pierces the sky.

The fragrance of the *saru* trees replaces the acrid odors of the alley; halfway down the street, light from a street lamp brings into relief the Ali Baba Café.

A narrow path veers past the wire pens that hold Hagas's chickens in abeyance for the night. Omar brings the car to a stop before an open shed with a rusty old truck wedged to one side. A steep staircase hugs the back of the building, leads to the small veranda on the second floor.

The frantic chickens begin to squawk, their privacy invaded. A woman's face suddenly unfurls above the corner of the hedge, eyes luminous, mouth slightly ajar. Clara whispers Omar's name in warning, but when he turns to look, the face disappears into the shadowed dark.

As they begin to climb the stairs, Omar gives Clara his hand. "Once we lock the door behind us," he says softly, "we'll be safe from prying eyes."

He turns the outer key, clicks open the door. Inside, a single light bulb illuminates the hallway; its threadbare runner, crafted in Afghanistan, separates Hagas's room from Sylvia's room—theirs for the night. Clara unhinges shutters and flings open windows, then draws flowered chintz curtains shut, for privacy.

Omar stands, absorbed, before a painting of a smiling clown, framed and hanging on the wall—as if yellow, red and blue balloons held a portion of his dreams. Curtains billow, flap against window bars and rocking chair, absorb the muted silence of the room. As Clara moves a fingernail across his back, Omar turns swiftly to take her in his arms. Their only audience: the ragged, button-eyed bear perched in the chair; the smiling poster-clown.

Afterwards, as Omar's wiry fingers tighten over Clara's hand, he begins to chant a little tune under his breath, the tale of a man whose beloved was whisked away in the middle of the night. If I could break the rules, he sings, we'd ride together on my horse to the ends of the earth and back. For I am a creature without air or sun—when I am away from you....

"Marry me," he says now, "and I promise to break any rule you want...."

Clara no longer believes in promises given in the heat of passion, prefers to disengage reality from the dream. "But, why spoil a near-perfect relationship?" she asks.

Despite Omar's protests, she leans back, content, against the crook of his arm, and listens as he chants his melancholy song—chants it hoarsely, like a man dying.

To block out sound, Clara presses her face against his chest. As his hand begins to stroke her back, she moves toward him and they make love again.

"Marry me, and we'll make love with the rise and the setting of the moon," he says. "We'll banish loneliness forever."

She laughs. "My mother will tell you—marriage is for more than just making love. It's mainly for making babies."

Yet she clings to him, this foreigner wanting to marry her—a woman already married—as if it were a matter uncomplicated and without risk.

Omar's eyes probe hers. "And where are your babies, my sweet Clara?" he asks.

"No babies for me," Clara says. "George won't let them near this cold cruel world. He is convinced bringing babies into this world is perfidy.

"'Look at Johnson in Vietnam; also Mao and his Madame and their Cultural Revolution. And now...,' George said just the other day, 'that hothead Nasser just itching for a fight.' George blames the Nassers of the world for the mess mankind is in. And for not making babies."

"If you marry me," Omar says, unrelenting, "we'll make beautiful babies together."

She smiles at him, decides to play his game. "We'll have to take them to the States. My mom will be glad to help...."

"Why can't we raise our children here, in Beit Nuba?" Omar's belligerence catches Clara by surprise. The game, transformed, has become too serious for her taste.

"This part of the world," she says thoughtfully, "is too volatile for raising children—especially now, with Nasser rocking the boat."

"Nasser," Omar says, triumph in his voice, "has finally taken a stand."

Clara's mind, resistant, weaves its own path around Omar's arguments—and Jeremy's warnings. "Think of it..." she says, "the Soviet Union is in this knee-deep. War could be a threat to... to the free world—to democracy!"

He moves his head toward hers, says soberly, "Who knows? Perhaps, if war does come, we'll win back what we lost in '48. Then, we can make our own democracy...." He gives her a conspiratorial look. "Like making babies."

"Not quite, I'm afraid."

His hand tightens on her shoulder. "With the latest in Russian arms, Nasser can certainly hold his own." As Omar's fingertip begins to map out the outer curve of her mouth, Clara closes her eyes, erases argument from her mind. No dastardly plot here—nothing subversive to put her on guard. She gives in to the luxury of a few blank moments—sinks into a void where thought is suspended for a while.

But jarring thought resumes when Omar whispers into her ear, "What will you do, dear Clara—if war comes?"

The silence between them is a thin and airless space. She says, her eyes still closed... "Turn tail and run—the only thing I know to do...."

"But how could you bear to leave...or even think of it?" Bitterness in his voice.

"I'm a coward, let's face it."

"Ah, Clara!" As Omar holds her prisoner in his arms, her flesh and spirit lose their cowardice, begin to revive.

Faint but persistent knocking on the outer door seeps into Clara's consciousness as she lies trapped in Omar's arms.

She holds her breath. "Did Hagas forget his keys?"

"Hagas is not one to forget keys."

Omar sits up, begins to put on socks, underwear, and the rest of it. Passion distilled—replaced by economical, unhurried motions.

Clara resists a childish urge to snatch Sylvia's button-eyed bear and hold it in her lap. Instead, she begins to dress, a robot doll with mechanical body parts.

When knocking finally ends, and footsteps recede, they move cautiously toward the window. A woman stands at the bottom of the stairs, the glint of moonlight on her face. Out of the dark of the *saru* grove a man emerges. Heads bend in greeting, hands touch.

Back in Sylvia's room, Clara and Omar sit on the edge of the bed and wait. After an eternity of time, a key turns, the outside door creaks open. They hold their breath as footsteps in the hallway pause briefly at their door, then turn and walk away.

This little room that has held their banter and their love-making in trust a few minutes before, now holds their movements in separate balance, each preoccupied, a formality between them.

"Could it have been the woman you saw earlier this evening?" he asks.

She laughs, a bitter laugh. "Maybe she, too, has an arrangement with Hagas...?"

Clara reaches for the fallen bear, takes a seat in the rocking chair; she stares into button eyes, and begins to sing oh so softly an old revival song.

"I was sinking deep in sin..." she sings slightly off-key, "far from the peaceful shore..." Flat, her mother said. Please stop singing and just mouth the words. No use spoiling the song for the rest of us.

"Love lifted me..." She sings, bouncing the bear on her knee. "Love... lifted... me..." she sings, louder still.

The words shift, rearrange themselves. Her inner song, transformed, has a gentle rhythm, an old-fashioned melody prancing in her head.

She watches as Omar makes the bed, tucks in corners, folds back the chenille bedspread.

The pensive sound of the mandolin from across the hall rouses Clara from lethargy.

"It's Hagas," Omar says.

Clara gets up, props up the bear against the pillows on Sylvia's bed. Before they leave the room, she closes the shutters, pulls down the shade.

Nasser announced last night that Egypt has decided to close the Gulf of Aqaba to all ships flying the Israeli flag or carrying strategic materials to Israel....

The London Times, May 23, 1967

President Nasser's showdown move against Israel at the mouth of the Gulf of Aqaba is read here [at the U.N.] as a direct challenge to the U.S. and other Western Powers....

The Christian Science Monitor, May 24, 1967

CHAPTER FIVE

Alya

"SMASHING PERFORMANCE," Dick Brandon says, "didn't know you had it in you."

Alya's wound has been gouged out, made public, bystanders splattered with her blood, and yet she walks with a lightness in her step as if cords around her ankles have been cut.

"You've heard of righteous wrath?" she says. "It can make one brave—even reckless."

Mist shrouds the Manarah Circle of lights, drifts around parked cars and shuttered stores, and small trees or bushes sprout out of the soil of sidewalk squares. A dog barks, another takes up the call. And from a far-off house, the rhythmic voices of men rise in song, the ululating *zaghareet* of women in joyous celebration.

Celebration for her well-played role. For bravado?

Euphoria, like the mist, replaces guilt, settles in the labyrinth of her soul. She barely hears what Dick Brandon says, is forced to repeat.

"Will your headmistress look askance at one of her teachers causing a 'scandal' in the Beit Nuba teapot? Off with her head, and all that?"

Alya says. "Miss Whitney may pretend the Mission Board controls her every move. But she pays little mind to gossip, takes most of it in stride."

They turn the corner toward the Hotel Semiramis, pass Badri's house, its fig tree a specter against the sky. No band music plays this Sunday night to titillate the senses, to disturb her mother's fitful sleep.

Alya trails a finger across the damp fender of Mr. O'Connor's rented Ford, parked crookedly near the hotel gate. Mr. O'Connor comes to Beit Nuba twice a year, to stock up on religious artifacts for his import shop in Texas.

"I'm a fallen Catholic in the eyes of the Church," he confided to Alya once, "with not even an excuse of 'invincible ignorance'...."

As they walk briskly toward the glass vestibule of the hotel entrance, Dick says, "Sorry... can't stay for your upcoming scandal, old girl. But, as Nawal can certify, I've paid in advance for my hotel room. I'm also leaving a few things on the shelf...."

"... with the promise that you'll be back?"

"With the ardent hope that I'll be back ...."

"Say hello to the Egyptian general for me," Alya says.

Dick smiles. "Only if there's a lull in the conversation." He adds, "I think I'll take a quick walk around the grounds—to help clear my soggy brain." They shake hands efficiently, like soldiers parting. His footsteps recede, his apparition melds with the trunks of trees.

Alya waits for euphoria to subside, for thoughts to readjust. Earlier that evening, a creature, other than herself, disrupted conversations, jarred the ambience of Madam Alami's party.

A creature, much like herself, bent on reprisal.

Inside the *liwan*, she finds Mr. O'Connor, in animated discussion with Maddie and Josh Johnson from Virginia, while Nawal, behind her desk, hides a yawn.

"...but we look forward to Armageddon," Maddie is saying. Despite expert camouflage, her face still reveals the small fissures of middle age. "Surely, you read the Bible? It's all there, in black and white...."

Mr. O'Connor's round lashless eyes focus on her face. "But in what language, my dear lady, does God communicate His predictions? And how can *we*, mere mortals, accurately interpret that holy writ?"

Her husband says, conviction in his voice, "Believers have special powers to interpret His Word." He glares at Mr. O'Connor. "And how can you possibly deny God's Truth and remain in His good graces?"

Mr. O'Connor's fleshy jowls quiver, his eyes narrow. "Ah, yes. God's indomitable Truth on the page. All in black and white."

"To deny is to... to..." Maddie looks, wild-eyed, at her husband.

"Roast in the fiery pit?" Mr. O'Connor asks mildly.

"To deny is... blasphemy!" she says, relieved, perhaps, that words have come.

"Faith," says Josh Johnson, "is *believing* in your heart that Christ is Lord. That He, in his glory, died for our sins, and will return to save all believers on Judgment Day...."

"Alas!" laments Mr. O'Connor. "I'm afraid I'm one of those souls who pleads skepticism of matters religious...."

"And yet...."

Their voices trail after Alya, filling in the blank spaces of her mind as she approaches the hotel desk. Nawal looks up from her *Redbook* magazine, points to the well-coiffed blonde on its cover. "Don't you think she looks like Miss Madding?"

"The American who reads the news in English from Amman?"

"Both blonde. With the same arch of the eyebrows."

"Could be." Alya glances at her watch. "Where's Omar?"

"A Mrs. Brown called...." A small hesitation as gold bracelets clink against Nawal's wrist. "Omar asked if I'd take his place until *you*... or Mustapha showed up."

Alya smiles. "I bet I'm the lucky winner of that prize...."

The front doors swing open and Dick Brandon strides

through, calls out a cheerful "Cheerio!" before taking the stairs to his room.

"He's leaving for... Sinai in the morning," Nawal whispers.

"He might even visit Gaza...."

Nawal emits a small sigh, pulls at a strand of limp brown hair. "Although she grew up in Askalan, my cousin Wadia has lived in Gaza since '48—nearly nineteen years! But, if I met her in the street tomorrow, how would I recognize her... a grown mother of four boys?" Nawal's eyebrows furrow over her thin, aquiline nose. "My mother prays each night that God will send me a worthy husband, so I may bear many sons—like my cousin in Gaza."

"Mothers often dream dreams and see visions." Alya smiles, thinks of her own mother's dreams.

Before Alya takes over the desk, Nawal says, "Earlier in the day a friend of yours called from Jerusalem. He mentioned a sister, Julia, but did not leave his name."

No doubt it was Sari Pappas, the potter, whose sister helped him at the shop. A month ago Alya had stopped by on her way to her rendezvous with Majed. She had a hurried cup of tea with Sari, and a quick hug for Julia, who trailed after her, complaining about the secret voices in her head.

It's a good thing that Nawal lives nearby, that her street is well lit. Still, Alya worries about her walking home alone at night. Maybe, with a little friendly persuasion, Mr. O'Connor would gallantly offer to escort her home.

"Be glad to," Mr. O'Connor assures Alya—despite Nawal's protests that she's a big girl, and lives only ten minutes away.

After Alya takes over the desk, the Johnsons bid her good-night and wander off to their room. But a few minutes later, Maddie reappears in a pink chenille robe, sans makeup, her face glossy with cream.

"I've got a doozy of an upset stomach," she tells Alya plaintively. "It's either the *falafil* I ate earlier or, more likely, the discussion with Mr. O'Connor that did me in...."

"I might have something that'll do the trick," Alya says, and heads toward the kitchen. She returns a few minutes later with a hot cup of *maramiyyeh* herb tea.

"I can't stand the way Mr. O'Connor puts down religion," Maddie says as she sinks down into the corner couch. "Even though I'm not really sure *what* he believes...." She sips her tea and begins to confide in Alya the many steps of her arduous spiritual journey over the last few years.

"Faith is a tricky business," Mr. O'Connor says, walking back through the front door. "At least for *some* of us...." He nods at Alya. "Nice girl, Nawal. I delivered her safe and sound to her parents...."

"But now that we've found 'faith' there's no doubt in *our* minds...." Maddie says.

She and her husband, she's told Alya, have come to the Holy Land to walk in the footsteps of Jesus, to experience the wonderful peace of Jerusalem.

Mr. O'Connor excuses himself. "I think I'll leave the discussion of religion to you, ladies—obviously a hardier breed than I...."

Before she leaves, Maddie relates to Alya her experiences on Friday following the Way of the Cross on the "Via Dela... Dola...."

"Via Dolorosa...." Alya offers.

"But the *crowd*, dear Jesus, I almost had a heat stroke!" She drains her cup. "You *do* believe in Jesus, don't you, dear? Your mother, I hear, reads the Bible day and night...."

"As an Orthodox Christian, my mother is certainly a believer...." Alya says.

"Bless her heart," Maddie says, beaming.

"But my dad was Muslim," Alya says. "But that complicates things, doesn't it?"

"I'll pray for you, dear." Mrs. Johnson pats Alya's arm. "And thank you for that nice tea. I feel better already...."

The honeymoon couple from Bireh drift in, hand in hand, smile at Alya, bid her goodnight. When Mustapha finally appears, thirty minutes late, Alya—grateful for his presence—

reserves her inquisition for Omar.

A little past midnight footsteps sound in the adjoining sitting room, a key turns. Feet begin to pace the floor in Omar's room, finally lull Alya to sleep. She dreams of a live dragon spewing fire, of Dick Brandon, in a soldier's uniform, pointing an Uzi at her face. She wakes up with the ringing of the telephone.

"I won't make it to school today." Clara's voice is a sleepy echo from a distant place. "But stop by after school, and I'll fix us a cup of Nescafé...." She gives in to a spasm of coughing. "Those... cigarettes," she says hoarsely. "They irritate my throat even as they calm me down—just like all the other temptations in my life."

"Just for a few minutes." A small pause. "You okay?"

"I need a reprieve from chapel. Miss Whitney's sermons drive me up the wall."

Alya laughs. "Not *sermons*, dear Clara. Vignettes. Little stories with a moral she hopes will do us some good."

"Or make us feel guilty," Clara says and begins to cough again.

History Class

ON HER WALK to school every morning, Alya inevitably passes Nasir Hatimi's bookstore. But this morning, he does not wait in his doorway, grinning, his hair slicked over his bald spot, eager to share with Alya his lovelorn philosophy of life. Near Cinema Hayat, the loudspeaker from *Abu* Abdo's coffee house blares the news of U Thant's proposed visit to Cairo.

"But what good will U Thant do?" demands the radio commentator in loud and flinty tones. "How can he bring justice to our brothers, the Palest...?" A car honking interrupts the speaker's rhetoric. "We must take our destiny in our own hands," continues the announcer in his Egyptian accent, "or die honorably for our cause...."

At the top of Al-Majnuna Street, the Crazy Woman's Street, Hani, who dropped out of school last year, tempts potential customers with thyme, and bread-necklaces of sesame-*ka'ik* piled high on his wooden cart. For Hani, at thirteen, school is but a memory for a working man. He grins at Alya when she returns his "Good morning: *Sabah el-khair!*"

The tempting, heady aroma of *ka'ik* follows her into the school gates of the Girls' Mission School, and into the *liwan*-hallway of the main building. In chapel, students and faculty are singing "*Yu hibbuni, Yu hibbuni...,*" an Arabic hymn about God, the spiritual lover of humanity: a hymn for believers and nonbelievers alike.

Alya takes a seat on a corner bench, outside the auditorium, and waits for chapel to end. Black-and-white photographs of past graduating classes hang in rows on the wall facing her. No frivolous smiling faces here; only girls of the most solemn purpose are worthy of graduating from the Girls' Mission School of Beit Nuba.

Miss Whitney's crisp, Midwestern voice in a Bible reading drifts through the auditorium door; her "sermonette" follows. As young voices finally lift in communal prayer, Alya leaves for her class: a small and crowded room with wooden desks, her own table and chair, and a single window to her right.

The girls drift into the classroom, talking and giggling among themselves. Their dark green tunic-uniforms harness firm young breasts, conceal the curve of buttocks. Once inside, voices turn muted as each girl takes her seat. Young faces lift to Alya's, see themselves reflected in her eyes.

Obviously, they have not yet heard the news of her *own* misdemeanors.

The tinny sound of the school bell signals the beginning of class—the end of frivolity.

"Good morning, Miss Habeeb," their voices sing out in unison—as if life is orderly and free from barbed wire pressed against the throat.

Today, the class will review the causes and results of the

French Revolution. Nahida Salim—unsuspecting bride-to-be of Majed Alami—sits near the window, her wheat-colored braids hanging limp on the pages of her history book. I could warn her, Alya thinks, tell her about the *other* woman in Majed's life.

Jumana, square-bodied, square-faced, a sardonic smile curling her lips, raises her hand.

King Louis, she says, was preoccupied with hunting wild game, with pleasing his wife. The starvation of his people did not hurt his conscience—or hers.

After class Jumana sometimes argues with Alya about her grades. Her father, in Hebron, expects more than an almost-A. As a boarder at the Mission School, Jumana struts around the school grounds, a small clique of friends in her wake.

Alya pinpoints blonde, curly-headed Suhad with her eyes. "What else can you add?"

Suhad wrinkles her brow, fumbles with a pencil, looks toward the pine branch outside the window. The nobility were untaxed, she says cautiously. The *proletariat* and the peasants bore the brunt of it.

Nahida raises her hand once more. "The *bourgeoisie*," Nahida says, pronouncing the word perfectly (hadn't Alya given them a vocabulary list?), "wanted more say in their government. But Louis kept changing his mind... until the radicals took over." Her light brown eyes gaze at Alya without suspicion.

Ah, Nahida. How soon will you, too, turn radical?

Huda, a slight girl with worried eyes, answers the next question about the role of the Church. "In reward for unending patience," she says softly, "the Church promised the poor a slice of Heaven." Huda's face twists into a grimace; her voice breaks free, "But what use is Heaven when your belly aches with hunger?" she demands of Alya, of the world.

Uneasy silence—as young minds filter this sudden outburst of indignation. Alya smiles at Huda to help ease her pain, to affirm her identity. Yes, she says with her eyes. You are quite right.

Alya scans the young faces before her, feels a wrenching sadness for the young. "Was revolution, then, inevitable?" she asks.

Nahida tugs at the golden map of Palestine that dangles from a chain around her neck. She wears it like a good luck charm—wears it for all the world to see and know what is in her heart. But how will Majed—grown jaded with his truth—deal with the fervor of Nahida's daydream?

"An oppressed people must revolt," Nahida says crisply. "It is their inherent right."

Heads nod, and a murmuring, like the rustle of wings, flits through the classroom.

Alya persists. Were liberty, equality, fraternity worth all the bloodshed, the terror?

"The French certainly thought so," Jumana says without hesitation. Giggles. Whispers in the back.

"But you, Jumana, what do *you* think?"

Jumana's eyes dart toward Nahida's, seek her approval. "When all else fails," she says, "a revolt... a kind of uprising, is *necessary* to call the world's attention to injustice... to suffering."

"But at what cost?"

More questions churn in Alya's mind, unasked, unanswered. You ask too many questions, her mother told Alya when she was Nahida's age.

Questions can be dangerous.

God's will, after all, is sufficient for contradictions.

But surely there are ways of untangling the will of God from the schemes of men and women... A sign, a clue, perhaps?

Alya and Clara

THE MUSTY ODOR of stale cigarettes permeates Clara Appleby's living room. Her array of dolls, six or seven she brought with her from Memphis, sit in the glass cabinet like quiet, docile children. And on her coffee table, Fulbright's *The Arrogance of Power* lies across a *Life* magazine with a torn cover. At her elbow, a vase with beaded flowers.

"There you are!" Clara, in pink flowery housecoat, greets

Alya at the door. "I won't be a minute."

She brings back two mugs of hot water, two packets of Nescafé, sugar, spoons, artificial cream. An Indian guru in blonde curls, Clara sits cross-legged on the couch, facing Alya in her chair; she picks up the vase with beaded flowers, holds it for inspection.

"Last night I threw that sucker at George's receding back." Smiling, she runs a finger across its hairline crack, touches petals of a beaded flower. "Missed, darn it!"

"The men in our lives prefer their women tucked away in corners... like your dolls." Alya says. "Fortunately, we women *intrude*, sometimes spoil their plans."

Clara's earrings quiver with spasms of laughter, swords dancing. She sips her Nescafé, says, with laughter ending, "You've probably figured out by now that last night, the mysterious 'Mrs. Brown' whiled away her time with your brother, Omar... in glorious sin." A scowl rearranges lines and dimples in Clara's face. "Would you believe? He wants me to throw out dear old George and make babies with him...."

Alya thinks of Omar, secretive, self-righteous, judging her, reserving judgment for himself. She recalls the tie clip she broke, its inscription revealing more than she cared to know. She says quietly, "What are your real feelings for Omar?"

"Except for his politics, Omar's a sweetheart."

Alya fixes a thoughtful gaze on Clara's face. "But what happens when love-making ends?"

"Your brother's too damn serious about love *and* politics." Clara lights a cigarette, inhales, flips the matchstick onto the ashtray nearby. "I wish he'd keep his politics to himself. I'd rather *not* know that he considers Nasser a hero." She shrugs. "So tell me, how do *you* manage to rise above politics?"

Alya laughs a rueful laugh. "Concentrating on vain, self-centered men has given me little time for serious stuff. Besides, I was only eight when we lost our home in Katamon. We came to Beit Nuba... with a detour to '*Ammi* Musa's house. But Omar was fourteen. He remembers hordes of people fleeing their homes, with bundles on their heads. And children... lots of children. For him, it was a *nakbeh*. For me, at eight, it was just a game."

"Omar's devotion feeds my ego." Clara looks up, blows smoke rings in the air. "It also scares the hell out of me."

The price one pays, Alya thinks. Like the smoking of cigarettes.

Nothing was ever resolved in Alya's confidences with Clara; everything hung by a thread. And although blood was thicker, she knew, friendship still had its place.

As she makes her way back to the Semiramis, Alya hears the loudspeaker at *Abu* Abdo's coffee house blare out the lament of Egyptian singer Fareed Al Atrash for his lost love. Even the stars of the night wept for his pain, he sings in a husky, mournful voice.

Her own pain was frivolous, a lost illusion of loving and being loved. The party at Madam Alami's was her catharsis—the cleansing of her life from debris.

This time, she finds Nasir Hatimi firmly fixed on a stool in the doorway of his bookstore, reading the newspaper, sipping a glass of tea. When he sees Alya, he smiles expansively, holds up his glass. "This is my lucky day, *Sitt* Alya..." His free hand pats the waxed strands of his hair into place. "As I was telling my sister, Samiha...." Nasir Hatimi's eyes shine with the gleam of a lovelorn suitor. "Tea is only a small substitute for love."

To deflect ardor, Alya asks, "And how is your son, Bahi?"

"Ah. The motherless waif—the *karut*...." A sigh transforms itself into a spasm, contorts his pudgy, docile features. "You see, at age eleven, he still...." His voice grinds to a stop. "But, here I am, a literary man of means, acting like a... a simpleton. A donkey!" The glass of tea trembles in his hand, spills onto the U Thant-Cairo headline lying unceremoniously on the pavement.

He gives Alya a melancholy smile. "You see before you a widower in his prime, in need of a woman at his side to ease his loneliness, to bring him contentment...."

And to take on the roles of wife, instant mother, and sister-in-law to Samiha?

A large woman in *thobe* passes by with three noisy children in tow. A man in business suit pauses to inspect the cover of *Rose El Yusuf* magazine in the display case.

Nasir Hatimi extends his beggar's palm toward Alya. "I would be the happiest man on earth if you would consider...." A wrenching shudder: a small earthquake in a middle-aged body deprived of fleshly love. With a son who....

"Beit Nuba is filled with women who would be delighted to marry you," Alya murmurs.

"If only you were one of them...."

A schoolboy of ten or so stops to ask about an old geography book.

"A book with a yellow cover," he says, "with maps of America and Africa, and even Palestine...."

"Maps... *before* 1948?"

"Before I was born, the teacher said."

"I will have to look."

Before he re-enters his bookshop, Nasir Hatimi casts a pleading glance toward Alya. Until the next time, his eyes seem to say. And don't worry, I'm a persistent man.

Shaking his head, he says aloud, "Ah! The changes in our world recorded in old geography books...."

This is what I may need, Alya thinks: An old geography book—with maps—to recreate the past. To point the way.

In front of the Bata shoe store, she passes an old man with a small boy in monk's cassock. Once again, the *nidr*—a promise made to God and priest. To survive serious illness, even death, is a miracle to warrant a child's austerity for a year.

The boy reminds her of the image of the child Majed, unwitting child-monk held prisoner in a photograph. Yet Omar, who has never worn such garb, has survived so far without miracles— his love for Clara and Palestine, a frenzy in the blood.

But, what promise will Sari Pappas give, what sacrifice will he have to make—to elicit a miracle for his sister Julia?

Middle East:

The new ambassador to Egypt, Richard Nolte, arrived at Cairo airport May 22. He said, "I would say that crisis is too strong a word for the present situation." He hoped for "improvement" in United States–United Arab Republic [Egyptian] relations.

The Christian Science Monitor, May 23, 1967

Greece:

"The objective of the government [the military junta] is to cleanse Greek life in general...."

Newsweek, May 8, 1967

"From now on," declared Interior Minister Pattakos [of the Greek military junta] "no traveler will be allowed to enter Greece if he has a beard, scruffy clothes, or less than $80."

Time, May 19, 1967

Greece drops the ban on visiting beards in response to travel agents....

The New York Times, May 16, 1967

CHAPTER SIX

Alya and Sari

ALYA'S RESOLVE to visit Sari Pappas and his sister Julia in Jerusalem came toward the end of a class discussion about the French Revolution on Monday. "The guillotine," she said in her firm teacher's voice, "was the invention of a doctor who believed in a more *humane* sort of... murder." The girls of the Mission School looked up at her from somber eyes, afraid perhaps that their own necks were in jeopardy.

Alya decides to call Sari from the second-floor parlor between Omar's and her room at the Hotel Semiramis. Asleep on the window seat, Bisseh, her mother's three-legged cat, flicks the stub of her tail as if to discount a cat-dream; and the canary, its cage hanging from the arch above Alya's head, falls silent.

Fortunately Alya's brother is nowhere around, and her mother, cloistered in her room a few feet away, is probably reading her Bible, or taking an afternoon nap.

"You were on my mind last night," Sari says when he hears Alya's voice. "I was hoping you'd come by to see me and Julia this time—and no one else...."

"I'll drop by later this afternoon. I promise."

"Has Majed been taking up most of your time?"

"Not anymore." A pause. "I called to make sure you'd be home...."

Sari laughs his guttural laugh. "What do you take me for? A gadabout like you? I'm either in the ceramic shop or upstairs in my flat. On some evenings, I wander over to Uncle Sam's for a game of backgammon." A pause too short to interrupt. "Once in a while, I meet someone interesting. And if I'm lucky—it may even be a woman."

Absurd, Alya thinks, this bragging about chance encounters, of women passing through. "Does Julia get to meet the friends you bring home?" she asks.

When he finally answers her, Sari's disembodied voice seems to come from a distant land. "When I ask her to come up for a cup of tea, she always refuses—preferring to come later, in secret. She climbs the stairs to the patio-roof late at night, talks to the doves, peers through my windows like a spy...."

When Alya first met Sari—a few months before her father's death—he was more intense, more desperate—as if, at thirty-six, life was passing him by. Age mellows us, Alya has heard, read somewhere. Seven years later, at age forty-three, Sari has become transformed, like the pottery he crafts, along fluid, less brittle lines. His is a jaunty stoicism, a resignation to Julia's presence in his world.

"Have you run across any interesting women lately?" Alya asks to distract him.

"Yes. A woman from Finland who seemed to know something of Greek history and politics." He adds with a chuckle, "I wanted to bring her home, to show her my pottery. To make love, even. But in the end, it didn't happen...."

"I'll have to take the bus to Jerusalem," Alya says, "since Omar no longer trusts me with the car." Reluctantly, she tells him of her accident on Salah-uddeen Street a few weeks ago. She was on her way back from seeing Majed in Jerusalem when she hit the street-vendor's cart with its load of oranges. Children gathered to point fingers, to laugh at her—a woman behind the wheel. The man with his broken cart and spilled oranges cursed her and threatened to call the police; but regained his good humor with the help of a few *dinars*—all that was left of her schoolteacher's paycheck that month.

"I've missed you," Sari says wistfully. "It's been ages since I saw you last."

"Surely, not more than three or four weeks?"

"One week is a long time for a small boy—or an aging bachelor."

She assumes her expository voice, "Teaching... and keeping track of Omar at the Semiramis, take their toll on my life." He already knew about her preoccupation with Majed—even during the intervals when she did not see him.

A small silence like a shadow flickers between them. "If you like," she adds to pacify him, "I'll also cut your hair and trim your beard—unless you've been transformed into a shorn lamb behind my back."

His laughter reverberates in her ear. Occasionally, when she and Majed got together at the Pensione Al-Ahram in Jerusalem, Sari acted as buffer zone—giving Omar invented excuses, to keep him at bay.

Last time, when Omar called to ask about Alya's whereabouts, Sari told him that she'd gone over to *Abu* Mahmoud's in the Old City. "But you know how she is. She takes her time, likes to bargain, even listens to his long Juha tales...."

Fortunately for Alya, because there were many "*Abu* Mahmouds" in the Old City, it was nearly impossible for Omar to trace her there.

As a reward, a kind of gift, Alya offered to cut Sari's hair, which, at first, he accepted reluctantly, later asked as a favor. Alya fell into the habit of it, this barbering, whenever she came to see him, finding him ragged, the gray of his hair and beard meshing.

"Have you heard the latest?" he asks now. "The ban on men's long hair and straggly beards at the Athens airport has finally been lifted."

Sari—dejected over political insanities in the land of his

fathers, his voice looping around her like barbed wire. Greek tourism, he explains, apparently had been in jeopardy because of the ruling by the Minister of Public Order.

"I suppose," Sari continues, "the minister was finally persuaded that hippies and bearded old men may have *some* money to spend on Greek tourist attractions after all. But the ban still holds on women's miniskirts." His laughter is caustic, cynical.

"Any news from your father since the coup?" she asks.

"One small letter... a week ago." Sari pauses as if to anchor his thoughts. "'The objective of the coup,' my dad wrote, 'is to reshape and purify the government from radical elements.' Pure jargon, don't you think?"

Before they hang up, Sari asks, "How can a middle-aged son tell his dad—without rancor—that he and the junta should take a running jump into the Aegean Sea...?"

At 4:30 that Monday afternoon, a rattletrap of a Volkswagen bus, its driver a man who whistles under his breath and smokes Pell Mells on the sly, careens down Nablus Street in East Jerusalem and deposits Alya in front of the YMCA.

Alya wears low-heeled Oxfords for walking on slick sidewalks chiseled out of stone. The thick mane of her hair, forming a chignon, is held in place by a bright cloisonné barrette. Her tawny hair absorbs the afternoon sun, appears almost rufous. From Aramaean, Phoenician and Arab ancestors—with a token offering of Crusader blood—Alya inherited a prominent nose, a sensuous mouth perhaps too large for beauty, and deep-set eyes, inquisitive, often stubborn, looking beyond appearances.

She walks briskly past schoolchildren in uniforms, avoids a thin black cat that darts her way; taking her cue from the cat, she darts across the street just as a taxi speeds by. Near the front gate, a woman sits cross-legged with a basket of grape leaves and a mound of squash, and hawks her produce to passersby. Squatting nearby, a small barefoot boy draws pictures in the dirt with a thin, crooked stick. Small islands of blue and purple petunias flank the flagstone path that leads up to the side entrance of

Sari's ceramic shop.

In the nineteenth century the building housed Russian pilgrims to the Holy Land. But when Sari Pappas bought it, nearly ten years ago, it had stood empty, its plaster peeling, its windows broken. Its original owner, a woman from old Kiev, lies buried in a corner of the garden. Alya has seen the cross with its Slavic writing that marks her grave.

She has also glimpsed the back room where the kiln and potter's wheel are kept. An alcove in the back wall holds the icons of Christ and Mary, set in plaster. Below the icons, Julia has taped a faded print of Rublev's Icon of the Old Testament Trinity.

The building's gray stones sprout occasional weeds and moss between grooves once crisp with kohl cement. A glazed yellow plaque on the door announces in black script "Pappas Jerusalem Pottery. Open: 9–5. Closed: 1–3 and all day Sunday." A hairline crack runs diagonally across the decorative word "Jerusalem."

Alya pulls at the frayed rope and hears the hollow sound of its inside bell. Footsteps shuffle to the door, the door creaks back on its hinges. Julia's small figure appears in the unlit hallway like a ghost, a black scarf framing her aging child's face.

Julia glances furtively at the staircase to her left, then takes a step or two back to allow Alya entry.

"I was in the middle of loading the kiln when I heard the bell." Julia gives Alya a quick, uneasy smile. "I made sure the clay was well dried so it wouldn't explode... like the last time...."

"How've you been, Julia?" Alya asks. A question safe, without commitment.

Julia's hands flutter in the air like Sari's caged doves, fall motionless to her side. The small, narrow mouth flies open.

"But how could I *help* it? I mean, what I did later. A customer like him deserves worse." Julia's breath comes in short, uneven gasps. Perspiration glistens on the soft fuzz of her upper lip. "He came in, reeking of smoke, demanding to see his name plaque. You'd think he was an oil sheikh or something!" She sucks in her breath, lets it out slowly. "What right did he have to hurl insults in my face? I spent hours on the script, trying to keep my hand from trembling... trying to block out the voices. But he *refused* to pay. Just stalked out, cursing my poor dead mother...." Panic cuts across Julia's face. "'Why a lion that looks like a pussycat?' he screamed. But after all, his wife insisted...."

Alya touches Julia's shoulder. "And when did all this happen?"

Julia's glance shifts downward toward the pink fuzz of her slippers. "Today. Or maybe yesterday? When Sari cooked the stew. The meat was tough, too salty for my taste...." Julia's sigh, a winter's wind, fills the corners of the narrow hallway.

Alya reaches out to fold Julia in her arms, to comfort her, to keep her from harm. But Julia pulls away, holds her arms rigidly against her waist.

"Sari refuses to play backgammon with me anymore. He says I take too long to decide. That I sometimes cheat." Her frantic glance skims Alya's face. "But how, oh how will I *ever* hope to win?"

A door creaks open above the stairway. Julia darts back into her room, slams the door shut behind her; the key clicks shut.

"I thought I heard voices...." Sari looks down at Alya from the top of the stairs, adds, smiling, "Ah, Alya! *Ahlan wa sahlan*! Welcome! So you came at last."

The stone staircase, Alya is convinced, was built for giants. At the upper landing, Sari takes her hand, helps her across the threshold and onto his patio-roof.

His grip tightens. "So glad you're here!"

Alya pauses to catch her breath, looks into Sari's narrow, sun-drenched face with its straggly hair and beard. Despite middle age, Sari still retains a lean athlete's build beneath a blue, paint-spattered shirt. A Greek ancestor, a discus thrower or craftsman, perhaps, on his father's side. His mother's people, Palestinian farmers, descended from a small clan near Nazareth.

Two cushioned rattan chairs and a small table piled high with newspapers face each other just beyond Sari's L-shaped roof apartment. Various-sized pots, set back against the parapet, hold ferns and the mint and basil herbs Alya gave him nearly two years ago. To the far right, tall cages enclose the doves and pigeons that keep Sari company.

He steers her toward the tall cages, his hand now light on her wrist. A pair of snow-white Indian fantails occupy the bottom half of the cage; one perches on an upper berth in meditative silence, while the other struts on pine needles, a jaunty angle to its feathered cap.

In the upper cage, a beige ring-neck dove huddles stoically on its nest, while its mate circles the periphery of the cage making soft, cooing sounds. Sari reaches into the upper cage and lifts the dove gently off its nest to reveal a pair of squirming, pink-skinned doves, smaller even than her thumb.

"Two days old today," he says. "Both parents take turns keeping them warm. They feed them that special milk they spew up for the occasion."

"I bet Julia must be entranced...."

He re-hooks the latch of the wire door, turns around to face her. "She wondered whether *she* was as ugly when she was born. I assured her most babies improve with age."

They move the rattan chairs away from the shadow of the house and into the bright May sun, for warmth. Sari pulls the table with its clutter of newspapers and books near to his chair.

Beyond the parapet, a *saru* tree from the garden extends its branches above the rooftop, partially blocks St. George's Cathedral's turret and a nearby minaret from view. To their left, palms precariously balanced on tall ragged stalks fan out against the sky. A man hawks his steamed corn in the street below, and a child's wail rises, like smoke, above the rooftops. But, for a time, the cooing of doves blocks out a restless world.

"Tea?" Sari asks. Without waiting for an answer, he strides over to the wooden crate and pulls up a sprig of mint. She follows him inside, across the hand-loomed crimson Es Samu rug of the front room, through the clutter of his bedroom, to the kitchen in the back. Despite an odor of burnt onions, the small kitchen is clean, the dishes washed and piled in the porcelain sink to air-dry. He puts the kettle on, moving mechanically in his own private world, independent, unmindful of her presence, gathering cups and saucers and sugar bowl on a round brass tray. From a shelf above the sink he takes out the ceramic teapot, with its drawing of anemones, and Julia's black initials writ boldly beneath green stems. The light-blue anemones are the work of a younger Julia, he tells her, her hands skilled then, without tremors. After he pours boiling water over tea leaves and fresh mint, Sari carries the tray outside and sets it on the table's edge. He disappears inside, returning with a bowl of cookies in one hand, scissors and comb in the other.

She asks, "Did something happen recently to liven up your life—and Julia's?"

As Sari gives his version of events, Alya seams it to Julia's, to give it perspective… like history. The customer, Zaid, was enraged because his wife ordered a plaque with his name below butterflies, and a lion yawning. The lion, Julia's drawing on bisque, was copied from an illustration in a children's book.

"'My wife giggles at me behind her hand,' Zaid complained. 'And now this latest humiliation: this new plaque, with crooked lettering. Besides, who wants a sissy of a lion at his door, above his name? I refuse it, throw it back in your face!' Forming a fist, he banged it on the counter, making the plaque rattle, breaking off a corner."

"That's when Julia flew into a rage." Sari smiles wryly, leans back in his chair. "As Zaid turned to go, Julia aimed the plaque… and hit him in the rear." Sari chuckles. "But what can I tell you about the righting of wrongs—about revenge?"

Alya sips hot minted tea and thinks of doves and pigeons imprisoned in cages, looking out. Perhaps used to it by now.

Reaching for a small, leather-bound book from a nearby table, Sari props it up on the angle of his knee. He looks up. "Before you came, I was reading poems from ancient Greece… May I read a line or two?"

At her nod, he begins to read out loud, translates:

"'In that radiant moment of victory, a man stands on the edge of the absolute narrow line separating mortal from god.'"

He looks up. "From fifth-century Greece I give you Pindar, poet of victory."

"Why not a poet who writes in praise of Athenian and Spartan *women*—forced to stay home and slave over hot coals?"

His eyebrow lifts. "In those 'unenlightened' days, wars and athletic games were the exclusive domain of men." He leans back in his chair, ponders a clear blue sky. "I wonder what Pindar would say about our little 'manly' coup in Greece?"

The question, unanswered, hangs between them like an opaque screen, blocking vision. What answer can she give—she who cares not a whit about modern politics, who, in the past, lay awake at night thinking not of a coup in Greece, or the latest shooting on the Syrian border, but tried to recreate, instead, the amber of Majed's eyes, the bristle of his face against her skin. Love, Majed told her once, was a mirage to dazzle, a golden net to trap birds on the wing.

Sari, bereft of human love, sets Pindar's book back on the small table, takes a gulp of tea. He picks up one of his Greek newspapers, spreads it open across his knees, smoothes out its edges.

His eyes search out the pockets of her resistance. "You've probably heard? The publisher of the *Athinaika* is now in custody of the junta. Labor unions and other 'leftist' groups are outlawed." His smile turns rueful, spreads across the arid lines of his face. "And my own father, in Athens, asks, 'Isn't censorship, after all, for the public good?' Why not beggars in asylums and off the streets, skirts set at 'decent' lengths and beards snipped off?" He fingers his own beard, pulls at its straggly edges. "I suppose," he adds, "the only bearded men my father will tolerate are our church Patriarch and his Merry Men."

Sari's indignation taunts Alya with its passion, dares her to disagree. But the surge of her own emotions focuses on people she knows, events close to home. She refuses to pick up the mantle or accept the challenge he offers, prefers, instead, to sip her tea, listen to the doves and ponder her life, realigned.

"No one at Uncle Sam's Bar and Grill—or anywhere else for

that matter—cares a fig about the loss of civil rights in Greece today," Sari gives her a pensive look, "…especially now, with 'incidents' on the Syrian–Israeli border and Nasser's latest move in Sinai."

"I hope," Alya says warily, "we won't have to test that narrow line your Pindar writes about—at least, not in a bloody war."

Alya's attention span for current events is measured in centimeters, comes from an occasional look at an *Al-Quds* Jerusalem newspaper, or a *Newsweek* or *Life*—borrowed from Clara's supply of months-old magazines. Dick has also introduced her to his "liberal rag," which she reads reluctantly and only at his insistence.

For Alya, history-in-the-making is too volatile for her blood. But history, past, like one of Clara's day-old cakes, its ingredients risen and now cooling, is more palatable, more to her liking. Abd al-Malik. Napoleon. Bismarck. Saladin—their deeds framed in space and time, exposed from a distance to the world's judgments.

And wars past, their causes and results as clear as ink on paper. Yet, if they knew then what we now know, would they ever have….? And what of wars that never were? An *almost* war or revolution? Governments or factions pacified in the nick of time, turmoil abating. Glory, honor, greed, insecurity, even despair, given brief respite?

Until the next time.

As Alya bends over Sari's docile head with scissors and comb, the murmuring of doves imposes its own rhythm on the convoluted affairs of men and nations—on the queries of her life.

Hesitantly, almost reluctantly, (does he take her for a mother confessor?) Sari begins to talk of Julia, his voice muted, drained of passion. For several weeks now, Julia has been docile, taking her pills. Or so he thought. But, from the beginning, *tawla*—the backgammon game they both loved—seemed to trigger in Julia a fierce rivalry. She would fling the dice on the board, he says, as if tossing *milleem* coins to beggars, throwing them with a ferocity that made the dice jump, roll on the floor, lost for a time under table or chairs or at carpet's edge. Lost, until one of them, crawling on hands and knees, rescued the ivory dice from dust in the corners of the room.

And Sari, promising the game would end with Julia's next tantrum, would begin anew at Uncle Sam's, with a stranger, perhaps, tranquil, sipping *arak*. Or with one of the regulars, nursing his *arkeelah*, inhaling calm and the odor of burnt charcoal, throwing dice that did not jump or spill on floors and hide in corners. Playing for the love of the game, not out of adamant rivalry—or even terror.

"But what if I should lose?" Julia demands of Sari. "Would you go away, like father?"

She lost that last game (when she was winning before, for days on end)—all because of a stupid, imprecise move to test her luck. Precision and luck, their father said, were inevitably intertwined.

As a boy, Sari learned the *tawla* game at his father's knee, watching the dice clatter on the wooden surface of the board, counting black numbers on white. Fate turned the tables, startled, showed its power, their father—who was leaving Julia behind—said that *last* time. And she, lurking in the shadows, waited to catch whatever fate the dice would bring.

"The trick," their father said, "is to maneuver your way back home."

"I finally stopped playing *tawla* with her," Sari says now, moving his head sideways, patient with the snipping of her scissors. "Those last few times she placed her chips in awkward places, her eyes narrowed, watching my every move. And Monday, when she hit my wooden man, triumphant, slamming him across the ridge, I reminded her that six and one did not add up to eight. Trembling, as if life itself depended on the throw, she swept the pieces to the floor and stomped out—blasting me with epithets—returning moments later, penitent, to pick the chips up, begging to play once more. But this final time I stood firm, boycotting this and future games—to make my point."

Sari cocks his head, yields to the slight pressure of Alya's hand as she snips at the ragged edges of his beard to restore symmetry. Shadows lengthening enclose them both: shadows of wire cages and birds and potted plants and the slant of the house. Silhouettes on cement, over pebbles, against the parapet and the top of the *saru* tree and the palms. In a few more minutes she will leave him here, with his Pindar and his newspapers tangled in the shadows, leave him with Julia and go back to reconstruct her life.

She hands him comb and scissors, brushes clumps of graying hairs from his shoulders to the floor. Easing herself back into her chair, Alya pours herself a cup of lukewarm tea, and extends bare legs into a patch of sun. She smiles at Sari reflectively above the rim of her teacup.

The air is cool and smells of basil. A warbler lands on the parapet, flicks the black and gray-white tail, the jabber of his "zerwit" interrupting her musings.

Sari excuses himself, disappears inside, perhaps to consider his shorn image in the mirror, to bring back a broom and dustpan. Returning, he sweeps checkered locks into the dustpan, looks up dejectedly.

"Almost any girl will marry you now," Alya assures him. "All you have to do is ask."

He runs his fingers through the shortened hair, pulls at the newly trimmed beard. His thin, grooved face, less grizzled now, seems almost boyish in its new packaging.

"In all my forty-three years of living," he says, "I've fallen in love twice; asked three women to marry me. Each one had an excuse worthy of the gods."

"All fools," Alya says.

The warbler flies to the dome of the storage building, makes his whirring sounds, like the clattering of a wooden toy. Downstairs, the sound of a door slamming startles it into flight.

Sari leans toward Alya, takes her hand in his.

"I hope," Sari says, clearing his throat, "that Majed is worthy of your ardor and all the risks you take."

"Risks to my reputation, you mean, in a town like Beit Nuba?"

"That—and other risks."

"Love, my mother has often told me, is for fools. Now I believe her."

"When did this cynicism happen?"

"Saturday evening, when Majed told me about his mother's plans for his life." Alya attempts a smile. "And on Sunday, I discovered... he didn't quite fit into mine."

She disengages her hand, picks up her purse, and holds it against her breasts as if to ward off further intrusions into privacy.

"Next time you visit your *'Ammi* Musa in Jerusalem, stop by. Don't forget we're on the way to *Bab el-Amud*. Julia and I would love to see you more often."

"*Insha'Allah*: God willing." She gives him a piquant smile. "This could mean yes or no—or even maybe…."

For now, her own will—not God's—was in flux, adjusting to the feel of things—to the discovery of who she was, what she would become in a day... or a year from now. With puppet strings cut, her legs would have to develop stamina for the dance.

Sari follows as she walks briskly past the cages with their tenant-doves, toward the stairway landing. She pauses long enough to note the purple stem of a caper vine as it winds its way across the parapet wall, roots embedded in stone crevices. White-petaled flowers with reddish stamens are perfectly at home here, stranded on the wall.

This is what I am, what I've become, Alya thinks now. A woman clinging to the steep incline of walls, roots embedded in stone. Making do.

Downstairs, Alya knocks on Julia's door, calls her name. But Julia's locked door yields only an echo in response.

At the front gate, Sari turns to face her. "Call when you have time," he says in a disembodied voice. "I'll call when I must."

"When you call next time, feel free to give your name. That might convince Nawal you're not a Mossad... or CIA agent."

Sari leans against the gatepost and stares at cars passing. The man (or was it a boy?) with the cart of steamed corn, has gone home. But honking cars and people walking home from work and cats and a stray dog or two remain to clutter up the road.

"Thanks for the haircut," Sari says. "And for listening to my meandering talk of politics and Julia...."

"Give her my love." Alya hesitates. "Bring her to the hotel some afternoon. The change might do her good."

His melancholy eyes, incandescent in the late afternoon light, hold the mystery of himself intact. He says wistfully, "A change will do us *all* good."

Alya makes her way down the narrow sidewalk past the American consulate. In the consulate garden, a man and a woman are huddled on a bench near a rosebush, filling out an official form. Despite gas fumes from cars, the fragrance of roses trails after Alya, lingers, even when she nears the American School of Oriental Research.

She pauses at the window of a travel agency to grimace at her reflection in glass, to tuck in a strand of unruly hair. Propelled by imprudence, by an inexplicable yearning, she quickens her pace down Ibn Khaldun Street to the familiar corner of the Ritz Hotel. She turns right on Ibn Battuta Street, and stands for a time on the sidewalk, gathering courage—across from the pink and white facade of the radio station with its skeleton of a tower. She ponders the shuttered windows of the recording studio, considers its balcony. Majed is probably in his cubicle, signing off, ending his broadcast for the day.

She recognizes Nidal, twelve. He stands in the doorway of *Abu* Abdo's coffee shop across from the radio station and swings his coffee tray by its pyramid-handle and watches other boys his age play tag in the middle of the street.

A smaller, younger boy runs frantically across the street, trips and falls on the asphalt road, scrambles away just before he's caught. As Alya begins to cross the street, he sprints toward her, pauses long enough to grab at her skirt. She stares down into the small, bruised face, feels the thump of his forehead against her legs. A small terror takes hold—her childish dread of moving shadows outside windows at night, the howls of foxes in the valleys beyond Beit Nuba.

And even when the boy, laughing, bolts back toward the sidewalk after his friends, the residue of terror remains, like an aftermath of a bad dream. Alya squares her shoulders, takes a deep breath and, trailed by a cacophony of children's voices, walks away from the Hashemite English Broadcasting Station and Majed Alami.

President Nasser said replacement of United Nations Emergency Force troops in Sharm el-Sheik commanding approaches to Israel's port of Elat "means confirmation of our rights and sovereignty over the Gulf of Aqaba...." [He] spoke as U.N. Secretary-General U Thant flew toward Cairo in an effort to avert a Middle East war....

The Christian Science Monitor, May 24, 1967

Sixteen people were killed when a booby-trapped Syrian car exploded at the Jordan post of Ramtha. Jordan accused the Baathist regime of "premeditated sabotage"....

Time, June 2, 1967

CHAPTER SEVEN

Lunch and Politics

AS ALYA APPROACHES the Semiramis parking lot, Omar's Sheltie, asleep near the gate, opens one eye, lifts his head, then readjusts his muzzle between his paws. Alya pauses to catch her breath, to shift books around. Just then Badri sprints past, nearly stumbles over the prone body of the Sheltie. The dog lets out a yelp, and the book under Badri's arm falls to the ground. Lined papers with Badri's lettering flutter toward a black Jaguar with Amman license plates; a sealed envelope lands at Alya's feet.

But before Alya can bend down to pick up the envelope, Badri snatches it away and sprints past her, toward the hotel.

An old-model Mercedes taxi stops outside the gate. Passenger and driver emerge, retrieve suitcases from the trunk. Each carrying a bulging suitcase, the men walk purposefully toward the hotel.

The noonday sun has etched a shimmer of light over men and women clustered around tables on the patio and under the pines. Beyond the veranda, near potted white dahlias, a woman with honey-blonde hair sits at a table next to a man in tinted glasses, his arm draped across the back of her wicker chair. Alya recognizes Jaleel Hawa, producer of television programs in English, here with Priscilla Madding, English news anchor on Jordan television.

Jaleel is already on his feet and striding toward Alya, arms open wide. But Alya is grateful for the barrier of school books, since here, in Beit Nuba, he must restrain his ardor at seeing Alya after nearly eight years—no longer a girl, gullible, yearning for a thick-waisted, middle-aged professor, but clear-eyed and, despite her twenty-seven years and *almost* spinsterhood, attractive still.

"Alya Habeeb! Even more beautiful than ever!"

His smile stretches the dark, even line of his moustache, brackets the corners of his mouth. He wears his expensive suit casually, as if, after all those years, he has grown used to affluence.

Alya nods toward the table. "What is it this time? Romance... or business?"

"A little of both, I hope." His voice turns confidential. "I've always had champagne taste in my women—even when we were both at the University...."

Alya asks, sarcasm in her voice, "So, how did Samia fit in?"

"Easy prey to my charm, I'm afraid." He shrugs. "In those days I wanted *you*, but found, instead, your willing roommate." He smiles indulgently at her. "Tell me. Do you still hear from your venerable Professor Antone?"

"He wrote constantly when I first left. But I never wrote back. How could I? I was too busy watching over my father as he lay dying."

A lie—to save face—since Professor Antone wrote her only one letter. And that, in reply to her own.

Jaleel Hawa says now, "Would you convince Priscilla to stay for the hotel dancing this evening? And even better: try to persuade her to spend the night...."

"But aren't you the one with persuasive charm?"

"I tried that on her a little while ago," Jaleel says, "but it didn't seem to work...."

He touches Alya's elbow. "Come," he says, "I'll introduce

you."

Priscilla smiles up at them as Jaleel Hawa introduces Alya Habeeb.

"Jaleel and I were old college friends in Beirut many moons ago," Alya says—"when I was young and foolish."

Priscilla's cool green eyes focus on Alya's face. "Some of us may not be so young, but we're still foolish...."

Alya notes the well-manicured nails, the bracelet of jade set in platinum on her slender wrist. "Priscilla Madding, news anchor on Amman TV...." She flashes the professional smile of a television anchorwoman. "I am she-who-reads-the-news-as-others-write-it—censored or uncensored."

Jaleel pulls out a chair for Alya, takes his own seat between them. Priscilla makes a sweeping gesture toward hotel and grounds. "Tell me. Who *owns* all this?"

"Once upon a time all this belonged to my maternal uncle," Alya says. "My uncle's widow in Brazil now owns it." Alya laughs softly. "My brother, Omar, now runs the place, and once in a while, I help Omar at the desk, or in emergencies. Or—from his viewpoint—help create them."

"Was the summer dancing *your* idea, then?"

Alya nods. "I finally convinced Omar—much to my mother's dismay! But believe it or not, it seems to work."

Jaleel's eyes graze Priscilla's profile turned away from him, the seductive curtain of blonde hair across her cheek, lancing her shoulder. His glance shifts back to Alya.

"Why not describe the wonderful band, Alya? And tell us how comfortable your beds are...." Jaleel's hand rests lightly over Priscilla's arm; his voice becomes a plea. "Since you already have a fill-in for tonight's newscast, why rush back to Amman?"

Priscilla's shoulders stiffen beneath her tailored jacket. "Separate rooms, then?"

He leans toward her, says quietly, "But why keep up this farce of propriety in Beit Nuba? In Amman, after all, everyone knows...."

Priscilla stands up, turns to Alya. "I'd like to wash up before lunch. Would you... show me where?"

"I'll take you up to my room if you like," Alya says.

Priscilla gives Jaleel Hawa an antiseptic smile. "Try to stay out of mischief while I'm gone."

He winks at her. "I'll do my best."

Alya leads the way through the maze of tables on the veranda and into the cool, high-ceilinged *liwan* of the Semiramis. Nawal looks up, gives Alya a small wave.

A stocky, balding man in his mid-fifties stands near Nawal's desk, his red tie askew. Next to him two bulging suitcases lean against each other, as if for comfort.

Nawal looks up at them from worried eyes. "This is *Sayyid* Rasheed," Nawal says formally. He came by taxi a few minutes ago from the Kalandia airport." She hesitates. "He's come all the way from Brooklyn, he tells me, to... to...."

"To find myself a wife." *Sayyid* Rasheed rolls small, marble eyes their way, makes a sweeping gesture toward the *liwan*. "This is a fine place you have here. Real fine. Almost as good as the Holiday Inn." An effusive sigh. "As my wife, God rest her soul, used to say: 'The Holiday Inn is tops.'"

Alya's glance takes in the fleshy face, the thinning hair. "We're glad you like our hotel," she says, in her most diplomatic voice. "How long do you plan to stay with us?"

He lifts his palms toward the ceiling. "It's all in God's hands. You see, ladies...," he makes a small bow, "I've come to Beit Nuba not only to find me a wife—but also a mother for my *kawareet*—my poor motherless children."

"And how many children do you have?" Alya asks.

She regrets her question as soon as he gives names, ages, and detailed descriptions.

"Will the chosen wife also have to sing?" Priscilla asks under her breath.

"...To sing?" he repeats.

"As in 'The Sound of Music'...."

Sayyid Rasheed studies Priscilla with an appraising eye. "I have no conditions about either voice or beauty. Character is above all."

"Happy hunting, *Sayyid* Rasheed," Priscilla says.

"But why this formality between us?" His hand flutters in the air-space between them. "Although Rasheed is the name my father gave me, in Brooklyn they call me Rick. You can also call me Rick...."

Alya thinks of Nasir Hatimi, widowed owner of the bookstore, who still remains unsuccessful in his search for a wife and mother to his children.

"An American passport," *Sayyid* Rasheed says, allaying all doubt. "This is what women in Beit Nuba will find most attractive." He looks up coyly. "Not my four children, or my thinning hair."

In her bedroom, Alya points to the bathroom and hands Priscilla a clean face towel. "Make yourself at home," she says, and proceeds to follow her own advice. Depositing her books on the desk, she kicks off her shoes and leans back against her bed pillows.

"Nice place you have here," Priscilla observes. She glides around the room, looking at photographs, picks up a blue ceramic cat transformed into a paperweight, contemplates the drawing of a man and woman in profile on the wall.

She spins around. "Why the woman's downcast eyes? Is she afraid to look, to see what he's *really* like?" Her face looks ravaged by the thought.

"She probably was... a year, a week ago. But since then, she's learned a thing or two about life. About herself."

Priscilla moves stealthily toward Alya. In her cool green eyes, a storm is brewing.

"I never learn, do I? Never want to learn." Her voice, self-mocking, spins on air. "Two years ago, in San Francisco, I fell madly in love with Bill. Margie, I convinced myself, was just a girl he knew at work. Besides—brown eyes never turned him on. Green, he assured me, was his favorite color." A short, bitter laugh. "Here I go again. Same line, different accent. And me—

never knowing when to say No! or Stop! or even 'Give me time to think it through.'"

But how, Alya wonders, does one analyze love's consequences and calculate its risks? "You've got impeccable control on that magic tube," Alya says now. "I would never have guessed...."

Priscilla flashes Alya her television smile. "'Born to keep up appearances' should be tattooed on my forehead. But it's the bathroom I came for—not to burden you with my True Confessions." She rummages inside her purse, produces a miniature hairbrush. "Hi, ho! It's off to the bathroom I go... to touch up my faltering image."

When Priscilla reemerges, her face is scrubbed clean of makeup. She tosses a sleek blonde head. "We've got a quirky relationship—Jaleel and I. He makes me happy... or utterly miserable." Her eyes focus inward. "We have this power struggle between us. I hate to give in—especially when he tries to manipulate. And he never gives up trying."

"But as a modern American woman," Alya says, "surely you're liberated and can do what you please."

"Not really. I'm a wimp. I stand there like a puppy, hang my tongue out and beg."

Priscilla studies her face in the mirror above the dresser and skillfully begins to reapply her makeup.

In one of Alya's college photographs, Jaleel Hawa stands by their college water fountain, a straw hat tilted at a rakish angle across his squinting eyes. During his college years, he had inspired ardor in the breasts of several ex-virgins; yet had failed to lure Alya away from Professor Antone—a seasoned philanderer and seducer of impressionable coeds like herself.

After she left Beirut and came home to her ailing father, Alya wrote Professor Antone from Beit Nuba to protest a too-generous grade in his class.

"But you *did* work hard, my sweet Alya," Professor Antone wrote back in his precise handwriting. "You say you were distracted, but that was quite normal—given the circumstances. I, too, was distracted—by your gazelle-like eyes. But it was your youthful innocence I cherished most—that, and a willingness to be taught...."

The letter, signed with an initial, was in a shoebox in the back of her closet, next to Alya's sociology paper on 'The Passionate Attachments of Man'—a paper on the marriage and burial rites of the ancient Babylonians—for which she had received the high grade she did not deserve.

She tells Priscilla an abbreviated version of her memory. They laugh, ripples of laughter building into wild crescendo, hooting laughter pouring out like a water spray. They catch a glimpse of themselves in the mirror—rag dolls, lacking dignity. And laughter, abrasive, cynical, begins anew.

When Priscilla finally leaves Alya's room, a bond had been formed.

A knock at Alya's door. Omar, formal in tie and suit, says humbly, "The guests are all here, waiting. Will you come?" His glance settles briefly on Alya's wounded cheek. "I'm sorry for Saturday night. I didn't mean to...." Pain now apparent in his eyes.

"I didn't mean to break your tie clip," Alya says. She does not mention Clara, or the message she had read.

"Any jeweler can repair it," he says.

She meets his glance. "Did you get the letter Badri was in such a tearing hurry to give you?"

Omar's face is a mask. "It was just an invitation to dinner at Lutfi's house in Nablus. A business matter...." He hesitates. "Miriam thinks flowers from the garden would add color to the luncheon table...."

Pity overwhelms her for this man, her brother, who walks the razor's edge in his love of another man's wife. A man willing to give advice on business matters to other men—impractical and volatile men like Lutfi Abdul Kader.

"I'll bring carnations," she says, to reassure him.

❧   ❧   ❧

A pale silk blouse and black skirt will lend her an air of dignity, Alya decides as she forms her auburn hair into a chignon. She adds bright amber beads for a noonday meal, and hopes that politics will disappear from the talk of men and women at special luncheons. Afterwards, she will walk back to school for her afternoon art classes.

She takes the back stairs to the garden where pink and white carnations grow next to the greens of mint and parsley. A few minutes later, in the kitchen, while Miriam takes out roasted chickens, Alya arranges long-stemmed carnations in an Indian brass vase.

In the dining room, a baroque sideboard stands near the door, its clawed feet planted firmly on the tessellated floor, its beveled mirror reflecting glasses and dessert dishes and the angled heads of diners.

Omar and guests sit near the tall arched windows, overlooking the veranda.

"Carnations from our garden," Alya announces, and sets the ceramic vase down next to the platter of individual meat-and-parsley "pizzas" called *sfeehas.*

"Ah, lovely flowers!" Madam Salwa Jaber exclaims. But despite her girlish delight at fresh carnations, Madam Jaber—fiftyish, with hair tightly rolled at the nape of her neck—retains an austere dignity as principal of the Government School for Girls in Beit Nuba.

From his seat at one end of the table, Omar points Alya to the chair on his right. He introduces her to Fahd Abdul Nabi, assistant to the Minister of Education in Amman—also known informally as *Abu* Mazen. A rotund fellow in his mid-sixties, with a *hatta*-and-*agal* head-dress, he half-rises to his feet, spreads stubby fingers across his chest in greeting. "A privilege," he says, his moustache expanding like an uneven fringe above his upper lip.

Across the table, Priscilla gives Alya an enigmatic smile, her mask in place. Jaleel, on Priscilla's left, nods his formal acknowledgment of her presence.

While Alya ladles rice, grape leaves and stuffed *kusa* squash onto individual plates, Omar begins the ritual of cutting up and serving roast chicken. All help themselves to the platter of *sfeehas* in the center of the table.

"Last time I tried to make *sfeeha*," Priscilla says, "I used Bisquick. And forgot the onions." Smiling, she catches Alya's eye. "Cooking was never my best subject."

"A little garlic," Madam Jaber says. "My mother always used a little garlic."

Abu Mazen bites into a *sfeeha*, chews slowly. "They tell me the dough must be made from scratch. And my dear wife gets up before dawn to prepare and knead the dough."

Alya passes the bowl of yogurt with a sprinkle of dried mint to Priscilla. She glances over at Omar, senses his restlessness with this talk of food.

"You've probably heard about the Syrian car bomb at Jordan's Ramtha checkpoint?" Jaleel Hawa says during a pause in the conversation.

Heads nod; several murmur their condemnation of the deed. Alya, who listens to news only when compelled to by loudspeakers in the street, looks puzzled.

"No sense in it," *Abu* Mazen shakes his head as if to dispel a gnat from his whiskers. "Sixteen of our people killed. And several wounded!" He takes in a breath, lets it out slowly. "And why *now*... even though his majesty, King Hussein, has declared full support of Egypt, Syria and the Arab League Council?"

"Nasser is never satisfied with King Hussein's moves... however conciliatory," Priscilla says, her green eyes searching out each face, as if for confirmation. "I bet Nasser's the *real* culprit behind this latest bombing at Ramtha....."

Omar half-rises from his chair. "Just because both Syria and Egypt were once members of the United Arab Republic does not mean Egypt is to blame for Syria's misdeeds."

Abu Mazen leans forward, his tie ballooning precariously over his plate. "Nasser's moves in Sinai and the Gulf of Aqaba have created, I'm afraid, an added crisis for us all."

"It was Amman radio that egged Nasser on," Omar says, his

voice rising. "The Jordan radio accused Nasser of 'cowardice,' of hiding behind U.N. troops it labeled 'a pane of glass.'" Omar glares at *Abu* Mazen. "But, whatever Nasser chooses to do on Egyptian land and waterways is his own business—as head of a sovereign state. And, since Sinai is Egyptian land, Nasser has every right to replace the U.N. force guarding the Sinai border between Egypt and Israel with Egyptian troops."

Priscilla's green eyes narrow as she contemplates Omar's face. A small silence, a clearing of her throat. "But Nasser's stirring the pot *does* open up some unpleasant possibilities, don't you think?"

"Nasser's a fool," *Abu* Mazen declares. "With Egyptian soldiers embroiled in Yemen's civil war, he can't afford to taunt Israel—a country backed by the military might of America."

"I'm sure Nasser is not anxious for war with Israel," Omar says, sarcasm in his voice. He glances over at *Abu* Mazen. "Don't forget. Last month—despite a defensive treaty with Syria—Nasser did nothing, beyond rhetoric, when Israeli jets attacked Syria."

Priscilla's gaze is steady on Omar's face. "Western governments worry about anything that might upset the equilibrium in the Middle East."

"I read somewhere," begins Madam Jaber, "that Britain has given Israel a renovated World War II submarine...."

"Shouldn't Britain's generosity also extend to Jordan?" Jaleel Hawa says with a smile. "Who knows? Jordan might find some use for a submarine...."

Muted chuckles. But *Abu* Mazen, unmoved by humor at Jordan's expense, mutters something about Jordan's army being second to none, "...even though it was Glubb Pasha, a Britisher, who helped create the Jordanian army."

"That explains the bagpipes," Priscilla says with a grin.

"Yes. The bagpipes," Alya says. "But don't forget our very own Lawrence of Arabia. He rallied the Arabs to fight on the British side—and against the Ottoman Turks—with promises of independence and self-rule."

"Promises all broken," Omar says bitterly, "especially here, in Palestine."

Alya glances warily at her brother's rigid profile, notes the indentation in his jaw—as if words were being chewed and swallowed whole. She reaches for the stuffed *kusa*-squash serving dish, passes it to Madam Jaber, then offers it to Omar as a distraction.

"I like its tartness," Madam Jaber says as she ladles one plump *kusa* onto her plate, with a drizzle of tomato sauce. "But I could never duplicate...."

"But surely, *Sayyid* Omar," *Abu* Mazen interrupts, "in this year of 1967—you do realize the Jordanian government is *your* government as well?"

"Not *chosen*, but imposed on us in '48," Omar says, "the very year Palestine was dismembered... and we Palestinians lost our land!"

An uneasy silence follows as others at the table mull over Omar's remark, brace themselves for confrontation. This time, Alya knows—a rock, replacing pebbles, has hit the bottom of the pool.

"But how could what was left of the Palestinian West Bank possibly have *survived* without Jordanian leadership? At the time," Jaleel Hawa adds in a pacifying tone, "*some* kind of union with Jordan seemed inevitable."

"But why should we, Palestinians, remain dependent on other governments?" Omar demands. "Given half a chance, we can manage our own affairs, and create an independent state of our own...."

Madam Jaber directs her appeasing glance at *Abu* Mazen. "As a professional woman, I owe much to Jordan's Majesty King Hussein, and as a Palestinian, I'm grateful I still live on the sacred soil of my own land."

"But I thought," Omar says, derision in his voice, "your people originally came from Jaffa on the Mediterranean coast?"

A pensive look touches Madam Jaber's gray-flecked eyes. "Yes." A sigh. "My grandfather owned an orange grove in Jaffa, my father a pharmacy. But, even before the war of '48, they were forced to leave Jaffa. As refugees, they ultimately settled here, in Beit Nuba. But, as the saying goes, 'Half a loaf is better than none.'"

Abu Mazen picks up a stuffed grape leaf, pops it into his mouth, and wipes his fingers on his linen napkin. He glances over at Omar.

"Surely you know, *Sayyid* Omar," he begins, now relaxed, almost expansive. "Your Palestinian West Bank is of *equal* importance to our own land *east* of the Jordan River. After all, we consider the holy *Al-Haram ash-Shareef*, or Noble Sanctuary, in Jerusalem as one of Islam's most sacred treasures."

"Israel... and the Western world call that the Temple Mount," Priscilla says.

Omar shrugs. "They can call it what they will."

"Are you aware," *Abu* Mazen continues, "that your Palestinians make up at least one-third of Jordan's population?"

"And yet," Omar says now, "Jordan refuses to give us arms for our own self-defense, and has even banned the Palestinian Liberation Army from its soil."

Abu Mazen ignores Omar's outburst, says in conciliatory tones, "But don't forget, our Jordanian soldiers were killed fighting to defend the Palestinian village of Es Samu...."

"The people of Es Samu," Omar says, his voice rising, "had no arms to repel the attack on their homes. And the Jordanian soldiers arrived too late to do any good."

Butrus, the waiter, appears with a pitcher of water to refill empty glasses. A man at a nearby table begins to laugh; across the room, a stylish woman in a blue dress and a rotund man in a beige suit get up to leave.

"Here in the Middle East, one can never guess when a small skirmish can escalate into war," Priscilla says with a shrug. "It's also a pity that U Thant did *not* consult with other countries before dismissing the U.N. force from Sinai and Sharm El-Sheik—at the entrance of the Red Sea. Because of this, Elat, and all of Israel, may be subject to Nasser's whims."

A vein in Omar's temple throbs to a melody with no rhythm, no discernible sound. He gets up slowly from his seat, points a menacing finger at Priscilla's face. A baton, it slashes at air, directs the flat, contemptuous voice. "It's Egypt that's been subject to America's—and Israel's—dictates." Omar's rage and accusations spill over, leave nothing behind except Priscilla's hollow green eyes and painted mouth clamped shut to stifle screams.

"Omar...." Alya's urgent voice throbs in the space above her head. "Omar...." Alya pulls on his arm. "Please remember, Americans don't always reflect their government's politics...."

At the next table, an older couple pause, forks in mid-air. Heads turn, curious eyes search out the riddle.

Already on his feet, Jaleel glares at Omar. "A gentleman," he announces, "must *never* insult a woman—especially a *guest* in our country. What sort of image would she get of a people unable to listen to a viewpoint other than their own?"

Jaleel—transformed suddenly from Playboy of the Eastern World to Defender of Western Womanhood, Alya thinks.

Omar sits down heavily in his chair, covers his face with his hands.

"Here we are," Alya says, "amateurs all, giving expert opinions on politics, arguing about events over which we have little—or no—control." She stirs uneasily in her chair, searches the faces around her—faces in need of security, of one perfect answer. "I much prefer history," she adds. "At least history gives us the benefit of hindsight."

Alya wonders now at her dubious role as pundit—she who lacks wisdom about her own life. For beneath the veneer of eloquence, a small tremor of panic remains—the scraping of sand against glass.

Omar lifts his head. "History tells us of the struggles between the powerless and the powerful," he begins. "But winners usually write the history books, while losers are forced to accept their verdict." He directs his glance at *Abu* Mazen, who sits impassively in his chair. "Our fate, as Palestinians, lies with those who've long meddled in our lives...."

"The Jordanian government, I'm sure, has our best interests

at heart," Madam Jaber says in a conciliatory tone. "And for this we should all be grateful."

As if woken from sleep, Priscilla redirects a crisp look at a spot near to Omar's left ear. "Alya's right," she says slowly. "But if I disagree with you, that doesn't mean your opinion of 'Truth' has more substance than mine...."

"Truth is a tricky word," Alya says. "Our opinions don't always consider the 'truth,' and our assessments are often subjective."

"In today's world," Omar interrupts, exasperation in his voice, "any fool can give an opinion. But for an opinion of substance, one must have knowledge and experience...."

"And a little wisdom," Alya says.

"Wisdom is a rare commodity in today's market," Madam Jaber says with a sigh.

"I'm very sorry, I didn't mean to...." Fragments of Omar's apology to Priscilla cling to air like steam rising. Omar, Alya knows, has become expert in spewing words of repentance.

Coffee is served in the formal living room, east of the *liwan* front room. *Abu* Mazen, slumped in a red velvet armchair, describes his wife's baked chicken *musakhan* dish, on *taboun* bread, with lemon and *sumac* herb. He holds the tips of his fingers against his puckered lips, smacks his approval in pantomime.

"The *sumac* plant *I* know," Priscilla says, "turns brilliant red in autumn and, some say, is poisonous...."

"The *sumac* plant *we* know is an herb with a lemony tart taste," Alya says. Politics is forgotten for a while as talk now shifts to educational priorities and the media. While Alya nibbles at a sweet piece of *baklava*, *Abu* Mazen argues the value of memorization. The old system was best, he says. New ideas appeal to those who abhor real study—especially the young. "How would I recite the *suras* from the Koran—without memorization?" he asks rhetorically.

"Modern ideas have *some* validity—but only in their own place." Madam Jaber touches a napkin to her lips. "Yet, surely room exists for both old and new?"

"Back in Richmond," Priscilla says, "we're still debating the dictum of 'Spare the rod and spoil the child.' It's a never-ending argument."

"With boys, it may be a good thing to occasionally use the rod," Madam Jaber hesitates. "But for *our* girls, a look, a strong word may be enough."

Jaleel Hawa nods his agreement.

Before Alya goes up to her room to change back into her teaching clothes, Priscilla catches up with her. "We're meeting to decide crucial issues in education," she tells Alya. "We plan to put on an 'all things to all people' educational TV program. Sure you don't want to attend?"

"I have an afternoon art class to teach, and I can't keep my little girls waiting," Alya smiles, "or they become restless." She recalls Priscilla's dilemma. "So, have you made plans for tonight yet?" she asks.

Priscilla's green eyes meet Alya's. "I'm still waiting for that bit of wisdom...."

"Aren't we all?"

Alya sits on the edge of her bed and ponders her incongruous life at the Semiramis. She thinks of Omar, and the swell of anger embedded in his own life. Returning from her room, she pauses midway down the stairway, and catches a glimpse of Omar and *Abu* Mazen through the partially open living room door. They huddle on the red velvet couch, an envelope between them. *Abu* Mazen reaches for the envelope, tears it in half, throws it on the rug at his feet. Omar bends down and picks up the pieces, puts them in his pants pocket. He stands up abruptly and, without a backward glance, heads for the door.

Later, when he sees Alya, Omar tells her, his voice a fierce whisper, "*Abu* Mazen is a pompous old fool who thinks he knows everything. How can you reason with such a man?"

Alya smiles, says nothing.

Later that afternoon in art class, as Alya bends over the clay piece of ten-year-old Basma, she points out ways of roughing up the smooth edges of the dragon's tail to form the needed scales.

"But I wanted to make a bear instead," Basma says, on the verge of tears. "I've never seen a *real* dragon... have you?"

"Only in picture books," Alya says. "And in your imagination...."

"Do dragons have wings?" Basma asks, her small pinched face lifted to Alya's.

"Once upon a time..." Alya begins, and Basma's face brightens up and her fingers rest lightly against the bear-turned-dragon as she listens, wide-eyed, to the tale Alya now spins. But other girls in the class demand Alya's time and she must pay *them* attention—these girls of nine or ten who are learning to voice their doubts about authority—and dragons.

Taxi Waiting

IN THE HOTEL parking lot, a taxi driver leans against his old Mercedes, cigarette dangling from his mouth, eyes half-closed. But as Alya passes by, returning from school, he snaps to attention, waves her to a stop.

"*Sitt* Alya, please tell the American lady I tired of waiting?" He glances at his watch. "I wait for two hours already." He flicks his cigarette into the jasmine bush, lifts a gloomy face toward Alya's. "Ten minutes ago, when I go in to ask, a man in dark glasses he tell me to leave. But the American lady said not to go away. But now it's nearly 4:30, and I'd like to drive the forty-five minutes to Amman before dark."

"I'll find out what I can," Alya says.

As she is about to walk into the vestibule, Alya nearly collides into Priscilla, who stops short and looks up at Alya from reddened eyes.

"Well, I did it. One small step for womankind." She gives Alya a self-conscious grin. "'What's wrong with a little dancing, with sharing a room?' he argues, reminding me how he came to my defense—as if I owed him one. 'Not at the risk of *my* reputation, *my* feelings,' I said, and this time I stood my ground."

"You'll be making one impatient taxi driver very happy," Alya says.

Priscilla hesitates. "A friend of yours just called, and left a message with Nawal. Something about his sister's disappearance...." She gives Alya a quick hug. "Well, let's hope political sanity prevails, that the Mideast doesn't blow up. I'm not quite ready for Armageddon."

In the parking lot, an impatient taxi driver loudly honks his displeasure at waiting.

The State Department urges American citizens to avoid travel to Israel, Egypt, Syria and Jordan and advised American citizens without serious business to leave at the earliest opportunity....

The New York Times, May 23, 1967

Americans were advised not to travel except for urgent reasons to the UAR [Egypt], Syria, Jordan or Israel....

The Christian Science Monitor, May 24, 1967

War precautions pushed in Israel.... Pupils Sandbag Jerusalem Schools. Tourists Leave.

The New York Times, May 25, 1967

CHAPTER EIGHT

Sari

PERCHED AT THE COUNTER, she wears her skirt above her knees, flaunts ample bronzed thighs in the dim light.

"This Uncle Sam's is not too bad... for an Arab watering hole," she says, and gives a little laugh.

"Its Jerusalem owner was once a taxi driver in New York, even served in the U.S. army," Sari says, "which might explain the name."

Her caramel eyes appraise Sari like a cat's. "You're a native, then?"

Sari fashions a reply for a woman he's met by chance. "Born in Jerusalem... forty-three years ago. A Greek father. A Palestinian Arab mother. So, take your pick."

She sips the white smoky *arak*, says, after a while, "I've no prejudices against Arabs—whole, or half-something like yourself."

Her name, she tells him, is Fiona Kooperman; she is of English and German descent. "Works almost as well as Arab and Greek," she adds in her Oxford-tinted accent.

He considers her chance intrusion into his life, reflects on possibilities. "What brings you here?" he asks. "I'd think Western watering holes were more your style."

She smiles. "I wanted to discover for myself the *native* lures of this town." She sets her glass down, her bracelets shimmering as if in a special signal. "Besides—I also write 'Adventuring!' a travel column for a small London rag. I try to give my blue-collar readers a sampling of exotic, out-of-the-way places they may never get to see."

"Ah. A writer, then?"

"Of sorts. I've also written poetry... and a novel, once—about a British spy. But I've lost the knack." She looks forlorn, as if the loss is more than she can bear.

As she readjusts her legs, her body sways toward him—as if a gust of wind has caught her unawares. The smell of her, a heady autumn scent, wafts his way, breaks down mental resistance.

"A British spy?"

"A handsome, dashing sort of fellow... who stays out in the cold."

"I see...," he says, but does not see at all. His glance strays toward the line of bottles reflected in the mirror behind her, takes in the outline of her breasts—harnessed under a silk paisley blouse—moves back toward her Anglo-Saxon face, her startling dark eyes.

She asks, "So—what is it you do?"

He takes a sip of aromatic tea, smiles back at her. "I work as little as I possibly can to earn my daily bread. I make pottery for tourists like yourself." His smile widens. "And despite the sign at my door, I keep erratic hours."

"And what do you do—between firings—to pass the time?"

He rearranges sentences in his mind, discards them, decides to simplify. "I read avidly. I worry about Greek politics. And when I get tired of reading, or worrying, I come to this 'Arab watering hole'—to play backgammon, to sip *arak*, or tea, or thick coffee and bandy talk about."

He does not add, I sometimes wander the *souks* of Old Jerusalem, like Julia, absorbing sounds and smells... make friends with shopkeepers and urchins.

And think of Alya.

Fiona touches his sleeved arm. "You're not married, then?"

"Unlucky in love, I suppose."

She shakes her head. "Luck is a phantom word with little meaning for *my* life. It's what I set my mind to do that counts."

"Luck... or the lack of it," he says cheerfully, "is the corner-stone of mine."

She smiles a quirky, hopeful smile, touches a ruffle at her neck. Re-crosses her legs and waits, as if in the waiting, bravado might return. She asks softly, "You live nearby?"

He meets the challenge in her eyes. "Just down the road a bit. Above my shop."

"I'm looking for a special piece. Something original to give a friend." She flashes a radiant smile. "Would you show me... what you have?"

He chuckles. "It's too late for pottery. Besides, my sister Julia's room is across the hall from our shop."

"I don't mind sisters-in-close-proximity," Fiona says. "She might be nice to meet." She levels a glance at Sari, slides off her stool. "Well?" Her word, a reprimand for the unsure, for the weak of heart. She smiles brightly in his face, her mouth offering him a prize better, even, than Jaffa oranges.

"Why not?" he says at last, a query to challenge all doubt.

Alya's phantom dogs his footsteps as he walks with Fiona the short distance to his place. At the door, she pauses to inspect the plaque, "Pappas Jerusalem Pottery," runs her finger across the hairline crack. She waits for him to lead the way past Julia's locked door and upstairs to his patio-roof where a billion stars converge, like pinpricks, in a cobalt blue sky.

Fiona murmurs her greetings to the doves, looks past corners and over parapets. "You're just a stone's throw from Mandelbaum Gate, and on the edge of 'No Man's Land,'" she says.

"A strategic location, I would think." He smiles. "Wasted on the likes of me."

She walks back past chairs and table, with books left there

since Alya's visit, looks into his face. "Have you stopped to think—if war comes—boundaries may change and Jerusalem may turn seamless overnight?"

He shrugs. "The thought has come, and gone. And occasionally returns."

Would his own mind coalesce, turn seamless in the night? he wonders as he unlocks the door of his living room, flicks on the lamp. Fiona crosses over to the Picasso print. "A gift of flowers," she murmurs, "that's all I want of life."

Alya's apparition hangs, like cobwebs, in the corners of the room. He stands, frozen in place, until Fiona takes him by the hand, kisses him lightly on the lips. "Time's fleeting," she whispers in his ear.

"Any moment now," he says pensively, "carriages might turn to pumpkins, and kisses into drops of rain...."

"It's perfectly obvious," Fiona says as she runs her fingers through hair Alya trimmed a day or two before, "some *other* woman is on your mind... besides Julia. But try to concentrate, love, on this dewy English skin: royalty—not peasant stuff."

"Worry," Sari says dejectedly, "drains ardor and the rest of it."

"Not to worry." Fiona laughs a brittle self-conscious laugh. "Indulge tomorrow in worry about Julia... and the other women in your life. But not tonight."

He borrows one of Fiona's cigarettes, inhales smoke as if it were a special elixir. Tonight, he must erase guilt and Alya's apparition from his mind, and concentrate, instead, on this woman within reach.

"That's more like it, love," Fiona now croons in his ear. "Tonight, it's you and me, love—and no one else—before I go on to other assignments, other lands."

But the transparent dark outside his room holds more than pine and mint scents, cradles ghosts that flit across gaps in the bedroom curtains. He holds his breath and waits for imagination to dissipate as shadow-fingers tap their coded message on the window pane.

But when Sari leaps up to call "Julia!" into the night, only the doves coo their muted reply.

Fiona says against his chest, "Is Julia your albatross, love? A millstone around your neck—to keep other women at bay?"

Later, before she leaves, Fiona promises to return "next time I'm in town." The only pottery she has asked to see is the ceramic ashtray on the floor.

Alone, in his Fiona-scented bed, Sari lies awake and yearns for Alya. With Majed gone from her life, Alya, he thinks dejectedly, has cloaked herself with Invincible Virtue—drawing barriers against Men-kind. Against him.

Relatives and Strangers

"ALYA DOES NOT love you, never will," his sister, Julia, the oracle-giver, tells Sari the next morning before she locks her bedroom door. "Is that why you brought the English girl to giggle in the night, to moan, to throw her arms around your neck and mold herself to you? I saw through the curtain slits. I heard, saw everything last night."

At noon, he knocks on Julia's door and calls her name, but she refuses to answer him. In her fury, she has bolted her door shut against all intruders, has locked herself back into the past.

"We need to talk, like adults," Sari calls out. "Don't you think we can manage it?"

"Go away." Her voice is faint, spent of emotion. "Go away!"

"Julia's logic is twisted, her emotions unwieldy," Dr. Murad tells Sari time and time again. "The one thing you can do for her—and for yourself—is send her back to the Bethlehem hospital. For, how can you ever live your life with Julia's dinosaur stalking your shadow?"

"Alya is more *my* friend than yours," Julia said the other day. "Yet I know you want her in place of all the *other* women you make love to...." She sucked in her breath, her face taut with the effort. "How does one make love?" she wanted to know, looking forlorn, without love.

He said flippantly, "Nature has her ways...."

Julia sat primly in her chair, neither gesturing nor holding conversation with the wind. "'The forbidden fruit,' my mother said, 'not worth the screw.'" Her face contracted into a grimace. "She told me it comes at you like a rock falling—especially that first time."

Sari ambles toward his bedroom to look for evidence of last night. In the unmade bed, the indentations of heads, like two giant thumbprints on beige pillows; the ceramic ashtray on the floor, piled high with Fiona's cigarette stubs.

He settles in the rocking chair in his living room, stares dejectedly at the Picasso poster on the facing wall. Thoughts of Julia, like signals in the brain, make way to yellow and coral and orange petal-smudges. After a while, his glance drifts toward the sprightly deer woven into the fabric of the rug, settles on the *Akropolis* newspaper at his feet.

Hope remains an illusion—despite a headline that reads, "Junta will draft a new constitution within six months, King Constantine declares."

For what do kings know? The world of politics turned upside down and his own brain too clogged to absorb details. Papandreou, the elder, under house arrest; the son, 'safe' in jail awaiting trial for treason. Words, like scorpions, crawl across the page; facts melt into half-truths and innuendo.

And halfway round the world, a Greek actress is entertaining New York audiences in *Illya Darling*! Melina Mercouri can't go home to Greece again, will not be allowed that privilege in a Greece ruled by the junta.

Home—where Julia hides, locked up in her room.

Sari drops the newspaper on the rug, stands in the doorway, looking out; a desolation, like ashes, drenches his patio-roof, hovers over buildings, clings to the palm and *saru* trees.

"I wish," Sari had said not long ago, flinging words into Julia's face—regretting them later. "I wish I'd never left Athens and returned to Jerusalem. For here, I've no real friends to define who, or what, I am...."

Julia, who lives her social life in dreams, has myriad friends. Her list includes Mr. Balat, manager of the Aelia Capitolina Hotel, shopkeepers in the Old City, a handful of nuns and priests at the churches where she sometimes goes to pray.

My need is to hear other voices, Sari tells the caged pigeons, who listen, heads cocked. To break *my* barriers lest I go mad—like Julia. I must get away for a while: not to Uncle Sam's—where they suspect the truth about Fiona and last night—but to a place where nuggets of Hebron glass form chandeliers, and the mosaic of the Tree of Life is recreated in miniature on the wall. A place with corner seats where one can sit and meditate on the follies of our world, and observe the flow of tourists, like Bedouin tribes, passing through.

In the wide-open spaces of the Aelia Capitolina Hotel, Sari will sip his *arak* and dream of clear Aegean waters. With Mediterranean sun drenching his skin, he will watch Alya, who reclines on a rock, humming. This is what I'll do to make you love me, he'll say—like a schoolboy listing and numbering miracles. But Alya, turned mermaid, will not accommodate love; hates men's legs against her fins. Swims free.

Sari pauses in the garden of the Aelia Capitolina Hotel to admire a ruffled fern without a name. Three elderly women in hats sit around a glass table on the patio, sipping lemonade and discussing purchases.

"I'm a sucker for bargains," the thin one says, and displays her woven camel saddle with pockets on the sides. "But my dear! Half-price he offered... Can you *imagine*...?"

The other can hardly contain her excitement. "One

shopkeeper followed me halfway down the street... But why, I ask you, would I want to *buy* that ridiculous thingamabob?"

Talk eases to a stop as curious glances dart Sari's way. But as animated talk resumes, heavy glass doors sever the women's voices.

Inside the hotel lobby, tourists mill around a maestro in a straw hat with 'Al-Quds, Jerusalem' stamped in purple on a white headband. Bags and parcels lean against each other, form uneven pyramids near seats and corners of walls. The guide in the straw hat waves his arms in the air, his voice a shriek above the babble of other voices.

"My pastor warned me about this," one disgruntled voice resounds above the rest. "Last time *he* came, an explosion put the fear of God...." The tourist's voice trails, begins anew. "And now, our government advises us to leave. 'Warn' is more like it. Jerusalem is supposed to be the city of peace. Yet, any moment now, a war...."

"War," the guide's voice climbs an octave higher, "is only in the imagination of your State Department." His hat tilts precariously to one side. "Mini-crisis, yes. We live with those daily, and somehow, manage to survive." He readjusts his hat, lowers his voice a little. "Life, you see, has toughened our Palestinian hides. But you? Mere visitors, barely arrived. Why in such a hurry to leave?"

Reasons crowd upon reasons, push back rationality. One man pats the folded map in his shirt pocket. "I *still* haven't seen the manger where Jesus was born. I promised my Emilia I'd light a candle there, someday...."

A woman with white fluffy hair shakes her head. "I'll probably die and go to...." She hesitates. "Who knows *where* I might go before *I* light a candle in the Church of the Nativity?"

The hotel manager, Mr. Balat, sits in his arched cubicle overlooking the lobby, his pink balding head bowed over his ledger. A young couple in blue jeans slouch against the seat that circles the front column, staring vacuously at the flurry of older tourists. Nearby, Sari considers the merit of corner seats, calculates distance from sound.

In the far right of the lobby—away from milling tourists—a woman in pale-green pantsuit occupies one arm of an L-shaped seat; the other side is vacant. As he approaches the coveted corner, she looks up through the camouflage of her cigarette smoke.

"Well. Hello."

"May I?"

She loops her cigarette in the air. "It's an *almost* free country, isn't it?" she says in a Southern drawl. "And this is an *almost* public place."

"An almost public place, yes." He takes the empty seat, and with a nod toward the woman, returns to the spectacle of tourists cut off from the security of schedules, from their well-programmed lives.

The waiter who takes Sari's order has a stoic, unsmiling face. His eyebrows are in disarray, in contrast to his slick and shiny hair. With amazing speed, he brings back a bottle of *arak*, green and black olives, a variety of salads swimming in olive oil, and bread.

The woman exhales smoke like Fiona, head thrown back, pinpointing cobwebs in ceilings. He has to live with it, this cloud of smoke, a gauze curtain to hide her ravaged face. A woman in her late forties, with transparent skin rouged beyond endurance. Her mouth curves into an introspective smile, as her glance darts at intervals toward the outer door.

In the center of the lobby, bags are picked up or are pulled on wheels, packages balance precariously over other packages, as tourists move, slug-like, toward the front door.

Their guide's desperate voice strains above the din, "...and when you're back in Idaho or Alabama or California, remember our sunsets and the sounds of our church bells and the *muezzin's* call to prayer. Don't forget us *samideen*—those of us who must stay here. But please, come back and bring your friends. And your dollars. It's my livelihood, after all."

"Who has seen my Gaza rug?" a man's voice booms. The

young couple, still seated at their column, glance stoically at their watches, at each other.

Sari, sipping *arak* and nibbling at olives, thinks of Julia locked up in her room, hiding from him, from voices in her head.

Last year, in a frenzy of revenge for some remark or other, Julia set fire to the brocade drapes in his living room.

"Why burn curtains?" he asked, pushing her out of the way, pouring dishwater on the blaze. "What have curtains done to you?"

"The voices," Julia said then, "make me smear designs and colors, names even... on pottery. They told me to set the fire."

First curtains, then a house and all who live in it?

"The doctor's pills will make your voices go away," Sari reassures her. "Surely you and the voices know that?"

"No medicine for me," Julia says, defiance in her voice.

But fear of being locked up in Bethlehem—where a silver star marks a holy birth—has caused Julia to lock herself up in her room.

No one can get me now, she probably thinks. Not Dr. Murad. Not even you.

Nearby, the woman sips her coffee and leaves purple marks on the cup. Her glance assesses Sari's proximity, settles on his face. What brings *you* here? What are *you* hiding from?... lies dormant between them.

Smoke loops around her face, drifts toward him unchecked. He clears his throat.

"Does it bother you?" She gives him a ritual smile to match her question.

He recalls Fiona, and his lone cigarette last night—the breaking of a fast of four or five years. "Yes—and no," he says and looks the woman in the eye.

She props her cigarette on the edge of her ashtray. "At one time my husband thought smoking was up there with life and taxes. But now that he's given up the weed..." a burst of heady laughter, "he's changed his mind."

"I'm Sari Pappas. And you are...?"

"Amanda Kelby." She offers her hand. "Johnny is my husband's name, although he prefers Jonathan...." She inclines her head. "Johnny's gone to buy us plane tickets to Cyprus... where we plan to wait out this miserable fiasco."

A tall, spare figure of a man enters the lobby; Amanda gives Sari a conspiratorial glance. "That's my Johnny. Listen, if you like. But pretend we haven't met."

The man strides toward them, his suited, elongated torso like a runner's, pitched forward. He plants a quick kiss on his wife's cheek, slides next to her. Age, erased from his face, lurks in the slack of his neck, in the elastic folds under his eyes.

The man gives Sari a wary nod. He unbuttons his jacket and, from an inner pocket, produces an official-looking voucher, hands it over to Amanda.

"So... we're all set?"

He leans toward her, lowers his voice. "I've got *your* ticket, dear. But since my UNRWA work is at a crucial stage, I may have to stay a little longer...."

She looks up. "So your plan, dearest, is to send me off to Nicosia, *alone*, while you face danger by your lonesome?"

He gives her a worried look. "We *both* know how this war-talk affects you. How your nerves easily...." The word swallowed up, taboo. His arm encircles her shoulder reassuringly, "Nothing may come of all this. Hussein, after all, is a sensible fellow and not easily trapped into Nasser's schemes."

"The real reason for this little sacrifice of yours," says his wife, sarcasm in her voice, "is that you want me out of your hair... while you carry on with nurse what's-her-name."

"My God, Amanda...." His voice is taut with outrage. "Nurse Muna is someone I *work* with, period. Besides, what could I *possibly* offer her that she doesn't already have?"

She pats the sleeve of her husband's jacket. "Your *passion*, my dear Johnny. Your passion. The one thing you've kept from *me* all these years."

Sari, pouring more *arak* into his glass, watches furtively as Amanda folds the ticket in half, tears it up, drops the pieces into the ashtray and, before her husband can stop her, presses the lit end of her cigarette into the layers of paper. The small blackened hole flares up into an uneven orange blaze that lasts a few moments before dying out.

Amanda watches the charred remains of the ticket in the ashtray with clinical interest. "If you stay, I stay," she says cheerily. "Better here than there—wondering what you're up to. Worrying about my house, my bed... and *who* could be in it...?"

Sari, eavesdropping, averts his gaze, smears *hummus* on bread; contemplates escape. But before thoughts have a chance to jell, Amanda gathers purse, jacket, cigarettes, and scrambles out from behind her husband's knees. With heels clicking, she makes her way toward the front door.

Amanda's husband gives Sari a sheepish grin. "Women! I tell you. 1967 is a bad year for men's rights. And the month of May is even worse." His glance steadies itself on the chunks of bluish-green Hebron glass that hang from the ceiling, pulls back toward Sari. "It might be Vietnam after all! Dry rot in the middle of our lives. And me, Jonathan Kelby, a middle-aged wonder from Chicago, trying to manage a small portion of a humanitarian bureaucracy. Limbo, that's what we're in—your refugees and me. No light at the end of *our* tunnel." He sighs—a vibration strong enough to scatter the charred remains of a small fire. "Personally, I prefer the days when man was lord of his cave. And women knew their place...."

"And when the word 'chattel' had a nice ring to it?" Irony in Sari's voice.

Chortling, Jonathan Kelby slaps his thigh. "Yeah. The good old days." He extends a hand. "Glad to meet you, buddy. Sorry you were witness to the underbelly of our marriage." He shrugs. "I suppose I'll go to Cyprus with Amanda. But first, I'll have to tell Nurse Muna about the change of plans. I hope she'll understand."

"Good luck. To the *three* of you."

"Being in the middle of all this," Amanda's husband says cryptically, "I'm afraid I need it most."

After he leaves, Sari, sipping his *arak*, considers the tyranny of unyielding and self-righteous men; and tyranny reversed.

The *mezza* salads show only insignificant indentations from his nibbling; the bottle of *arak* is still two-thirds full. This early afternoon drinking merely anchors Sari's mood—as if what he attempts to blot out is magnified, turned querulous.

When Sari stops by the cubicle to pay his bill, Mr. Balat, frowning, confides, "I can't believe this sudden exodus." His glance takes in the young couple now pacing the floor of a lobby that has emptied itself of crowds. "Tourists in panic because of *rumors!*" He shakes his head. "But when *I* look up at skies I see no ominous signs. No omens." He laughs suddenly, as if pain must be covered up. "Yet you and I must hold our ground. Even my dear old mother will not budge. 'If war comes,' she says, 'and if planes drop napalm on our heads, I'll turn to ashes and mingle with the holy dust in the *souks* of Old Jerusalem.'"

Discordant voices echo through the lobby. "This trip was *your* idea!" Her young woman's voice is brittle with frustration. "I didn't have to come, did I? What do you expect me to do all day? Sit around and wait for bone fragments to congeal?"

Rage dissolves into tears: the flood, reenacted. The young man's arms circle her waist; heads, necks, bend toward each other, form a protective arc.

Mr. Balat pulls his gaze back to Sari's face. "Ah, impatience—the privilege of the young!" He props his elbow onto the ledger, oblivious of fresh ink markings. "We older ones must pray for patience since we have even less time to sort things out." A deep intake of breath. "By the way, have you heard the latest from Amman?"

Sari shakes his head

"Yesterday, in parliament," Mr. Balat begins, "Jumma'a announced Jordan's support for the closing of the Straits. And in his anniversary speech, the king said that Jordan is now 'ready to make sacrifices'...." Mr. Balat raises tufted white eyebrows. "What sacrifices does he mean?"

"Mere rhetoric," Sari says. "For, behind the scenes, Western Powers are scrambling to appease the fragile egos of certain governments. And, who knows? By next week, tourists may return, and business will go on as usual."

"*Insha'Allah!*" A melancholy smile. "Only if God wills it." Mr. Balat cocks his head. "Haven't seen Julia since that last time when she told me you no longer play *tawla* with her." A clearing of the throat, eyes lifted discreetly to Sari's face. "She also told me that same 'villain' plans to lock her up in the Bethlehem hospital." He shrugs. "I listen. I offer sympathy. What else can I do?"

"She's been difficult lately," Sari says. "Cheats at *tawla*, then denies it. Has her rages—even with customers. And then there are those voices... that drive us both mad."

Mr. Balat inclines his balding head. "Ah, women. They can be difficult. That's why I choose to live alone."

In the driveway, a taxi honks. The young couple pick up suitcases and packages, scramble toward the front door without a backward glance.

As Sari takes his leave, Mr. Balat's fingers flex themselves into a halfhearted wave. "God be with you," he tells Sari. "God be with all of us."

Sari walks out into the mellow mid-afternoon light where a dusty old Mercedes taxi with open trunk is swallowing up suitcases and packages.

The weathered taxi driver in a *kaffiyeh* leans against the side of his taxi, and watches the young man in jeans heave one last package into the trunk. Sari briefly notes the "Get out of Vietnam" button pinned to the young man's shirt pocket.

"How can I help it?" the taxi driver tells Sari in exasperation. "When the authorities close the road to the Kalandia airport, I'm *forced* to be late! And if I break barricades, I might get run over by a plane...." His spurts of laughter elicit a disgusted look from the young woman, who is busy rearranging packages in the back seat.

"A private plane, this one," the driver adds, for mystery.

❁   ❁   ❁

For a few moments, *arak* turns whirling school-papers into leaves, the road *almost* swirls, but finally steadies itself as Sari, whistling to keep his courage up, makes his way home. He fumbles with the iron key, lets himself in. Once more, he knocks on Julia's door, and calls her name, yet she won't answer him. But when he tests its handle, the door gives way, as if he's heaved his muscle to it and sprung it open.

Julia's nightgown lies in a heap on the braided rug, next to her lavender chenille bedspread. Momentary chaos swirls, like leaves, inside Sari's brain, gives way to guilt. He murmurs her name, as if she were a kitten tucked away somewhere—afraid to startle, or put her on guard. But Julia is neither in bathroom, nor craft-room, nor working at the kiln; has vanished into air.

In their cage on the roof, the ragged baby ring-necks lift their heads in startled greeting; male dove sits passively on his perch, his occasional cooing in counterpart to female dialogue. Nothing has changed here; no alarm has yet disturbed tranquility.

In Sari's kitchen, dishes are washed and neatly stacked. Julia's watch lies innocuously on the sill. He sees it then: the halves of the glass money jar, like jagged eggshells, nestled in a corner of the sink.

Spare money, in case of crisis, he told Julia months, years before, hoardings, like olive oil or rice, to tide us over in time of need. Filled with *piasters* and *shillings* to anchor it, the jar was wedged in a corner beneath the sink.

Not long ago, Julia secreted her *own* wage for making pottery, spent it on pistachios from Theodore's, baubles of Hebron glass and a *thobe* from Askalan, worn out and patched clumsily. Toward dusk, she reported, a Sister of Zion took Julia into the underground grotto of their church and showed Julia ancient grooved flooring where Roman soldiers once played their dice games.

"Next time...," Julia smiles her secret smile, "I'd like to go to that *other* church down El Mujahideen Road they call St. Anne's."

❁   ❁   ❁

St. Anne's, near *Bab Sitna Miriam*, was his mother's favorite church. A day or two before his father whisked him away to Athens, his mother took him there on a pilgrimage of sorts. He sat on a hard wooden bench, a boy of seven, anchored in place by the dank smell of ancient stone and his mother's sighs. His mother, on her knees, began to wail in argument with a wooden statue, her voice still resonating in his head.

His own father never wept for his inconsistencies—walking the streets of Athens with frigid face set against his sins. Bleeding for it, he stitched the wound calmly with his own hand—a master surgeon performing miracles.

Men's insecurities, Sari knows—their fear of flowers and soft colored things made them hard. Men wept without tears, going stoically to work as if it were a healing balm to anesthetize pain.

The young boy, Sari—noting his father's obsession with the woman not his mother—resolved he would never marry until he was sure of love.

At seventeen, Sari returned with his father to Jerusalem, his childhood home. Julia, twenty-two and in her prime, scowled at male relatives lost to her when she was barely eleven.

Ex-husband and son listened grimly to a discarded wife's lament. "A phase Julia's going through, those voices she pretends to hear. What else could it be?"

Hunched over a scarred wooden table, his mother slices the ends of green beans without looking up. "And yet we've managed, Julia and I—without men to disrupt our women's lives." As his mother's threadbare face lifts to contemplate Sari's youth, her words explode, "Men! It's either their bellies or their balls...."

At seventeen, Sari's passion centered around soccer and history books. No girls had yet traipsed through the thicket of Sari's life, since 'Enter at your own risk' was enough to keep them at bay.

For Sari, at forty-three, women remain an incongruity. His own impulse to hold a woman in his arms was not without peril—especially when, in making love to one woman, he longed for another.

But now, the one woman on his conscience roams the *souks* of the Old City with her coins in search of sanity among the *thobes* and pistachios and the aroma of spices and freshly ground coffee and *hale*.

Sari mixes his own coffee—without *hale*, but with sugar—in the dented brass pot, adds water, concocts a witch's brew. Boiling, it overflows and spills into a murky puddle on the stove. He sips what coffee is left to clear his head for thinking, to renew courage.

Guilt dogs his footsteps as he trails after his misplaced sister, who wanders the Old City *souks* weighed down with *piasters* and *shillings* in search of herself. He passes the alleyway of the Protestant Gethsemane garden, crosses Sultan Suleiman Street toward the Old City walls, zigzags through the beehive of cars and humanity into *Bab el-Amud*, Gate of the Pillar. Inside the gate, moneychangers are busy in their cubicles, and the tall Sudanese in his white robes sells roasted peanuts in cones formed out of the discarded homework of schoolchildren. Sari nearly slips on slick cobblestones, regains his balance as he hurries past magazines and newspapers plastered on the wall and a crowded sidewalk coffee shop.

He stops at Theodore's to ask questions—and to inhale the aroma of roasted sunflower and watermelon seeds and pistachios and almonds and mounds of *fustuk*. A woman complains about the price of roasted garbanzos, bites into one. With a scowl, she turns on her heel and walks away. Standing behind the mounds of roasted *fustuk*, Theodore wrings large peasant hands and mutters epithets under his breath.

Anger discarded like a peanut shell, he turns toward Sari. "What brings *you* here in the middle of the afternoon, during business hours?"

"Looking for a lost sister...," Sari says gloomily.

Theodore shakes his head. "I did not see her today. But she stopped by several weeks ago, sipped the tea I offered, and confided her misery." His eyes stray toward the near-empty street.

"Near tears, she said you were holding her prisoner in her own house, that, by some miracle, she managed to escape." Theodore plunges his scooper into the mound of roasted garbanzos, gives Sari a cursory glance. "But how could I believe that Sari Pappas has turned devil behind my back?"

Sari picks up a pistachio nut, breaks it open, swallows it whole. He smiles ruefully, "Monsters—both of us—you might say?"

Theodore rubs an unshaven chin, emits a labored sigh. "A pity she has those... unfortunate spells."

Two nuns pass by, gesturing, talking melodiously in French; others follow. A man bent double, with half a dozen cane chairs on his back, follows close behind. Man turned donkey is guided by the aromas of food and condiments, by the glimpse of doorways, by the shoes or bare feet of others in his path. "*Aw'a—* Watch out!" his cry, repeated at intervals, miraculously clears his path.

Theodore chews on a roasted almond, says suddenly, "Have you noticed how most foreigners have fled our city in panic—as if tomorrow might be Armageddon?"

Sari takes his leave, veers left toward *Souk el Wad*, where hand-embroidered *thobes* flutter overhead, and where shops, crammed full with pottery, offer him stiff competition. Men, fingering prayer beads, perch on low stools in front of souvenir shops, call out to the few shoppers, and gaze apprehensively at barefoot boys playing tag in the narrow street.

"Who's chasing you today, my friend?" Awad calls out to Sari and motions him to stop. A rotund, grizzled man, he stands behind his display case with its clutter of silver trinkets and the many-sized wooden camels arranged in pyramid-style on the lower shelf.

"I need more of your pottery to sell." He smiles amiably at Sari. "Nothing expensive or esoteric, mind you. Just your everyday ceramics for the *average* tourist." He adds wistfully, "Although lately, the ranks of tourists are thinning out.... But you're empty-handed, my friend, and in such a tearing hurry. Are there *djinn* at your back?"

"The *djinn* have whisked Julia away," Sari says dejectedly, "and I'm trying to find their hiding place."

Awad presses the bulge of his stomach against the counter. "If only your sister were married...," a delicate clearing of the throat, "...she would not be quite as *restless*, shall we say?"

Sari laughs, as if laughter were a balm in Gilead. As if problems could be harnessed like wooden camels, or strung as beads and offered up to God in prayer.

"Marriage," Sari begins cautiously, "may cure some ills, but can also create new ones." A rote answer he learned at his father's knee.

Loud, skeptical laughter. "But how can *you*, a bachelor, know anything about marriage?" Awad's eyes light on a young woman in a flowered dress. "A small happiness, this—to watch the pretty ones in their flimsy attire. Naturally, I look but do not touch." A melancholy sigh. "My dear, devoted wife, sadly, is unreasonable on that subject. She has absolutely *no* tolerance for any type of... flirtation."

Sari's more serious flirtation interrupted last night—with Julia staring into his window, spying on him.

"I hope you find her, my friend." Awad's voice trails after Sari's receding back.

Here, in the Old City, an amalgam of religions is woven into the dusty texture of ancient stone and artifacts, leaves its imprint on his blood. Sari quickens his footsteps, makes his way under Hadrian's Ecce Homo arch, passing the Muslim Umariyya School—considered, in Christendom, the site of the first station of the cross. Several meters short of *Bab Sitna Miriam*, on El Mujahideen Road, are the words, inscribed in stone: "Sainte Anne. Pères Blancs. Séminaire Grec-Catholique."

His mother's grip tightens on his trapped fingers. "Tomorrow," she whispers in his ear, "your father will spirit you to Greece. But today, you and I will pray at this church for strength to bear the suffering that may lie ahead."

Inside the gate, a *bulbul*, startled into flight, flits from a palm to a eucalyptus tree, his fluting staccato song measuring eternity, and in a flash of yellow, glides above the Pool of Bethesda and what is left of a Byzantine ruin, into an open sky.

Sari pauses to gaze up at convent windows near the New Gate, wonders whether Julia has taken refuge with the Réparatrice nuns. A brown-robed Melkite seminarian sweeps the entrance of the church, ignoring the Arabic script above his head. A Crusader church, converted for a time into a Koranic madrasa—a Muslim school of a bygone era when sacred buildings were sometimes interchangeable, renamed to accommodate victory or defeat.

Inside St. Anne's, voices in harmony spin out a hymn that resonates around the marble statue of a young girl at her mother's knee. Harmony lifted like bird-wings, caresses fissures, peers into tiny light-filled holes in place of windows, reaches the alcove with its wooden statue, the girl now transformed into the regal mother of a holy child, hand lifted, holding what?

No longer boy, the man, Sari—at the cusp of middle age— sits on a hard brown bench and absorbs harmony and black-and-white patterns at his feet, temporarily erasing Julia and Alya and angels with wings and statues from his mind.

A Nasser aide told this correspondent [John K. Cooley], "We have restored the situation as it was before the Suez War in 1956. We want nothing more for now. But we will not budge from this position. Anyone who wants to test us can try."

The Christian Science Monitor, May 27, 1967

Israel announced that it would consider a blockade of the Gulf of Aqaba "an act of war"....

Time, June 2, 1967

Pope Paul VI calls for prayers to "exorcize the scourge of new conflict" in the Middle East....

The New York Times, May 26, 1967

CHAPTER NINE

The Old Woman and the Cause

THE OLD WOMAN squats in the shade of the apricot tree and munches on the *falafil* sandwich Miriam, the Semiramis cook, has prepared. This time, she did not stop at Badri's house, but came straight to the hotel— on instructions from Lutfi Abdul Kader.

She waits, her jaw barely moving, her elbows resting on her knees. In the last week or two, she has become a courier of secret messages—her bodice a pouch for letters. As the mother of Amin, the *fedayee*, she is called *Um* Amin in Nablus, trusted above all others who work for the Cause. Her son Amin—barely nineteen years old—would give his life for Palestine. All Lutfi has to do is ask.

She was forty-seven years old, and heavy with child, the year their village of Ein-Yalo was erased from the face of the earth. Then she was called Nazha. Go, the soldiers said to the villagers. You have twenty minutes to gather whatever belongings you can—and leave.

No one was rich enough to own a car in Ein-Yalo, although the *mukhtar*, the village leader, owned two mules, three sheep and a donkey, which he loaded with the youngest of his children, bedding, and food. Halfway to Nablus, the *mukhtar*'s wife remembered her gold dowry, hidden beneath a floor tile in a corner of their bedroom.

Although her husband flung epithets in her face when she told him, she took in his tirade without protest; his anger, she knew, was directed against his humiliation and their forced eviction from their home and village.

"Someday," the *mukhtar*'s wife confided to Nazha as they trudged along their path through the hills, "I'll return under cover of darkness to our village, and retrieve the gold."

"*Fil-mishmish*," Nazha said with a shrug. "Never in a million years."

It was odd that the *mukhtar*'s wife told Nazha what she did about returning to retrieve the gold. Perhaps she had not heard that the soldiers would dynamite the houses in the village and plow them under, so that barely a trace would remain. And only later would the soldiers find her gold in the rubble and consider it booty in time of war.

"The child under your ribs," the wise woman of the village had assured Nazha months before their eviction, "is sure to be a boy. No more *Um banat* for you, my dear."

Um banat, meaning "mother of girls," was the name the villagers jokingly gave Nazha behind her back, before she became *Um* Amin—the mother of Amin. Yet she was proud of her five daughters who obeyed her implicitly, and who helped around the new stone house her husband and his brothers had built for them in Ein-Yalo.

A few kilometers into their trek from Ein-Yalo, Nazha, weeping like a child with weariness, begged to be left behind. But her husband would not hear of it, for he, too, had believed the wise woman's prediction.

"No son of mine will die because his mother chooses to give up," he said. She saw his resolve in the dark pupils of his eyes, saw it in the quiver of his moustache, felt it in the hand that gripped her elbow, propelling her over rocky soil, and with each step farther away from her life in Ein-Yalo.

Along the way, they stopped in an almond orchard to rest, and ate green almonds to sustain them. The owner of the orchard looked on helplessly as the evicted refugees swarmed over his land. But in the end, he allowed them to eat, and to drink the water from his well; he was one of the lucky ones whose home and land were still intact.

These days the memory of their trek is a blur in Nazha's mind, but she still recalls the midwife's words even now, "A miracle... that the boy was born at all!"

A greater miracle that he continued to live—despite the trickle of milk from her poor sagging breasts. Amin had fought for his life—and won.

In Nablus, Nazha lived in the casbah, in a cousin's house. Her husband's joy in his son's birth lasted through the next two years of his life. But then, even the Nablus doctor, with a degree from Lyons, France, couldn't explain why a man of fifty-four, and in good health, would drop dead in the middle of the street.

After her husband's sudden death, Nazha began to work at people's homes—to wash, to clean, to earn a meager wage. At home, her daughters took care of their brother Amin, who continued to sprout, a tall weedy plant, restless, always into mischief. Relatives and friends called him *karut*, their nickname for a boy without a father. At sixteen, Amin dropped out of school and found work as the cobbler, Talal's, assistant, going to work early mornings, returning home late for supper and a dreamless sleep.

Nazha's work took her to the Masris and the Nabulsis, the old families of the town. Five months ago, she also began work on Wednesdays at Lutfi Abdul Kader's modest home. One afternoon, when Lutfi dropped her off near her home, he met her son Amin. Long after Nazha went inside, Amin remained hunched over the car window, talking to Lutfi. Afterwards, Amin began to ply his mother with questions about their eviction from Ein-Yalo, and about the war.

Odd, that a rudderless boy, a *karut*, could be transformed overnight into a man with a purpose. Amin began to come and go at will, disappearing, sometimes, for days on end. He would return, bone-weary, caked with dust, confiding little, if anything.

Once, a messenger boy of thirteen or so came by to give Nazha the news that Amin was in the hospital, recovering from a flesh wound. Nothing to worry about, he said. He'd come for a change of clothes, but told her not to visit—since Amin would be coming home in a week or two.

After Amin was home for a few days, soldiers came to her door in the middle of the night, and—despite her protests—took him away without explanation. Lutfi came over the next morning to reassure Nazha of his unconditional support.

When Amin finally returned home several weeks later, he walked with a limp, and a dullness had replaced the sparkle in his eyes. He refused to tell her why the soldiers had picked him up in the middle of the night. For the next few weeks he did not leave the house, or drive the truck that Lutfi sometimes asked him to drive. But even after the leg wound healed, Amin spent his time lying around his room, reading books and magazines his friends would bring.

The next time Lutfi stopped by, he barely spoke to Nazha, asked only for Amin. Behind the closed doors of Amin's room, voices grew louder, turned to shouting. "Leave our movement, if you like," she heard Lutfi say. "Do you think you can hide here forever? Any commitment can be broken if you're not man enough...."

As she heard Lutfi's words, her mother's heart shriveled inside her chest. What did he mean to imply? That Amin was a coward?

This morning, when Lutfi gave her the letter, he had stressed its importance—as if their very lives depended on it. Don't forget you're *Um* Amin, he said, the mother of a *fedayee*—a man willing to sacrifice his life for the Cause.

Compared to Amin's, her own life is of little value. Her sacrifice is not in delivering clandestine letters, but in the acceptance of her only son's dedication to justice, at the risk of his own precious life.

She chews the last bite of her *falafil* sandwich, savoring the taste of garlic and nutmeg, wipes her mouth on the back of her hand. From a slit in her belt, she takes out the snuff box, brings a pinch of *z'ut* to her nostrils. She sighs heavily. Her old woman's bones are tired of this interminable waiting; her knees are stiff, the muscles in her thighs pulled beyond endurance. This is the last week in May, and, despite a cool breeze from the east, the noonday sun is brighter, warmer, even, than yesterday.

Omar Habeeb opens the kitchen door and steps outside. He attempts a smile, his greeting stilted, a mere formality. As his veiled dark eyes settle on her face, she can see his disappointment in her presence, a nondescript old woman in faded black *thobe*, not worth his time.

She lifts her head. "Lutfi Abdul Kader sent me. In the past, he's asked me to give the letter to Badri... who in turn..."

"Yes, yes. I know." Impatience in his voice.

She holds onto the trunk of the apricot tree, pulls herself up from her squatting position. "I've been here since 10 this morning. It's now after 1." Her shoulders sag against the tree, her breath comes in spurts. "Lutfi considers this an urgent matter," she says after a while.

"I didn't mean to keep you waiting," Omar says in conciliatory tones. "I hope Miriam offered you something to eat?"

"She took pity on an old woman and made me a *falafil* sandwich."

"Ah!" He looks at her, his hands in motion, fingers flexing.

She takes out the wrinkled white envelope from inside her bodice, smoothes it out between her hennaed palms. Her eyes lift furtively to Omar's face. "Lutfi insisted I bring back your reply—before I leave today."

Omar

HE SHOULD HAVE at least asked her name, this woman who reminds him of his mother, her green hooded eyes measuring character. And when he finally asks, she recites her name in two versions: Nazha first, then *Um* Amin—confiding her origins in the village of Ein-Yalo. As she rambles on about daughters and an only son, Omar skims over Lutfi's letter, rereads it a second time. Her glance pulls away and she falls silent, busies herself with sniffing *z'ut*.

Since the king, Lutfi writes, has ignored the request from *Abu* Ammar to arm the Palestinians on the borders, Fatah will accept Omar's offer of a storage shed on the Semiramis grounds.

"Our good friends have cleared the truck—which came by way of Syria—both at the Ramtha checkpoint and the Bridge. The merchandise, in crates, was hidden under inlaid boxes, brass trays, and woven Damascus rugs. In Jericho, we plan to replace this elaborate camouflage with a load of oranges and *khush-khash*.

"We hope to deliver the boxes by midnight, Thursday. As soon as you confirm this plan, I'll tell Amin, driver of the truck, and son of Nazha, our letter courier.

"Alert your handyman, Mustapha, to receive the goods, since he also works for our Cause. Ask him to secure the shed in preparation of delivery. If anything should go wrong—God forbid—Mustapha and Amin will accept total blame."

As Omar takes in the familiar lightning zigzag of the *Al-Assifa* emblem, he considers the implications of the letter. Not to worry, Lutfi implies, since Omar can claim ignorance of the plot.

Yet for Omar—a worrier from birth—an impossibility, for how could he, in good conscience, allow others to bear the brunt of it?

"Well?" The old woman's eyes, fixed on his face, wait for a signal.

"A small matter I must first deal with...."

"So—how much longer, then?"

A peevish old woman, Omar thinks, irritating in her questions.

"Not long," he says to pacify her. "I will ask Miriam to make you coffee while you wait."

"Coffee will keep me awake for the trip back to Nablus."

In the kitchen, Miriam, hunched over the counter, is busy

cutting up parsley and green onions for *tabbouleh*. Omar asks her for the favor, humbly.

Miriam's glance strays toward the old woman; she nods her acquiescence, even as her knife continues its staccato beat on the cutting board.

He finds Mustapha in the courtyard, stacking chairs on tables, getting ready to hose down the cement and tile floor.

Mustapha grins, revealing a flash of gold molar. "So you've come to tell me about *Um* Amin...?"

"You know her, then?"

"I know her son, Amin, even better." Mustapha moves to another table, pauses in his task of lifting and stacking chairs. "So... will you allow the shed to be used?"

Omar hesitates. "Lutfi writes that you and Amin will take full responsibility."

"I'll secure the shed, and wait for the shipment, which Amin will bring at the appointed time."

"Surely, your wife will worry about your safety?"

"Children and work keep my wife from worry." The lines of the craggy face deepen. "Besides, she knows only that I work at the Semiramis. Nothing else."

They exchange glances. "What if—*la samah Allah*, God forbid—you...." Omar falls silent, unable to utter the hated words.

"God will provide. Besides—I'm sure my oldest son will do his duty toward the family."

Omar, who has no son, gazes at Mustapha with admiration and a tinge of envy. Mustapha, a muscular man with a face shaved haphazardly and clumps of graying hair, like uncut weeds, across his jawline.

When the task of stacking chairs ends, they make their way past the veranda and the kitchen through a cluster of pines toward the shed. A gray, low-slung building, with a tin roof that holds the accumulated debris of pine needles and twigs. Walls, of crudely cut stone, sprout weeds where mortar once filled cracks. The wooden door leans back on rusted hinges; outside the door, earth has been scraped smooth, and a block of flat rock is transformed into a seat. The windows with their broken glass bring to mind a monster's large, jagged teeth.

A newspaper kite with a ragged paper tail leans against an inside wall; a skeleton of twigs lies next to an unwound string where marbles and peanut shells form random patterns in the dusty cement floor.

While Mustapha examines the lock and inspects broken glass, Omar makes his way toward the back, ducks under a door lintel that barely clears his head. As a teenage boy, he lay awake in this tiny room listening to his father's snores, and longed for the Katamon home he had left behind. Omar now reaches out toward a section of the wall, feels with palm and fingers for initials he once carved there; his hand is tangled in a spider web. A mouse scurries across the windowsill, pauses to inspect the giant-man before it disappears into the dark. The dank, musty smells of his past penetrate his nostrils, settle in his lungs, make it hard to breathe. He turns on his heel and quickly escapes back into light.

"In the next few days," Mustapha says, "I'll install a lock, repair the door, board up windows. Will you allow it?"

"Yes," Omar says, all qualms set aside.

Mustapha smiles his relief. "The guns and ammunition will be used in self-defense—in case of possible attack or war. At the appointed time, we will transfer them to the border villages...." Mustapha thrusts his face closer to Omar's. "You must pretend to know nothing. And tell no one. No one at all."

Exhilaration, an antidote against pain, surges through Omar's blood. He curbs the urge to call out to the heavens, to declare it from the rooftops: Our destiny is in our hands at last!

Mustapha repeats the words softly, in Omar's ear. Distinctions blur as the men embrace, affirming their secret alliance.

"I must give *Um* Amin my reply," Omar says, and walks slowly back toward the kitchen.

"I would like to say to the Arab countries... that we harbor no aggressive designs, we have no possible interest in violating either their security, their territory, or their legitimate rights. We on our part expect the same principles to be applied to us."

Levi Eshkol, Israeli Premier, in a speech before the Knesset, *Time*, June 2, 1967

"He is a disgrace to the people and the nation. He does not know how to distinguish between truth and untruth. He should be fired."

Ben Gurion, of Premier Levi Eshkol, *Time*, June 9, 1967

President Nasser now holds the initiative in the Middle East. He is firmly maintaining his blockade of Israel's Red Sea access route. But he is planning no further move at present unless attacked... This is the sober assessment of many top Egyptian officials and... Western diplomats here....

The Christian Science Monitor, May 27, 1967

CHAPTER TEN

Julia

AT FIRST, Julia had the whole back seat of the bus to herself, until the peasant woman and her baby got on at Beit Hanina. The woman, now crooning her baby to sleep, glances from kohl-rimmed eyes at Julia as she clutches her purse with unusual ferocity. With each jolt of the bus, Julia's body lurches forward, coins clatter.

Julia begins to hum a tune that melds with the bumps and rattles of the bus. But as words begin to spill out of their own accord, the peasant woman jerks her head, scowls into Julia's face.

"...Love is a golden dove"—sings Julia off-key. "It flies beyond the vales and hills of home and holds my heart in its beak...."

Julia smiles to herself. Her resolve to report Sari and Dr. Murad to the Beit Nuba police hardened soon after Sari threatened to admit her to the Bethlehem hospital. Perhaps in Beit Nuba the police will finally listen and arrest Sari for his crimes.

In Beit Nuba, Julia plans to visit Alya at the Hotel Semiramis. Julia went there with Sari once, and still recalls tables under pines, scented geraniums and a black, three-legged cat.

And should Alya ask where Sari was, Julia might say, "How should *I* know? He's old enough to fend for himself."

Clusters of gray rocks in hennaed earth whirl past Julia's window; houses skim by in disconnected patterns, making her dizzy. She leans back against her seat, closes her eyes. Maybe in this bus, away from scrutiny, the voices will finally leave her alone.

Brakes screech and the bus comes to a sudden stop; the child near Julia lets out a piercing wail. A herd of sheep has drifted into the road, encasing cars and buses like oozing oil—halting all traffic to Beit Nuba. A shepherd boy of ten or eleven stands in the middle of his flock, his arms flailing helplessly.

Cursing loudly, the bus driver stomps out of the bus. Julia holds her hands against her ears, tries to block out discordant voices and cars honking and the baaa's of frightened sheep. The mother near Julia unbuttons the top of her *thobe*, pulls out her breast, and inserts a nipple into the tiny, puckered mouth. The baby's wails miraculously cease, replaced now by rhythmic gurgling sounds. Julia averts her eyes, grateful that, at forty-eight, she may be too late for motherhood.

Restless children begin to chase each other in the bus aisle. As one trips and falls, wailing begins anew. Julia's hands, now folded over the purse in her lap, begin to jerk like fresh-slaughtered chickens.

When in control, Julia's hands can sew the delicate seam of a brassiere, or wedge clay until its variegated colors blend perfectly and the clay becomes free of air bubbles. They can pull a pitcher handle in rhythmic, stroking motions, or throw a bowl or a jug on the potter's wheel, guiding its final form into perfect symmetry. They can draw intricate designs, or write names and dates in calligraphy.

When the road is finally cleared of sheep, their driver returns, takes his seat. As the bus lurches forward, Julia's bones begin to clatter, feel like blown pieces of a tin roof.

Sari's voice intrudes into her mind, wielding threats, demanding—as if she had no right to privacy—"Why did you throw your pills away?"

What business was it of his? Why should she tell him anything?

Alya and Julia

WHEN THE TELEPHONE CALL from the police station comes that Thursday afternoon, Alya, just arrived from school, is sipping hot minted tea to soothe frazzled nerves and revive energy.

"Do you know a certain Julia Pappas from Jerusalem?" The man's voice on the other end is guarded. "Yes?" Relief evident in his voice. "Miss Pappas is at our police station, waiting for you. But would you first assure the distraught lady of your coming?"

Julia's voice is a tremulous echo over the phone. "I took the bus from Jerusalem. I brought *shillings* and *piasters*. But the policeman wouldn't... wouldn't...."

"Wouldn't... accept the gift?"

"...wouldn't help me pick up the money when it spilled on the floor... even though I got on my knees to... to...." Julia's words give way to muffled sobs.

The policeman who meets Alya at the gate smiles warily, rubs thin, bony hands together. He is a dark, slightly built man with a handlebar mustache. "Your friend Julia wanted us to arrest her brother in Jerusalem. She even tried to bribe me with *piasters*." He gives a short laugh. "After her coins fell on the floor, she said, 'Everything you pick up is yours.' But I told the poor woman that a Jordanian officer of the law could not be bribed—at least never with *piasters*." He smiles an impish smile, twirls his handlebar mustache. Before he unlocks his office door—where Julia waits—he lowers his voice. "Is it true, what she said... about her brother's cruelty?" He looks away—embarrassed for asking.

But how can she explain Julia's emotional turmoil to this respected member of the Jordanian police force—whose world of law and order makes little allowances for disorders of the spirit?

Julia shuffles behind Alya into the Semiramis *liwan*, moves at her own pace. Nawal, too busy with the Johnsons of Virginia, pays little attention as they pass her desk and make their way upstairs to Alya's room.

Julia takes a seat on the edge of Alya's bed facing the dresser mirror, tucks one leg under her. Afternoon light paints tiger stripes across her ruddy child's face, pinpoints wrinkles and blemishes. She pushes a gray strand of hair under her scarf, looks up, startled—a cat, unused to mirrors.

"Sari has *spies* to watch me." She gives in to an involuntary shudder. "At night I see their shadows outside my window. I hear them whispering, plotting behind my back."

In the past, Sari had confided, he was forced to confine Julia to the Bethlehem mental hospital for treatment. But the 'cure' was temporary, the disease recurring like a fever in the blood.

"Sari plans to lock me up with all the other crazies at the hospital," Julia says. "But, if you let me stay, I promise not to listen to those other voices anymore...." She flashes a smile, a childish promise to be good.

"Sari can't always solve problems alone," Alya says gently. "He needs your help. He needs your doctor's help."

Julia lunges forward, claws at Alya's arm. "Why defend him when you don't know the truth? How he spends his nights— thinking I don't see? Sari's women!" She spits out the words like venom in her throat. "Creatures of the devil, placed on this earth to tempt stupid and unwary men."

Alya takes Julia's hand, contemplates the distraught face. But Julia wrenches free, drops to her knees. Her fists pound against her thighs, her voice rises like a funnel cloud.

Miserable creature of God—with no one to love, to tempt, even. Alya reaches out to comfort her, holds Julia in the circle of her arms... until anguish is spent. A tattered leaf, motionless, fallen to earth.

Alya says in the space above Julia's head, "I must tell Sari you're safe with me. And when I do, he might want to take you home." She waits for words to settle, for ideas to take hold. "If you like," Alya adds, as an afterthought, "I'll go back with you to Jerusalem."

Julia asks, sanity restored, "Will you let me stay the night?"

Alya thinks of Dick Brandon's vacant room down the hall, thinks of possibilities. "There's a room... an English newsman's room. Since he's away, you could stay there if you like." Alya adds quickly, "But just for tonight...."

Julia lifts her head, nods wearily, without resistance. She extends her limbs across the bed, lies motionless, a string unwound, and begins to snore, her mouth open, a rhythmic nasal snore that perforates the silence of the room.

Alya decides to call Sari from the parlor near her room. He answers at the first ring.

She asks, "Are you, by chance, missing a sister?"

A sound akin to a wedding whoop reverberates in her eardrum. He says, when calm returns, "I looked for her all over the Old City, even at Saint Anne's Church. I thought of calling the Jerusalem police... She'd vanished, taking with her a bagful of *piasters*."

Alya laughs. "The police in Beit Nuba would have been more helpful. They'd have told you exactly where she was. And what she was doing."

"Filing charges against an abusive brother, no doubt?"

"She tried to bribe the police officer with *piasters*," Alya smiles. "But only *dinars*, I suppose, would have convinced him of your villainy."

A chuckle. "I'll be there to pick her up as soon as I can."

"I think she'd like to stay the night," Alya says. "But, if problems come up... I'll call to let you know, and to ask for advice... if I need to." What if Julia decides to run away, again? Alya adds after a silence, "I told Julia I'd go back with her to Jerusalem, if she needs me to. I might also drop in on *'Ammi* Musa there...."

"Thank you." A long pause. "But how could I... we ever repay you...?"

"Rubies would be nice." Alya laughs. "But only if we weren't good friends."

❊ ❊ ❊

As Julia continues her fitful sleep, Alya turns on the short-wave radio on her desk and flips through in search of soothing classical music: an étude, a concerto, or even a somber Chopin nocturne might help wipe out any lingering fears in her head.

Radios and blaring headlines these days make Alya uneasy. But in her own school, this breathless waiting for events to happen has created a euphoric kind of suspense. They expect a miracle: a genie-war to help regain a lost Palestine—to make up for past humiliation and defeat.

But how can rhetoric win battles or ensure justice? *They* have modern weaponry and the will, Alya thinks dejectedly, while *we* lick our wounds and vow revenge.

The faint and scratchy strains of a Tchaikovsky concerto come to her from some far-off place, drift away into a din of static, are replaced suddenly by a gravelly voice.

"...Arab nations," says the voice, "have declared that an attack against one would be considered an attack against all...."

Alya thinks: War—a tremor in the earth—spews out bones and flesh and young men's and young women's dreams. Nothing left but this clinging to moving earth as if it were one's home.

"...The twelve Arab nations who signed the joint declaration are the UAR, Syria, Iraq, Saudi Ara...."

But on the other side—in Katamon, West Jerusalem—a *saru* tree holds the imprint of Alya's child-feet as she gazed beyond rooftops at the ice factory, and saw roses and a stone angel in a neighbor's yard.

"...Lebanon, Jordan, Kuwait...."

One world lost, another regained, here in Beit Nuba, in this spot, pretending the loss of that other does not grate. Camps—hovels for men and women and children who once had *saru* and orange trees. And now survive on memories.

"...the United States, rather than Israel, is the Arab people's enemy. No one...."

Even here, in Beit Nuba, a world apart, life survives tremors and hurricanes as memories harden into rock.

"...Philippe Entremont, pianist, and Leonard Bernstein,

conductor...."

She could weep for the loss of Tchaikovsky, for Julia and Sari—for herself. But tears, trapped, sear her eyes and throat, can't wash away shards of glass embedded in the soul.

Julia stirs from sleep, lifts her head, looks at Alya from reddened eyes. "I heard a voice. A man's voice...."

"The radio was on," Alya says.

"It *must*'ve been Sari. Did he come... to take me back...?"

Without waiting for Alya's reply, Julia begins to weep, heaving sobs as if her heart had splintered into a thousand pieces.

An urgent knock on Alya's door. *Um* Ramzi's worried voice asks reasons why.

"Julia Pappas is visiting from Jerusalem," Alya says in partial explanation as she lets her mother into her room.

"The potter's sister?"

Alya nods. "Her brother, Sari...."

Um Ramzi shuffles toward the bed. She clasps Julia's shoulder, looks down into the tearstained face. "Has anyone fed you yet?" she asks solicitously.

"Anyone" looks up guiltily. Nearly 8 o'clock, and hunger pangs for both Julia and Alya erased from memory.

"Bring the poor thing something to eat from Miriam's kitchen." An imperial command. She looks at Alya. "And where will the poor child sleep tonight?"

"For quiet—Dick Brandon's room down the hall. I don't think he'll mind...."

Um Ramzi shrugs. Her sharp features quiver, her eyes now focus on Alya's face. "Go now. I'll stay with her until you get back."

Downstairs, the disembodied voice of the Egyptian singer *Um* Kalthoum floats toward Alya from the radio in the *liwan*. "...We're going back like morning after a dark night," sings *Um* Kalthoum in her smoky contralto, "The tragedy of Palestine pushes you toward the borders...."

Nawal bends over the radio, barely looks up as Alya passes by.

Alya crosses over to the front window, sees her brother Omar near the trellis in animated conversation with Mustapha. He pauses to greet a man and woman strolling, arm in arm, toward the courtyard.

In the kitchen, while Miriam heats up chicken and rice for Julia, Alya, her hunger revived, nibbles at a cold chicken drumstick, munches on *taboon* bread.

Um Kalthoum's song has come to an end, and Nawal clicks off the radio. "The Johnsons from Virginia have checked out," she says cryptically as Alya passes with Julia's food tray. "Mrs. Johnson is frightened, I think, that war is imminent...."

Um Ramzi and Julia, in pink pajamas, huddle on her bed, with a docile Bisseh, the cat, between them. Alya waits in the doorway as *Um* Ramzi reads a Psalm Alya recognizes from childhood.

> "...Insolent men rise to attack me,
> ruthless men seek my life;
> they give no thought to God.
> But God is my helper...
> ...and I look on my enemies' downfall with delight."

The last spoken with particular fervor.

Um Ramzi looks up as Alya enters the room with the tray. "I wanted Julia to hear God's precious words." Her eyes hold Alya in abeyance as Bisseh, her equilibrium disrupted, jumps from the bed, scurries toward the door. "I found the pink pajamas in one of your drawers. And an old pair of slippers in the closet." She clears her throat. "Julia would like another dress to wear tomorrow... Hers is stained, needs washing."

Julia's unshod feet are poised above an old pair of Alya's slippers; her toes flex, ankles cross. She looks up shyly. "I want a dress with flowers and lace to make me look pretty...."

Um Ramzi crosses herself. "Pretty is in the eyes of God...."

Julia breaks into sudden, caustic laughter. "Ugly feet, aren't they?" Toes wiggle, feet dance in mid-air. "As big as watermelons... Long ago in China, my father told me, they bound a baby girl's feet. 'A lady must have small feet,' he said. ' But only peasant feet for you....'"

Alya's armoire reveals staid dresses and skirts galore to delight a mother's heart. But Julia's eyes light up as she spies the green dress in the back.

"I want *that* one!" Julia says, and claps her hands with glee.

"But it's a dancing dress. An *evening* dress."

Julia's mournful eyes meet Alya's. "I'll take good care of it. I promise."

Julia follows Alya down the hall to Dick Brandon's abandoned room—with green chiffon pressed against pink pajamas.

Will the pink apparition metamorphose—turn butterfly before Alya's eyes?

"I'll lock myself in, for safety." Julia's glance is secretive as it takes in the room.

"Sleep well," Alya says. "Let me know if...."

The door slams shut behind her. Returning, Alya hears movement in her mother's room. She knocks, cracks open the door. *Um* Ramzi stands before the dresser mirror plaiting strands of gray hair into a single braid. Perched on the dresser, Bisseh looks on as Alya takes a seat on her mother's bed.

"I worry about her," *Um* Ramzi says after a silence. "No husband, no child to comfort her. Although children of *this* generation..." An eyebrow raised, a pause meant to instill guilt.

"She *does* have a brother who cares."

"Why, then, does she run away from him?"

"This is part of Julia's illness," Alya says. "She hears, talks to voices in her head; and believes what she *thinks* they say...."

Julia's Vision

THE ENGLISHMAN'S SCENT hangs above Julia's bed like an invisible cloud, permeates the room. Clock-hands point the lateness of the hour. An older face looks down at Julia from an oval frame, a smiling woman's face with rouged cheeks. Julia spells out the English words, barely makes out the script.

"To Dick, love through thick and thin, Aunt Millie."

Thick and thin... what? Julia ponders the puzzle, ponders sleep. But how can she fall asleep in this room that holds a noisy clock with silver hands, and an Englishman's belongings in neat piles on the corner desk?

She eases herself out of bed, pads over to the narrow, wood-frame mirror, stares at her image in pink pajamas. Why not try on pretty green chiffon, with lace and tulle instead?

Despite a zippered waist that will not close, and the dragging of her hem, she will dance around the room, limbs light as air. She lifts her hem, bows at her image in the glass, and glides past Aunt Millie's portrait watching her, past piles of books and papers the Englishman has left behind to guard the room till he returns. She spins around the room, a dizzying, whirling dance, bumping into walls and desk and window ledge.

"To you, my lovely one," sings Julia,

"Wear your wedding dress and wait for happiness.
After my wedding bath I'll come to you
in my finery.
Love is a golden dove that hovers on your windowsill,
It holds my heart in its beak.
I've waited a lifetime for this moment.
You are, and always will be —
my one true love...."

Maybe, after this, sleep will settle in her limbs, and longed-for rest will come.

She leans against the window ledge to keep her head from spinning. Turning toward the window, she catches a glimpse of apparitions on the ground below. She presses her nose against the windowpane, looks down as their shadows slink back into the night.

Holding her breath, she waits, a spy who must catch moving shadows unaware, but night has swallowed up their path and left no clues. Yet, as a creature of the night, she must stalk their trail and discover for herself their hiding place.

Outside her door, a pool of light pinpoints an alabaster pot of ferns and the top of the spiral staircase. A different kind of dance, this twisting down a stairway to find herself at last in an unlit room with cooked garlic and onion smells, a window that frames the black trunks of trees, and a shrouded courtyard light.

Phantoms slink by the window, first one, then two, with box-shapes molded to their heads; muffled voices whisper a coded message in Julia's ear. Despite the hammering of her heart, she feels her way gingerly along rough plaster walls, past counter-top and stove to the outer door in the farthest corner of the room. She fumbles with its iron key, but the key refuses to budge, trapped in its place.

Molding herself to the window sash, she holds her breath and waits... until the phantom-ghouls reappear. As she taps a sig-nal on the windowpane, heads turn, eyes glitter in the dark. Her glance traps a face she's seen in dreams, another new to her. But elusive shadows quickly melt into the misted dark, and only dis-embodied voices remain to clamor in her head.

Alya's Discovery

URGENT TAPPING on her door disrupts sleep, startles Alya into wakefulness. Julia's child-face looks up at Alya.

"I saw moving shadows," Julia whispers through the opening in Alya's door. "I heard men's voices...."

Groggy from interrupted sleep, Alya ushers Julia into her room, listens to a muddled vision of ghosts and voices in the night.

"I give you my word," Alya says, "the Semiramis is free of ghosts and ghouls."

"I saw shadows. They were carrying boxes on their heads...," Julia persists.

"Shadow boxes? What kind of boxes?"

"How would I know? I tried, but couldn't open the outside door."

"Sleep," says Alya with a sigh, "is the best antidote for ghosts and apparitions."

She reaches for Julia's hand, leads her back to Dick Brandon's room.

"Please try to get some sleep, before the *muezzin* wakes us up at dawn," Alya says.

Julia's disembodied voice persists, drifts toward Alya through the closed door. The thuds of staccato footsteps punctuate her words, "I'll be glad when my enemies are destroyed! They lay a trap for me. Trap, trap...." Words fade, return with an urgent plea. "Hear me now, dear God. Erase the voices in my head... hear me now...."

But does God hear voices trapped in rooms, calling out for help?

"Please unlock the door," Alya says. "We need to talk."

Julia's words give way to humming—a kind of droning of bees formed in the throat.

Alya picks up the master key from an unattended *liwan*. Where has Mustapha vanished to? In the hallway upstairs, the young son of the sheikh of Oman cracks open his door, and a small brown face peers out at her.

She looks on as a barefoot Julia in green chiffon glides past— one arm outstretched, the other lifting a trailing hem. Head thrown back, frizzy hair across her brow, Julia grins impudently to herself as she stares past Alya at some secret vision, her face glossy with perspiration—grown miraculously young.

She says happily, still in her trance, "I can dance, can't I? Can't I? My father always said he liked the dancing—despite my watermelon feet." She stretches out a stocky leg, inspects a humped big toe. "I thought I'd make him love me if I danced. 'Dance!' he'd say, and clap his hands and stamp his feet. 'Faster! Faster still!'"

Julia falls in a heap across the bed, laughter gurgling in her throat. Alya touches her shoulder beneath the fallen strap, gazes at the worn and glistening face. Bending down, she strokes Julia's hair, caresses the warm damp cheek. A shudder, a gasp—and Julia's tears begin to fall on green chiffon, on arms and feet and woven Gaza rug.

Each of us, Alya thinks, needs a buffer zone—the presence of another—to separate us from the darker side of truth.

"*Hayyou 'ala-assalaah!*"

The amplified call to prayer breaks into Alya's early morning sleep, makes her nostalgic for the days when the *muezzin*'s voice—unaided by electronics—woke the faithful with a lyrical sound, rather than a resonant blast.

This is Friday, a Muslim holy day, and—along with Sunday—a temporary reprieve from school. But morning comes too soon to suit Alya, brings with it the day's complexities. She lies motionless in her bed, a burning behind her eyelids as fragments of the night's events compete with the *muezzin*'s ubiquitous presence in her room.

This time, she will call Sari from the *liwan* telephone... so as not to disturb anyone. She dresses quickly, goes downstairs.

Mustapha is asleep, his grizzled head resting across a newspaper on the desk. Alya ponders the lax, unshaven face, the small bird-of-paradise tattoo on the wrist, his hands.

He lifts his head, blinks at Alya from bloodshot eyes.

"I need to use the phone," she says, then hesitates. "I came down earlier, but couldn't find you...."

He scratches his head. "I may have stepped outside to check on a stray dog...."

A refugee from Jaffa, Mustapha settled in Beit Nuba soon after 1948, and became the indispensable handyman and night manager at the Semiramis.

After Mustapha leaves, Alya takes his seat, dials Sari's number. What can she tell Sari of voices and shadows in the night? Of Julia dancing in Alya's green chiffon dress?

"Glad to know she came to see you!" he says, relief in his voice. "So how did you survive the night?"

"We've had an hour or two of sleep. Barely enough to restore sanity."

"Do you want me to come now?"

"As soon as you can. But you might have to wait until my mother convinces Julia to wear some other dress...," she laughs, "...besides green chiffon."

Mustapha returns with a tray of steaming brass coffee pot and two small cups. He pulls up another chair, and watches intently as Alya pours coffee for both of them. She inhales the aromatic scent of the *hale* bean and allows the dark brew to work its magic.

Mustapha holds up a newspaper headline. "What do you think of Nasser's closing of the Straits of Tiran?"

Before Alya can divert thought, and come up with an opinion, Mustapha plunges in, "My own fervent hope is that my son, Amin, return to Jaffa to reclaim his grandfather's orange groves." He adds, with a fervor that surprises, "May Allah help us avenge those nineteen years of exile."

For Mustapha, Omar and the rest—the gossamer promise of return hangs by a thread.

"But why would Allah permit our tragedy in the first place?" she asks, to challenge him.

Mustapha squares his shoulders, sets his coffee cup down. "How could the suffering of His people be the will of a compassionate God?" And yet, the Devil is always at work, spewing evil in his trail... "But we *will, insha'Allah*, return someday to our lost lands and homes in Palestine!"

Always *insha'Allah*—"If God wills it"—the miracle phrase. A two-tiered word, meant to shift blame—to link destiny with fate; an expression pliable and obedient without risk of failure or success—untroubled by wars and rumors of wars. If war comes, so be it. For does not God will it so?

But despite her father's faith and her mother's indoctrination, Alya has stripped *insha'Allah* of its assigned meaning and given it her own interpretation.

For while God waits in the wings, humanity, Alya is convinced, wills it so—concocting its own misery with little, if any,

divine intervention. And regardless of the will of God, the devi-
ous continue to manipulate the gullible—even as Majed Alami
has misused her love.

Alya rotates her drained cup, turns the cup over in its saucer
to allow it time to form wrinkles and fine brown dollops—to
clarify destiny through the scrutiny of coffee grounds. A road to
adventure? A letter from an old friend? A welcome stranger in
her life? All possible in the intricate mappings within the dried
grounds of her coffee cup.

And: *insha'Allah!*

Alya stands in the doorway of her mother's room, looks on
as *Um* Ramzi knots her braid at the back of her head, deftly
inserts several hairpins to secure it. She turns her head to meet
Alya's gaze.

"Last night, long after the music ended, I heard moaning
from the poor girl's room. When I went to her door I heard her
in conversation with angels or *afreets*...."

Um Ramzi takes out a black scarf from her dresser drawer,
tucks it around her head. She stands in silhouette against the wall
where Christ hangs on a silver cross, his crown of thorns embedded in his brow.

"Each has a cross to bear," *Um* Ramzi shakes her head, as
if to dislodge thorns. Her glance shifts to the crucifix on the
wall. She walks toward the bed, adjusts pillows as if adjusting
thoughts, lowers herself onto the edge of the bed.

"I saw Majed Alami's mother yesterday at Dr. Munir's clinic,"
Um Ramzi looks down at her hands. 'And how is your son, the
radio man, these days?' I asked—out of politeness. She glared
at me as if I were her maidservant, then walked out, muttering
something about 'bad blood'—slamming the door in my face."

Um Ramzi lifts a puzzled glance to Alya's face. "You assured
me once your friendship with her son would lead to marriage."
She sighs heavily, throws up her hands. "But even if we lived
here a hundred years, we'll always remain, in *Um* Majed's eyes,
homeless refugees, not of her kind...."

"Let *Um* Majed think what she will; it no longer matters."
Alya throws a furtive glance at her mother's face, decides to return to the subject of Julia. "Last night," she says, "your presence with Julia worked a miracle. This morning, she'll still need your help... to dress, to eat—before her brother, Sari, takes her home."

Alya hands her mother the key to Julia's room. "I locked her in this time," Alya says, hesitating. "I worry about her running away...."

Um Ramzi's breath catches, a look of panic crosses her face. "At any moment now, the poor girl may wake up in a locked room."

At different times in our lives, Alya thinks, we, too, wake up in locked rooms.

"I plan to go back with Julia to Jerusalem," Alya says. "I might even visit *'Ammi* Musa there."

Um Ramzi shrugs. "The old man will chide you... and complain about you and your brother Omar—for being still unmarried. Last time he came here, he told me that the only other times he'll set foot in this town are on your wedding days....."

"This mountain, I'm afraid, will then have to go to *'Ammi* Musa."

Slivers of light stain the couches by the window, form elliptical patterns on the *liwan* floor. Mr. O'Connor, seated near the door, looks up at Alya from his writing pad. "Top o' the morning to you!" he says cheerily. "Both of us seem intent on getting the early worm, I see."

Smiling, Alya returns his greeting. She walks out into the brisk damp air, blinks against the webbed smatterings of morning light behind the trunks of pines. Despite tufted mist still in the valleys, night has been transformed into dawn.

At the gate, Omar's dog readjusts his paws, growls in his sleep. A fine mist shrouds cars in the Semiramis parking lot, envelops the milkman as he lumbers up the hill on his mule. A nearby rooster's cock-a-doodle-do fragments her thoughts.

Alya waits, pensive, by the gate. Does she expect Sari to fly?

Driving cars surely takes time.

Restless, she wanders toward the courtyard where, a few days before, she danced her dervish dance to block out terror from her life. Chairs, upside down, cling like fingers to the edges of tables stripped of tablecloths. She moves stealthily past the bougainvillea vine and the trellised geraniums, to the table where she and Majed sat that last evening, at the dance.

A gray-striped cat, crouching on Majed's chair, watches Alya with yellow eyes; poised tiger-paws leap to earth, scatter pine cones, scramble past other tables. Nothing left here but pine needles in haphazard patterns on table and chair. Alya sits down gingerly, watches a long-legged spider race toward the table's edge, dangle spider-rope toward Majed's empty chair.

She sees Majed in parts: eyes, mouth, cigarette hands; can't manage to see him whole. Amber eyes, bland and without guilt, imprison hers; his voice gives logical reasons for perfidy.

Images shatter as Sari strides toward her with his loping gait, his beard, she notes, already in need of trimming. Bloodshot eyes, face haggard in the early morning light. He sits in Majed's chair, takes her hand as if it were a gift.

"Almost had an accident near the furniture factory," he says. "Lucky my Peugeot's brakes held!"

"My mother is seeing to Julia's needs." Alya smiles, relieved Sari is here, intact—assuming responsibility. "My mother chants Bible verses, Psalms, whatever comes to mind, to calm her down."

A *hud-hud* bird lands a few meters away, distracts, its curved dark bill hammering earth. Crest flares: black on white-cinnamon feathers, like fingers waving, snap back into sharp-pointed crest. Flying low, it melts into the dazzle of sunrise.

"Not only did Julia hear voices this time," Alya says, "but she also saw moving shadow-boxes, ghosts, even."

A dark, effusive sigh. "My mother knew a woman once who spoke gibberish, imagined ghosts in closets. Cured, she said, when an Orthodox priest prayed with her, cast out the *afreets* in her soul...."

"Why is it," Alya asks, "that priests and witch-doctors in some distant land know perfect remedies—while our educated doctors only guess at cures?"

Dappled light flickers across Sari's face, accents the strain evident in his eyes. "And how have *you* been?" he asks at last.

"I was thinking of Majed—of being a fool."

He gives her a rueful smile. "Welcome to the Kingdom of Fools and Villains—and other assorted characters...."

Grass grows in cracks, caper vine on walls. Life is askew, she thinks, and ponders disarray.

"I hope Julia won't make a scene—for *both* our sakes. And for the sake of your paying guests."

Alya smiles. "Scenes are my specialty. Just ask *Um* Majed... known in social circles as Madam Alami. Ask Omar... and all our paying guests." A donkey brays, asserting its presence beyond the southern wall.

"Your uncle stopped by last week and ordered a name-plaque from Julia. You should see him now—with his latest eye patch, and his new vocation."

"Possibly, old age could bring liberation," Alya says crisply. "And, at his age, *'Ammi* Musa is free to make what he will of his life."

Sari's shoulders sag under his shirt. He contemplates Alya's face, says wistfully, "When I take Julia to Bethlehem—will you also come with us?"

"I might consider it...."

Alya pauses near her mother's room. *Um* Ramzi is placating Julia with hot tea, *labaneh* sandwiches, and verses from the Beatitudes.

"'Blessed are the poor in spirit, for they shall see God,'" she reads in her singsong voice.

"'Blessed are they who mourn, for they shall be comforted. Blessed are the meek....'"

Julia is silent, her eyes closed, the hands in her lap miraculously stilled.

For modesty, Alya changes into a long-sleeved dress; twists her hair into a sedate chignon at the back of her neck—to impress *'Ammi* in Jerusalem. She chooses for Julia a shirtwaist dress with tiny blue flowers and leather belt.

"Would you try the dress, for my sake?" Alya asks.

Julia looks up coyly. "No."

"No?"

Weightless and without form, the word bobs on the surface of Alya's mind.

Julia wraps her arms around her waist, holds herself prisoner. "I'll wear the pretty, green one to Jerusalem. Nothing else."

Children's eyes watch green chiffon pass by. Giggles—and a father's reprimand. A muffled sound as hand makes contact with flesh; weeping behind a closed door.

Downstairs, the warm aroma of newly baked bread wafts from Miriam's kitchen, rouses hunger pangs. Mustapha's discreet smile holds in words better left unsaid.

"If Omar should ask... tell him I've gone to Jerusalem with friends," Alya says. "That I will visit *'Ammi* Musa there."

Alya clasps Julia's hand, moves purposefully toward the door.

Mr. O'Connor, still in his seat, looks up from his pad.

"Ah! Who do we have here?"

"A friend from Jerusalem," Alya says.

"Enchanted!" Mr. O'Connor nods at Julia, makes a little bow.

"I saw them last night," Julia's voice is a whisper. "Dark shadows... with boxes on their heads."

Mr. O'Connor smiles broadly. "Where did the boxes go?"

Julia jerks her hand free from Alya's and, trailing green chiffon, she dashes through the vestibule, past the verandah, toward the kitchen windows. She stands there, triumphant, points toward an opening in the trees.

"There!"

Alya and Mr. O'Connor stop in their tracks, look at Julia, at each other. He nods his head.

"Exactly!" he says, and gives Alya a wink.

Alya will not have to explain Julia's condition to this amiable American with an Irish name. He already understands.

As Sari's disheveled ghost-image strides toward them, Julia's grip tightens on Alya's arm. Courage is slow in coming, and now, despite herself, the kernel of Alya's being—soft at the center—has turned to mush.

Tourists have complied in increasingly large measure with the U.S. government's advice to leave Israel, among some other Middle Eastern states, in view of the "seriousness of the situation."

The New York Times, May 25, 1967

"It is not difficult for the situation to deteriorate into war, but we have to be strong enough to try all other means."

Premier Levi Eshkol of Israel,
Time, June 9, 1967

British Foreign Secretary George Brown has urged the Soviet Union to use its power in the Middle East in such a way as to see "that the peace of the world is maintained."

The Christian Science Monitor, May 26, 1967

CHAPTER ELEVEN

Alya and Sari

THEY STAND IN THE DOORWAY of Julia's bedroom and look down at the sleeping figure beneath the bright orange quilt: her face in shadow, the form, curled like a fetus in its mother's womb. Small shivery sighs break the rhythm of her nasal breathing, serve as a backdrop to their talk.

Sari turns toward Alya. "If you'd let me," he says, "I'd fall in love with you."

"Your way of saying thanks, no doubt?"

"Among other things...." He winks at her, as if to allay suspicion.

For Alya, friendship for now will suffice. She dismisses possible ardor with a shrug, holds up a fragment of 'Ammi Musa's plaque that Julia, in illogical rage, had hurled against the kiln.

Frowning, Sari takes the fragment from Alya's hand, studies it as if to decipher its puzzle. "What excuse will you invent for 'Ammi Musa?" he asks, trepidation in his voice.

She smiles at Sari's fear of reprimand. "I could say—during an argument about the Greek junta, you waved your arms around.... Or—we were analyzing U Thant's visit to Cairo when your elbow accidentally jabbed...." She giggles, despite herself.

Sari's eyes are somber on Alya's face. "Her tantrum was in revenge for Fiona and all those *other* Fionas who've wandered into my life...."

"Poor, muddled Julia." Alya looks back at the sleeping figure on the bed. "First a father who leaves her behind, then a brother who can't quite give her what she craves...."

"I suppose it might please Julia if I led a hermit's life," Sari says in a rush of emotion. "If she had her way, I'd have to end all friendships. All potential love affairs." His glance settles lightly on Alya's face. "I sometimes have this urge to find refuge in some Aegean island where neither Julia nor the junta will ever find me. But then I step out onto my patio-roof at dusk, and look up at swallows wheeling against the Jerusalem sky and hear the *'Allah-u-Akbar* of the *muezzin's* voice—or the bells of St. George's Church—and I know that *this*, after all, is the prison of my choice."

He takes Alya's hand in his. "I also choose to stay because *you're* only a few kilometers away...." He smiles at her, an artless grin that dares her to protest. But she's already preoccupied with leaving, with thoughts of *'Ammi* Musa.

He locks Julia's door, turns hesitantly toward Alya. Through the filtered hallway light, dark semi-circles seem permanently etched beneath his eyes.

"I need to go...," she says, urgency in her voice.

They walk out together into the bright mid-morning sun. "Would you pick up a newspaper or magazine in the Old City for me?" he asks. "English or Arabic will do."

"Culture, or politics?"

He gives her a somber glance. "Politics, of course."

They wend their way past clusters of petunias toward the gate. He asks, "When did you last see your uncle?"

"He showed up one morning two months ago at our door and stayed an hour or two. 'Just an old uncle still waiting for invitations to Omar's and Alya's weddings,' he told my mother. As if we'd concocted a plot to deprive him of that pleasure...." She smiles at the memory.

Alya's special bond with *'Ammi* Musa is woven with bits of childhood images recreated on ceilings and the borders of walls.

Sari's hand rests on the gate's rusty diadem; his nail scrapes off flakes of loose paint. He gives her a pensive smile. "When you give *'Ammi* Musa my apologies for the broken plaque, try to be discreet."

Discretion, Alya decides as she walks down Nablus Street, is for diplomats, and spies.

The sun has transformed the grayish patina of Suleiman's crenellated walls into a newer version of the old. Cars honk, and schoolchildren, freed from uniforms for a time, skip down the road, careless of what will soon happen in their lives.

But another breed of children Alya sees every day have learned the grown-up need to earn their keep. Children with wizened, sunburned faces who hawk newspapers, *ka'ik* sesame bread, ears of corn and a variety of plastic toys for those *other*, more fortunate ones.

Like an honor guard, *service* taxis line up at the gate of *Bab el-Amud*, their drivers calling out their destinations.

"Al-Khalil! Al-Khalil!"

"Beit Nuba! Beit Nuba!"

A woman in azure dress is ushered into the "Al-Khalil" Hebron taxi, her thin gold bracelets glistening in the sun.

Inside the Old City gate of *Bab el-Amud*, a Sudanese man in white robes sells freshly roasted *fustuk* *"ala kaifak"*—"as you wish"—its warm and tantalizing aroma trails after Alya as she passes the cubicles of money changers.

A woman in black veil nursing her child on the steps calls out her beggar's cry: *Hassaneh lil-lah!*—"The good you'll do is for God!" Alya, pausing to pat the baby's head, drops a coin into the tin cup.

Racks of newspapers and magazines, their languages and color vie with black-and-white headlines, hang from strung-out wire, line the outer wall. Alya stops to browse under the watchful eyes of a boy with buck teeth.

Her glance skims over headlines.

"U Thant arrives in Cairo for talks to Nasser."

"Pope Paul urges prayers to avert conflict in the Middle East."

Will he pray for a miracle?

And on the cover of a *Life* magazine, an astronaut. If one can't stand the earth, then why not fuse with the sky?

Leafing through the magazine, Alya discovers photographs of the "First Lady of California."

"Nancy Reagan's principal regret about being a governor's wife," she reads, "is that the hectic social schedule gives her little time to dress as casually as she likes...."

My hectic social life, Alya thinks, is like the woman with a covered face, asking for alms in a corner of the street.

"Mao's wife Chiang Ching," declares another journalist, "glorifies worker-heroes of the New China in her new opera."

And in Greece, a child is born—an heir to the shaky throne of King Constantine.

Would half-Greek Sari care?

At the Cairo airport, the new U.S. ambassador to Egypt assures the press, "I do not share the sense of crisis that some people feel...."

Yet, each day brings another crisis, Alya knows as she returns the *Life* magazine to the young vendor standing guard. Sari may not care to see Nancy, wife of Governor Reagan, in a red dress, or read about her social agenda. And Hill 881 in Vietnam may not interest him as much as his own political crisis closer to home. She decides to buy the *Al-Ahram* Cairo newspaper, and *Rose El Yusuf* magazine for herself, rolls them up, and tucks them into her straw bag.

Walking down el-Wad Road, Alya reflects on veils and footbinding and a thousand other things that have kept women in their place.

And in California, a woman in a size 6 red dress bemoans the formality of her social life. What kind of power, Alya wonders, does *she* have?

Joan Baez's recorded voice drifts toward Alya from the

Armenian pastry shop, laments the death of young men in war. Fragments of her song trail after Alya as she makes her way down el-Wad Road, past shuttered souvenir shops and hostels and the Orthodox Prison of Christ, where ancient shackles have etched their mark in stone. A man bent double under a load of straw mats, emerges from Via Dolorosa, calls out his *"Aw'-a!"* a warning to passersby to stay clear. A dog licks crevices of an ancient stone where food has been spilled.

Alya weaves her way around the western periphery of the Muslim *Al-Haram ash-Shareef* into the narrow *souk* where shops and layered houses cluster around courtyards in the shadow of the Western Wall. The Wall, *'Ammi* Musa has explained, where El-Burak, the Prophet's horse, was tied before his flight to heaven.

She turns abruptly down an alleyway across from Mugharbeh Gate, makes her way through a maze that will eventually lead her to *'Ammi* Musa's courtyard. Small children squatting around a game of knuckle-bones pay her no mind. Alone on a facing stoop, a small girl tugs at her skirt to cover her knees and ankles, grins shyly up at her.

Making her way through this labyrinth that weaves its path around people's lives, Alya tries to find her way by instinct or sign or number or the way an old wall sags. She finally recognizes the narrow gate on rusted hinges, its crescent and star intact, allowing anyone to come into the courtyard, to explore, to see for themselves how Old City residents live in clusters here, in almost harmony—except for chickens and cats and *Um* Azmi with half a dozen children, and *'Ammi* and his weeds—all a stone's throw from the *Haram* wall.

Inside the courtyard *Um* Azmi squats in her doorway, and boils coffee over a charcoal *kanoon*. She motions to Alya, who approaches warily.

"Tell your old uncle," she scowls, points to a peeling green door, "to mind his garden—or erase it from the face of the earth before I...."

Chickens scurry away from *Um* Azmi, peck at corn kernels

scattered on the cement. Other faces peer at Alya from windows and doorway-openings, their eyes like birds hovering. A child of three or four throws a ball at Alya's feet, stands near a lavender plant, arms poised, waiting for its return. She dribbles it back, sees that he encircles it in his arms, then moves toward a patch of earth near *'Ammi* Musa's stairway. Crouching, Alya inspects tomato and cucumber plants—barely visible for the weeds.

She looks up at the man in striped *kumbaz* robe and *hatta* and *agal*, now perched on the upper landing. "Your garden weeds seem healthier than your tomatoes," she calls to him. "*Um* Azmi couldn't help but notice."

He blinks at Alya above the staircase from his one good eye, his left patch gleaming in the sun. "Why should she complain when her own chickens run loose in the courtyard?"

Once, before her time, *'Ammi* wore Western clothes: ties and jackets and *pantalones*. Alya has seen old photographs of that "Western phase" of his life. One hangs on his living room wall, a strangely domestic portrait of himself, with wife and son of years before... taken of him at *Deir Yaseen*.

Climbing stairs, she comes face to face with his newest eye patch and, etched in its center, the word *salaam*. Peace.

He tugs at his beard, his luminous eye intent on Alya's face. "Ah. You've come for this unexpected visit... to inquire about my health?"

"That, too." She shifts her glance to the crescent carved in stone above the doorway, the *Higra* date, along with a great-grandfather's name—original builder of this home. And does not "*Al mulk lillah*," in stone, proclaim that God, who owns real estate—owns life?

Months have passed since Alya last visited *'Ammi*'s small house. A tree once grew in the middle of the house, cut down years before to expand living space, to make room after a baby's birth. Above the couch in the front living room, she notes the portrait of *'Ammi* as a young man, with two eyes instead of one—and wife with baby boy.

Death of *'Ammi*'s wife and son blur in Alya's childhood

memory, reverberate in disoriented, pain-filled voices.

"Will you be going to prayers at *Al-Aqsa* today?" she asks now.

He shakes his head. "Most days I manage it. But today my joints are too stiff for going anywhere. Something in the air, perhaps, has seeped into my aging bones." He lowers himself carefully onto the worn damask couch, pats the place to his left. "Besides, you're here today to bring me... good news?"

Light finally dawns. "No news of marriage yet, I'm afraid— not for me, or for my brother, Omar."

She looks over at the calligraphy of the Koranic *sura* on the facing wall, reads out loud, "'In the name of God, the compassionate, the merciful...

"He who forgives the sin, accepts repentance....'"

They sit, each in his corner on the worn damask couch, angled to face the other, to reread the *sura* on the wall, or to speculate on the ceiling rimmed with faded vines and the calligraphy of Koranic verses.

Alya rests her hands on the bag in her lap that holds a newspaper, *Rose El Yusuf* magazine, and the wrapped ceramic pieces Sari has sent with her to *'Ammi*. "Sari, the potter," she says cryptically, "sends both greetings and regrets."

"Regrets?"

"He *meant* to have the plaque you requested ready. But a crisis interfered."

'Ammi's fingers moving amber prayer beads pause in their task. "I'm a patient man. I'll wait." He shakes his head slowly. "I'm too old to worry about a crisis any more. I've had my share."

She tries to explain, but he shrugs, does not reply. "If you like," Alya says after a while, "I'll help you weed your garden before I leave."

He looks at her, a twinkle in his one good eye. "We'll do no pulling of weeds on this holy Friday. But soon after my noonday prayers, I'll bring out whatever food scraps I have in my kitchen, and we'll break bread together. And afterwards, I'll show you my painting of the Dome."

They talk, a casual discussion of world events, until the *muezzin*'s call to prayer. He gets up, and goes into his room to wash, to pray—leaving Alya behind to contemplate vines and calligraphy on the upper edge of the living room wall.

Nineteen years before, the child Alya, seeking refuge with her family at *'Ammi*'s house, stared at calligraphy in the almost-dark, and despite the staccato sound of gunfire, was hypnotized into sleep. The trek from Katamon to *Harat el Mugharbeh* (where *'Ammi* Musa still lives) to Beit Nuba, changed the direction of their lives.

After noon prayers, *'Ammi* emerges with *hummus*, tomato and mint salad, black olives and bread. Alya eats hungrily, watches him nibble at food, chew meditatively.

Afterwards, he disappears for a minute or so, returns with a large package wrapped in brown paper. He unwraps it carefully, props it up on the round brass table near the couch.

He says, "This old man has managed to paint a likeness of the Dome of the Rock. See for yourself."

The oil painting is of the Dome burnished in early morning light, its mosaics brilliant blue and gold. In a lower corner, a tiny bird sits in the enclave of an arch with lines and empty space—for what?

"A wonderful likeness," she exclaims. "And all those years, you've hid your talent from us. Why?"

"Old age has stirred creativity... has given me the chance to make a modest living." He hands her a print, a replica of the original, mounted on cardboard. "I sometimes stand outside Mugharbeh Gate or just beyond the Wall and wait for tourists. And when someone buys a print, I write his name in *Kufic* calligraphy inside the lower arch, below the tiny bird." He adds reflectively, "In the last few days, less tourists come by. Talk of war, I suspect, has frightened them away."

He fingers amber prayer beads in meditative silence.

"Legend has it," he begins, translucent eye fixed on Alya's face, "that the sacred rock beneath the Dome once extended twelve miles heavenward, its shadow reaching all the way to Jericho. And those who lived in Balkh, Afghanistan, could spin their wool at night by the light of a ruby set at its pinnacle."

"That same rock from which the Prophet went up into heaven?"

He nods. "For you, a history teacher, *facts* may take precedence over legend... or even tradition. But we, the students of this world, also know that 'facts' *must* be given in context—and are subject to interpretation, and viewpoint."

"Yes. But in this case...."

"Both facts and tradition create our Muslim truth. A valid truth that has convinced millions. Even as *your* mother's Christianity has interpreted a different truth for its own millions." He sighs. "And here you are a rebel, skeptical of both."

The weathered face expands into a smile. He says quietly, "I will only tell you what *I* know is true. Facts a good history teacher *ought* to know." Hunched over his prayer beads, he gives her an added lesson in a segment of history she only knows in parts.

"On the *Al-Haram ash-Shareef* site, nearly two thousand years before, a Jewish Temple was destroyed by Romans—except for one retaining wall." He clears his throat, sighs audibly. "The Jews call it their temple wall, and we, Muslims, call it the wall of El-Burak, named after the winged horse on which Mohammad ascended into heaven. On that same site, a pagan temple of Emperor Hadrian was once built—and destroyed. And under Byzantine rule—before Islam—that site became a garbage dump."

Gnarled fingers stop moving amber beads, lie still on his knees. His radar one-eye seeks Alya's face.

"Tradition tells of the Muslim *Calipha* Omar's shock at the discovery of the holy site turned into a garbage dump; and how, with his own hands, he helped his men clear the site where his architects built the modest Mosque of Omar."

She knew, read somewhere, that the Mosque of Omar had preceded the Dome, now mentions it, displaying knowledge.

"Yes," he nods his head. "In the Christian year of 687, the *Calipha* Abd al-Malik replaced Omar's Mosque with the magnificent Dome we see today."

Alya watches *'Ammi's* mouth half-hidden by straggly whiskers, hears a tale of Crusaders who placed a cross above the Muslim Dome, claiming it as their own—renaming it Templum Domini.

"Even the artist Raphael painted the Dome in one of his paintings as a Christian Church."

This, she confesses, she did not know.

But Alya, of dubious faith, must see the imprint of the Prophet's foot upon the Rock, and study the Raphael painting in Milan's Brera Gallery—to be convinced.

Later, as he talks of saffron and *khuluk* and the attar of roses—once used to perfume the Holy Rock—Alya enters her own reverie of scent and the chanting of "Kyrie Eleison" of the church of her childhood. She waits—a small girl, compressed between the thighs of older women—hypnotized into acquiescence by priestly ritual and the smell of incense.

Angels, saints and devils populated her childish days, played havoc with her nights. Would she, asleep, be whisked away to dance, barefoot, with angels? Or play tag with devils intent on snatching her soul away?

'Ammi Musa looks into Alya's face. "Have I told you enough to satisfy curiosity? Or has your mind drifted to another place?"

"But only for a moment."

She doesn't mean to offend, to cast doubt on her uncle's faith. But she is a woman without home or country—caught between two faiths—in search of her self.

"In the next months, even years," she says now, "I'll weigh what I learn of my father's faith, and will consider my mother's Christian beliefs. Only then will I try to decide what I will... or will not believe."

'Ammi lifts his head, gives her a conspiratorial look. "I'll forgive your inattention, my dear Alya—but only if you make us a good cup of coffee."

She rummages in the kitchen cupboard, finds coffee where it was myriad years before. Measures coffee, sugar, seeds of *hale*, watches seeds somersault in the dark foam, boats on a raging sea—like lives.

They sip coffee in companionable silence, wait for thoughts, like coffee grounds, to settle.

"A woman who knows how to brew a good cup of coffee should have been married long ago." He heaves an extended sigh. "Look at you and Omar... both without mates! And why, my dear Alya, allow unborn children to languish in your womb?" His one good eye glistening, a flare of anger in his voice.

But how can she explain it? What can she say about the betrayal of love? Of her faith in Majed Alami?

Before the ritual of their parting, she bends her head and kisses the parchment hand—a gesture of respect for the old man who is her father's brother. He walks her to the door, touches her forehead lightly with his palm—a kind of blessing.

"Next time, when you come, bring Omar with you. Both, then, can help clear weeds from my garden." He smiles. "And may Allah clear debris... and weeds, from your life and mine...."

In the courtyard, Alya nearly trips on a chicken scurrying toward the gate. From an open doorway, a child is weeping. *Um Azmi* calls out above the din, "So... is the old man going to clean up his garden?"

"*Insha'Allah!*" Alya says.

Alya

AT NEARLY 3 O'CLOCK that Friday afternoon, Alya makes her way back from the narrow *souk* of *Harat el Mugharbeh* at the Western Wall, to the northwest corner of the *Haram*, where a crowd has spilled out of the Umariyya School and into the Via Dolorosa. Brown-robed Franciscan monks, carrying a wooden cross, chant their "Miserere nobis Domine," reviving in Alya a reverence for the ardor of the faithful. The crowd engulfs her—a woman dispossessed, seeking asylum from her lack of faith. As their chant overflows into the souvenir shops and *souks*, she is propelled for a time into that other, safer world where guidelines for Heaven and Hell are clearly defined.

In her own world, innocence, abandoned long ago, hangs in

tatters on the line, and Heaven and Hell are fused into a murky gray. But devils and demons, turned pussycats, no longer hold her in their grip—stand back to let her pass.

She eases out of the crowd veering left, turns right into el-Wad Road and makes her way back toward Damascus Gate. The Sudanese with his roasted *fustuk* has vanished; in his place, a young boy sells honeyed sesame candy from a wooden stand.

A man of medium height in Western suit hurries past, and for an instant, his stride and the longish cut of his hair resurrect in Alya a fleeting image of Majed Alami. But when he pauses to consider the tray of sweets, he turns his head, revealing a sharp profile in a ruddy, alien face. Boys pass her by, jostle one another, their laughter reverberating in the street. They stop to ogle the candy tray, the suited man, to dig in pockets for some change. One almost trips, reaches out to steady himself, pulls at the man's sleeve.

"*Wlad sharameet!*" the man hisses under his breath.

Alya flinches at the vehemence of the man's curse. The chant of the "Miserere nobis Domine" echoes in her head, becomes a portcullis against an ominous dread that settles, like fine Gaza dust, over her mood.

She threads her way out of the Old City, past taxis and the surge of humanity and the woman in black seeking alms. Crossing the intersection, she turns to the right and walks toward the post office and Salah-uddeen Street. She passes a handful of open shops and families in their Friday best and finds herself, as if by appointment, across from the Ritz Hotel. She stands on the corner and looks up at the radio station, its tower filigreed against an azure sky.

Has she suddenly turned spy, covertly watching out for lovers grown cold?

Alya and Sari

ALYA WENDS HER WAY back past the Ritz Hotel, and wanders into a bookstore, for refuge from the absurdity of her life. Inside, dusty, unread books crowd walls, reach nearly to the ceiling. The man behind the desk lifts furtive eyes above his *London Times*. She meets his glance, asks for a book she knows he will not have. He shakes his head, returns to his hiding place behind the news, allows her to browse to her heart's content.

For Alya, the feel and smell of each book is the censer of the black-robed priest of her childhood days—spewing incense and blessings across the aisles. She flips through pages, savors pictures and words, inhales the scent of bound paper as if it were the sweet fragrances that once bathed the Holy Rock. A book on exotic birds entrances, another tells the tale of an earthquake in San Francisco; one is in a woman's voice—the first to learn the habits and habitats of chimpanzees. And when she picks up an American book titled *How Love Can Change your Life for the Better*, she begins to laugh, searing laughter to cause chimpanzees to hide and exotic birds to fly from harm's way. The man at the counter glances up from behind his paper at this frenzied display of hilarity, asks, caution in his voice, "You find the book amusing?"

"More than...." she manages to say, and begins to laugh anew.

She leaves the bookstore, decides to walk a marathon walk to the Palestine Museum and back—as if in the movement of legs answers will come to dissipate fog, to guide her path toward grace.

An aching weariness settles in her bones, a lightness in her head. Leg muscles strain, pull robot legs toward a juice stand with two sidewalk tables, one already occupied by a disheveled calico cat that eyes Alya with guarded suspicion.

Behind the counter, a man with a sallow, unshaven face squeezes oranges into a speckled glass. "If it were up to me," he says, "I'd offer you Jaffa oranges. Nothing sweeter than an orange from the Jaffa grove my father once owned. Owns still."

Alas, he no longer owns, his eyes confess.

"Jericho oranges will do as well, for now," she says.

What once was, belonged to... has vanished. We've lost what we once thought was ours: orange groves, homes, lives—even love. But how do we learn to integrate the raw wounds of loss into our lives?

Dusk has begun to whiten the sky, wraps itself around ancient walls, meshes into the sharp corners of the street. As Alya looks out on moving cars, she tries to distill vulnerability from her blood.

With the newspaper for Sari still tucked inside her handbag, Alya meanders back to Nablus Street, crosses the familiar street toward Sari's house. A straggly ghost on the stoop gets up to greet her.

He says, "It's been a while. I was afraid you weren't coming back...."

"My detours—and my visit to *'Ammi*—took longer than I thought." She takes out the folded paper from her handbag, gives it to Sari. "The *Al-Ahram* newspaper—with all the latest news."

He flashes a boyish grin. "If I had a bit of wisdom, I'd stay away from the news and other things hazardous to mental health."

"So... how's Julia?" she asks.

"After you left, she had a tantrum, tried to set fire to her curtains." Sari gives Alya a condensed version of Dr. Murad's visit. After a pause, he adds, "He told me I had some hard decisions to make."

"Hard decisions can also be hazardous to mental health," Alya says flippantly.

"It's *indecision* that can drive one mad." He gives her a wry look. "But please come in? Water for our tea has been simmering for a while now."

Alya follows Sari inside. He glances briefly at Julia's closed door. "Before the doctor came, I made soup for both of us. She poured her portion in the sink, convinced I'd poisoned it...."

"Poor Julia...." Alya takes in a breath. "I wish I could be of better help."

On the patio-roof, the scent of mint clings to cool evening air. Doves flutter in their cages, startled by guests. In Sari's living room lamps are lit, but curtains are still open to the sky. A shard of *'Ammi* Musa's broken plaque lies on the glass coffee table, next to clay figures of man and woman, arms intertwined, with staring eyes in tiny, smiling faces.

"Wait here," Sari says. "I won't be long." He tosses the newspaper on the low-slung chair, leaves Alya to take off her shoes, to study Picasso's "Hands with Flowers" poster behind the leather couch. She notes colored smudges of paint for petals, the outline of hand holding stems. Her own hand trembles as it takes the cup from Sari; tea almost spills. A weariness has taken hold of her hands and fingers, has settled in her bones. She tucks one leg under her, flexes sore toes.

"*'Ammi* Musa and I had a good visit," she says finally. "We discussed history and legend, even weed-infested gardens. One tradition has it that the Holy Rock was once twelve miles high, and that, at night, the people in Balkh, Afghanistan, could spin their wool by the light of a ruby set in its pinnacle."

Sari shrugs. "If Moses can part the sea, the walls of Jericho can come tumbling down, or Christ can walk on water... why not the legend of the Rock?"

"Only if you believe in miracles...."

"I believe in possibilities...," he says as he settles into the facing corner of the couch, extends his legs. He watches with a bemused glance as she sips her tea. "You must have had a long visit with your *'Ammi*," he says after a while.

She looks up. "Did you know he also sells prints of his Dome watercolor to tourists, even writes their names in calligraphy?"

"Aging artists must eat, you know."

"When I told him about the plaque, he didn't seem half as upset as by news of Omar's and my continued unmarried status."

"If I were *'Ammi*," he says, "I'd arrange a marriage for my favorite niece with a man of integrity and wit. Religion and financial status won't matter. I'd pick a poor but honest man who'd lay down his life...."

She laughs a light and airy laugh, resists an impulse to cover eyes and ears against miracles. She sets her teacup down, looks up into Sari's bearded, unsmiling face.

"I stopped by the radio station to spy on Majed—the man I thought would lay down his life for me. I did this on impulse, as if magnets directed my feet to walk there—despite logic and common sense." She drapes an arm across the back of the couch, rearranges her legs.

Sari's gray eyes scrutinize her face, "Were you expecting to see Majed? To grant him a pardon?"

"In my fantasy, I see him fall on his knees before me, grovel, beg forgiveness... and assure me he would defy his mother for my sake. But I would naturally turn him down...." She rests her head in the crux of her arm, looks out beyond the window at the darkening sky. "An English king once begged forgiveness of the Roman Pope—groveling on his knees in the snow." She laughs. "It must've been a pretty sight."

Alya sips her tea and reflects on impulse gone astray. "I've been a woman scorned, but I can't bear the thought. I tried to do my bit for revenge at his mother's house, but it left a bitter taste." Her gaze settles on the small, ceramic couple on the coffee table, their eyes wide open as they seem to weigh the hazards of love. She gets up on impulse; picks them up, makes her palm a pedestal.

"Are you still in love…," he hesitates, "… in love with Majed Alami?"

She sets the ceramic couple down, turns to face him. "Once, I suppose, when I was less cynical... I thought I was."

"Once—a week ago?"

"A week, or even an hour... can make a mirage vanish. I suppose I'm in mourning for what I *thought* I had—the love of the man of my choice."

She returns to her corner on the couch, falls silent as she ponders the gritty residue of passion gone awry.

"At the advanced age of forty-three," Sari says, "I've become convinced that all we ever have are our own reactions to life's ironies, and the possibility of miracles." He leans back against the cushions, gives Alya a rueful smile. "If we really believed this, we'd then learn to love without expectations. Or cynicism."

Alya sets her cup down with a clatter. "What about free will, and choice—*with* expectations?" Her hand creates a fist, pounds against the edge of the coffee table, rattling teacups. "*Our* will, *our* choices should define who we are—and pinpoint what happens next in our lives."

"*Interaction* of 'wills' and 'choices' might better do the trick." Sari turns toward Alya, his shoulders stiffly braced against the pillows, and presents his case. As she tries to decipher words and hidden meanings, her attention weaves in and around nuances, shifts toward the window, where night has begun to settle on the irregular rim of the sky.

And why does he wear the navy blue shirt with silver buttons—reserved for special occasions, his hair smelling of *Nabulsi* soap and combed neatly into place?

Why does he demand much more from her—besides a weightless and uncomplicated friendship?

He says with a vehemence that catches her off guard, "I'm afraid I've *chosen* to fall in love with a headstrong woman who has grown cynical about love." He gives her an oddly pensive look. "Or is this beyond my choosing?"

"After my visit to the radio station," Alya says, biding her time, "I stopped to browse at a nearby bookstore. An American book about 'how love can change your life for the better' made me laugh—too loud, I suppose, to suit the manager of the place."

A secret breeze manipulates the blackened crests of the tall, graceful palms. And, despite the faint rumble of traffic below, Alya can hear the cooing of doves, awakened from stupor, and the occasional flutter of their wings.

She gets up abruptly, pads barefoot to the window and looks out at the gray-tinted sky, at a scattering of stars, and tries to organize emotions. Friendship, she knows, is a constant thing, to savor for a lifetime. But love's unpredictability—she thinks with sudden panic—could ruin a friendship and undo the careful outline of her plans.

Thoughts of Professor Antone unravel themselves in her

memory. A younger Alya then, vulnerable, easily seduced. Their trysts—scheduled for his conference period or sometimes after school. But sometimes, when he forgot to come, he winked at her in Sociology class, murmured apologies. Once even scribbled "Please forgive this absent-minded...." on her paper, "Religious Practices of the Maoris," right below her grade.

She looks at Sari. "All these months we've been friends. Isn't that enough?"

"I've always loved you," Sari says now, his hands moving in cadence to the anarchy of his words. "But how could I bring it up—knowing Majed was central to your life—and Julia, to mine?" A sigh. "I'm a foolish, middle-aged man, in the grip of schoolboy emotions. All these months, I've waited for the courage to let you know...."

"For me," Alya says, "love means giving up the small securities of life. And I'm not sure I want to take that risk."

She sits cross-legged on the couch, and begins to relate to Sari her memory of the puppet game she and her friends played in Katamon, Jerusalem—as if it held the clue to future skepticism. "We'd run as far as we could, and at the word 'Freeze!' we weren't allowed to move or smile or show emotion—turned into puppets—moving arms and legs at our own risk. When we broke the rules, we had to climb the *saru* tree in a nearby empty lot and stay there until dark."

Sari reaches for her hand, holds it, palm up. "That's not the kind of game we'd want to play, is it?" he says.

Alya resists the impulse to snatch her hand away, allows it to lie in his, uncaged. Years before, she recalls her father's parchment hand in hers as he lay dying.

"But surely friendship can *also* be a part of love?" Sari's hand closes tightly on her own. "I want you near me, to touch, to hold. To show you who I really am—without the mask. To know you as you are."

She needs time to consider this curious offering at her door; time to decipher her own responses. The possibility of Friend turned Lover is a phenomenon to weigh, to meditate upon.

"Why not an island of our own where our own wills prevail?" Sari waves his arms about in emphasis. "One where convention and the rules of society don't apply—where we could create our own...."

She thinks: ...with orange trees, and caves with friendly, harmless bats... And where snakes, like eagles and sparrows and hyenas, are never used to tempt men and women into sin.

Her hand—a small segment of herself, detached, impersonal—lies quietly in his, the filigreed gold of her grandmother's ring burnished in the light.

"We need a safe haven—far away from wars or rumors of wars." She smiles a bitter smile. "Where we wouldn't be forced to watch, while hawks swallow up doves whole, spit out their bones." She asks suddenly, "*Without* an island, what other choices do we have?"

Her question, a spider on its thread, unobtrusive, testing the air.

"You speak *politically*, I assume?" At her nod, he says, "All we *can* do is bide our time and adjust to the choices of men in power that may affect our lives."

"So we're no more than cats or dogs held on a leash, or tied to other people's fences?"

"It's in the *adjustment* that we make our choices," Sari says with a shrug. "What we think, how we act—or react—as we wait for the dam to break." His glance is impersonal, turned inward. "And afterwards, if we're still intact, we can choose to accept or reject the changes that will come."

She pulls her hand away, touches fingertips above her skirted thighs, lifts her head. "We must also resist with every fiber of our being what is demeaning or unjust. To resist logically and without hate or even violence—but with the conviction that your intrinsic self *will* remain intact."

Outside the window the deepening blue of evening has absorbed the sky, and seeped into the corners of the room. Her terror defused for a time, replaced by the plop! of pebble thrown into the well, its echo singing in her head.

Sari gives her a melancholy smile, bends his head, a medieval courtier to kiss a lady's hand. He holds his palm against hers, as if to measure size and texture, to explore the reality of warm flesh. Like figures in clay, reaching out, touching.

She holds her breath as his talisman fingers smooth back a strand of her hair. He leans toward her, his eyes focused on hers, and for a fleeting second, she sees Majed's face; eyes, nose, mouth, seduce—compel response. Miraculously transformed into a craggy, bearded face. Face hovering, Sari kisses her, a fleeting kiss that barely leaves its mark.

A thought intrudes, scurries like a gecko on a screen. Tomorrow, a school day like any other, is only hours away. Mustering will Alya rummages for shoes, bag, stands up shakily, her legs slightly apart, for balance.

"I've got a *service* taxi to catch," she says, "and many miles to go before I sleep...."

He ignores the logic of her argument, instead, clicks off one source of light and moves toward her, blocking her escape. Shadows in the room swaddle furniture and poster on the wall. The disarray of wilted roses in their ceramic vase emit a diffuse gentian glow. He stands close enough for Alya to smell the *Nabulsi* olive-oil soap in his hair and beard, the hard muscle of his arm pressing against her back, cuts through nebulous shadow, blocks out the light. A bittersweet melody pulsates in her head, a malagueña of sorts, its rhythm penetrating her defenses. But why does she cling to him, her feet nailed to the floor, when the music intoxicates, compels her to dance?

The ticking of the kitchen clock provides a certain comfort. But other sounds intrude, and somewhere in the recesses of her mind, a door creaks open, closes stealthily.

Sari says, with a certain urgency, "Will you take me as I am, and still allow me to be your friend?"

His rib cage pressed against her breasts quells what answer she could give.

A frantic rustle of feathers and the barking of a far-off dog, intrude. Her fingers lose their grip, and her handbag falls noisily to the floor.

Compressed against the angles of his body, she seeks what once was lost, rediscovered by chance here in this room. An avalanche of tears break through barricades meant to hold them back. Outside, shadows dance against the sky, creep slowly toward the ledge, take on human shape. But for now, the cooing of the doves and a dozen other night sounds blot out doubt and human apparitions.

I could lose myself, Alya thinks. Even learn to love again.

A scraping of nails on glass intrudes, disrupts both thought and reverie. Alya looks beyond the window pane at clawed fingers aimed, like daggers, at the darkened room. Aimed at her.

"What was that?" Sari murmurs his question into Alya's hair.

She turns him toward the window so he can see Julia's nose flattened against glass, marble eyes searching out their hiding place.

"Dear God!"

Julia's ghost moves swiftly from the window, melts into the murky night.

Sari calls out Julia's name. But his voice, hollowed out, falls back to earth with a thud. His fingers caress the hollow of Alya's neck, outline her mouth. Does he seek to assess her reality—suddenly grown blind? Alya prays a silent prayer to the Guardian Spirit of this Earth—to watch over Julia and keep her from harm.

Sari closes the curtains, turns on the lamp. "I'm sorry. I didn't mean to... But I felt this urgency...."

...for mysteries to be solved and miracles to happen?

The memory of a gritty storm lashes against the sanctuary of herself. Glass breaks, metal twists in howling wind. Sand sears her eyelids, burns her face. The hollow sound of grief breaks through the iron portcullis that holds back the world's injustices. She clings to the hard bone of Sari's shoulder, his arm steadying her, granting her temporary reprieve. The silhouette of the Katamon tree cuts into the frantic desperation of her mother's voice. Impersonal shovels dig into rubble, into tombs of the once-living. The hotel that once was, is no more.

And a cheerful English tune hovers overhead—the soldiers' dirge for the living and the dead.

She huddles against him and waits for the storm to subside. Nothing remains now but a ragged portion of herself, devoid of memories, even tears.

He lifts her chin with the crook of his finger, looks into her face. "I'll take you home," he says formally.

"I'll manage on my own. Please stay—for Julia's sake."

He hesitates. "I asked once before. But if I take Julia to Bethlehem, will you come with us... for *my* sake?"

Once more, she gives her promise reluctantly, fearful of promises. He takes her hand in his, brings it to his lips. "Shall we pray for a miracle?"

But the swallow has come and gone, leaving its imprint in the sky.

Dressed in a slate blue pilot's uniform, [King Hussein] signed the treaty [with Nasser]. The King piloted his own civilian plane, [a Caravelle... to Cairo] from Amman.

...Shukairy, leader of the Palestine Liberation Organization, arrived on the same plane with the King....

The New York Times, May 31, 1967

On June 1, Major General Moshe Dayan, commander of the Israeli forces in the 1956 Sinai Campaign, was appointed defense minister... to the satisfaction of the hawkish elements in the government. Israeli forces were placed on a war footing.

The Book of Knowledge Annual, 1968

CHAPTER TWELVE

Clara

THE MOMENT Clara saw him, she knew. He was the Voice on the Telephone—the warm, amiable voice enticing her into revelation.

"I suppose you found him attractive?" the Voice had said surreptitiously.

"Short, dark and passionate. How could I resist?"

"But you *did* say you'd help us...?"

"A possibility," she told him. "But never a commitment...."

There had been seven or eight calls during her eighteen-month stay in Beit Nuba. Always the same Voice, friendly, coaxing, with a Southern accent. It was connected to the name Phil. Phil X, he said, like Malcolm.

Yesterday he called for an appointment. "I must see you. Preferably alone—since you've told me your husband doesn't know...."

"He's happier that way...."

A clearing of the throat. "I hear your husband will be off on a short trip to Emmaus, the village Kubbebeh. That will give us privacy... and a time to chat. Tomorrow afternoon, then? Shall we say 3 o'clock?"

"Four would be better."

A pause. "Your husband might come back sooner than expected, and we don't want him to realize...."

"...that his wife is a potential spy?"

"Too blunt a word, ma'am, since you haven't given us any clues yet... about anything." An uneasy laugh. "Or anyone."

"That's the way the ball bounces," Clara says cheerfully.

"Only if there's air in it, ma'am."

He stands at her door now, tall, about forty-five, with receding brown hair that has a reddish tint to it. His eyes behind silver-rimmed glasses look pained as if he must get used to looking at people instead of documents. Although he reminds her a bit of George—the academic part at least—he seems more relaxed, has a guarded but friendly smile.

As he walks into Clara's living room, his glance takes in the dolls in the cabinet, the books and magazines on the coffee table. He picks up the *Life* magazine, eyes the sketch on the cover, thumbs through it casually.

"Remarkable man, that Leonardo," he says as he takes his seat across from her couch, and balances the magazine across his knees. "Remarkable horse... that bit about being melted down. A great pity."

"George would certainly agree...."

He lifts his head as if to gain perspective. His name, he tells her now, is Phillip McCarthy Giles. "I'm a paper-pusher at the consulate. Not very exciting work, I'm afraid."

She lights up a cigarette, smiles at him through the haze of smoke. He looks slightly rumpled in a pin-striped suit, a size too big and in need of ironing.

"So... you've come in person to try and extract those little secrets you think I've kept from you?" she says amicably.

"Any stray bit of info is helpful, ma'am." He inclines his head, his brows furrow. "But I've also come to urge you to leave Beit Nuba right away. For your sake, and for ours."

"We've been mulling it over—George has, at least." She

shrugs. "Hussein making up with Nasser, and now Dayan at Israel's helm... really worry him. But I've been holding out. No logic to it... but it's difficult to end an affair with a passionate man." She smiles brightly at Phil's obvious discomfort, asks without warning. "Are you a passionate man, Phil?"

She notes a reddening of his neck, a stain creeping to his temples. A cerebral man, she decides, with passion repressed—at least in her presence.

When he mutters something about "an inappropriate question," she presses on, "Married?"

"Divorced," he says. "Fortunately, no children."

"I'm married... but without children."

He clears his throat, studies her thoughtfully. "Surely this man Omar has other... interests?"

"His interests revolve around the hotel, his sister's antics, and me. But his real passion is Palestine... this mythical land he carries with him like an albatross around his neck."

"He's told you this?"

"More or less." She clasps her hands, reaches above her head, stretching. "American men have obsessions like football, or baseball or even the books they plan to write. Not Omar. His one obsession is the Palestinian cause."

"Does he have any plans for this... Palestine?"

"He spouts ideas with little logic. I sometimes fall asleep listening to his endless monologues...."

Phil's eyes narrow; he says softly, "Any specific threats aimed at Israel?"

She gives a short laugh. "He never mentions it by name. Merely alludes to it... as if saying the word 'Israel' might make it real in his mind...."

"Does he...." Phil leans forward in his chair; a hand flexes itself over Leonardo's horse. "Does he use threats... or suggest any acts of terrorism?"

Clara shakes her head. "Not that I've heard." She is silent, searching out past statements. He's mentioned Es Samu, where a Nablus friend once lived. His house had been blown up. He alluded to Fatah, but never quite explained it. Not that she wanted to know.

"Tell me about his sister, Alya Habeeb."

Clara takes a drag from her diminished cigarette, sets it down on the edge of the ashtray. "Alya doesn't get into politics," she says now. "Besides, she has her own personal problems to work out... like the rest of us."

"A teacher, I hear. And quite attractive."

"You probably know all that... from other sources?"

He nods. "But Omar is the one who interests us. And his possible connection to Fatah." He sits back in his chair, gazes at her from narrowed eyes. "Surely, you've seen or heard *something?*"

Without giving him the benefit of reply, Clara gets up, walks over to the cabinet, and picks up her latest ethnic doll—a cloth doll in robes and head-dress, its beard a tangle of brown woolen loops.

She returns to her corner, props up the doll in her lap, readjusts its headband. She turns the doll around to face Phil. "So... what does it remind you of?"

"Some character from the Bible." Impatience in his voice. "But what has this to do with...?"

"Passion?"

He heaves a weary sigh, his glance intent on Clara's face. "Has he mentioned a Fatah operation to you?"

"Omar Habeeb is too busy with taking care of the hotel," Clara says haughtily, "...with keeping an eye on his Alya—and me—to have time for any so-called 'operation'...."

Philip McCarthy Giles lays down the *Life* magazine on the edge of the coffee table, then stands up. To Clara, he looks worn out, tattered at the edges.

Poor thing, she thinks now. I gave him a rough time.

"Once more," he says softly. "Y'all make sure you leave Beit Nuba soon." At the door, he hesitates, turns around to face her. "In the meantime, if something concrete comes up... call the number I've given you. You still have that number?"

"On the back of my banana bread recipe card."

Clara returns the doll to the cabinet, walks over to her kitch-
en. On a narrow shelf above the stove, her recipe box sits next
to a bowl of sugar, and a small ceramic cat, tail dangling over the
edge. Rummaging through the box, she pulls out the recipe. On
the back of the card, she verifies the penciled number she'd written down that first time he'd phoned.

She takes the card with her to the back porch, sits down on
the top rung of front steps and lights up her cigarette. She takes
a couple of puffs, fills her lungs with it. Pressing the corner of
the card to the lit end of her cigarette, she exhales slowly. Bap-
tism by fire, she decides, as tiny flames, like rat's teeth, begin to
gnaw at the card, forcing her to drop the charred remains in the
grass.

Nawal

THE LOBBY of the Hotel Semiramis is deserted this Friday
evening, but soon Hagas's band will begin to play, and Janan will
sing her bittersweet songs of love, and the night will acquire a
surrealism of its own.

Although most of the foreigners have vanished, a few hardy
souls remain. Mr. O'Connor, for one. And "Rick" Walid from
Brooklyn, who—despite his American passport—has not yet
found himself a wife and mother to his orphaned children. Others from Arab countries are here to enjoy a summer much cooler
than Saudi Arabia, or Oman, or Kuwait can provide. Several
honeymooners pass Nawal furtively, sit for hours on end under
the pines before returning to the privacy of their rooms. The
rest are locals who come here to enjoy the ambience and the
music—who will try, for a little while, to postpone the reality of
their world.

Nawal folds over page 151 of the Agatha Christie story in
her April *Redbook*, and turns on the black-and-white television
on the counter. She listens vaguely to the American couple in the
commercial sing the praises of Lux soap in Egyptian-dubbed

dialect, and waits for the news from Amman.

But, instead of Priscilla Madding, Jaleel Hawa begins to give the evening news in English for the first time on Amman television.

But where is Priscilla Madding's familiar Midwestern accent, the honey-blonde hair, the confident smile? When Nawal lies sleepless in her bed at night, she imagines herself reading the evening news—her straight brown hair transformed into wavy blonde tresses, her nondescript eyes sparkling with jade-green highlights to dazzle even the most stubborn of viewers.

Perhaps even someone like Omar Habeeb.

"...new defense installations on the outskirts of the Old City...." Jaleel Hawa clears his throat, looks down at the papers in his hand, nervously strokes one end of his dark blond mustache. "...not far from the Inter-Continental Hotel...."

When the telephone rings, Nawal tries to ignore it as she continues to watch Jaleel Hawa's erratic reading of the news. Her eyes still riveted on the screen, she finally turns down the volume, picks up the receiver.

Although Nawal recognizes the voice as that of the mysterious "Mrs. Brown," the caller identifies herself as Clara, wife of George Appleby, the American professor. Nawal briefly met Clara a year or so ago, recalls a round, pink face, gypsy earrings. Despite a breathless urgency in Clara's voice, Nawal continues to stare at the wiggle of Jaleel Hawa's mustache as he informs his viewers of Shah Pahlevi and Empress Farah's latest visit to West Germany.

"Student demonstrators threw eggs at the Shah's motorcade," continues Jaleel Hawa gloomily. "Security was tightened...."

"I'm trying to get hold of Omar Habeeb," Clara says into Nawal's ear. "But, when I call him upstairs, either no one answers, or else he hangs up on me." She takes a deep breath. "But I must talk to him. Damn it! I want him to know I'm not a free agent—that, under the circumstances, I'll have to do what *they* say."

"They?"

"The boys in Washington. They think they know best."

Certainty—confirming hearsay and gossip—surges through

Nawal like a cold shaft of steel. She knows now what she once suspected, will no longer tilt at windmills in the night.

Clara then—despite her own marriage vows—has penetrated Omar's fantasies, has even helped create them.

"His Majesty King Feisal of Saudi Arabia has ended his visit to Great Britain...," reads Jaleel Hawa. And: "'Life in the Soviet Union is unbearable,' says Stalin's daughter, Sve—Svetlana Alli —" he smiles awkwardly into the camera, "—lu-yeva, who defected...."

"Omar can be pig-headed," Clara says loudly, disrupting Nawal's concentration on the news.

Nawal considers the implication of the word "pig" in all its aspects. The people of Beit Nuba have little, if any, affection for those rotund "unclean" creatures of God.

She murmurs her protest in the English she has studied at Beir Zeit College. "It may be probable that something upset him, that may have caused him to become impatient...."

As if she knew the secret workings of a man who compliments her efficiency and hard work, but fails to notice her womanhood.

"If he won't talk to me over the phone," Clara says, exasperation in her voice, "I may have to come to the hotel...."

Jaleel Hawa stares seductively into Nawal's eyes, says solemnly, "Nasser has sent a pledge to world leaders that he will not commit a first strike. The message went to...."

The front door swings open and Omar walks in with Mr. O'Connor at his heels. Nawal covertly relays this information to Clara, asks her to hold the line.

"What you're saying is *not* an accurate assessment of the truth," Mr. O'Connor is saying to Omar's receding back. "Besides, I can show you scars in places my own mother couldn't guess at."

Ignoring Mr. O'Connor, Omar continues doggedly toward the stairway.

"But you *must* try to understand our dilemma," Mr. O'Connor protests. "*Everyone* seems to have a 'just cause' these days. The Palestinians, the Irish, the Kurds, the Armenians...."

Omar stops short a few paces from Nawal's desk, turns swiftly toward the little Irishman—his body alert, poised for combat. He slams his fist into the palm of his hand like a hammer. "A little justice... that's all we ask for. Justice from those Westerners who gave our land away, and those who took it gladly. Justice from our Arab brothers."

"But who's to say what is just and unjust?" Mr. O'Connor asks. "The Jewish cause, after all, has been on top of the list for decades. The Holocaust, as you well know...."

"You have a phone call," Nawal interrupts. As Omar walks back to Nawal's desk, the Irishman makes his escape.

"Tomorrow, June 3, 1967," a newswoman now says on the small television screen, "will be sunny and warm, with early morning mist. Sunday will be—"

"Would you turn down the sound?" Omar says brusquely as he picks up the receiver.

Nawal turns off the set, and her eyes refocus on the chic blonde on the cover of her magazine; she pretends not to notice as Omar, wordlessly, slams down the receiver.

As she scans Omar's glowering, tight-lipped face, her breath feels constricted—as if all the words she has practiced secretly into the night have wedged themselves into her throat.

Light and shadow flicker in Omar's narrowed eyes. "She has her *own* loyalties; I was a fool to think it may have been different...."

He turns abruptly toward the stairway, climbs the steps two at a time to the second floor.

Nawal now understands. Clara is leaving with the rest of the foreigners—deserting Omar—returning with her lawful wedded husband to higher ground. A certain relief washes over Nawal—gives her an airy sense of euphoria.

For at age twenty-six—and despite approaching spinsterhood—Nawal is still in love with Omar Habeeb.

From her purse, she takes out comb and mirror, and like

a scientist bent on discovery, studies her features. She stares at her introspective, narrow face framed by lethargic hair, considers possibilities of refurbishing. In American magazines, mousy women are often transformed—through makeup and hairstyle—into ravishing lovelies. Browsing through her magazine, she wishes that a "Kenneth" or a "Mr. Thomas" could shape her own lackluster hair into "wide and curvy lines, brushed on one side with a pert flip." In the do-it-yourself mode of Americans, page 38 has detailed diagrams of what *she* could do to add glamour to her own appearance.

Perhaps even her life.

But vanity, her mother insists, is not becoming in a daughter who must accept with grace what God has failed to provide.

Sighing, Nawal returns to Hercule Poirot and *Third Girl*.

She reads, "'Your moustache,' said Norma immediately. 'It couldn't be anyone else—'"

Not even Jaleel Hawa's.

The honeymoon couple from Zerka saunter down the stairs, she in her scarlet dress and golden bracelets, he in his pin-striped suit, his hair slicked back. They greet her shyly as they walk past her toward the front door. They will probably take a turn or two in the garden before settling down at one of the courtyard tables to wait for the evening festivities to begin.

Nawal contemplates the possibilities of her *own* honeymoon, thinks: Only for Omar Habeeb would I give up my virginity, would give in to his male cravings. The thought of it sends a shiver through her frame, makes her blush.

Carnal thoughts subdued, she returns to Hercule Poirot and reads words her mind must try to absorb.

"'You've been having me followed.'"

"'No, no....'"

The front door swings open and Badri's round, freckled face emerges from behind glass—followed by arms, torso, legs. He runs toward Nawal, plants himself in front of her, and extends a closed fist; he opens it slowly, revealing three lone marbles in variegated colors. His eyes deflect toward hers with the patient obstinacy of a stray dog whose presence will not be ignored. He emits a jumble of sounds as his hands now form urgent diagrams Nawal must try to decipher.

Tears bubble up, etch a path across his face. Once more, his hands flex themselves in an urgent pantomime of what he insists she must know.

As Nawal steps out from behind her desk, Badri grabs her hand, pulls her reluctantly across the *liwan* toward the front door. Once outside, he sprints to their right. Looking back to make sure she's following, he runs ahead, past the oak and *askadinya* trees through the pines—an *afreet* genie, light as air. She finds him standing guard by the old, abandoned shed, a small dark shadow, one foot thumping the ground with quick, staccato jabs.

The sounds emerging from Badri's throat spill haphazardly into the evening air, get tangled in the trunks of trees. Once more, he takes her hand, this time to point out boarded windows, to show her a lock that was not there before. His angry fist bangs against the wooden door as if to break it down. He spins around to face her, to repeat what she finally understands: that his treasures—his kites, his cache of marbles, are all locked up inside his play-shed—turned fortress.

And he locked out.

Nawal uses awkward gestures to comfort him, to promise what she can. She must gather courage to ask questions of Omar, of Mustapha even, to discover why.

Back at her desk, Badri holds up a marble with amber veins, its pattern imbued with light, thrusts it toward Nawal.

She smiles warily, allows the marble to roll along the grooves of her palm, daring it toward the edge. What will she do with a boy's love when it's a man's love she craves?

As she inadvertently tilts her palm, the marble drops to the floor, rolls down past the coffee table toward the door. As Badri scrambles on hands and knees to retrieve it, the door swings open and Clara nearly collides into Badri's prostrate figure on the floor.

"Damn!" she says loud enough for Nawal to hear. "What's that boy doing on the floor?"

Perspiration glistens above Clara's upper lip. Her shirt-waist dress with clover leaves is wrinkled; one stocking has a run in it. As she turns her head, the silver chain of her earring shimmers in the artificial light.

"Looking for a marble," Nawal says.

"So—where *is* the illustrious Omar Habeeb?"

A pause, like sticky resin, inserts itself between them. "I think... upstairs in his room."

Clara stares distractedly around the room. "He's got to listen to reason. At least to *listen*...." She lifts forlorn eyes toward Nawal, runs her fingers through the short, disheveled curls. "I suppose I *could* go upstairs and cause a scene. Or wait until he comes down—which might get my adrenaline going. In either case I can't be responsible for what I say—or do."

Nawal considers responsibility and "scenes," thinks of Abd, a distant cousin on her mother's side, who told her Juha folk-tales when she was ten or twelve that made her laugh.

Once, at a family gathering, he stopped her in the corridor of his parent's house and grabbed at her budding breasts. Nawal shudders at the image of his face close to hers, his eyes red-veined, his hand invading her privacy.

She had, inadvertently, create a *scene*—humiliating her poor mother, who told Nawal later that a well-brought-up young lady *never* raised her voice, never used words to make a ruffian cringe.

Since then, Nawal has practiced the virtues of "modesty" and "self-control" as penance, discovering along the way that soft-spoken words, honed to a fine edge, could be manipulated to do one's bidding—express hurt, even outrage... all in a ladylike manner.

Nawal says now, "You've come to say goodbye?"

"That—and to explain a few things."

She kicks off her sandals, lowers herself onto the couch, tucks one foot under her. She fumbles with matches, lights her cigarette after the third try. As she inhales, blowing smoke rings in the air, Badri's eyes focus on the disintegrating wisps of smoke.

As Clara leans over to massage the bottom of her free-swinging foot, Nawal's glance takes in its small, near-perfect shape, its manicured nails. A pampered foot, Nawal thinks, envious.

Badri inches closer, holds out his palm toward Clara, and displays his two other marbles as if to entice her—to win her favor. She smiles back at him, pats the cushion next to hers. But he scurries to the other side of the coffee table—as if to assert his squatter's rights.

Nawal says, "I'll go upstairs and tell Omar... you're here to see him."

At her knock, Omar cracks open the door, asks irritably, "What is it you want?"

"It's not her fault," Nawal says, "this sudden panic to flee our part of the world. Our land has brought mightier men and women to their knees."

Omar looks at her with sudden interest, takes in an incongruous reality: Nawal turned mediator.

"Badri's also in the lobby and refuses to leave," Nawal adds, to divert attention. "His playthings are now locked up in the abandoned shed where he once played, and he doesn't know why."

She waits for Omar to explain, but he merely blinks as if to erase an opaque screen against his eyes. "The boy has a home, a yard. A tree to climb," he says coldly. "He should not play on Semiramis grounds." He shrugs. "But I'll speak to Mustapha."

What business is it of Nawal's, anyway—why a shed is locked up, its windows boarded?

As they walk back toward the stairway, Clara's high-pitched, cheerful voice drifts toward them. A-one, a-two, a-three, a-four. Thump, thump. Atta boy! Clap! Clap!

Downstairs, Clara is calling out instructions to the dance, while Badri concentrates on its mimicry. They stand in the middle of the floor, right legs pointed toward invisible partners. Tra la la, sings Clara. Tra la la. She lifts Badri's hand high above his head, and spins around, her sandaled feet a whirl.

She sweeps past them, eyes flashing. "Come join us!" she calls out merrily.

Omar pauses stiffly, his hand on the balustrade; his eyes glint with a sharp-edged light aimed at Clara's face.

Bowing low to Badri, Clara brings her impromptu dance to an abrupt close.

"Why did you bother to come—a busy woman like you?" Omar asks, sarcasm in his voice. "I'm sure you have a lot of souvenirs to pack—mementos to bring your friends back home." He smiles contemptuously. "In a few days, you'll probably forget most of this 'unpleasantness.' And you'll probably erase from memory this insignificant spot of earth we call Beit Nuba."

He takes a step or two toward her, thrusts his face close to hers. "But once in the States you may need to change your ways. You'll become the dutiful wife; and the only strays you might pick up will be mongrels and stray cats."

His voice, aimed at Clara, skims the surface of Nawal's mind, settles, like ice, between its cracks.

Pity for the man Clara will discard, pity, even, for Clara, replaces Nawal's relief for her leaving. Pity for humanity, discarded, left to rot in hovels.

Nawal moves toward Badri, takes his hand and steers him toward the front door. Pulling free, he barricades himself behind the coffee table, still watching—a spectator at a tennis match.

Nawal attention veers toward the crescendo of Clara's voice and the sweep of Clara's arm as her hand makes contact with Omar's face.

Badri's laughter crackles in the silent room. But before Nawal can stop him, he takes aim—and like a discus thrower—flings a marble across the room at Clara's legs.

Clara flinches, lets out a cry, her eyes suddenly filled with tears.

"*Akroot!*" Omar calls out the insult for all Semiramis to hear. But Badri has already bolted through the door, and Miriam, Badri's mother, is unable to hear through thick kitchen walls.

Clara hobbles toward the couch, props up her foot on its

edge, and rubs her ankle as if to dislodge a stain. She turns toward Nawal, gives her a telephone number. "Ask George to pick me up at the parking lot gate, will you?"

Omar, turned solicitous, hovers over Clara, blurting apologies she ignores. She limps toward the door, walks outside; Omar, following, calls out her name, pleads for her to stay.

When he returns a few moments later, he stops at Nawal's desk, as if to collect thoughts. Bitter laughter converts into an odd conglomeration of sound akin to Badri's attempt at communication.

He looks at Nawal from bloodshot eyes. "You must never tell anyone about this...."

She nods wordlessly, averts her eyes from the residue of Omar's humiliation and grief. "Alya should be here by now," she says, adjusting her voice to a casual pitch.

But he does not hear her, walks away toward the stairway, a man suddenly grown old.

As Hagas and his band begin to play, Janan's voice drifts toward them, blots out images and pain. Janan sings a Fairuz song, a fast-paced waltz. In the privacy of her own room, Nawal imitates Fairuz's style—sings of being neighbors with an elusive moon, sings of what she can only imagine to be so—a man's arms around her waist, holding her up.

But should the rope slacken, she would lose her footing and tumble to earth—to lie there, bleeding, with no man to weep for her wound.

The telephone rings. A man's agitated voice asks to speak to Alya Habeeb.

"She's not yet here. Is... there a message?"

"What can I tell her? That my sister Julia set fire to the curtains? That I need to talk to her...."

"Your name and number, please?"

"She'll know. I'm a friend. An old friend. Just tell her to call. And ask her to keep Sunday open."

The phone clicks shut. Nawal picks up her magazine, tries to block out the image of fire, burning curtains, of a man's voice in distress. She flips back to her mystery, begins to read where she left off.

"'They think I'm crazy,' she said bluntly. 'And—and I rather think I'm crazy, too. Mad.'"

"'That is most interesting,' said Hercule Poirot, cheerfully.'"

Alya

EVEN BEFORE the taxi rounds the corner and begins the ascent toward the Semiramis, Alya hears the music: the lilt of Hagas's mandolin underscoring Janan's voice in her imitation of Fairuz.

The taxi driver lets her out in front of Badri's house, thanks her profusely for the extra *piasters* she places in his outstretched hand.

She makes her way past the sweet-scented jasmine and the bougainvillea vine toward the pines. Checkered light streams through the lattice work, stains chairs and table tops and the trunks of pines. Camouflaged figures to her left hug the edges of their table, hiding, even as she now plans to hide.

She can see the dancers through the lattice screen, catches a glimpse of Janan, who sings of love and heartache with a fervor born of experience. But this time, Fairuz's lyrics of "Being Neighbors to the Moon" call for a playfulness, a frivolity Janan fails to render.

A small, dark figure, half-boy, half-elf, scurries past the fountain toward the parking lot, is swallowed up into the night. Alya looks back at the gate, shrugs, allows the music to blot out distractions. Tonight, no wine dilutes her blood or eggs her on toward the dance floor. Not even Majed's face in mottled light, its grin suspended like a cat's, can work its miracles.

A chill wind seeps into her bones, drowns out the melody. She shivers, holds her shawl tight against her breasts, and thinks of Sari, brittle in his loneliness, reaching for a spark of fire to warm him, to keep him sane.

But she—who once dangled by a thread—fears the cracking of walls as wind pierces mortar and stone.

Longs for solid earth beneath her feet.

The glass doors of the vestibule swing open and a woman moves toward the flagstone path, her face set against the night shadows and the music. Despite her limp, she walks with fierce, determined steps toward the gate.

Alya recognizes Clara's impatient tilt of the head, the dress she wears. But before Alya can move leaden feet, Clara is whisked away in George's shadowed car and carried back into her own world.

Alya thinks: As females, we are pitted against the world, reaching for warmth. But clutch, instead, angled skeletons in the dark.

A human shadow, bent and distorted in the shrouded light, meanders down its solitary path. Hesitating near the rosebush, it turns to survey the entrance of the hotel.

And, as the door is flung open, takes flight.

Omar's voice, torn from him, calls out Clara's name from the vestibule, but Janan's plaintive song intrudes, distorts Omar's words, follows her past the gate, beyond the parking lot and into the black road.

Poor Omar—unsuspecting of Clara's duality: this rise in temperature in his veins he mistakes for love. Real love, after all, was a cicada breaking free from earth, filling the air with a cacophony of celebration.

But did not the sound of love, turned inward, gurgle in the throat, break—even as a tie clip breaks?

The most drastic effect of the crisis has been the departure of tourists. Hotels and shops in the Holy City (of Jerusalem) are empty and some have begun to close....

You sit on a roof in the Old City and look out over the shadows of No Man's Land to the lights of the new, Israeli city and watch the people and cars moving....

You can hear the dogs yelp on both sides of the border, basically the same breed of yellow mongrels. The Israeli dogs yelp and the Jordanian dogs answer. They, at least, have no difficulty in communication... [according to one hotel manager in the Old City].

The New York Times, June 5, 1967

CHAPTER THIRTEEN

The Long Road to Bethlehem

FROM HER UPSTAIRS WINDOW Alya can see Sari's Peugeot above the rise in the road. It turns into the Semiramis parking lot and eases into the empty space between the Austin and Rasheed Walid's rented Ford. Badri's small ragged figure bounds from his yard and skips across the road toward the parking lot gate. He pulls himself up on the gate's ledge and, crouching, drags one foot against the pavement. The gate swings slowly forward, stops, swings back again. The rays of morning sun, like a giant, gold-spun web, cling to car hoods and asphalt, create uneven patterns of sequined glitter.

The ringing of the parlor telephone breaks into images and reverie.

"I'm calling to say goodbye," Clara Appleby says in Alya's ear. "I came by Friday night, but you were gone."

"I was in Jerusalem that day, and I stayed longer than I'd planned." Alya decides not to mention what she saw or heard that evening, says instead, "You're leaving then?"

"Your brother and I... well, he thinks I'm bailing out...." She adds in a rush of words, "But when my country warns me it's no longer responsible for my safety... what else could I do? Besides...," the crisp, defensive voice wavers, gives in to a muffled giggle, "I've got certain wifely obligations...."

"Wifely obligations," Alya says carefully, "have certain priorities."

A small silence. "What will you do if...?"

"...if war breaks out?"

"To put it bluntly...."

"Keep a sense of humor, and think of my history lessons. You know—the causes and results, the rise and fall... and all that."

"I'll write, I promise. Please, write back and let me know how things are with you and... Omar. And thanks."

"Have a safe trip," Alya says, and means it.

Clara has decided to escape, to abandon what frightened her of love and hate and a world where men and women lived in memories—tangled roots that stretched beyond rock and earth into the hollowed-out places of their lives.

In her own room, Alya scrutinizes her image in the mirror as if to confirm her formal reality. Her hair tied back in a paisley scarf and pulled back from her face gives her the austere look of high resolve. Only the intermittent flicker of her eyes betrays the inner disparity of herself.

When she comes downstairs she finds Omar at the desk, his face ravaged by lack of sleep—by Clara's abandonment.

But, what could she do for him who has chosen to love the wife of George Appleby almost as much as Cause and Country?

Omar folds the newspaper in his hands, lays it across the blotter on the desk, near his coffee cup. He looks up at her.

"So—where are you off to so early this Sunday morning?"

"To Bethlehem... with friends. Julia Pappas and her brother, Sari."

"Why Bethlehem now? When our world is on the brink?" Omar's voice, harsh with pent-up anger, scrapes against the hard casing of her resolve.

Alya laughs cynically, "We can't put our lives on hold just

because we're on the brink of something or other, can we?" She meets the scowl in his eyes. "Even if those we *think* we love decide to go away...."

"What business is it of yours... who goes away, who stays? Worry about your own life for a change... and that Majed fellow who strung you along—without commitment." Omar's clenched fist hits the desk, knocks over his coffee cup, spills its contents onto the newspaper. "And who is that Sari Pappas anyway? Why should you risk your life and reputation...."

"A good friend. His sister...."

"Loyalty to family comes before loyalty to so-called 'friends.' Friendship—even love...," Omar pauses to clear his throat, "can be as nebulous as summer clouds. I've learned this lesson well. Why haven't you?" His fingers flex against the edge of the desk, curve inward, hold onto the frayed lifeline of his argument.

She listens, trapped in the elongated shadows of barred windows, waits for fury to dissipate like smoke.

To be freed of cravings and desire, Alya is convinced, is to inherit the earth.

The residue of Omar's anger now filters into the flat logic of his voice, fills her with uneasy dread—as if he could be right, after all. He talks to her like a child—with no sense or will of her own; and when she interrupts, he stares at her as if she were a creature with sawdust in her veins.

"I'll try not to be late." Alya's voice is conciliatory. "If you like, I'll watch the desk for you this evening."

Omar says suddenly, "A postcard came for you with a Cyprus postmark. It's from that Englishman Brandon."

She takes the postcard from his hand, glances down at the photograph of an old church, turns it over.

"I hope to be back when the excitement settles, and sanity is restored," Dick writes. "Soon—I hope."

She looks up. "You've read it?"

He nods. "He's probably on *their* side...."

"Dick's paid for his room in advance," she assures him. "Some of his things are still there... although Julia stayed there one night."

"I know. Nawal told me."

Outside, the fluting, staccato song of a *bulbul* rises like a signal from the garden. Alya sees a flash of yellow against dark brown feathers as the *bulbul* takes flight. Dew drenches the bougainvillea vine on the courtyard trellis, and in the garden, daisies, fuchsias and sweet peas glisten in the morning sun. Cool, pine-scented air propels her past the fountain, down the flagstone path toward the parking lot.

Sari emerges from the Austin, walks toward her. His herringbone jacket and black-striped tie give him an air of propriety, of solemn mission. For he will, after all, be depositing Julia into safekeeping at the hospital in Bethlehem—with the hope that the doctors would extract her personal devils and restore her to sanity—at least for a while.

He holds out his hand. "I like your hair," he says in greeting.

"Tied back in a scarf like this?"

"It gives you an aesthetic look—as if you're about to perform a pirouette or two."

She laughs. "Never at this hour—when even the milkman and his mule are barely awake." She glances back at Julia asleep in the back seat. "So—what magic trick did you conjure up to get Julia to come peacefully?"

"The only magic—the pills the doctor prescribed after the burning of the curtains—and the promise of a picnic at Solomon's Pools." He laughs softly. "Last night, we made *labaneh* and cucumber sandwiches—enough for a small tribe."

Badri, lurking a few feet away, scampers to the other side of the car, presses his nose against the glass. At Sari's sharp warning he pulls back, leans against the Austin's trunk and covers his face with splayed fingers.

From inside the car, the harsh sound of Julia's coughing splinters the quiet of morning. Before Sari can stop him, Badri opens the car door, drops a marble into Julia's lap. Retrieving a second marble from his pocket, he begins a rhythmic tattoo on car window. Julia, her eyes riveted to the window, to the motions of Badri's hand, picks up the marble Badri gave her, and begins an intermittent clicking on glass in counterpoint to Badri's staccato beat. Her small ruddy face, its mouth pursed in concentration, reflects her wonderment at this invented child's play. In a little while giggles turn to spurts of laughter, replace the hacking cough of a few moments before.

From somewhere beyond the garden the soft gurgling of pigeons cushions laughter and the clicking of marbles on glass. The marble game comes to an end when Julia slips the marble into her purse, and takes out a half-moon sandwich. With Badri watching, she begins a pantomime of eating, of hunger satisfied.

"Come to our picnic!" she calls out and holds the sandwich closer to the glass. The scarf and embroidered blouse she wears give her the air of an aging gypsy queen. She cranes her neck toward Sari, who stands on the other side. "Ask him to come!"

"Three for a picnic—isn't that enough?"

"Why not four?" Alya says now. "His grandmother will be grateful for the reprieve."

They find Badri's grandmother in her kitchen, bent over a wooden bowl, kneading dough. A small woman, she has pale leather skin that holds a sprinkle of freckles in the folds of her cheeks, her neck.

Her glance appraises each face as if it were a puzzle to be solved. "So... you want to take him away for a few hours?" Her wiry hands, immersed in dough, pause in their task. She glances at Badri's disheveled shirt, looks back at Alya. "I worry about him. Getting into trouble, throwing things. A *karut*—his father dead, and Miriam and I his only family, and this small house—all we have to give, to leave behind. A house my father built when I was not yet twelve."

She makes a vague motion toward the window that overlooks her yard.

"At daybreak—following prayers, my father would sit crosslegged under the fig tree near the wall and chisel at blocks of stone, shaping them into rectangles, smoothing down their roughness. Sometimes, when I brought him water, or food to eat, he would pause in his chiseling to recount a Juha tale, or a story of foxes and hyenas in the days when Beit Nuba was under Turkish rule."

Some of the stones of the house have since become gray-veined, a few turning black with age. Below the steel shutters, rust stains are embedded in stone; and grasses sprout where mortar is cracked or missing. But the small house retains a quiet dignity, its tiled dome marking its age like the lines in an old man's face. And "*Al mulk lillah*"—chiseled above the doorway—still proclaims God as the true owner of the house.

Badri's grandmother washes her hands in the sink, takes Badri away, returns a few minutes later with a grinning Badri, his hair slicked back, wearing a bright plaid shirt. One hand cups a few marbles, the other swings a drawstring pouch.

"When his marbles were locked up," the old woman says with a shrug, "he wouldn't give me peace until I got him a few more."

In parting, she kisses him on both cheeks, admonishes him to behave. He drops his marbles into the pouch, scrambles into the back seat next to Julia. As they drive off, a grunt and an occasional squeal are Badri's contribution to Julia's intermittent chatter.

But the cadence of rhythmic breathing soon replaces chatter, and as they pass the refugee camp on the edge of town, Alya glances back at Julia, now asleep, her mouth slightly open.

Except for the occasional clicking of marbles they drive in relative silence past hills where morning light drenches houses built on terraced hillsides, and is absorbed into rust-colored earth. On the side of the road, crimson poppies intersperse purple thorns and clumps of grass. An old man on his donkey flashes a toothless grin, waves them on, and Alya, awakened from reverie, waves back—too late for him to notice.

"Omar thinks I'm risking my reputation—or what's left of it—to drive to Bethlehem with you and Julia," Alya says.

Sari grins at her. "Omar flatters me!"

She sighs, looks down at her hands. "Since Clara deserted

him, he's become a small boy afraid of being left alone in the dark."

"I've known that raw terror a few times in my life." Sari gives her a sidelong glance. "It may become more acute if you decide to abandon me... for more lucrative options."

"Our options are limited, wouldn't you say?"

His fingers flex on the steering wheel. "'Options'... implies more than one—at least two. And if I had the choice, I would easily defy the 'sensible option' for the more radical, more personal one." He pauses as if to allow her to savor those possibilities, adds quietly, "And although society dictates our *outer* response, our inner impulses, even our consciences should dictate the other."

She says skeptically, "But in *most* cases, we still give in to what society decrees...."

"'In most cases' sounds pretty drastic to me."

"A sadder Omar insists—family above friends and lovers. And he gives a convincing argument." She glances at Sari's profile, notes the intensity in his eyes focused not merely on the road. "But loopholes certainly exist," she adds, smiling, "like small hotels in Jerusalem where the proprietor is discreet...."

He gives her a quick wink. "...And where the alibis of good friends help shield you against the wrath of society's defenders—the Omars of the world?"

"I suppose," she says, ignoring his implication, "society's rules are meant 'for our own good.' Ignored sometimes at great personal risk. Rules, for instance, that pertain to morality."

Ahead of them an old truck chugs along at thirty kilometers an hour. Sari makes an effortless loop, passing the truck, resumes his earlier speed.

His eyes still intent on the road, he says after a moment or two, "I'm convinced the separation of religion and society is a myth—even in countries which make that claim. One inevitably dictates the other."

"You mean as in: 'Thou shalt not covet a man's wife or his oxen?'"

"Or you might be trampled by a herd of camels!" He laughs. "In biblical times, as you well know, a man's wife and his oxen were considered his own personal *chattel*—to do with as he pleases."

"That might explain why 'Thou shalt not covet a woman's *husband*' is missing from biblical records?"

Sari's eyes narrow as they pass a man with a dog, a woman trailing behind, a basket balanced on her head. "Another possible theory may be that women are the nicer, more moral sex—who would *never* covet another woman's husband."

She shrugs. "Only if we're angels in disguise."

He slows down as they pass a bus on the side of the road; several passengers mill around the driver as he changes a flat tire.

"And in *every* society," Sari continues, gives her a sidelong glance, "fools like me covet independent, stubborn women. Such fools lie awake at night, scheming—and in the morning get cold feet."

"Wisdom cometh at dawn," she says smiling.

"Thou shalt not, O fool! I keep reminding myself. But what do fools know?"

A red Volkswagen from the opposite lane skims the road, veers into their own lane. Swerving to the right, Sari comes to a sudden stop. In the back seat Julia lets out a yelp as marbles clatter to the floor, and a collision is barely averted.

As the red car passes them by, the driver waves amiably. "He should be driving a donkey instead!" Sari observes dryly.

He turns on the radio, flips the dial from one station to another. As the voices of newscasters embedded in static (and why does she imagine the voice of Dick Brandon among them?) radiate from London, Amman, Cairo, and that *other* Jerusalem, Alya's mind wanders through the maze of news and commentary, skims over bits and pieces of a world in trouble.

According to Premier Ky, says the well-oiled voice of the commentator, the purpose of censorship in South Vietnam is not to create dissension or disunity—but to crack down on anti-government propaganda. *The Vietnam Guardian*, suspending its publication, was not permitted to—

The radio voice continues with its news.

—the U.S. attack carrier *Intrepid*, ordered to go through the Suez canal, was en route to an assignment in Vietnam—a test case, the American government declares, of how serious Nasser is about the closing of the canal.

But since a technical state of war exists between Israel and the U.A.R., Egypt affirms her right to bar—

Click. Click. Go Badri's marbles.

—In Cairo, Heikal, editor of *Al-Ahram*, says that Israeli forces were mobilized on the Syrian frontier—

Alya thinks of Omar waiting for war to solve the problems of humanity. A "just" war to restore a homeland.

On the mound above Jerusalem, Jordanian soldiers stand guard over their subterranean barracks. As she turns her head, she catches a long-ago image of a younger, barefoot Omar—his swollen, dirt-encrusted feet jabbing at earth, his game tight under his arm. But before he is swallowed up into the belly of the mound, he turns his head and she catches a glimpse of ghost-eyes staring past her at some invisible place.

Alya draws in a quick, sharp breath. As the Peugeot careens down the hill, she looks beyond the mound of ghosts to the clean façade of the French hospital across from a soccer field where a younger Omar once kicked a ball to team-mates in blue-striped shirts.

They turn left from Nablus Street in East Jerusalem, pass Salah-uddeen Street and the post office. Bypassing Bethany, they skirt the eastern flank of the Old City wall with its Dome burnished in the morning sun. At *Ras el-Amud* the road turns sharply to the right, winds its way around the bulge of No Man's Land, and veers into the gorge of Wadi-an-Nar—the Valley of Fire. High above them looms Jabal Al-Mukaber, its U.N. flag marking the British High Commissioner's house where once a pre-1948 Mandate carved its alien decrees in blood. A mood of desolation settles over Alya to match the bleak desolation of the ancient, limestone hills. If she should cry out now, her disembodied voice would hover, suspended, above the narrow, tortuous road, would follow the swallow's flight above cactus and dusty olive trees that cling like tentacles to rocky earth. But who would give her answers to questions she dare not ask of *ins* or *djinn*—of man or spirit?

Does God, in his High Commissioner's house, demand obedience—subservience even—of those who call his name? Does the babble of voices distract, bring him out of purdah to raise his giant arms above the hills and decree silence? Who is this God who sits upon his mountain, and—watching the games—refuses to take sides?

Who are His people now? The quiet, humble ones who live in hovels by the side of the road? Or the well-armed confident ones who depend on man-made miracles? What language does he speak? Why will He not answer her woman's voice in this vast desolation?

Those who obey, *them* will I favor, says the God of the Mountain. Thou shalt not. Not. Not. Slap my face and bring me to my knees. Learn to obey. My laws are carved in stone. Transcribed by men who know my Voice.

What do mere women know?

The tortuous road to Bethlehem begins its climb out of the valley of desolation, clings like a ribbon to the hilly ridge of the village of Sur Bahir. In the back, Badri jiggles his marbles in rhythm to the newsman's voice and Julia, huddled in the corner of the back seat, mutters in her sleep.

Sari, impatient with the clicking of marbles, scowls at Badri, demands silence.

—In a thirty-five-minute presentation before the U.N. (continues the BBC commentator) Gideon Rafael declared that Israel was "determined to make its stand on the Gulf of Aqaba"—

—But Pope Paul the VI fears the destruction of holy shrines in Jerusalem—

Who fears for the people? wonders Alya now.

But surely war could be averted since Nasser is sending his vice president to Washington to discuss "The Emergency" with President Johnson....

To discuss, after all, meant to meet face to face and speak in diplomatic tones. To try and work things out.

But Alya had heard, read somewhere that at Rhodes after 1948, the American mediator—frustrated by the stubbornness of Muslim and Jew—exploded in righteous indignation, "Why can't you act with a little more *Christian* charity...?"

Or words to that effect.

But first, you must believe and be saved!

Saved from what, Lord?

Saved from yourself, O infidel!

News ends, and the voices of John Lennon and Paul Mc-Cartney drift toward them in a song that laments the end of a mythical yesterday when "troubles seemed so far away..."

Afterwards, the announcer introduces Joan Baez, who, he says, will sing a protest song that reflects the mood of some... about the Vietnam war. Not many, mind you, he implies. Just those misguided ones.

The car radio sputters the words, chokes on the melody, but Joan Baez does not flinch and her rebel cry reverberates, like a guitar string, in the barren wilderness below them.

Where have all the tulips and the anemones gone? Where are all the vibrant young men? she asks.

Entombed in earth, turned to dust in their prime—sings the mournful voice.

In a world turned upside down.

As static drowns out the music, Sari clicks off the radio, gives Alya a sheepish grin, "At times like these, one can become obsessed with the sounds of radio. With worry about world affairs."

Alya smiles back at him. "Obsessions come in different sizes and shapes. So why not the sounds of radio?"

"If only we weren't so well chaperoned," Sari says now, his voice barely audible, "I could wipe out all politics from my life... with thought of you."

She laughs. "If I were you, I'd choose the 'sensible' option for now—or even later."

He gives her a rueful look. "I'm not yet reconciled to 'now.'

'Later' has its own priorities."

His hand touches hers resting lightly in her lap, caressing palm, fingers, wrist, as if each were a separate entity—pliant clay to mould according to an artist's need. Fingers, coaxed into life, curl around his, palms touching, her woman's will snared, as if it were a small bird in a net.

But the bird manages to break free as practicality takes hold, and guides his hand back to safety on the wheel. Behind them, Julia springs to life, leans forward, drapes an arm over their car seat, allows it to swing like a pendulum between them. Sari, pre-occupied with a curve in the road, pays her no mind, but Alya scrunches up against her car door, and looks beyond the wall of cactus and the olive trees at the squat houses and the minaret of the village of Sur Bahir.

On the far side of the road, an old man herds his goats with the help of a small black dog. The goats, darting in and out of the asphalt road, are barely held in check by the snap of the old man's cane and the dog's persistence. A speckle-faced goat with long, coppery hair scampers into the road just as a jeep filled with Jordanian soldiers appears round the bend. Slowing down, Sari eases toward the dirt shoulder of the narrow road and out of harm's way.

Brakes screech and a string of curses foul the air as the goat darts into the path of the jeep. The driver-soldier, his red-check-ered *kaffiyeh* askew, his black walrus mustache bristling, waves a clenched fist at the creature now lying motionless in the road.

"Keep your bloody goats out of the streets!" the soldier calls out. "*Nush-kur Allah!* Thank God! the jeep did not fall into the valley below. If we'd been killed, you'd have had to answer for such a crime before... before his Majesty the King!"

Off with his head, the king would decree. The goat-herd-er is a menace to society and a danger to proud Jordanian sol-diers destined to defend the land from napalm dropped from the skies. And show your gratitude to these soldiers—trained in British discipline by the successors of the Englishman, Glubb

Pasha—who will lay down their lives for *your* country... that you may have a semblance of life.

Yet we must be discreet about the soldiers huddled in Saint Anne's Church, seeking refuge from napalm. And we'll speak only behind closed doors of the soldier in woman's dress escaping with hordes of Palestinian refugees across the Allenby Bridge.

Surely his covered face revealed nothing except the panic in his eyes....

But these soldiers in their jeep in Sur Bahir—the village that straddles the road to Bethlehem—are in a tearing hurry. They have an appointment with destiny—whatever that happens to be.

"Here's a *dinar*," says the soldier to the old goat-herder. "It will help pay for the goat's injury." His narrowed eyes take in the gathering crowd. "But if the goat does not survive the blow, you could always make a meal of it and invite your relatives for a feast."

The paper money dangles from the soldier's fingers like a flag at half-mast. But the old man, irascible as his goat, holds his cane firmly against the asphalt and stands motionless in front of the jeep, blocking its way.

"You've killed my favorite goat, my Salwa." The old man's voice is cold with emotion. "It's better that *you* were dead."

Children and youths and men and women are gathering to watch *Abu* Salwa (for that seems to be the old man's name) confront the Jordanian soldiers. They've also come to watch a goat die in the middle of the road of Sur Bahir.

Alya, Sari and Badri watch the spectacle from their car; Julia's eyes flutter open and she, too, sits up and takes notice.

"If I were not a reasonable man, I'd shoot you down," the soldier says through his walrus mustache. Folding the *dinar*, he returns it to his pocket, his bravado erased.

One can already see him in his woman's dress, his face covered, escaping over the Allenby Bridge.

"We must be on our way," he says to other soldiers in the jeep. "We can't afford to waste any more time...."

As the soldier guns his engine, the crowd parts silently. Women and children form one ragged line, with a tattooed woman holding an infant near Sari's Peugeot; the other line is interspersed with men and goats, the small black dog and the grieving goat-herder, *Abu* Salwa. Wheels squeal and the jeep jerks forward as if brakes have lost control, loops around the prone body of the goat and takes off in a trail of gas fumes and dust.

The thin, hairy body of the goat shudders with life passing through. *Abu* Salwa shuffles toward the body of his goat, and crouching low, he places a sunburned hand across its back and begins to caress the long, coppery hair. Alya can see the stubble of the old man's face twitch and his mouth work itself around incoherent words.

The woman with her infant walks back toward *Abu* Salwa, swaying as she walks as if a gust of wind might catch her unawares.

"You have other goats," she says above her baby's head. "And surely, you have family and friends?"

In the back Badri wrenches the car door open. Before anyone can stop him, he scurries out toward the goat, and hunkering down near the old man, he thrusts a marble at him as if it were a magic potion or a remedy for grief. But the marble drops from the old man's fingers onto the asphalt, rolls down and disappears into a clump of yellow dandelions.

A dusty Mercedes taxi, rounding the corner, comes to a sudden stop. Craning his neck, the driver demands that whoever is responsible for the mess should clear it up.

"An accident, can't you see?" a young man calls out. "You can still go round...."

Sari gets out of the car. He takes off his jacket, his tie, drapes them across his seat, and makes his way to the road. Crouching, Sari lifts the goat in his arms and carries it like an offering to the side of the road. He walks back toward *Abu* Salwa, extends his hand, and pulls him to his feet. He offers his arm to steady him, guides him back to safety.

No blood or other sign of death marks the asphalt road: only the old man's dog, still unconvinced, sniffs at invisible stains.

Alya stands by the car's door and waits for interruptions to end, for Sari to return.

This time, the woman—her child nestled against her shoulder—returns. "It was Allah's will," the woman says with a sigh. Alya can see the delicate green filigree tattooed in an arc below her mouth.

But why put the blame on God for human carelessness—even error? A *compassionate* God, Alya is convinced, abhors wars and pestilence and violent death. *That* God comes down from his mountain and lives among the humble ones and shares their olive oil, their bread.

And weeps when a goat is killed without good reason in the middle of the road.

The woman caresses the matted curls of her sleeping child, shoos away a fly. "May you and your family prosper," she says softly. "May no evil befall you."

"*Insha'Allah*," Sari answers, walking up to the car with Badri. "For you. For *all* of us."

The tower and walls of the monastery of Deir Mar Elias stand like a fortress on the hilly ridge at the northern edge of Bethlehem. The barbed wire of No Man's Land shears through the olive grove that surrounds the monastery. At the crossing, they turn left onto the old Bethlehem road; to their right loom the secluded heights of Tantur, once hospice of the Order of Malta; and in 1938, given to the Sisters of Cottolengo of whom Alya knows nothing at all—except names. She pictures women in black, heads bowed, walking down long corridors, whispering prayers—resigned to whatever God, in his infinite wisdom, would demand of them.

To become a nun, her mother told Alya once, was of the highest callings. Orthodox, or even Latin. To know one's place—to have one's tasks defined within the periphery of prayer—

would remove all insecurity and doubt.

But never to rail against the world's injustices? Or call God to task for the imperfections of his Creation?

"Mysterium salutis," Sari says, following her glance.

"Ah!"

"The old Salesian motto for Tantur."

To their left, a field of stones with a legend of petrified peas. In this, the land of her birth, myth and religion intertwine, dance in the slightest breeze.

Mysterium salutis?

They pass Rachel's tomb and wind their way around the periphery of Bethlehem toward the Pools of Solomon.

Except that Solomon had nothing to do with them.

Shallow waters shimmer in the rectangular, slab-edged pools, and on the far side, boys play tag across the terraced rock. As Sari parks the car on the shoulder of the road, Badri motions excitedly toward the water, scrambles out of the car and breaks into a run.

Birds scatter as he comes to a stop at the water's edge. He flops down on his belly, dangles one hand in the water, then settles cautiously near the water's edge, his bag of marbles at his side. Oblivious of other boys, of sparrows and doves overhead, he twists his neck to stare at a yellow cat that makes its secret way along the periphery of the pines.

In the back seat, Julia taps Sari's shoulder, suddenly asks, "Will I stay long at the Bethlehem hospital? A month? A year or two?"

"You'll come home... when you feel better. When the doctors say you can," Sari says.

His shirt smudged from lifting *Abu* Salwa's goat, his tie askew, he turns to face her, penitent, asking forgiveness for what he is compelled to do.

Julia's mouth begins to twitch, and Alya, staring into the dull anguish of her eyes, hears the portcullis slam shut between them. She pushes open the car door, slides out, and stands frozen in the morning sun, her ruddy, girlish face beneath its scarf as ancient and as barren as the hills.

"*You* and your need for women!" Julia's voice is shrill with malice. "And I—always in the way." She drops the picnic sack at her feet, and watches, unmoving, as an orange rolls away, stops at a moss-covered rock.

Alya retrieves picnic sack and orange, takes out hers and Sari's share, and hands Julia the rest. "You and Badri might want something to eat," she says, to distract her.

The sack nestled in the crook of one arm, Julia turns on her heel and makes her way toward Badri's sun-dappled figure near the water's edge.

Dear God of the Mountain (Alya prays), come down from the heights and cast out the devils of thy servant Julia—whom no one loves and who loves only with her need and her desolation. Lift her up from the Valley of the Shadow. Unto Light. Amen.

Dear God of the Mountain—Alya, who has known prayer by rote, prays again—I, too, need light to see the road ahead.

As they watch Julia perched on a slab of rock under a *snober* pine, Alya's odd-shaped prayer clings stubbornly like a gecko, in a corner of her mind.

Badri scurries toward Julia, sits, cross-legged, at her side; together, they munch sandwiches and watch a pink-breasted dove a few feet away. Later, Julia flings bread crumbs in the air—laughing merrily as doves and sparrows scramble to retrieve the crumbs she scatters, helter-skelter, on the wind.

Sari follows Alya to another crop of rocks near the farthest ledge. As they settle down in the shade of a *saru* tree, her glance pulls toward Julia feeding birds.

"I hate to put her away...." Sari's pewter eyes shift uneasily to Alya's face. "But what else is left to do, when even doctors work on faith... and miracles?"

"Faith," she says glibly, "can move mountains."

He smiles, "My faith—or yours?"

"Mine can barely cover a needle's head." She takes a deep breath. "So you think war is inevitable?"

"The props are in place. The musicians are tuning their instruments."

But why hasn't Dick Brandon warned her? His latest note, by way of Cyprus, tells her nothing.

"When will this alleged war... happen?"

Her question flaunted out of cynicism merely assumes that Sari is up to date on the plans of other men. But one must face reality, after all, and she must prepare herself to look the monster in the face, touch his leather skin and feel his pulse.

Sari's voice is laced with a cynicism to match her own. "In a week or ten days. Next month or next year. Or even tomorrow."

Expect a lightning war, a modern blitzkrieg, he might tell her—*if* he knew. Mirages and Mystères, with the help of Johnson's photographic Phantoms, will wipe out Egyptian air power on the ground and rain napalm and white phosphorus on the brave desert men of the Arab Legion who will fight in vain at Tel-el-Ful and Sheikh Abdul-Azeez and Biddu and Nabi Sumueel near Jerusalem, and will hold for a few hours Jabal Al-Mukaber and its U.N. headquarters.

But *their* Centurions and Shermans and Pattons will swallow up the Pattons of Jordan—after the last Hawker Hunter jet is destroyed. Flares and spotlights will light up the nights for their jet fighter-bombers to pound pockets of resistance, and brave men will lose their courage and their lives, and those who seek haven at Saint Anne's Church with the women and children will speak of it behind closed doors, and only in whispers.

And *Abu* Salwa's dead goat will not matter then—its sacrifice in vain.

Tomorrow:

When Mystères and Mirages will smudge an innocent sky, their victory assured.

But how can Alya surmise this, today, at the Pools of Solomon, nibbling at her sandwich as if it were an apple or a plum? She leans against the stone embankment and stares at the terraced rise beyond the pool and thinks: They should take war-mongering politicians and those who egg them on to an isolated spot, give them rusty swords, and let them fight it out.

And leave the rest of us alone.

The yellow cat near the edge of the pool slinks toward a sparrow pecking at crumbs, hunkers down, waits. A cat with no wings to match the sparrow's must catch him unawares. But a cat with wings could be a disaster to bird-kind, Alya thinks, as the sparrow lands on a branch and out of harm's way.

"Would you fight for a Cause?" she asks Sari now, "for honor and country?"

He takes her hand, gives her a conspiratorial look. "Only if *you* insist I offer my wits and my uncoordinated self for Cause... and what is left of country." He smiles back at her. "And you, my dear Alya—if you had a choice—would you kill or be killed... for justice? For freedom?"

Raucous laughter interrupts thought and Alya's reply. Julia, crouching on her rock, waves excitedly at Badri, and points toward the yellow cat. "Look!" she calls out. "The cat got the stupid bird!"

But Badri, cracking pine nuts on the ledge, can't hear, can only see the cat slink away into the woods with her prize.

"There *must* be other ways to resist... to make a point." Alya hesitates. "But Omar, I'm sure, will go willingly. Gladly. Believing we will win. Only in armed struggle, he thinks, will we regain our dignity, our freedom."

"We all have illusions and dreams—winners and losers both." Sari's eyes graze the hard shell of her resistance. "But there are instances when winning can be even more hazardous than losing."

She shrugs. "To kill and be killed—what's the sense in it?" For how else to thwart Omar's argument and the logic he has imposed on her secret fears? She adds, "We could always go to the World Court and plead our case. And hope someone will listen—and act—before it's too late."

"You mean you and I and the hordes of others—refugees... or citizens of other lands?"

"You and I and Julia and my mother... at least for now."

Sari shakes his head, smiles cryptically. "Julia may not want to come. As for your mother—I'd think the Bible will have all the answers she might care to ask. And I...." He clears his throat. "Do you really need to know?"

She nods. "I'll have to make *my* plans."

Tomorrow will limit her choices and impose its own structure on her days. But for today, details must take precedence, and plans must still be made.

For how else could she possibly survive tomorrow?

He says, "If you'll have me, I'll follow you to the ends of the earth and back." He grins, kisses the palm of her hand. "Even to Geneva."

"It's settled then," she says, almost convinced.

I've looked at life from both sides now,
From win and lose, and still somehow,
It's life's illusions I recall,
I really don't know life at all....

Joni Mitchell

"In June 1967, we again had a choice. The Egyptian Army concentration in the Sinai approaches do not prove that Nasser was really about to attack us. We must be honest with ourselves. We decided to attack him...."

Prime Minister Menachem Begin
address to the Israeli National Defense College
August 8, 1982

CHAPTER FOURTEEN

Um Amin

WHEN THE JORDANIAN SOLDIERS came in the middle of the night, *Um* Amin refused to open the door. "If you don't open up," the sergeant roared, "we'll break down the door, and take you *both* to prison."

Despite her protests, it was her son, Amin, who finally opened the door.

Earlier that Saturday evening—before Amin's arrest—Lutfi Abdul Kader stopped by to talk to Amin, and to give them both details of the operation.

They sat around the narrow kitchen table, and over strong, aromatic coffee, Lutfi confided his premonitions. With Moshe Dayan as Defense Minister, Israel, he was sure, would plan to swallow up the rest of Palestine—under the pretext of self-defense.

"We can't rely on the Jordanians to protect our people," he said with a vehemence that intensified her own resolve. "Not after Es Samu. We must do it ourselves."

Amin, Lutfi confided, would drive the empty truck to the Hotel Semiramis, arriving there at midnight Sunday. Both Mustapha and Omar would load the truck, but only Mustapha would help Amin drive the truck with its cargo of weapons to the border villages. The operation could easily extend two or three hours into the early hours of Monday, June 5—but should not go beyond the *muezzin*'s call to prayer at dawn.

Tomorrow, *Um* Amin would make her trek to Beit Nuba to notify Omar Habeeb and Mustapha of the details of the plan—by word of mouth, this time, for safety.

Before he left, Lutfi mentioned in passing that the day before, his wife, Amal, gave birth to a daughter. "We've named her Palestine."

As she now makes her way uphill toward the Hotel Semiramis, *Um* Amin thinks of a tiny Palestine suckling at her mother's breast, unaware of loss and defeat and the convoluted plans of men.

Her old woman's bones creak, and sweat drenches her brow as she trudges past the flower shop, pausing to wipe her face with a large white handkerchief. From the corner of her eye she sees the boy, Badri, in his yard, but decides to ignore his frantic waving, continues on her way.

A moment later, brakes screech as a car pulls up near her and comes to a sudden stop. Looking up, she recognizes Omar Habeeb behind the wheel.

He calls to her, "Has Lutfi sent you?"

"Why else would I be here?"

He unlocks the car door, motions for her to get in. "It'll save you a few steps," he says in conciliatory tones.

She scrambles without protest into the front seat. "I'm an old woman," she says wearily. "A walk uphill takes its toll."

He parks the car under the branches of a *snober* pine in a far corner of the parking lot, then turns to face her.

"Well? What is it?"

Last night, she had stifled screams, her woman's rage damned up, her mother's heart frozen into place. This morning, she is mere conduit for messages she must give.

"The Jordanian soldiers arrested Amin last night." She speaks matter-of-factly, without emotion. "'Dirty *Baath* Socialist!' they called him before they beat him up, and hauled him away. They took his books and papers—for evidence, they said. And when I protested, the sergeant, a burly man with a hedgehog bristle for a mustache, nearly knocked me down."

"If they knew he belonged to Fatah—it would have been much worse"

"Hounds on the wrong track," she says irritably. "They concocted this charge to suit their purposes."

"The government is on the rampage against *anyone* who does not give whole-hearted obeisance to Hussein's monarchy," Omar says dryly.

She looks beyond the roof line of cars at the Semiramis courtyard. "Amin reads, writes too much. I asked him once what it was he wrote. 'A tale in poetic meter about our cause,' he said." She shakes her head as if to dislodge a gnat. "His father, God rest his soul, was a lover of words. He memorized scraps of poems, and could quote much of the Koran by heart."

"What work did *Abu* Amin do?"

An effusive sigh. "His lifelong work? The cleaning of the streets from rubbish...."

Omar's melancholy eyes search out her face. "So... what message do you have?"

"Water first... before I can say another word."

She follows him through the parking lot, past a man with a ruddy, foreign face who nods at Omar, throws her a curious look. They make their way past the vestibule toward the kitchen in the back.

"Wait here," Omar says. "I won't be long."

She lowers herself on her haunches under the apricot tree, closes her eyes, and tries to block out Amin's bloodied face from her mind. "In the name of God the compassionate, the merciful," she prays, "take pity on my son, Amin, and bring him home safe."

A sudden wail is wrenched from her, clings to the branches

of the apricot tree, before it dissipates into the morning air.

Omar brings back a jug of water, a tin cup, hands *Um* Amin an orange, a small knife.

Ignoring the cup, she tilts the jug above her head, aims a stream of water at her throat. She drinks heartily to quench her thirst, wipes her mouth with the back of her hand. "Bring Mustapha," she says. "My message is for both."

"I can always tell him later...."

She looks up from green-hooded eyes. "Not later. Now... face to face."

Omar leaves once more, and after she waits the length of time it takes to score and eat her orange, Mustapha appears, trailing after Omar. Stooped and unshaven, Mustapha makes the usual inquiries about her health.

"My health is in God's hands," she says.

Mustapha gives her his hand, helps *Um* Amin to her feet. A stalk shaken loose from earth, she leans against the tree trunk to steady herself, to catch her breath. Last night, with little sleep, she had called Lutfi Abdul Kader to give him the news; soon after, she called her grandson, Raja, to tell him of Amin's arrest.

"Let's walk toward the shed, for privacy," Omar suggests now.

She trudges after them, her flat hard heels crunching pine needles underfoot until they come to the low-slung shed, its rusted tin roof hammered into place, doors and windows boarded up. Near the door, a pile of marbles, a kite, its tail looped around a wooden stick, a muddied geography book, a piece of string.

"I unlocked the shed last night and took out Badri's things," Mustapha says. "*Sitt* Nawal suggested it."

Were these the marbles she gave the boy, Badri, as a bribe? She lowers herself on a nearby stump and stares beyond the legs of the men at the striped *hud-hud* bird pecking at earth.

The men stand before her, waiting.

"Since Amin is in prison...," she speaks deliberately without emotion, "my grandson, Raja, will take his place."

"How old is Raja?" Omar asks skeptically.

"Seventeen... old enough to become a *fedayee*."

Mustapha looks at her, nods, light dawning.

"If all goes well," she continues, "Raja will drive the empty truck to the hotel—arriving tonight at midnight. Lutfi asks that you both help load the truck, but only Mustapha will drive back with Raja to the border villages."

The son of her eldest daughter, Raja, at seventeen, has learned to drive his uncle's old truck to bring back slabs of stone from a hillside quarry—good training, she knows, for driving a truck on a Fatah mission.

She will not mention her fears for his safety.

"I'll begin my wait here at 11:00 this evening," Mustapha says, "until the truck arrives." He glances over at Omar.

Omar nods. "Since we must not arouse suspicion, I must first make arrangements for the desk before I can load the truck. Once this is done, I'll do all I can to help...."

Um Amin notes a glazed brightness in Omar's eyes, a look she has seen in the eyes of men intent on winning the soccer game.

"Tonight, I'll wait in the shadowed enclave of the *saru* tree... just beyond the gate." He adds—almost as an afterthought, "I'd also like to help Raja drive the truck with its cargo back to the villages."

Um Amin lifts her head, looks beyond their faces at an iridescent sunbird hovering above a sage bush. "Lutfi has already made his decision." She clears her throat. "Mustapha will help Raja drive the truck. No one else."

Omar Habeeb, she thinks as she trudges back toward the road, has a dark and secret pain, greater even than my own.

Omar

SO FAR, Alya has suspected nothing.

But as soon as she gets back from Bethlehem at God knows what hour, Omar will confront her with his request. He will try to convince her to give up a few hours of sleep to man the desk—until Mustapha returns. A small sacrifice for the cause.

Despite Alya's impetuousness and her unrelenting stubbornness, she may still possess a sense of loyalty and a buried instinct for patriotism. He'll count on this tonight when he asks her for this favor.

He hides in his room in an attempt to sort out the tangle of his thoughts, to clarify his goals for tonight. He paces his room, pausing to look out beyond the lemon tree outside his verandah at the stray figures wandering through the grounds and seated under the pines.

Fortunately, Hagas and the band will not play their music this Sunday evening in the Semiramis courtyard. Instead, Hagas, with his café open to customers, will cook his food, and play his mandolin music there for anyone who cares to listen.

Omar looks at his watch. Already 2 o'clock, with barely time for a late lunch. But instead of hunger pangs, a kind of disquiet supplanting need for food has blocked his appetite, has sharpened fervor. The burning of self-will to produce the flame, the sacrifice, he thinks now, takes precedence over the love of a woman.

Even Clara.

And why allow Mustapha—husband and father—to risk his life, when he, Omar, could easily take his place? With Mustapha and Nawal's help, he is convinced, his mother and Alya could manage quite well—with or without him. To be a *fedayee*, he thinks wistfully, would free him from the mundane worries of his days, and give meaning to his life.

What argument could Omar give Mustapha to change his stubborn will? The poster on his bedroom wall gives its own answer. Allah is the light of the heavens and the earth. Allah is....

But man, himself, must make decisions, create change. And he, one man, must do his best to convince Mustapha of his view.

Clara's iridescent eyes stare at him from walls and ceiling, her earrings dance. Why so intent? they ask. This cause has given you enough anguish to last a lifetime. Lighten up a little. All thought and little play make Jack dull dull dull....

"My name is Omar," he says now to the empty room. "Not Jack. Never Jack...."

He must leave this haunted room and air the mildew in his brain. A visit to Hagas, perhaps. Something to drink, a bite to eat, even, despite lack of hunger. A word or two.

Downstairs, in the *liwan*, Nawal is talking to Rasheed Walid, temporary import from Brooklyn in search of a wife. Rasheed, elbow propped up against the counter, thrusts his hand toward Nawal in a gesture of supplication.

As Omar approaches, Nawal calls out his name, faintly, like a child drowning. He has yet to give up, Omar thinks with cynicism. Besides, Nawal is too self-sufficient for marriage. He nods his greetings, says in his business voice, "I'm walking over to Hagas's café, and might stay a while. But when Alya returns, please tell her I need to talk to her...."

"I'll be glad to walk with you," Rasheed Walid says. "A question... a problem I want to discuss...."

"Tomorrow," Omar says. "Better then."

"Always tomorrow." Rasheed Walid shrugs. "Mañana, the Spanish say. But today is what we have. Only today."

"Sorry. But our discussion will have to wait."

He pats the shiny strands of hair arranged skillfully over the dome of his head. "I'll have to put my problem 'on hold,' as the Americans say." He nods, eyes meeting. "Tomorrow, then."

A walk to Hagas's café will do him good, Omar thinks now, might clear his head from Clara's phantom. He threads his way past cars and humanity that clog street and sidewalk, but an imprint of Clara's presence, like the blare of radio news, trails after him beyond Main Street into the narrow alleyways of the old town, to the café.

He turns abruptly into the backyard where Hagas's chickens, roaming free, scramble for hidden seeds in the dust.

He came here with Clara only a few nights ago. Or has it been months, an eternity? Her presence beckons on the stairway to the second floor, glides toward the upper landing. A woman's face vanishes behind the fence, and later a knock on the door. A spy?

Hardening himself against apparitions and memory, Omar walks into the smoke-filled kitchen. His back to him, Hagas stands over the old stove, the bristle of his gray hair caught in the light. He is browning liver and onions in a large iron skillet, the smell permeating the air.

Hagas turns his head. "So... what brings you here in the middle of the afternoon... and alone?"

Omar, without appetite, looks away from onions wilting in the pan and floured liver in olive oil. "Clara has left for America," he says.

As Hagas stirs the onions, his small eyes peer at Omar behind the smoke. "Does she plan to be back?"

"It doesn't matter what future plans she makes."

Hagas shakes his head. "Nothing lasts when you fall in love with...."

"Another man's wife?"

The door between kitchen and restaurant opens. A small boy with a wizened old man's face appears with a tray full of dirty dishes, which he sets down with a clatter in the sink.

"The man wants to know when his food will be ready?" he says.

"Take this," Hagas says, pointing to a *tahini* salad and a loaf of bread on the counter. "It may help stifle his hunger pangs for now."

As the door swings back behind the retreating figure of the boy, Hagas gives Omar a philosophical smile. "The heart has few guidelines, follows its own course. And women add the spice to our lives. In my youth—how the years roll by—I fell in love many times. Even with married women. We are eternal, we think, defying death, and can do what we please. But nothing lasts," he adds, resignation in his voice. "Today, I have few women in my life. My wife, God rest her soul, has left me with a daughter, Sylvia—a restless spirit. Too restless to settle down in Beit Nuba. A widow, a neighbor who lives on the other side of the fence and cares for her aging father, sometimes comes late at night and asks me to hold her in my arms. She came once when you and Clara were in Sylvia's room, knocked on the hallway door, probably gave you a fright...." He laughs heartily as he flips over liver and onions, turns off the flame. He heaves a sigh. "Here I am, a man of middle age, with my music... and my wife's chickens to keep me company. But you. Still a young man in the prime of life, with much to live for...."

"With a mother who insists that only marriage can solve life's problems, and a sister who defies convention... who left for Bethlehem this morning with a man and a sister with illness in the brain...."

"Not Majed Alami?"

Omar shakes his head. "A potter from Jerusalem. An old friend, she says."

"Majed was not worthy of her. He was a simpleton."

"We are all simpletons...."

Hagas gives Omar a wink. "Only in matters of the heart." He slides the contents of the pan onto a plate rimmed with blue flowers. "I'll take this to our hungry customer. Make yourself at home here. I won't be long."

Omar takes a seat at the small wooden table near the wall, stares at wilted petunias, at old cigarette stubs. He hears Hagas say loudly, "But why discuss the strategy of war over good food? Why not music instead?"

The muffled strains of the mandolin revive in Omar a dread that the hard core of his being could crumble, turn to mush. Restlessness and an urgency to escape propel him toward the back door. He walks outside into the bright afternoon sun and, barely avoiding a chicken scurrying in his path, makes his way back onto the sidewalk.

Clara's image... no longer a burr that clings to the cavity of his mind, exorcised, her ghost melted into chicken feed.

But to prepare himself for tonight, he needs to reaffirm strategy, resolve.

An urge to walk longer, farther, through the hills of Beit

Nuba, to follow the twists in the road, away from the hub of
town where shops and taxis compete for passing humanity, away
from the dust and papers whirling in the street into meandering
roads that hug the edge of hills, past, even, the walled Christian
cemetery where no Muslim is allowed burial.

But here is the burial place of his grandfather on his mother's side; a hard, self-righteous man, his mother told him once,
who drove her away for marrying a man of Muslim faith.

Omar climbs gingerly through an opening in the barbed-wire
fence, and weaves his way past myriad tombstones toward a corner of the cemetery where his grandfather is buried in an Orthodox grave. Its headstone, a large fallen stone cross, now rests on
its side where vandals had tipped it over... years before.

He had tried once or twice before to dislodge it from earth
and weed, to push it back into place; tries again now, crouching,
heaving his muscle to it. Straining, he draws in his breath, tries
once more, barely budges it.

He looks around for flowers. A caper plant clings serenely to
the nearby wall, waves pink stamens in the breeze. He bends a
prickly stem, breaks off a flower, places it on the Bible verse, engraved in the slab of marble that holds his grandfather's bones.

"He who has faith, has everlasting life...."

Faith. To believe without proof, without logic. A premonition of the heart? To believe in victory, in justice. Was that not
also faith?

His own Muslim father is buried in neighboring El Hilal in a
modest grave; his Koranic saying reads,

"He who forgives the sin, accepts penitence....

God the Great speaks truth...."

Penitence... from a man disillusioned with the world's hypoc-
risy and pain.

He was his father's son, an outsider, in need of forgiveness
for past apathy. Only his love of Palestine sustains him now,
gives him the will, the courage, to do what he must tonight.

A kind of euphoria settles over Omar's mood as he winds
his way back to the Semiramis. Passing the flower shop, now

shuttered, he glances at his watch. Already a few minutes past 5.

In a corner of the *liwan*, Rasheed Walid is playing backgammon with Mr. O'Connor. Nawal at her desk looks up briefly, gives Omar a self-conscious smile. Omar stands for a moment to observe the game.

"*Shaish baish* means the dice numbers are five and six," Rasheed Walid explains.

Mr. O'Connor looks up at Omar. "He's a good teacher, but a bit impatient with my moves."

Rasheed rattles the dice in his fist, spills them onto the board with gusto. "*Say-wa-do!*" he says triumphantly. "Three and two!" He slams his men in a corner, blocking his opponent's move. "Why not have the winner of this game play *Sitt* Nawal?" he asks reflectively.

"I don't think I'll be the lucky one," Mr. O'Connor says. "But one day soon, who knows? I might win."

"*Tawla* games are for men and women of leisure," Omar observes. "Nawal won't get off work till 6, when Mustapha takes her place."

"I'm willing to wait for an hour, a day, even a week. But no longer." Rasheed's laughter gurgles in his throat. "My visa expires by then."

Mr. O'Connor throws the dice, begins to count again. "Who knows? There's a chance I may still win after all...." He raises a speckled eyebrow, glances across at his partner. "So how's your wife-hunting coming along?"

The other shakes his head. "As erratic as this game, alas. But Rasheed Walid doesn't give up easily. Who knows? Maybe, in the last few hours of his stay, a touchdown!"

"Alya is not yet back from Bethlehem," Nawal tells Omar when he asks. She looks down at the scribbles on her pad. "But your '*Ammi* Musa called," she says cheerfully. "He wants to know when you and Alya are going to invite him to your weddings."

Omar shrugs. "It might take a while. Years, even, I'm afraid."

Nawal gives Omar a pensive look. "To give him hope, I said

to him, 'In a few months, a year at most....'"

Rasheed Walid's voice fills the *liwan*. "You must admit brains overcame my *say-wa-do*. But you're getting close, my friend. Too close for comfort. One day soon, I'm afraid, you will win this game."

"Yes," says Mr. O'Connor. "Sooner than you think."

As Omar climbs the stairs, he hears Rasheed Walid plead with Nawal, but can't make out her reply. He glances briefly at his father's portrait above the stairway, the gaunt dark face glistening beneath the skylight. He approaches his mother's door, decides to knock.

He hears her voice, opens the door gingerly. His mother, leaning back against the pillows on her bed, is repairing the satin seams of an old, frayed blanket.

"Still at it?" he observes.

"Why waste good blankets, and allow them to rot in some closet, unused?"

As usual, the curtains of her room are drawn to keep out the brightness of sun. "I prefer electrical bulbs," she said once. "They do not shrivel the skin."

Despite her age, her pale skin is smooth and unwrinkled. Only her sagging neck gives her away.

"Nawal tells me 'Ammi Musa called. Did you, by chance, talk to him?"

She says, defiance in her voice, "But why would he want to talk to me, an old woman, when he asks for his brother's children?"

Omar sits on the edge of the bed, says nothing for a while, watches as she pulls the pink thread taut, and makes small even stitches. She looks up from her sewing, her mouth pursed like a small dried rose. "Is something wrong?"

He shakes his head. "But tell me what is wrong between you and 'Ammi Musa," he says.

Her glance rivets to the photograph of the child Ramzi on her stand, the brother he has never known, lifts to Omar's face.

"After your brother's death, your uncle would come to our house in Katamon and sit, silent as a ghost in a corner of the living room. He drank the bitter coffee I offered him without comment. To him I was *kafreh*, an infidel, who, despite her marriage vows during the Writing of the Book, would never forsake her own faith. Your father, knowing this, did not condemn me for it." She emits a gasp, a choking sound like air escaping from a valve. "Because of your father's Muslim faith, I've endured ostracism from my own family, denied to see my own mother. Pain that shrivels up the heart. But my deepest anguish came with my little Ramzi's death."

Death had left its mark, an engraving on his mother's heart. And neither Koran nor Bible could translate its secret code.

His mother's weeping—water breaking through encrusted earth, creates a fissure in the rock. A day or two before, Clara's tears cut a swath into his rage at being discarded, broke through his resistance.

She massages a spot between her breasts as if to ease an inward pain. Her callused fingers press against his, form a crisscross pattern in the artificial light. Loosening her grip, she reaches for an embroidered handkerchief to blot out tears, and once more takes up needle and thread.

She says, a tremor in her voice, "Is Alya back from Bethlehem?"

"Not yet."

She looks up, her eyes glistening from recent tears. "Poor Julia. Instead of the Bethlehem hospital, the Muslim Sheikh Jabbar could break the spell underground demons have cast on her." A shiver of a sigh. "The poor woman obviously has a counterpart that wishes her evil."

Was the devil, after all, loose upon the earth, and demons, his subterranean kin, still wreaking havoc in the lives of men?

"But, is not the casting out of demons a Christian art?" Omar asks, recalling his mother's story about Jesus and the swine.

She shakes her head. "The priests in Beit Nuba do not condescend to give that cure. Only the Muslim sheikh refuses to discriminate against those blighted souls who come to him, seeking help."

Um Ramzi lays down her mending, reaches for the rosary

near Ramzi's picture, fingers it as if it were a lifeline against evil. Her lips move soundlessly, her shoulders heave beneath her gown.

She says now, "A woman I knew gave birth to three children... each dying soon after birth. In desperation, she consulted the Muslim sheikh, who advised her against wearing the color red, and ordered her to stay away from funerals. He also scribbled a coded message on paper only he and the underground *djinn* could decipher, and asked her to bury it under a certain pine in the back of their house. And even when her own mother died, she refused to attend the funeral." Omar's mother looks up, triumphant. "In the next few years, the woman gave birth to several healthy children... alive to this day!"

"But why, then, didn't you consult the sheikh when Ramzi became ill?"

"My priest forbade it," she says with vehemence. "Besides, I was young then, and without wisdom...."

He persists. "Would you, an ardent Christian, have consulted a Muslim sheikh?"

"In a special case like this, what did it matter?"

Returning to his room, Omar flings open shutters, unlocks the side door, and walks out on the balcony. Beyond the empty and silent courtyard, the faint lights of Jaffa on the Mediterranean stain the horizon.

In the silent courtyard, through the trellis, Alya's lone apparition in its dervish dance whirls as if the spirit of the earth has broken free from chains, has welded the human to the spirit world—*ins* to *djinn*.

Although, earlier, he'd tried, but failed, to weld Clara's broken tie clip that once anchored his world in place.

But tonight, without consulting sheikh or priest, he, too, will dance his secret dervish dance, breaking free from demons of the past. Tonight he will become Omar, the *fedayee*, all for the love of Palestine.

Knocking persists as Alya's voice comes to him as if in reverie. He opens his eyes, pulls back from the pillows on his bed. On
the bedcovers is the book he was reading before he inadvertently
fell asleep: *History of the Ottoman Turks in Palestine.*

The time on the small round clock on his dresser is 9:32 p.m.
Two and a half hours till midnight.

Alya's voice cuts into her intermittent knocking. "Are you
hiding from the world?"

He gets up groggily, unlocks the door, and stands, blocking
her way, trying to absorb her disheveled presence at his door.

She says, "Nawal left a note with Mustapha. Did you want to
see me... about something or other?"

"Come in." He moves away from the door. "I didn't realize
the time...."

She ambles into his room, drops into the cane chair at his
desk, extends her legs, and stares past him at the lemon tree beyond the balcony. Color is drained from her face, a glazed weariness in her glance... as if tears are held back by sheer will.

"How was your trip to Bethlehem?" he asks casually.

She tells him of the killing of a goat in the middle of the
road in Sur Bahir, of a picnic at Solomon's Pools, and of Badri,
sleeping all the way back, curled up like a *halazoneh* snail.

She shrugs, looks down at her hands. "Only at the hospital,
when Julia accused me of being the culprit for all her ills... did
my courage fail."

She'd failed to mention the man, Sari, and he dares not ask.

A momentary surge of pity at Alya's foolishness cuts into
Omar's impatience at her antics. "Illness in the head," he says
now, "rarely discriminates between truth and lies...." A guess—or
belated wisdom? to convince her, to convince even himself.

"I'd like a small favor...," he says, after a small silence. He
explains what he and Mustapha must do at midnight; but he does
not confide his other, secret plan.

"This 'operation' will endanger *your* life—besides Mustapha's
and the driver of the truck...." Her teacher's voice is matter-of-

fact, impartial, a conviction in her mind.

"A necessary risk," he says glibly. "But, the goal is to save the lives of defenseless villagers with no one to turn to in case of Israeli attack."

"Where are the guns now?"

"Stored in the old shed... our first home in Beit Nuba."

"Julia was right after all...," she says bitterly, her accusing eyes on his face. "The voices she heard, the shadows she saw the night she spent in Dick Brandon's room, were real—not imagined. When I later found her in the kitchen, she tried to convince me, to convince her brother, Sari... even Mr. O'Connor. But no one believed her. But how could we? Knowing poor Julia...."

"I was in my room that night," Omar says firmly. "I heard, saw nothing." But he does not tell her he already *knew*.

"So tonight you want me to see nothing... even when it happens before my eyes?"

"Mustapha will turn off all lights in the courtyard and at the entrance of the Semiramis. What moon there is may be hidden by clouds." He holds out his hands toward her; his voice becomes a plea, "All I ask is that you take Mustapha's place at the desk for an hour or two during the transfer of guns to the truck."

She gives him a skeptical look. "The end justifies... and all that?"

He sits on the edge of the bed, looks down at his hands. "Up till now, I've been a coward," he says in a rush of emotion. "But Clara's leaving freed me, gave me courage to do what I must."

Alya gets up from her desk chair, takes a seat next to him, on the bed. She says quietly, "In my *own* head, good and bad are blended like a stew, and 'must' gives way to 'maybe'...." Her arm circles stiffened shoulders, a bonding imposed against his will. He draws back, his body asserting independence from her woman's touch.

She gets up suddenly, stands for a long moment at the window, finally turns to face him, her eyebrows furrowing over her aquiline nose. "And even if you consider practicality, yours is the most impractical of schemes."

He speaks slowly, deliberately, "If I were you... I wouldn't consider myself an expert on practicality."

She laughs, and he sees the stubborn dervish dance in her eyes. "Or the smuggling of arms?"

At 11:20, when Omar comes to her door, he finds Alya wide awake and fully dressed. She follows him downstairs, her reticence in judgment over him, her silence holding him at bay. She brings her history book, papers, a red pen. Is he taking his leave of her forever, or for a mere hour or two—a sister who has caused him heartache in the past, now gives him her silence as parting gift.

"*Shukran,*" he says finally. "Thank you for your help tonight."

She stares at him, her head angled, as if to decipher motives, to discover causes and results. He can almost guess at the tangle of her thoughts, but is grateful for words left unsaid, for restraint. Blood is thicker... he decides, as he turns to go. Perhaps she is finally convinced of it by now.

While Mustapha waits near the shed, Omar crouches outside the parking lot, near the gate, his mind emptied of thought. He waits until the muscles in his legs are strained beyond endurance. But when he stands up, he remains in the corner, under the *saru* tree.

He looks at his watch. Almost 1 o'clock—and already the 5th of June—when he finally hears the rumble of the truck, and motions it to a stop.

A shadow emerges out of darkness, glides toward him. In the faint light, Omar sees a smooth-skinned boy's face, with fuzz on the upper lip, and green-hooded eyes.

"Raja," says the boy's voice, "And you?"

"Omar Habeeb. Mustapha waits near the shed."

They clasp hands, hold each other, like long-lost friends, like brothers.

Omar says, "You're late."

The boy whispers. "On the way here, the truck had a puncture. Changing tires took longer than I thought."

"The spare...?"

"As good as new."

"Mustapha is waiting," Omar says. With the boy following, he moves furtively past cars toward the Semiramis building and the narrow path that cut through the pines to the shed.

"A tire puncture," Omar explains. "That's all."

Again the ritual of welcome repeated. Mustapha turns toward the shed, unlocks the door, revealing the dark, crisp outline of stacked boxes.

He gives each a rag to twist and place on his shoulder to cushion the load of the box. They form a caravan of shadows moving stealthily between the trees, hugging outer walls, making their way toward the truck. The air, wet against their faces, smells of jasmine and pine; silence holds them like a thread.

Somewhere a donkey brays. Omar's dog, asleep near the gate, begins to growl. Omar pats his head, talks soothingly to him. Pacified, the dog unfolds himself, trails after them in companionable silence.

With the truck finally loaded, they stretch a tarp across the cargo of sealed boxes. No disguise of cargo needed this time, since there are no borders to cross, no suspicious agents to impose taxes on imports.

The dog, sensing the end of the loading, retreats to his spot near the gate. As Omar pulls at the rope, tying it to the truck's corner hook, a rush of euphoria obliterates the sharp aching of shoulder and back muscles.

"In each village," the boy whispers, "one or two men will wait for us near the entrance of the mosque. They'll know the password: "*Assifa...* the storm." He looks at Mustapha. "If you like, we'll take turns driving the truck. I've studied the map; I know the way."

Omar glances at his watch. Two o'clock on this Monday morning. Surely an auspicious time?

He takes a step toward the boy, but his eyes remain on Mustapha. "I have a better suggestion," he says with alacrity. "I would gladly help you drive the truck... instead of Mustapha. And I promise to follow Fatah instructions to the letter."

"Impossible!" Mustapha's voice is a small explosion in the night air. "*Um* Amin gave us specific instructions from Lutfi and Fatah. Besides, I've waited for this day—prepared for it in mind and heart. My family has given me unwavering support. How can I return to them like a dog with my tail between my legs?"

A rooster crows, as if in signal that time is passing, that decisions must be made soon.

Mustapha continues, "And if your mother and sister knew your intent, surely they'd oppose your taking that risk."

"I think for myself," Omar says, irritation in his voice. "I make my own decisions."

"I have many children—especially sons to carry my name," Mustapha adds, almost apologetically. "You, on the other hand, are still unmarried, without sons. You still have your life to live."

The boy, Raja, rummages for keys in his pocket. "Fatah has already decided," he says softly. "What right do we have to stray from their collective decision?"

Argument solves nothing, Omar decides. Action would provide its own logic, its own reasons.

Keys in hand, the boy climbs into the truck. A slight figure of a boy, a child, easily overcome. And despite rhetoric, Mustapha, used to taking orders, will not dare interfere.

A heady resolve holds Omar in its spell—goads him on. Martyrdom was his own choice, after all. Why should anyone deny him that right?

But the boy will not let go of the keys. Where does he have the strength to pull against him? He sees Mustapha, his nemesis, hold out an arm, sees teeth flashing.

A fist smashes into Omar's jaw, rattles his brain.

A thud. Then nothing.

Israel, starting on the night of June 4–5, mounted a rapid three-prong attack on its Arab neighbors. The Arabs were taken completely by surprise. Within six days the war that exploded upon the Middle East was over. A victorious Israel had occupied Gaza and the Sinai, Arab Jerusalem and the West Bank of the Jordan River, and the Syrian heights on the Golan Plateau.

The Book of Knowledge Annual, 1968

It thus took the Israeli forces slightly over 50 hours to rout the entire Jordanian army and capture the whole West Bank....

Ze'ev Schiff, *A History of the Israeli Army*

[Israeli Jews] push toward the mammoth blocks of the Wailing Wall... in a plaza created immediately following capture of the city [of East Jerusalem]. Rubble from [Palestinian Arab] houses razed by bulldozers edges the square....

National Geographic, December, 1967

CHAPTER FIFTEEN

David O'Connor

DAVID O'CONNOR discovers Omar's body in the parking lot half an hour or so before the *muezzin*'s dawn call to prayer. He crouches over Omar's body, looks for signs of life. Earlier—when O'Connor first heard the sound of a truck engine rumble away into silence—he clicked his Samsonite suitcase shut, picked up his flashlight, and walked out of his hotel room. To avoid scrutiny, he took the back stairs to the kitchen and wound his way through the pines to the shed. Just as he suspected, he found it empty, its door wide open.

Not too clever, those Arabs—leaving the door unlocked so his suspicions could be confirmed. But if all went according to plan, somewhere between Jerusalem and Es Samu, the truck would develop four flat tires—courtesy of his collaborator, Fuad Ibn Harami.

Yesterday, when he paid the bill to his hotel room and told Nawal he was leaving early the next morning, her thin intense face lifted to his. "Will you be back next year?" she asked in her business-like voice.

"Much sooner, I hope," he assured her, smiling.

For a moment, her puzzled look gave David O'Connor

pause. He felt sorry for Nawal, pitied them all—even Omar—who now lies at his feet on the asphalt parking lot. He moves the beam of flashlight over Omar's prone body, shifts it to his face, notes the purple markings on the jaw. Bending over, he tests Omar's pulse, lifts an eyelid.

Knocked out, he concludes—but still very much alive.

He looks up toward the southwestern sky for a premonition, for evidence. Despite his training in self-control, his pulse races, the hammering in his chest sounds like a dozen drums.

Dayan had given his assurance that Israel could win a war without the aid of foreign troops; David O'Connor was also convinced that "in every war, if you want to fight to win, you really must strike, and strike very hard...."

Any moment now, Israeli planes will be winging their way toward the Egyptian desert in a preemptive strike against Nasser's air force.

The straw that broke the camel's back... he smiles at the metaphor... was Nasser's closing the Straits of Tiran to Israeli shipping. Why would Israel win this concession in 1956 only allow it to be filched in 1967?

But despite President Johnson's worries about a Soviet–American confrontation, Israel—with its own self-interest in mind—preferred a surgical operation, a quick indelible lesson to the Arabs.

After Nasser was dealt with on his own turf, David O'Connor was confident, Hussein's newest treaty with Nasser would open up a second front, allowing the Israeli Defense Forces to break through, in retaliation, and reclaim Judea and Samaria.

And the rest of Jerusalem.

But why in the name of heaven was the American spy ship USS *Liberty* moving steadily through the Mediterranean toward El Arish and Gaza? Did the U.S. State Department not quite trust Israel, its one ally in the Middle East, to do what was best for America—as well as Israel?

David O'Connor smiles to himself. Although his own work is modest by comparison, he knows Chaim will be pleased with his efforts to monitor Fatah activities in the Beit Nuba area. Chaim will also applaud David's success in recruiting collaborators—like Fuad Ibn Harami, who became conveniently addicted to drugs with his first sniff of cocaine.

Using his Irish persona and his Los Angeles accent, David O'Connor has misled suspicious minds from his true identity—that of a case officer, or *katsa*, in Israel's intelligence agency known as the Institute, or Mossad.

His mother, Leah Schiff, would be proud. She dropped the "O'Connor" name soon after their move from Los Angeles to Israel. Although still in her early sixties, she lives in a home for the aging in the suburbs of Tel Aviv. These days, when he goes to visit, she nods her head at his tales of adventure, stares blankly into his face.

But he did come by his Irish blood authentically; his paternal grandfather was killed in the Easter Uprising of 1916. David's father, Pat O'Connor, immigrated to the States as a boy, later dropped out of school, and found a job at a corner grocery store owned by Yitzhak and Sarah Schiff.

The Schiff daughter, Leah, sloe-eyed and given to nervous laughter, spent her free time reading serious books about Zionism, or talking about Jewish destiny. For his part, Pat O'Connor tried his best to entertain her, telling her jokes that only made her grimace.

But somehow, the chemistry was right. And despite her parents' disapproval, Leah married Pat a year later—with a liberal Reform rabbi performing the ceremony.

David O'Connor was almost nine when his father was killed in a car accident. His mother, an ardent Zionist by then, took this as a "sign," decided, in 1951, to move with David to Israel.

His mother's zeal was integrated into his life... not as a flare of light, but as a steadily moving river, washing away obstacles in its path.

David O'Connor is determined to rid Israel of her enemies in any way he can. This was his promise to his mother, Leah, his vow to Chaim when he first asked him to join the Institute.

❀   ❀   ❀

A shudder courses through Omar's body, as he lies at David O'Connor's feet. Omar lifts his head, makes an effort to get up, sinks back with a groan.

"Luck of the Irish I found you," O'Connor says, suppressing a smirk.

"Where's...?" Omar's head bobs up again, his neck twists toward the road. A careful man, Omar will not dare betray Mustapha's name in front of David O'Connor.

"Would you like me to tell your sister about your... uh... little accident?"

Omar heaves himself up on one elbow, grunts his "No!" in Arabic. Shadows swaddle his head, extend between car tires toward the fence. Faint light now stains the eastern sky, glints on the roof of the rented Chevy. Once more David O'Connor searches the heavens—a fortune teller, intent on reading his people's fate in the stars. A good omen, says his heart.

But how can he be sure?

A recording of the *muezzin*'s voice reverberates in his head, jolts him back to the choices he must make. He will have to leave Omar here for now: a wounded mouse, allowed to play a little longer.

"I'm off to Jerusalem," David O'Connor says. "I have souvenirs to pack and shipments to make." He squats, bones creaking, looks down into Omar's face. "Sure you'll be all right?"

"I'm fine," Omar says in a fierce whisper.

"As you wish."

David O'Connor walks back to the car with a buoyant step. Once in Jerusalem, he will make his way through Mandelbaum Gate, then cut through No Man's Land into West Jerusalem. Chaim will be waiting for him on the other side with up-to-date details of the operation.

He already feels it in his bones: the war will be a glorious success.

Occupation
June 7, 1967

WHEN THE ISRAELI soldiers first arrive at the Semiramis, they round up the men and boys over fourteen, herd them to the courtyard. Hands lifted to their heads, the men wait in the June sun for elaborate questioning: Omar and Hagas and *'Ammi* Musa and Ali Cort from Nabi Sumueel, also the *mukhtar*—the mayor of the village of Yalo—and Rasheed Walid from Brooklyn, and Badri, who speaks only in grunts and symbols, and all the rest.

While Sergeant Abram struts on the periphery of the dance floor like a schoolmaster, barking his questions in his Israeli–Iraqi accent, a soldier on a nearby stool takes notes in a ledger balanced on his knee.

Full name? Date and place of birth? Father's name? Grandfather's first name? Religion? (Perhaps they will go easier on a "Christian?" But what if you were a Buddhist or even an atheist... how would you proclaim it to the world?)

Have you ever belonged to an organization that...? Do you own any weapons now hidden on the premises? Have you ever participated in...? And much, much more.

Women and children remain on the verandah, under the watchful scrutiny of Captain Mordacai, who asks those same questions in English, with Alya reluctantly translating into Arabic. A young soldier with kinky hair sits astride the parapet and jots it all down—stops occasionally to look up, to confer with Mordacai.

The youngest Cort, asleep in his mother's arms, opens his eyes, turns a deep pink and, with small arms flailing, begins to bawl. Her wail blocks out Sergeant Abram's relentless bark, disrupts Mordacai's well-ordered proceedings. The baby's sister, Muna, seven, clings to her mother's skirt, her brown eyes fixed on Mordacai's boots. A younger brother, four, suddenly emits a jagged howl that fuses with the baby's cry, wells up into the mellow afternoon sky like a signal for mutiny.

Their mother, Badia Cort, pushes disheveled hair from her

brow, glares, wild-eyed, at Mordacai, and flings a string of curses his way—curses aimed at life and fate and a callous world, erupting like pebbles at his feet. "May the monkey take you," she repeats over and over under her breath. And even when Alya reaches for the infant, to quiet her, to soothe away her fears, the baby's rebel cry begins anew.

Half-hidden by the trellised bougainvillea vine, Ali Cort—denied a request to urinate in privacy—forgets his grandfather's first name, is unable to answer any more questions. His large and pudgy frame begins to quiver, his hands slide from his balding head, fall uselessly at his sides. And, in clear view of Sergeant Abram and all the rest, he commits the ultimate act of humiliation.

Abram's laughter bellows across the courtyard in a relentless spasm of merriment that gives pause to Badia Cort's curses, to the cries of her children. When Abram's guffaws finally subside, Omar's voice, raised in angry protest, cuts into the momentary silence. He stands at the edge of the line, bruised, with a tremor coursing through his frame, but when he speaks, his voice is clear and in control.

"We are not beasts to misuse as you see fit. Our one difference is that *you* hold the guns for now...." His impassioned plea for justice, for human dignity, falters, loses its edge—is muddied in a flurry of name-calling, of incoherence.

Logic, after all, is victory, swift and without compromise; the agony of illogical men only stands in the way.

A *muezzin*'s singsong call to prayer eases itself into Omar's tirade, affirms to victorious and defeated men that God is great, and undoubtedly merciful—despite appearances. Victory, or defeat, after all, is an illusion, a freak happening, that can be reversed at a moment's notice.

The *muezzin*'s call reverberates around the stone houses of Beit Nuba, swirls through the olive groves and vineyards of the faithful, is whisked down the deserted alleyways where the fetid odor of the carcasses of dogs and cats clings to walls and gardens; moves regally down Main Street, where cars, flattened by giant tanks, lie shimmering in the sun.

But Sergeant Abram's fury at Omar's defiance superimposes itself on this afternoon call to prayer, is punctuated by the muted thud of fists in contact with yielding flesh.

The next day, when she is finally allowed to see him, Alya can barely recognize her brother's face.

1967 Occupation - A few days later

BISSEH, *UM* RAMZI'S three-legged cat, can't tell the difference between Occupation and Freedom. She merely understands hunger and thirst and affection as she moves among the soldiers in the Semiramis grounds, swishing her tail, stepping gingerly on pine needles, and eyeing dusty army boots with a certain disdain.

And *Um* Ramzi, confined to her room, does not have to worry whether the cat is well fed, for Captain Mordacai has a tender heart and sometimes feeds Bisseh the scraps from his own plate.

A day after the Israeli occupation of Beit Nuba, and the interrogation of the men and women at the Semiramis, the soldiers—along with Captain Mordacai and Sergeant Abram—had an all-night party in the hotel courtyard. They wheeled out the Steinway from the dining room to the verandah, down the flagstone path, past the fountain and the pink rosebush—mangled in the process—to the middle of the courtyard dance floor. And while Captain Mordacai played the piano, the soldiers sang and danced and stamped their feet and let out whoops of joy and laughed and slapped each other on the back and told jokes about certain events in the war.

For it certainly was a victory for the books.

Just outside Nablus and on their way to Beit Nuba, some of the soldiers had come across a Jordanian column of about thirty American-made Sherman tanks blown to bits by Israeli French-made Mirages. It was the way the Jordanian tanks carried their gasoline, Captain Mordacai explained, that made it almost inevitable. Besides, the few measly planes of the Jordanian air force could not have provided air cover since the Israeli air force had destroyed them soon after the invasion began.

Captain Mordacai is of medium height with a receding hair-line and pale-blue eyes that appear coldly analytical. He is married to a woman committed to the orthodoxy of her faith. Sometimes, Mordacai suspects that his wife considers him second best in the order of things.

As a scientist in civilian life, he is used to peering through microscopes at specimens. He can also lose himself in the music of Mozart, and speaks Hebrew, which he learned as a teenager, a smattering of Arabic, and his own native English with a scholarly British accent.

Sergeant Abram, who grew up near Baghdad, speaks and understands Arabic quite well. But despite his skill in their language, Sergeant Abram has no affection for the Arabs, either in Iraq or in Old Jaffa, the old maritime quarter on the hill above the harbor, where he now lives with his wife and three children in a house that once belonged to Arabs.

In the early 1950s, the Iraqi government confiscated Sergeant Abram's family home when he decided to emigrate to Israel. Now, he laughs loudest when someone tells a joke about the stupidity of Arab villagers who mistook Israeli soldiers for Iraqis, greeting them with cheers and *zaghareet*. He likes to tell the story of routing a column of Jordanian soldiers marching slowly east, like robots.

"We started shooting and they scattered. But we got several of them in the butt." He laughs uproariously.

Although the soldiers have taken over the first floor as well as the grounds of the Hotel Semiramis, for the time being Mordacai has allowed Alya, Omar, and the others to retain their quarters on the second floor.

Rasheed "Rick" Walid from Brooklyn—whose last-minute flight to New York was canceled just before the war began—is now forced to share a room with Hagas, whose restaurant building suffered direct shelling. Along with Badri, Badri's grand-

mother and Miriam, Nawal and her mother and other unexpected "guests" like the Corts and the *mukhtar* of Yalo and his
family who have also sought refuge here, are now confined to
second-floor rooms, including the room formerly occupied by
the sheikh from Oman and his family.

'*Ammi* Musa is currently installed in Dick Brandon's old
room at the end of the hall. He walked the seventeen kilometers
from Jerusalem to Beit Nuba following an order by the Israeli
authorities to bulldoze his small house in *Harat el Mugharbeh* outside the *Haram*, adjacent to the Western Wall.

Because of the lack of a peace treaty between Jordan and
Israel after the 1948 war, Jewish worshipers have had no access
to the Wailing Wall—a retaining wall of the ancient Temple of
Solomon.

But in June of 1967, with East Jerusalem now under Israeli
control, small Arab houses and shops near the Wall were bull-
dozed to create a wide plaza where Jewish worshippers now
come freely to celebrate *Shabuoth*—not worried about displacing
Arabs.

On his trek to Beit Nuba, '*Ammi* Musa carried with him his
prayer rug, a parcel of clothes, bread, and his original painting
of the Dome—the one he has promised Alya after his death—
wrapped in his *abaya*, the flowing outer garment he wears like a
coat. A light load, compared to other refugees streaming toward
Beit Nuba and the east.

'*Ammi* Musa says little, looks beyond Alya's ravaged face to
his own personal losses. His family killed in Deir Yassin before
the war of 1948, his home near the Wall wiped from the face of
the earth.

In the dark privacy of his borrowed room here at the Semiramis, before the *muezzin*'s call to prayer, '*Ammi* Musa sometimes
ponders the losses of his life and allows secret tears to course
down his weathered face.

But the time will come, '*Ammi* Musa believes, when the con-
quests of men will be like dust in their mouths.

Panic—the fear of mutilation or death by napalm and phosphorus or shrapnel from bombs dropped from Mirages overhead or a blast from an Uzi submachine gun—has caused many Palestinians to flee the path of war.

The day after the war began, the Corts from Nabi Sumueel and their children arrived on foot at the Semiramis, seeking asylum.

The young wife of the *mukhtar* of Yalo and her husband and children—forced by the soldiers to abandon their village of Yalo—huddle one evening in an almond grove on their long trek to Beit Nuba. A kilometer or two away she hears the explosions that would turn her new stone house to rubble, watches black smoke rise like a banner.

Yalo, a border village, leveled to the ground for "security reasons"; her brother, refusing to leave, is shot. But tears, like her mother's milk, turn hard as stone when her baby son is unable to nurse at her breast.

The victors in the war provide the refugees fleeing in panic with free rides in trucks or buses to the bombed-out Allenby Bridge over the Jordan River—and to King Hussein. The fewer Palestinians in the State of Israel, their leaders decide, the better.

But, fortunately for the people of Beit Nuba, their town has been spared the fate of Yalo. For the time being, at least, the wells provide adequate water for the soldiers and the residents at the Semiramis. Because of air strikes, electric power fails to work at the Hotel Semiramis. But Captain Mordacai manages to "borrow" a generator from the nearby Cinema Jalal to provide electricity for his men at the Semiramis.

This is the second week of this "lightning war," and except for two or three hours every few days, Beit Nuba remains under strict curfew. During the brief lifting of the curfew, men, women and children scurry to the market or the homes of neighbors and friends to buy or beg for food and other necessities.

Captain Mordacai, a man of conscience, tries to keep his men from vandalizing the hotel and carrying off some of the brass ornaments and rugs or mother-of-pearl inlaid side tables, or even the sacks of rice and sugar in the storage room next to the kitchen. But not always with success. When he catches some-one red-handed, the captain's frustration, usually held in, flares up, and even Sergeant Abram is silent and does not argue with him. But Sergeant Abram believes that the victor in war has a legitimate right to its spoils. So when the filigreed brass lamp on the first floor disappears, or the blankets and some of the bed-ding or the embroidered linen cloths or the silverware is pilfered, no one seems to know who did it—and only when Alya brings it to the attention of Captain Mordacai will he make an effort to investigate. And not always with success.

Once, when Alya snatched her painting of the Bedouin woman from the hands of Sergeant Abram and jabbed him (ac-cidentally?) in the ribs with a sharp corner of its frame, Captain Mordacai, impressed with the flame of Alya's temper, quickly dismissed the sergeant's excuse that all he wanted was to study the painting in the outside light.

"I didn't know you were a connoisseur of the arts!" Captain Mordacai told his sergeant in Alya's presence.

"Why not?" The sergeant flashed a gold tooth at Alya. "Not a bad painting, as paintings go, of a Bedouin woman with tat-toos."

Sometimes, when Alya complains to the captain about other thefts, he shrugs his shoulders, for he does as much as he can under the circumstances. His pale eyes appraise Alya, note differ-ences in character and looks between her and the man Omar, her brother. The woman refuses to be cowed—despite the yellow tag that labels her "servant" he's asked her to wear. Its purpose, after all, is to allow her to move freely from her quarters to kitchen, dining room, and back. For there are mouths to feed here, food to prepare, the cleaning and washing to be done afterwards.

Although his soldiers usually take up one end of the dining room, they use a room beyond the kitchen to prepare their food of dried or tinned kosher foods.

After lunch one day, with the dining room nearly empty, Captain Mordacai apologizes to Alya for the mess his soldiers have created inside and outside the hotel.

He stands near the window with its African violets on the windowsill and watches her sweep imaginary bread crumbs into a pan. He adds, "So your Hussein expected help from Nasser, perhaps? A delusion—we'd have gladly told him. If he had bothered to ask."

He watches her face closely for a reaction to his comment. He does not mean to taunt her, but wishes to start a dialogue of sorts with this woman who does not accept the realities of victory and defeat.

"A pity," he persists. "If Hussein's soldiers had not shelled our positions first, we would have left him alone. It was his choice."

She pauses in her task of battling imaginary dirt, holds her broom like a shield.

"To choose means to be a free agent," she says in her teacher's voice. "To decide among options without outside pressure, without compromise."

Mordacai smiles. "Fated, then?" he asks, using the words of her people.

Her voice erupts in molten fury, "Why is it 'fated' that my people live and die in captivity? That those more powerful, more wily, decide the limits of our lives on this planet Earth?"

A few feet away, soldiers in a small huddle pause to speculate on Mordacai's timidity in the face of the woman's defiance.

Mordacai says firmly, "Ours was a war of self-defense." Thinks: Despite war-mongers among us. His eyes sift through the layers of her obstinacy, find nothing to retrieve. To egg her on, to parry with sharp-edged words—he means to win this argument—he adds, "Your intent, of course, was to push us into the sea."

Her glance strays toward the clay pot of pink violets on the window sill, settles obliquely on his face. Topaz, he decides, her eyes are made of topaz, changing color with each movement of her head. Distinctive high-bridged nose flared at the nostrils, mouth tightly wound. Not quite a Renoir, this woman's face—a ubiquitous presence, overlapping Sarah's.

She says, incredulous, "Mere propaganda, spread by idiots, signifying nothing. Yet meant to deflect reality."

A surge of pity for her predicament cuts through Mordacai, akin to the pity he felt at the quick and inevitable defeat of the brave soldiers of Hussein.

He dodges her sarcasm, says patiently, "We've listened closely to the braggarts among your people. Perhaps even more closely than you have...."

"Our own legitimate fear," she interrupts, unmoved, "is not of braggarts—but of those who've pushed my people into desert wastelands, who, like yourself, now occupy this strip of land we've dared call home."

"One day," he says, to allay her fears, "your leaders and mine will sit down and talk. Not secretly and in disguise, but face to face. Why not?" he demands of the skepticism in her eyes, "After all, if our Moses can part the Red Sea—if your Jesus can walk on water—and if Muhammad can fly into the heavens on a steed— miracles can happen. Even the miracle of peace."

"And will you give up the spoils of a man-made war... for peace?"

Her yearning hard-edged as stone, scraping at miracles.

He laughs self-consciously, considers his own predicament. "It's not quite mine to give."

Eshkol might, he speculates. Dayan would not. The military need is, obviously, for a buffer zone. And Sarah, of course, would not give up one inch of it.

But what can he tell her beside "security?" A word that covers ground like pine needles?

"And if it were?" she asks, moving the curve of her broom toward him.

If she were a man, Captain Mordacai thinks, I would fear for my life. "For peace," he says now, "I'd give most of it back."

"Even East Jerusalem?"

He shakes his head. "I'll take my stand there."

Her resolve seems to harden like lead. Her words, "So do I," are an echo of his own.

We are Semites, you and I, he thinks, angry with himself for conceding. Besides, it's not my intention to remain a Spartan all my life, a Spartan wary of helots.

"I was born in Jerusalem twenty-seven years ago," she says, as if reciting a poem. "Our home was in Katamon. And although my mother's ancestors came from Beit Nuba, my father's people lived in Jerusalem for generations...." A flick of her broom, a storm brewing in her eyes. "The bulldozing of *'Ammi* Musa's house at the Wailing Wall, this erasing of his physical bond with the land—is a travesty." She reaches for a violet stem, breaks it off, crushes it in her hand.

His mind selects the kernel of her words, visible and invisible, to chew, to spit out. "When I was young—six or seven, I think," he says, "my parents and other Jews sold all their possessions in Nazi Germany and bought passage on a ship bound for Cuba. When Cuba reneged on its promise to accept our ship of refugees, we sought asylum in the United States. But Roosevelt—despite his fine and airy talk—turned the ship away. The lucky ones ended up in England. And in 1946, we emigrated—by way of Cyprus—to Palestine. This is *my* home now."

And Captain Mordacai and his soldiers, having laid siege to this scarred and bleeding land, now claim it for their own. For did not God promise the land to the seed of Isaac—through Sarah?

With Ishmael and his mother, Hagar, outcasts—yet Abraham, the father of both.

But how would the captain, a nonbeliever, try to convince this woman of Palestine—with logic based on miracles—that it was so?

Sergeant Abram (his stomach bulging, for he's eaten more than his share for lunch) walks up to them and nods at Captain Mordacai, but does not salute—for this is an informal army of victors who are not sticklers for details. He hands Captain Mordacai an envelope with a scribbling that spells Alya's name in English.

They exchange words in Hebrew.

Sergeant Abram looks on as Captain Mordacai hands Alya the envelope. "He tells me he's opened it... a formality."

More talk in Hebrew. Sergeant Abram is dismissed.

Captain Mordacai clears his throat. "Of course, we don't allow notes to be passed out at random here...." He rubs his forehead at the receding hairline, rivets impersonal eyes on Alya's face. "Objectively speaking, we still consider you *'oyev*: our enemy."

An easy smile now, without threat—to ease his reprimand. "The letter is from an English journalist—a friend, I think...?"

She takes it from Mordacai's hand, turns and walks away. Her broom held upright like a sword, she marches past the sergeant and his men and the young disheveled guard lounging at the reception desk—past the portrait of the Bedouin woman, upstairs to her room.

The ghost-eyes in the mirror belong to a woman who has journeyed across parched desert sands in search of water. Her glance takes in the yellow tag pinned to her apron with "servant" inscribed in Hebrew. The word, reversed, is no longer alien to her, worn for nearly two weeks for moving around the hotel, for doing servant's work. She and Miriam wear it now—a badge of honor. Of defiance.

From across the hall, the high, thin voices of the Cort children drift toward her, explode in argument. A child begins to sob.

Behind the barrier of Omar's closed door, his footsteps pace back and forth—not briskly, but with the deliberate pace of one awaiting sentence. A sudden weight presses against her ribs, makes it hard to breathe; she recalls Omar's phantom—head bent, eyes trained on the tiles at his feet—after Abram had pummeled him with his fists.

Alya lowers herself on her unmade bed, glances down at Dick Brandon's letter written in lopsided script.

"*My dear Alya,*" he writes, "*hope you can read the scribbles I've written you with my left hand, since my right is in a sling. Severed tendons, they tell me—a mishap of the war.*

"*As you recall, I first left for Egypt a few days ago to see the changing of the guard at El Arish. Later, in Israel, and despite stringent censorship, I was able to wrangle an interview with an assistant to their new defense minister, Moshe Dayan.*

"*At the start of this bloody feud, some of us journalists were allowed to ride with the Israeli soldiers on half-tracks into Gaza, even Sinai. Halfway through the Gaza Strip a sniper's bullet wounded the machine gunner, an-other tore into my hand. Serves me right, you'll probably say, cavorting with the 'enemy' like this. But which newsman, in his right mind, would turn down an offer for a front row seat to the war?*"

A couple of sentences blacked out... possibly by the censor?

"*Interesting bit of news you may have heard?*" Dick Brandon con-tinues, "*The bombing of the USS Liberty—a U.S. non-combat ship bombed by the Israelis just before their attack on Syria's Golan Heights. Thirty-four Americans killed, 171 wounded. An 'accident,' they claim.*

"*But here I am, in this West Jerusalem hospital, wondering whether I'm in the right profession. When I get out of this bloody place, I may decide to change careers. Become a soldier of fortune or a secret agent, à la le Carré. The poor chaps in America still have their Vietnam albatross around their necks—despite President Johnson's rhetoric. Americans insist on saving the world for their own brand of 'democracy'—but in reality, they end up sup-porting a motley variety of dictatorships.*

"*I'm rambling on, flexing the fingers of my left hand, for practice. When things calm down and the curfew's lifted, a friend of mine will drop by to pick up the few things I've left behind at the hotel. His name is Michael Corey. Michael speaks four languages, including Arabic and Hebrew. If there's anything you need, he has connections and will try to help.*

"*I'm taking a chance, sending you this. Not even sure it will reach you. I hope you and Omar and your mum are surviving. Do hope life gets back to almost-normal as soon as possible.*

"*Still your friend, I hope? Dick B.*"

Once more the voices of the Cort children break into Alya's reverie, become entangled with their father's. A soft whimpering follows an uneasy truce?

Alya thinks: How long can they survive—parents and children, jammed into one small room?

"We must go back home to Nabi Sumueel," the Cort father, *Abu* Mejd, confides when Alya makes her rounds. Sounds desperate, this balding middle-aged man outnumbered by children. "We'll walk home—if we have to—the way we came. A permit or a written pass from Mordacai might be all we need to get us on our way.

"We must return to salvage pride and live as others do. We have the right." He draws his breath in to restore calm. Blows his nose into a large, striped handkerchief. In the telling, the elder Cort, who does not believe in tears, begins to sob.

Later that afternoon, Captain Mordacai knocks on Alya's door to tell her that she and the others will be permitted to eat together in the dining room, early evening, before the soldiers' turn. He stands there, making concessions, waiting for the gratitude she refuses to give.

"Even your brother can come with the rest," he adds, "as long as he does not tangle with Abram. As long as he keeps his defiance to himself."

Alya's mind, untangled, reflects on Omar's impotence; taken prisoner in his own place, refusing to concede defeat. He rarely eats the food she brings to his room, but on occasion he will sip the lukewarm tea and drain the coffee from the tiny rounded cups.

This time, Omar bolts his door from the inside. Alya stands outside the barricade of his door and tells him of Mordacai's concession—this, after nearly two weeks of eating separately, each imprisoned in his room.

Is Mordacai softening—or is this personal occupation of the Semiramis soon to end?

"No hard feelings," Mordacai, a gentleman, will probably say in parting, perhaps regretfully, guessing at the hard core of her anger, at her humiliation. "Perhaps we will meet again, under better circumstances—as equals?"

This is the first time Mordacai has entrusted her with the keys, without a soldier to watch her every move.

"Open the door," she says to Omar now, spewing tattered words of pleading through the thickness of the wood.

But when no answer comes from behind the closed door, she falters, begins to weep. Huddled on her knees, she weeps into the hallway carpet for herself, for Omar, and for Mordacai, who has taken them prisoner. Weeps for Sari, who is in Jerusalem: dead or alive—whom she could learn to love; and for Julia, locked away in her own private cell in Bethlehem.

She weeps for Hagas and *'Ammi* Musa and the Corts and for Miriam and Badri and Nawal, for *Sayyid* "Rick" Walid, who no longer thinks of marriage but of escape. She even weeps for her mother, *Um* Ramzi, consoled by her Bible, not needing Alya's or anyone's tears.

She weeps noisily—impatient with Omar's silence trickling like thinned blood beneath his door.

And weeps, in part, for the world's hypocrisies.

The pale hall light smears her arms and weary legs, as her father's portrait—with Omar's eyes embedded in older flesh—looks down serenely at her desolation.

What is expected of her—a woman on her knees—yearning for miracles?

The Cort children are shrouded with sudden quiet. In the courtyard, a hubbub of alien voices, still in celebration, accentuate the black hole of her despair. Finally, inevitably, the door yields and she is allowed across the threshold, into Omar's room.

She sees Omar clearly for the first time in days—his mouth slack, the stubble of his beard a mottled shadow across a ravaged face. He touches her elbow, steers her toward the balcony. She goes obediently past the dresser, hides in the curtain's shadow and looks out beyond the balcony and the lemon tree at the courtyard below. Soldiers in their khakis mill around the piano, a few lounge near the mangled rosebush, their Uzis, like heavy toys, slung casually across their shoulders. Soldiers stand guard at the gate (where Clara waited for her husband two weeks ago), keeping watch over hotel grounds, Badri's house and the empty street below.

A short, tousle-haired soldier lowers his Uzi to the floor, straddles the piano bench and begins to play a sprightly tune. Nearby, soldiers spring to life. Some drop their guns, begin to sing, to clap, to stamp their feet. Alya closes her eyes against distraction, allows the melody, stripped of words, to warm her blood.

Once more she whirls around the dance floor to Hagas's band. Pulled by invisible strings, she dances her dervish dance— breaks free from despair.

Omar says, interrupting her reverie, "Nasser didn't have a chance. He was betrayed by Johnson and his ilk. Reconnaissance planes, I'm sure, paved the way for them to pulverize Nasser's MiGs on the ground." Omar's compact body convulses, retching a poison he's been forced to swallow. "And what about Fatah... and Mustapha? What has happened to Lutfi's plans?"

"Rhetoric has been our game," she says, bitterness in her voice, "this endless weaving of words of illusion and promise. And where is justice when our leaders play games against those who keep changing the rules to suit themselves?"

Omar turns abruptly from Alya toward the wall where the black-scripted Koranic saying glows serenely in the lamplight.

Alya wonders now, will wonder a month, a year or two from now, why God, ruler of Heaven and Earth, watches in silence as men and women trudge on blistered feet, carrying their lost children across their shoulders like toy guns. How can he bear to watch... as women with tokens of their past bundled on their heads, cross their broken bridges and make their way, one by one, past men whose souls are lost to them?

Knowing nothing of what awaits, they only know what is left behind: a *taboon* oven for the baking of bread. A white mulberry, or almond tree, a vineyard yielding grapes in season. The rubble of a house—or a house intact, with Persian rugs and Damascus brass. The portrait of an old man who sits frozen in his chair. Solemn wedding portraits of sons and daughters, photographs of sons long gone, resettled in Chicago or Mexico City or Berlin or even London. Sons—and sometimes husbands—scattered to the wind. Men and women, and children, uprooted like olive trees, their roots scraping foreign soil.

Does God, ruler of Heaven and Earth (Alya speculates), who sees, knows all, take pity on the women with their children, even the men with the hard angry faces? But why is Spirit silent, blowing ashes in one's face, burning eyelids, even as tears trace out the edges of the world like rain?

Nothing left here but bones. Bones of children clinging to women's breasts, to hands, to legs like scorpions. Sunlit bones of lost children drifting away from shore. Leaving homes behind.

"When Abram came looking for 'illegal weapons,'" Omar says now to Alya, whose thoughts muffle speech, "he never thought to look on an inner branch of the lemon tree." Omar smiles a cunning smile. "These days, before I sleep at night, I often think of Clara, who ran away to save her skin." Omar laughs abrasively. "And yet she was never mine to keep. Only borrowed, on occasion, to give meaning to my life."

Before Alya can answer him, he says, "Last night I dreamed I was a boy of twelve, and a ghoul from the netherworld held me prisoner in his cave. 'There are no ghouls,' our father used to say. Yet I'm still not convinced."

Um Ramzi

UM RAMZI closes her Bible, sets it down on the stand by her bed. To her left, closed curtains billow out, flap against the window sash. Light and shadow flicker against the round straw *tabak* on the facing wall, dance lightly on its rim. Sighing, she closes her eyes, repeats—as if to steady herself, to form the world anew: "In quietness and confidence shall be your strength. In quietness and in...."

But turmoil, instead of quiet, lurks like sparking fire in her heart. Confidence wavers, dies, even as her child, Ramzi, died. And she, an old woman with dissipated strength, waits on the edge, throws pebbles into an empty well.

She, whose faith has been a bulwark against despair, is now despairing. And yet, are not the Hebrews the Chosen People of God? And is not their takeover of the land prophecy fulfilled?

And how can *Um* Ramzi reconcile Holy Scripture with the discordant presence of the soldiers at the Semiramis? Yet, didn't faith, after all, help cure the blind, the crippled, even bring Lazarus to life? She closes her eyes and looks inward at her precious baby son Ramzi, still alive, crawling on hands and knees, coming toward her. She sees the young mother, herself, bend down to lift him up, to hold him to her breast. Blessed, for a time, was she among women. Unblessed, the fruit of her womb....

Um Ramzi thrusts her arms toward the ceiling, then lurches forward, heaves toward the Heavens as if in rehearsal for her spirit's flight. Her prayers in supplication, in penance, pour out like rain from a blackened sky. When will God forgive past misdemeanors and alleviate the curse that holds her in its grip?

She falls on arthritic knees, prays loudly, above the voices of soldiers in celebration.

Dear merciful Mother of God (she prays), forgive my past sins, my grievous sins. Rescue me from despair, dear Jesus. Rescue me—She begins to sing, her lips barely moving, sings about God and love and hope and the forgiveness of sins. Her song— a lullaby to Ramzi, to all the Ramzis of the world, to mothers, grieving with their children's loss. She croons, rocking gently, still on her knees, swaying from side to side.

Restore this world to sanity....

A sharp knock on her unbolted door. Alya's voice disrupts the rapture of her spirit, disrupts her prayer.

A key turns.

Alya is pale, and thinner than she was a week ago, or even yesterday; her eyes have lost their luster. Swallowed up in Miriam's apron, she wears the yellow tag with Hebrew writing, lopsided on her breast.

Bravado—that's what she's always had—even as a child. Caught, once, when she was five, dressed in her father's shirt, his slippers. Tripped and fell against the iron bed and skinned her knee and tore the shirt. No tears then, accepting punishment with tight-lipped defiance. Stubbornness in a child—especially in a daughter—is ground for the Devil's work, *Um* Ramzi is convinced.

Only God Almighty can eradicate stubbornness in sons.

Um Ramzi holds onto the bedpost, pulls herself up. She turns to face Alya. "So... how is your starving brother faring?"

"Barely surviving." A pause. "We have permission from Mordacai to eat together in the dining room early this evening. I hope you will join the rest? You will see him then."

Um Ramzi shrugs. "Appetite is a small thing with me. But naturally, I will come."

The piercing wail of the Cort infant invades small talk, makes its own statement.

"Why must we put up...?" *Um* Ramzi's voice falters.

Children not seen, but heard.

"The Corts will be returning to Nabi Sumueel tomorrow," Alya says. "Mordacai has arranged for their television to film their homecoming—a public gesture of 'humanity' to be flaunted to the world."

Um Ramzi says despondently. "Where has Bisseh, my cat, disappeared to?"

"Bisseh has switched allegiance to Mordacai and his men. She follows them around mewing for scraps." Alya sighs. "I can't decide whether she's a turncoat, or a mere beggar, like the rest of us."

Nawal

NAWAL HAS FINALLY washed her hair, in cold water from the sink. Nearly two weeks of unwashed hair is punishment enough—but her mother, bemoaning the dangers of pneumonia, insists it does not matter if hair goes unwashed for a while longer. She tells Nawal about *Um* George, whose husband gave up life at age fifty-nine and, in mourning for the dead, *Um* George went unwashed—body and hair—for thirty days.

At night, Nawal absorbs her mother's snores, falls asleep and dreams of hair washed in hot water in the privacy of her room. She dreams of Kenneth, transforming hair into "curvy lines," as he did for *Redbook* women. In her dream, Omar—seeing her—smiles warmly, holds out his hand.

Awake, she thinks: Loving someone like Omar can exacerbate the bleeding of the spirit. What joy is there in this secret loving, with hope embedded in dreams? Yet she prays for the healing of Omar's wound, and for survival—even as grandmothers survived a rule that forcibly carried their men to war. Women left behind, hauling water from a far-off spring, trudging across the hills and *wadis* to pick the olives, drying the figs, the grapes, and, with children clinging to their thread-worn *thobes*—weaving the cloth, baking the bread, and taking in other people's wash.

She wonders now: How does a man—his dreams flung to the wind—survive humiliation? How does he learn to do battle with dragons and *afreets*?

Her question tangles with the cadence of her mother's sonorous breathing, dissolves without a trace. She pads around the room, her wet hair turbaned with a towel, thinks: Rocks—even men—shatter when hurled against walls or bounced against cement.

And yet men like *Sayyid* Walid, their Fifis gone, revive as if by rote, their loss never too deep to scar the soul.

Before the soldiers came, he stopped by their house one evening, and with her mother dozing in a chair, he confided to Nawal the realities of his immigrant life in America. He and his Fifi had slaved those early years to make ends meet, to build up a nest egg.

"But with my poor Fifi with the angels, I must go on with my life." He'd reached for her hand and winked, an awkward wink, an irritation in the eye.

"Marry me," he pleaded, "and I'll treat you like a queen."

But as he cupped his hand over Nawal's, the strand of hair draped artfully across his scalp fell across his ear. Startled, Nawal slipped her hand away, jumped up, announcing—loud enough to wake her mother up—that coffee must be served.

Marriage is security for life, her mother says, and only when a woman marries will she find her place. "Men," she says, "are all the same under the sheets."

Now fast asleep, her mother is curled up on the narrow bed, her sleep an antidote to pain. For years, her mother's life was an endless waiting for a husband to return from *al-ghurbeh*: the foreign lands that swallowed up the men of Palestine, spit out their dreams.

A letter from Chicago—six or seven years ago—announced her father's fate. An accident, the writer said, and offered condolences. Her father, busy gesturing and talking to a friend, had ignored the "Don't Walk" sign blinking in his face.

Alya knocks on Nawal's door, tells her of Mordacai's unexpected "gift." "I've convinced Omar to eat with us," she adds.

A quick sigh—as if breath held in check would not give Nawal's secret away. Nothing, it seems, left of pride.

Nawal's towel unravels, falls across her shoulders, exposes wet limp hair—since Kenneth's artistry is missing from her life.

"I couldn't stand it anymore." Nawal laughs uneasily. "Washed it in cold water with what was left of the *Nabulsi* soap. Better than nothing at all."

"Pneumonia," her mother gurgles in her sleep, opens one eye. "Didn't I warn you from the start?"

Sergeant Abram

NOT ONLY does Abram dislike the arrogance of the woman Alya, who talks to him of thievery, but he also despises her brother, Omar. He's met his kind before in the streets of Baghdad, has seen the venom in the eyes. He is a Jew, after all, the

Rabbi's refrain from the Baghdad synagogue, "Next year in Jerusalem. Next year in Jerusalem," ringing in his ears.

"If we don't leave for Israel, they'll push us out," his father said over and over again; and so it came to pass.

They left soon after the public hanging of Shafeek Adas, a wealthy Iraqi Jew, convicted in an Iraqi court of buying military equipment from dismantled British bases and secretly transporting it to Israel.

The Iraqi government had labeled him a traitor.

This was a warning to those like Abram's father, the pharmacist, who worked in a pharmacy on Ar-Rachid Street... and whose loyalties had begun to shift. Unlike Abram's grandfather, the peddler, who took the bus every Friday mid-morning from his hovel in the suburbs of Baghdad to Haj Murad *Abu* Taha's house; to sit with his grandson Abram, in the company of Muslims, to talk of life and politics. But mostly to listen.

Abram's earliest humiliation was the memory of those visits—when, in leave-taking, Haj Murad slipped his grandfather a *dinar* or two, his Muslim *sadaka*—charity for the poor. In a clandestine pact between grandfather and his teenage grandson, Abram was sworn to secrecy, preventing him from reporting this to his father, who could have easily set up the old man in style. But, since his grandmother's death, his grandfather lived in a small room above a grocery store—resisting pressure from his son, the pharmacist, to elevate his position in the world.

And now, due to general harassment, and Shafeek Adas's public hanging, Operation "Ali Baba," transporting Iraqi Jews to Israel, by way of Cyprus, would reduce the more than a hundred and twenty thousand Jews living in Iraq to less than six thousand.

It would be *this* year in Jerusalem.

On that particular Friday, his grandfather, with a reluctant Abram in tow, arrives at Haj Murad's house to say goodbye for the last time. He brings with him a photograph, yellowed with age, of himself, a younger man, wearing the long striped *zbune*, with the white *tcharawyeh* wrapped around his head, Iraqi-style. He is seated in an ornate chair, its wooden back carved in the form of swans and inlaid with mother-of-pearl. And at his knee, his young son, Schlomo, father of Abram. The photograph is an embarrassment to Abram, who has argued with his grandfather about giving it away to an Arab.

For it is the memory of his grandfather's precarious friendship with Haj Murad that rankles Abram most. And—if it hadn't been for those Friday visits to Haj Murad's brick home with its lone eucalyptus tree—Abram wouldn't have had to suffer the mocking laughter of Muna, Haj Murad's youngest daughter. Two years older than he, she had managed—with her fluid hips and yellow-green eyes—to entice as well as repel the young Abram, who sat, imprisoned in the company of Muslim men.

But why was it his grandfather rarely offered an opinion? Was he ashamed of his Jewishness, wearing it like a hidden Star of David under his shirt?

When Abram confronts his grandfather with his questions, the old man dismisses them with a grunt and a wave of the hand.

"How can one learn without listening?" he inquires of the skeptical Abram. "In my silence I am invisible in their company and they talk more freely. But when, on occasion, I manage to drop by Haj Murad's house and find him alone, I speak my views, even as he does. We are like blood brothers."

His grandfather does not announce his leaving to the company of men, but keeps it secret till the end. No one mentions the fate of Shafeek Adas. The talk, this time, centers on the good days, before Abram's time, when Sasun Haskail, a Jew, was Iraqi minister of finance. As the men speak of it they nod, look their way. Abram, seated on the stool near his grandfather's chair, wishes he could be whisked away, longs for the company of his own father, who does not harbor his grandfather's sentimental attachment to the Muslim Arabs of Baghdad.

Toward the end of their visit, Haj Murad's daughter, Muna, appears with her ornate brass pot of black coffee and the small lotus cups and *smeed* biscuits, and sets her tray down before Haj Murad on the velvet-covered stool.

After the men are served, she brings her tray around to him, and makes her offering of coffee and biscuits from a blue-flow-ered plate, the level of her glance raised beyond the burning in his eyes.

But despite breakfast missed and hunger pangs, Abram's pride remains intact. He shakes his head and pushes the tray away. An impulse to stick out his foot and trip her on her second round is quickly deflated when one of the men gets up to take his leave.

"I'll see you at the gate of the mosque before noon," he says to Haj Murad.

One by one, as the rest of the visitors take their leave, the old man places his callused hand on Abram's knee and gets up to face his host.

"My son, the pharmacist, no longer feels secure here," he says. "He insists we leave for the Holy Land." A sudden and pe-culiar gap in communication breaks in, an inability to pronounce obvious words.

"...we will leave for Israel," Abram says, defiance in his voice.

Haj Murad shakes his head. "But Iraq has been your home for centuries. Ever since Nebuchadnezzar... or is it *Sayyidna* Ibra-heem, of Ur?" Sighing, Haj Murad holds out his hand. "Just be-cause one traitor was hanged, does not mean...."

No traitor, Abram thinks. But a lover of Israel who has paid with his life.

Haj Murad falls silent, digs into his pocket for his usual gift. But this time his grandfather's hand is faster than *Abu* Murad's, produces the photograph as if it were a colored scarf from a sleeve.

"A picture of my early years when our friendship first began, with my son, Schlomo, even before Nuri Es Sa'id...." Abram's grandfather is suddenly overcome with a spasm of coughing. Clearing his throat, he rubs his hands together as if in supplica-tion. "If it were up to me, I would not leave."

Abram's shame is now complete. His grandfather has abased himself before this Arab and his daughter with the yellow-green eyes.

In the custom of leave-taking between friends, the men touch bristled cheeks, the old to the younger; gray beard and black mesh for an instant.

And now: Abram's turn to shake hands, to touch cheeks the Arab way. Haj Murad bends his head and, smiling, extends his hand to the boy. But despite his grandfather's muddled thinking, Abram will take his stand without compromise. Rancor barely held in check, Abram holds his hand rigid at his side. No hands will touch. No words of farewell will pass his lips.

Thought is suspended for a time as older eyes appraise his judgment. And then, with a sudden, relentless blow, Abram's eyes blink their disbelief, vision blurs.

His grandfather's hand withdraws from Abram's cheek. His old sunken eyes register fury at his shame unleashed.

He hears it then, ringing in his ears, hears Muna's jeering laughter, taunting him, hears it as he tears down the path, past the eucalyptus tree and the children at play.

Abram hears it even now when he suffers the haughty glance of the woman Alya as she passes him in the *liwan*.

He has orders from Mordacai to remain outside the dining room and not to interfere as the Arabs gather for their meal.

Yet, with Mordacai gone for now, they will know that he, Abram, is in charge.

Mordacai has become soft in the head, Abram speculates. He has given in, allowed the Arabs to parade downstairs—as if Israel's war of survival was a mirage.

But it would never be the same—especially now, with *Kotel HaMa'aravi* in Jewish hands. Yet for nineteen years, the Kingdom of Jordan forbade Jews access to the sacred Wall. Waiting, an endless wait—before Jews would be allowed to say their prayers and shed their tears and mourn the destruction of Solomon's Temple by ancient Rome. The retaining Wall rebuilt, they say, by Herod, and later by a Sir Moses Montefiore... whoever he was.

The bulldozing of Arab homes and shops in *Harat el Mughar-beh*, next to the Wall, was necessary to create an open plaza for

Jewish worshippers. So what if their hovels were destroyed? Palestinians could easily be relocated to Arab countries. Welcomed even in Iraq. Abram is not moved by stories of Arab loss or tragedy. Refusing all these years to make peace with Israel, Arab governments must now shoulder the blame.

The old man with the ludicrous eye patch they call 'Ammi Musa, who looked me in the eye as if I were personally responsible for the bulldozing of his hovel near the Wall. Odd that I would think of my grandfather's death in 1956, the year of our invasion of Sinai. If it hadn't been for blackmail from Eisenhower, we would have taught the Egyptians and the other Arabs a lesson in manners.

Now my chance has come to make men like Omar understand who makes the rules. His face still bears the imprint of my fist. My personal autograph....

Gone is that fearful lad crouched on a stool near his grandfather in Haj Murad's house. Replaced now by the man who fears no one—his character molded during the Tel Aviv demonstration of 1951 against race discrimination. We, the Sephardim, will not allow the Ashkenazim like Captain Mordacai to lord it over us. Not even with the promise that soon the Temple will be restored on Mount Moriah.

Someday, when we are the majority in Israel, we will make policy. Others will merely follow our lead.

The Arabs in Judea and Samaria must learn to do what we tell them—without causing trouble. Or else get out. Perhaps an "Operation Ali Baba" in reverse? Better they pack their bags and move beyond the Jordan and Litani rivers to join those other Arabs.

The painting of the Bedouin woman above the first landing of the stairway reminds Abram in a strange way of his grandmother, Rebecca. Something about the eyes and the line of the mouth soon after a rambling lecture on Gehenna.

"Keep an eye out for your grandfather," she said the day before she died. "He can't see as well as he did once, becomes forgetful, is impatient. Even loses his way sometimes. And Baghdad is such a big city...."

Even before my grandmother's death in Baghdad, my grandfather paid his visits to Haj Murad, taking me along. He would tell her he might drop by the *kahweh* sidewalk café, to sit with his friends and play backgammon.

"But which *kahweh* is open on a Friday?" she asked.

"A Christian Assyrian runs this one," he said and winked at me, his partner in deception.

"Can't even write a letter to my friends in Baghdad," he complained to me when we first moved to Israel. He died a few months later—soon after our march in Tel Aviv.

My Iraqi grandmother's face looks down at me from the Bedouin woman's face above the stair landing. "Why is it you left him alone for two whole days?" I hear her chide.

And why involve yourself with demonstrations and such things?

Why not? Israel is a Jewish democracy after all, and we Jews must have our rights.

———————————

David O'Connor

WITH THE BLUE Israeli flag and its Star of David fluttering on the antenna of the old Chevy, David O'Connor drives slowly up the hill toward the Hotel Semiramis. Except for soldiers in jeeps or tanks standing guard at major intersections, no sign of life appears in this town under curfew. Flattened cars crushed by Israeli super-tanks hug curbs, rubbish swirls in the street. The stench from the bloated carcasses of cats and dogs assaults his senses. And as he drives by, he averts his eyes, tries to stifle breath. Life will get back to normal soon enough—but with new rules, and new hope for Israel.

For now, he will try to ignore the inconvenience, the lack of ambience in Beit Nuba, glad, for now, that he lives in Tel Aviv instead.

As he parks his car, a soldier ambles up to his window, asks for identification.

He looks briefly at the I.D. card. "Ah. The Institute," he says, and smiles amiably.

"I need to see your Captain Mordacai."

"He's gone for the moment. But in his absence, Sergeant Abram is in charge."

David O'Connor knows Mordacai, a decent man, a bit too intellectual for his own good. Analysis of motives and results in time of war can be a dangerous thing, he knows, which could lead to hesitation. To soft-hearted decisions.

Yet, he's glad Mordacai is not here to pass judgment on his own motives and decisions. "Your Sergeant will do for now," David O'Connor says.

Someone is playing a polonaise—Chopin, or is it Mozart?—the sound emanating from the courtyard. A clutch of soldiers stand around the piano player, savoring victory.

"Things seem to be going well?" he asks the soldier at his side.

The soldier's thin face expands into a smile. "Good enough."

If he were a poet, he would compose a poem celebrating victory. But he is a practical man who has no talent for writing poetry, little time for reading it. Yet years before, in his Los Angeles school, their teacher, Mrs. Spratt, had read his class a victory poem translated from some Greek poet. But he can't remember who.

Arab writers, he thinks now, will have to learn to write elaborate poems explaining defeat.

The cactus plant near the vestibule, now stripped of its blooms, looks a bit unkempt. As he opens the glass doors, *Um* Ramzi's three-legged cat scurries into the lobby. In an odd way, this is a kind of "homecoming" to a place where—as a paying guest—he watched and listened, preparing for this moment.

He waits, his eyes adjusting to shadows, to black streaks on the tile floor, to boisterous soldiers milling around the desk where Nawal once sat in demure austerity, keeping records, keeping track of hotel guests, reading her magazine.

"I'm Sergeant Abram. I understand you're from the Institute?"

David O'Connor looks into the small, round eyes of a stocky man about his height. He nods. "My identification will confirm it."

Sergeant Abram returns the card. "So... what can we do to help?"

"I need to talk to one of your Arabs here. Omar Habeeb... who managed the hotel before our victory in the war."

Light flickers in the recesses of Sergeant Abram's eyes. "If you prefer, I'll bring him down to you."

"Better I go where he is—for privacy."

"He's in his room on the second floor... under lock and key. A troublemaker," Sergeant Abram adds between his teeth.

"When we get to his room, I must go in alone. Please wait outside his door." He hesitates. "A small precaution."

"He may be volatile... but I've taught him a thing or two...."

David O'Connor nods. "I'm afraid he still has much more to learn."

As they begin to climb the stairs, Alya Habeeb suddenly appears at the top of the landing. She walks slowly down, as if in a hypnotic trance, pauses at the middle landing, and glances quickly back at the painting on the wall, as if to verify its existence. Turning, she stares, unblinking, at O'Connor as if to decipher the puzzle of his presence here. Her stark face and her hair, pulled back from her face, give her a look of austerity. In the past, he's admired her feisty spirit, fears it now.

She says, "So... you've come back to pay us a visit—despite the curfew?"

"Special privileges." His glance shifts from her face, lands on the servant tag pinned to her blouse, lingers there for a moment's respite.

"Special privileges?"

"I'm here to see your brother," he says formally. "To clarify a business matter."

An intake of breath. "So... you've been a spy all along?"

"Mossad." He makes an elaborate bow. "At your service."

Her eyes are coldly appraising. "And you're here to harass my brother, to add insult to captivity?"

"This is between Omar and myself." He shrugs. "Unless, of course...."

"Yes?"

"Never mind." He would not want to complicate matters. Not yet at least. It was Omar he was sure of. "Sergeant Abram and I don't want to keep you."

Despite the gesture to let her go, questions crowd his mind. How much did Alya Habeeb know of the plot to store weapons on the premises? What role did she play the night Mustapha and the boy drove the truck loaded with arms and ammunition to distribute among the villagers?

Alya says, mockery in her voice, "I could warn Omar of wolves who masquerade as guests. But he may not believe me— unless he sees for himself."

"Then we should give him that chance."

With Abram closely following, David O'Connor leaves her behind, crosses the familiar hallway past the door of his former room, and makes his way through the small sitting room to Omar's door.

"You know the way," Abram says admiringly.

"It's my job to know many things."

Abram scowls. "Up till now, Captain Mordacai allowed Omar the privilege of locking himself in with an inside bolt... although we had the outer key. But after the captain left this morning, I took it upon myself, for the sake of security, to dismantle it."

"Mordacai must be a generous man," David O'Connor observes dryly.

Abram turns the key, flings open Omar's door, then moves furtively out of sight. David O'Connor scans the darkened room; his eyes settle on the figure across the bed, head propped up against the pillows.

Omar looks up warily. "You," he says, his voice barely audible.

"Yes, me."

"What is it you want?"

Without answering, David O'Connor moves toward the balcony door, pulls open the shutters, and stands for a long moment staring out through the glass, beyond the lemon tree into the courtyard below. Where dancers once tangoed or waltzed to Hagas's band, soldiers now mill around a piano that he recalled once stood in a corner of the Semiramis dining room.

He turns around. "I have news that will interest you. I also have questions to ask."

Omar's face is a mask. "Very little interests me these days."

David O'Connor fingers the ring in his pocket as if to confirm knowledge. "I knew about the shed. I know about you... and Mustapha."

Omar sits up in his bed, drops his feet on the rug. His ghost-eyes fasten themselves on David O'Connor's face. "Tell me the news then...."

"Your friend Mustapha was killed by one of our collaborators... just north of Es Samu. But the young man with him got away." He takes the ring from his shirt pocket, offers it to Omar for inspection. "See for yourself."

His eyes narrowed, Omar studies the initials inside the ring, sets it down on the night-table near his bed. He looks up, his glance sticky resin on David O'Connor's face. "Instead of a businessman from Los Angeles, you've been, all along, a bloody spy? Mossad, I presume?"

"Good guess."

"*Ibn sharmouta!* Son of a...."

"Name-calling is the sign of a juvenile mind."

"Murderer...."

David O'Connor shrugs. "I take it you used the shed to store guns and ammunition to distribute for Fatah?"

Without warning, Omar sprints toward the glass door, pulls it open, and quickly steps onto the balcony, just as voices from the courtyard singing "Hava Nashira" invade the room. He stares, wild-eyed, at them, leans back against the railing, near a branch of the lemon tree.

A woman's shadow and the outline of her dress appear in the doorway. "Careful!" Alya's voice, aimed at her brother, is a plea. She eases herself past Sergeant Abram and David O'Connor, moves deliberately, her arms in a pantomime of an embrace, toward the balcony.

Singing ends abruptly, and in its place a sprightly piano piece. "They've murdered Mustapha in cold blood near Es Samu...," Omar calls out to his sister above the sound of music.

Turning, Alya makes a sudden move toward O'Connor, as if to strike. He grasps her wrist, tightens his grip until he knows he's made his point.

"Mossad...." She laughs a caustic laugh. "A special breed...."

David O'Connor scrutinizes her face. "You knew, didn't you? Why else would you give up your beauty sleep to keep watch at the hotel desk in the middle of the night?"

She shrugs. "Surely, the Great Infiltrator knows everything?"

As he eases his grip, she wrenches her arm free. Once, he had watched her dance alone in the courtyard, spinning like a dervish, in a kind of trance—until Omar appeared suddenly and dragged her away. Cinderella was forced back among the cinders.

Like now.

David O'Connor looks back at Omar. "Why not admit it?" he says, straining toward patience. "Both you and Mustapha worked for Fatah, a terrorist organization."

"*Your* Irgun was a terrorist organization," Omar calls out, his voice harsh with emotion. "Your Stern... even your Haganah that blew up our house in Katamon! *My* cause is Palestine... and liberty!"

The piano player now launches into a mazurka by Chopin. Someone in the courtyard roars with laughter. *Um* Ramzi's cat wanders into the room, sidles up to Alya, who pauses to pick her up; holding her loosely in her arms, she begins to stroke her fur.

David O'Connor rivets his eyes back to Omar—focuses slowly on the shotgun pointed at him.

"For *your* sake, I'd advise you to put the gun down," he says quietly.

Alya moves deliberately toward her brother. "If you don't, it will only give them an excuse to...."

A roar of gunfire, a small explosion of glass. With a yelp, the cat leaps from Alya's arms, scurries under the bed. A C minor note hangs suspended in mid-air.

Omar lies sprawled on the balcony floor, his bloodied face distorted for all the world to see. David O'Connor has barely managed to push Alya out of range of Abram's Uzi.

Loud soldiers' voices from below call out their questions.

Now on the balcony, Abram skirts the body, calls back in Hebrew, "Don't worry. Things are under control here."

In those other locked rooms, people bang on doors, call out their own unanswered questions. Children begin to scream; their irritating cries block out thinking.

"It was an old shotgun of my father's," Alya says softly. "I doubt if it even worked...."

David O'Connor's gaze settles briefly on the scene before him. Abram's Uzi obviously did not give second chances. "Stay away," he warns as he makes his way to the balcony, squats near the body.

Death—and martyrdom—were instantaneous. For Fatah, he knew, being a *fedayee* was the highest calling. He'd read it in their literature, discussed it with the collaborators. It makes our task easier, O'Connor thinks now as he pries the shotgun from his fingers, snaps open the cartridge chambers.

Empty.

The cat emerges cautiously from beneath the bed, scurries over shards of glass toward the balcony.

David O'Connor stands up. "We couldn't take any chances, now, could we?" He turns toward Alya Habeeb, but she has vanished into thin air. Before he has a chance to send Abram after her, she reappears in the doorway, with her mother, *Um* Ramzi, a black specter at her side.

The old woman lurches headlong toward the balcony, her wails rending the air.

Grasping her shoulder, David O'Connor tries to untangle her arms and hands, now welded to the body at her feet. But her bloodied hands claw at his chest as he holds her up, lest she give way and fall.

Moving swiftly to her side, Alya encircles her mother's waist and guides her firmly to a corner of the room. This time, David O'Connor decides, the sound of the old woman's grief is more deadly even than Abram's gunfire.

"Keep her in your sight," he commands Abram.

He hears the ripping of cloth and looks back, startled, as *Um* Ramzi, tugging at her bodice, has begun to rend her dress in two.

Alya says, her voice barely audible, "She had to know—to see for herself. He was, after all, her one remaining son."

Ignoring O'Connor's restraining hand, Alya pulls the damask cover from Omar's bed; it trails after her as she makes her way toward the balcony. Kneeling, she drapes the cover over the shattered body, cradles her brother's head in her lap, and rocking back and forth, begins to hum an odd little tune without melody.

"It couldn't be helped," David O'Connor says in apology to Alya. To the world.

"Obviously, it was self-defense," Sergeant Abram says reassuringly. "This is what we'll tell Captain Mordacai when he asks."

Clara

ON JUNE 8, 1967, Clara Appleby sat down to write a letter. *"Dear Alya...,"* she began and struggled for a long time over the words. *"Are you all right?"* she wrote, having read headlines about the war. *"Please give my regards...."*

But Clara knew Omar would not accept regards secondhand.

She crumpled the paper and began anew. *"Dear Omar,"* she wrote, *"I hope you've forgiven me for leaving suddenly the way I did. But try to understand... we had no other choice. I hope life gets back to normal for you real soon. Give my regards to Alya and your mother, and write when you have time...."*

Two weeks later, Clara's letter was returned—undeliverable. For in the space of six days, Beit Nuba had changed hands.

And destiny.

O, Allah, create us as a new nation without wounds, ancient agony and tears.

Abdul Rahim Omar, Palestinian poet

Peace demands the most heroic labor and the most difficult sacrifice. It demands greater heroism than war....

Thomas Merton, Catholic theologian

Then justice will dwell in the wilderness,
and righteousness abide in the fruitful field.
And the effect of righteousness will be peace,
and the result of righteousness, quietness and
    trust forever.

Isaiah 32: 16–17

CHAPTER SIXTEEN

Um Ramzi

HAGAS IS AT IT again, playing his mandolin. He plays for the caged chickens in the Semiramis courtyard, a little more loudly this morning, as if the music will liberate them and give them room to dance.

Yesterday, as *Um* Ramzi and Hagas sipped their tea on the veranda and watched Badri crouched near the petunia bed flicking marbles in the dirt, she told Hagas what she had heard—that after seventeen months in prison, her daughter, Alya, was being set free.

At the news, Hagas's glance lifted and he began to speak wistfully of his own lost daughter in England—as if she too would be returning home to stay. *Um* Ramzi listened to the prattle of his words as he asked once more about Omar. And when she told him for the hundredth time what he already knew, his head jerked and the gray tint of his eyes clouded over. But two or three days later, unconvinced, he would ask again.

Hagas, it seems, is forever waiting for events to happen, for people to return.

Her son, Omar, had forgiven Hagas his quirks—as if a secret alliance had been forged between them. But how could she ever forgive Hagas the many evenings her husband stayed away from home? Or the music Hagas and his motley band had played at the Semiramis courtyard late into the night—assaulting her nerves, keeping her from sleep?

But it was Omar who had initiated the open-air summer dancing at the Semiramis, and the shameful display of men and women gyrating to the decadent music of Europe and America.

And Alya, her rebel daughter—exposed to heaven knows what during her years in Beirut—had probably egged her brother on.

Alya stood before *Um* Ramzi, eyes flashing, and asked, "Why not give the people of Beit Nuba a little music, a little dancing, to ease the burden of their lives?"

Omar pleaded his case for the added income, appealing to logic, to his mother's common sense. Besides, *Um* Ramzi's own brother's widow in Brazil had approved the music for the courtyard, to help pay Omar's uncle's debts.

Omar, *Um* Ramzi was convinced, gave the people of Beit Nuba the Western music and served them the liquor to soften their brains, to keep them from thinking.

Despite arthritis in her elbow and a limp from a broken kneecap improperly set, *Um* Ramzi moves about the kitchen— not agile as she once was, but deliberate, economical—scooping up goat cheese from its brine, filling small bowls with olives and *za'atar*, ladling marbles of creamed yogurt in olive oil… without wasting steps. She fills the steel pot with water and sets it on the Primus stove to boil.

The sound of the mandolin drifting through her kitchen window no longer irritates her since it has become integrated into her days. But sometimes, when a sprightly tune eases itself into melancholia, it disrupts the passage of her thoughts and brings her closer to the phantoms of her life. She should be grateful, of course, that the soldiers leave her alone—an old woman minding her own business. The soldiers, instead, harass the young ones: students who shout slogans, burn tires in the streets or throw stones—all who dare challenge their authority. Alya refused to learn this from the start—although *Um* Ramzi warned her often enough about becoming involved with the antics of unruly schoolgirls.

Squatting, *Um* Ramzi pulls out from the lowest shelf of the cupboard the brass tray, and with her palm flat against the cement floor, she propels herself upward. Standing up a bit shakily, she sets the tray on the counter.

Words crowd into her head, snatches of the old songs, but the sounds she makes now, deep in her throat, are hoarse echoes of diluted memories. Like thieves, the melodies of her youth infiltrate her mind, words sung during the harvesting of figs and olives in the *wadis*—the valleys on the outskirts of Beit Nuba. The women—mother, grandmother, sister, aunts—sang them with a fervor that reverberated throughout the hills, urged them on in their work.

"I want to climb to the top of the highest mountain," (she sang)

"To greet the fresh sweet air of my country.
Dear God, if you fill the *wadi* with a downpour of rain,
I'll make my hands a bridge
And help you cross over to my side."

As a girl, *Um* Ramzi memorized the old songs, becoming at sixteen, almost as good as the older women, crooning their words as they spread out the figs or grapes on the flat roofs of the rough-hewn stone towers to dry in the sun.

They also sang of brides and bridegrooms, inserting her name slyly, causing her to blush, teasing her—a grown girl, old enough to marry.

Yet no one sang, or trilled the joyful *zaghareet* sounds at *her* wedding a year later, when she broke the Christian traditions of her people and married the Muslim, Ali Habeeb, and went to Katamon, Jerusalem, to live.

A few months later, when she felt the stirrings of new life beneath her ribs, she walked around the house singing to herself the old wedding songs in belated celebration. And with the birth of their son, Ramzi, the shadow of their marriage lifted for a time. Even her mother, defying her father's orders, came secretly to see her grandchild, Ramzi, in Jerusalem.

From then on they called her *Um* Ramzi—the mother of Ramzi—with his fine brow, hair the color of ripe wheat, and a smile to melt his mother's heart. To ward off envy and the evil eye, she hung a special blue-glass bead above his crib. And as she nursed him at her breast, she sang to him the old nostalgic songs.

Thinking of it now, *Um* Ramzi's hand trembles as she picks up the boiling pot and pours water onto black tea leaves in a pewter teapot. She reaches overhead for the china cups with grapevines painted on the side. Only three sets of cups and saucers are left from the original set of eight Alya brought home with her from Beirut. One dropped from Alya's hand when a lovesick suitor fell on one knee, proclaiming his undying love. And at Alya's rejection, vowing by his mother's head to remain a bachelor for life.

Yet two months later, apparently recovered, he sent Alya an engraved invitation to his wedding.

Alya's stubborn refusal to marry had brought *Um* Ramzi grief, but nothing to compare to that earlier anguish—the loss of Ramzi before his third birthday.

Soon after the death of her firstborn Ramzi—and despite Omar and Alya's births—a fog settled in the empty spaces of her heart, erasing the residue of old melodies, leaving behind bitter coffee grounds at the bottom of her cup.

She hears Hagas's fevered voice above the mandolin, his high notes creaking. Omar's dog begins to bark, and chickens squawk in apparent accompaniment. Hagas, hungry for his breakfast and impatient with the waiting, is probably playing his usual games with the chickens.

Um Ramzi tries to concentrate on slicing round thick bread into even wedges and unsealing a jar of marmalade. She tries not to think of chickens now in wire cages in a courtyard cubicle, where once men and women sat and drank *arak* liquor or sipped their mint tea, and listened to the strains of Hagas's mandolin late into the night.

A few hours before the soldiers filled the streets of Beit Nuba and occupied the Semiramis, Hagas brought the chickens to the hotel, the dead ones in a bloodied sack, the live ones, their legs tied with twine, dangling from his hand. *Um* Ramzi, watching from an upstairs window, heard the frantic call, saw her son Omar embrace Hagas holding dead and live chickens. Hagas, his voice hoarse with tears, told Omar of the small dog, sprawled in the dirt, killed by the residue of bombs. His café was half-demolished, he said. And Hosni, who worked at the post office, transformed into a mass of bloodied flesh, was carried in a burlap bag through the main street of Beit Nuba, with children, wide-eyed, following behind in silent procession.

Afterwards, Hagas and Omar went back to what was left of the café to rescue what they could. They brought back the mandolin, a portrait of Hagas's daughter at eight or nine, charred bedding, clothes, a pair of Sunday shoes. Omar gave Hagas the English newsman's abandoned room where poor Julia had earlier spent one night. The Englishman had left to write his war stories—even *before* the war disrupted their lives. A spy, nothing less, *Um* Ramzi thinks even now. Good riddance.

When the soldiers first occupied the Hotel Semiramis, no one was allowed to go downstairs. That first night, the soldiers made a bonfire in the middle of the dance floor; they sang their noisy songs and stomped the night into oblivion. Worse, even, than Hagas's band.

Um Ramzi arranges dishes of olives and *labaneh*, wedges of bread and marmalade, and the pot of tea and cups in an ellipse on the tray. She makes her way through the kitchen door to the outside stoop, pausing to savor the crisp damp air of a spring morning; she inhales its fragrance, fills her lungs with it.

Beyond the pines, the barbed-wire fence and the suburbs of Beit Nuba, lie the invisible valleys of her youth; their mist like cotton candy, soon to be swallowed up by the sun.

She squints against the dazzle of rays splintered against the trunks of pines, turns the corner and makes her way along the edge of the veranda. She walks with a halting gait—this woman in perpetual mourning for the dead—looks down to ensure her footing, careful not to step on larger pebbles, taking mental note of weeds between cracks in the flagstone path. Before his disappearance in the middle of the night, Mustapha took care of the weeds among other things, but now his eldest son works as a stonecutter instead—building *their* settlements—since it pays him more than she could ever afford.

She pauses near the water fountain to catch her breath, before making her way toward the cacophony of sound in the courtyard. Near the bougainvillea vine, she squints her old woman's eyes to bring them into focus, holds her breath at the sight of the frenzy of the lone chicken held captive by a piece of twine around one leg. Omar's dog, balanced on its haunches, barks intermittently, as the chicken dances its mad, drunken dance on the periphery of the dance floor.

As she approaches, Hagas looks up, but his sausage fingers continue to pluck at the strings of the mandolin in a flat and defiant melody, to keep her at bay.

Um Ramzi calls out above the sound of mandolin, of barking dog and squawking chicken, "Put that chicken back where it belongs. With all the rest...."

Hagas stops his strumming, drops his hand across his knee and gives *Um* Ramzi a melancholy smile.

"You should have seen her then, your Alya... whirling like a dervish across the dance floor, her hair aflame under the lights, her shawl trailing behind her. A vision, she was. Until Omar came and snatched her away...." His words tangle, dissipate.

The dog unfolds himself, moves toward *Um* Ramzi and the tray. With the hard toe of her shoe, she pushes against the dog's shins, stops him in his tracks. He growls softly, his mouth open.

"For God's sake, put that poor bird away and let's have some breakfast. Your tea is getting cold."

Hagas props up his mandolin against the curve of the stucco wall, gets up from his stool and moves stealthily toward the chicken. Squatting near the ledge, he tugs at the string, pulls the chicken toward him, scooping her up in his arms as if she were a child.

His hand caresses the feathered back as he says, a gruffness in his voice, "She's one of the old ones, past her prime, no longer laying eggs." He turns abruptly toward the cages.

Um Ramzi sets the tray down on a round wooden table in the next enclave, where moss has begun to grow on plaster walls.

"And how did you like my music this morning?" he asks as he takes a seat across from her and begins to coil the twine near the table's edge.

Um Ramzi shrugs, reaches for a teacup. "I don't understand your kind of music. You ought to know that by now."

Hagas takes the teacup from her hand and sips noisily. He looks up from a grizzled face, a glint of a smile in his eyes.

"So. You tell me Alya will be finally coming home. Like the old days. She and my Sylvia both. And Omar. Will he also return?"

Omar—safe at last with her little Ramzi. Death is a miracle, *Um* Ramzi decides, a coiled circle, like Hagas's twine.

Sighing, *Um* Ramzi shakes her head. She dips her bread into the oil and *za'atar*, chews meditatively, says nothing for a while.

Badri

YESTERDAY, his friends from the government school helped Badri make the paper kite, its green and black colors separated by a molten white, its dragon tail a brilliant red. "Fly it tomorrow at dawn," they said, "high up above the clouds... when the soldiers are still asleep."

Badri, his round freckled face now poised toward the sky,

could not hear their words, but understood their message from the motions of their hands and from a sketch of a stick-boy flying a kite, a sliver of a sun trapped between triangles, a bird hovering.

The older boy with brown kinky hair was Badri's friend, even before the war. He would sometimes come after school to play marble games or *takka wigri*, his stick-baseball game, or kick the soccer ball around.

A few weeks after the soldiers with their jeeps and monster-tanks occupied Beit Nuba—and soon after the curfew lifted—Badri and his friend climbed the fig tree in Badri's yard. They threw marbles at cans across the street, and stones at passing jeeps.

It was Badri, the marksman, who aimed and hit the soldier in the arm and made it bleed.

The jeep screeched backward in its tracks; three soldiers jumped out. While Badri's friend ran like the wind, one soldier scurried up the fig tree, caught Badri by the ankle and dragged him to the ground. Clubs hammered at head, shoulders, arms, as Badri lay curled inward like a worm. They tied his wrists behind his back and threw him in the jeep, head dangling. Before they drove away, he caught a glimpse of his mother's reddened eyes, her mouth wide open, her arms waving in the air.

Days later, when the soldiers finally let him go, it was the middle of the night.

The bruises on Badri's face and arms, the broken wrist, would finally heal, but not before the soldiers returned with tapes and meter-sticks to measure and re-measure walls and corners in their house. A soldier, his hand cradling his Uzi, squatted across from Badri, his face creasing into a smile. The soldier's face, with its pockmarks of lentils, was an older version of Badri's own.

Badri tugs at the string as the kite's bright tail snakes high above the Hotel Semiramis rooftop, high above the pines. The marbles in Badri's pocket roll and clink against one another whenever he moves his arm, but he cannot hear their sound.

He never heard *Um* Ramzi's wailing, saw only the tearing of her dress in grief. Even now he can't hear his mother's voice or Hagas's mandolin.

He never heard the blast that dismantled their house but, wide-eyed, saw stones and dense smoke erupt, and glass splinter, and felt the rumble beneath his feet—as if the belly of the earth had opened up and swallowed roof, beds, and pictures on the wall.

Badri, the ex-terrorist, now flies his kite on the rubble of the house his grandfather built. He is oblivious of the *hud-hud* bird now stepping cautiously between charred stones, the striped crest on its cinnamon head slightly askew. As his kite sails over trees, even birds, Badri feels himself lifted high atop wispy clouds, soars above the ceiling of the sky. Turned loose from string, he drifts over red-tiled roofs and the coiled streets of Beit Nuba, above hills and the vast blue waters of the Mediterranean where fishes hide.

Alya

IN ALYA'S DREAM, Badri's house does not splinter with the blast but unravels, like a rose, until petals fall, are blown away. Smoke does not sting her eyes or penetrate her lungs but soars, like Badri's kite, high above Beit Nuba.

She opens her eyes furtively, anchors an elbow to the floor, scans the empty corners of her cell. Only yesterday—or was it a week, a month ago?—other friends lived in this tiny room, shared the space of her sleeping, breathed in the same foul air. Women who kept the thought of children, husband, mother, like amulets on a chain around their necks. Women, like her, accused of 'disturbing public order,' of 'conspiracy,' and a dozen other real or invented crimes.

Alya's laughter spurts inside her lungs in spasms, lifts above the scum and urine odors, startles the gecko in his trek. They've vanished, the women who were her friends, dispersed to other corners, other cells. They've left her here with this expanded space to give her room to dance.

Alya's limbs flex, realign themselves. She stands up shakily, pushes her toes against the floor as if they were a broom; her arms embrace her cell, embrace herself in this, her prison dance.

She spins around the floor, a phantom in disguise. Tra la la! she sings, her voice a croak, tra la la! and sees faces, like moths, swirling inside her head.

Where is he now, her once-beloved? He with the amber eyes and the voice to break a woman's heart?

Bump, bump, flesh scrapes against stable walls, arms flailing. Why does Omar hold her back, his hand cupped against her mouth? Her brother, Omar, with the blazing, hollowed eyes, asleep upon the floor. Nothing would wake him up this time, no sound could disturb his sleep. O brother! she sings, and twirls around the room. Let me show you how to dance....

She leans against the wall to catch her breath, to slow the beating of her heart. And in the doorway, *Um* Ramzi weeps for a daughter gone astray; *Um* Ramzi with her cold white face, carrying her grief as if it were her son Ramzi, barely three.

Weeks ago, *Um* Ramzi dragged herself here on the bus, gave Alya a knitted yellow sweater as a birthday gift, brought Sari's note.

"These days," *Um* Ramzi said, "my life can easily crumble, turn to dust...."

She wept the waters of the Jordan River into the grooves of her face and neck, into her shriveled breast, confiding, "When your brother, Omar, was born, so soon after my little Ramzi's death, my milk turned sour, soon dried up...."

Six years later, Alya, the newborn rebel, refused her mother's breast oozing with fulsome milk, lived on thin custard gruel, and somehow managed to survive.

Hair flying, Alya whirls in the stench, recreates the blast of Badri's house. Pale slivers of light mark the territory of herself, the swollen arm, now healing. Her thoughts are suctioned to the ceiling like her gecko-friend, watching with bugged eyes.

We're prisoners, you and I (she sings in the near-dark); until one of us is let loose in the sunlight. Or dies.

Her hands fumble for Sari's note wedged between her breasts, the censored note her guards have already read.

Where is my one true friend? she sings, the one who kissed me in his rooftop home? Where is my dear sweet Sari now?

"Surely, friendship has room for love?" Sari told her once— as if he knew the longing of her bones for flesh. But his sister, Julia, came tapping on his windowpane to disrupt his life once more, to rend his heart.

Sisters, brothers, link arms, move nimble feet, and whirl like dervishes in a trance. Round and round in this crooked space, her legs like tender stalks in blustery winds.

Tra la la! Alya sings, melody gone astray.

Footsteps pause at her cell's door, iron key turns. Her other friend is here with curled eyebrows and a spider scar just below his ear. He brings her food, stale bread and *hummus* and black tea, lukewarm today. I'd like it hot, she said at first, with emphasis. And when he brought it back, he spilled it, steaming, at her feet, blistering her toes. What did she think he was, her genie-slave? And although she learned not to ask again, the tea transformed at times to almost hot, spilled only when her own fingers held the cup.

These days she asks for nothing from the guardian of her life save scraps of paper on which she scribbles thoughts and memories. And which he always reads.

"A teacher, eh?" he said when he first discovered it, then laughed. "You're *my* student now. And I'll teach *you* a thing or two about obedience."

She tries to picture her guard with curly brows and innocent eyes, before the fall.

"I heard your singing," her guard says now. "What do you celebrate?"

"A birthday... come and gone."

He eyes her skeptically. "Celebrate when they let you out." He winks. "When they let us *both* out of this infernal hole...."

"Yes," she says and thinks of Freedom, smiling, holding out her hand.

Her rebel teenage students, tired of wars and revolutions confined to history books, streamed out of her class, and spilled out into the street.

"Freedom!" they chanted, hands linked like prayer beads on a string. For what else did she teach in history class?

Her warning came too late. "They'll blast you with their power hoses and mark you with their dyes; they'll arrest your student leaders...."

They paid her little mind. "Didn't you say Liberty was our natural right? We've also read it in our books. Rousseau, Voltaire, Locke, and all the rest."

She followed them out into the street—made brazen by their chants. And when the soldiers finally stormed into their midst, she did not flinch or turn away from blows meant to teach lessons in subservience. Only later, in her prison cell, would little Nahida's bloody face haunt her waking hours.

Freedom, Alya sings now in her stinky cell, and claps her hands and tosses her oily mane around. Liberty, tra la! she sings, and points a toe. I'm free to dance and make a fool of myself.

Glossary

abaya, a loose-fitting full-length robe, a traditional garment worn by Muslim men and women

Abu, Father, or "the father of"

Addifaa, an Arabic newspaper published in Jordan, translates as "Resistance"

afreet, a supernatural creature, a demon, or a little devil

agal, a cord fastened around the head to hold a *hatta* or *kaffiyeh* in place

Ahlan wa sahlan, Welcome, you are among friends

akroot, a devil (not complimentary!)

Al-Ahram, a well-known Egyptian newspaper, translates as "The Pyramids"

ala kaifak, as you like it

Al-Assifa, Fatah's *nom de guerre*, translates as "The Storm"

al-ghurbeh, being away from your homeland or country

'Allah-u-Akbar, God is great

al-majnuna, the crazy woman

Al mulk lillah, All property belongs to God

'Ammi, Uncle

arak, a highly alcoholic anise-flavored drink

arkeelah, a hookah, water pipe, hubbly-bubbly

askadinya, a loquat

assifa, a storm

Aw'-a!, Get out of the way! (colloquial)

Baath, a political party

baba ghannug, an eggplant dip

Bab el-Amud, Damascus Gate (in the Old City of Jerusalem)

baklava, a Middle Eastern sweet pastry made with nuts and honey

banat, girls

Bedu, Bedouin, nomadic desert dwellers

bint sharmouta, the daughter of a prostitute

bulbul, a songbird, a warbler

calipha, a caliph, a spiritual leader of Islam

dabkeh, a Middle Eastern folk dance with a rhythmic stamping of the feet

dinar, a unit of currency (banknotes)

djinn, a genie

falafil, deep-fried balls made from ground chickpeas or fava beans

fedayee (plural *fedayeen*), one who sacrifices his life for a cause

fil-mishmish, in the apricot season (meaning almost never)

foolyeh, a fava bean dish

fustuk, peanuts

habla, not too bright

halazoneh, a climbing plant with a pretty flower

hale, the seeds of a bean, used to flavor coffee

Haram, an Islamic holy site of very high sanctity

Hassaneh lil-lah, The good you do is God's

hatta, a scarf wrapped around the head, part of a traditional head-dress

Hayyou 'ala-assalaah, Wake up so that you can pray

Higra, immigration

hud-hud, a hoopoe, a black-tipped crested bird

hummus, a dip of pureed chickpeas

ibn sharmouta, the son of a prostitute

ins, human

insha'Allah, God willing

kaffiyeh, a traditional Arab head-dress made from a square scarf

kafreh, an infidel

kahweh, coffee

ka'ik, bread made with sesame seeds

kanoon, a charcoal brazier

karmeed, a roof tile

karut (plural *kawareet*), an orphan

katsa, a field intelligence officer of Mossad (Hebrew acronym)

khuluk, a perfume made from saffron and attar of roses

khush-khash, bitter oranges

kibbeh, a patty made of bulgur, onion, and chopped meat

knafeh, a Middle Eastern dessert that is made of very fine pastry and contains cheese

kohl, a preparation used to darken the edges of the eyelids to outline the eyes

Kotel HaMa'aravi, the Wailing Wall or Western Wall (Hebrew)

Kufic, a calligraphic form of Arabic script

kumbaz, a long garment with stripes, a man's robe

kusa, a squash

labaneh, strained yogurt (like cream cheese)

La samah Allah, May God forbid

liwan, a hallway or room inside a house

malfoof, stuffed cabbage rolls

maramiyyeh, sage

Masjid Al-Aqsa, Al-Aqsa Mosque (in the Old City of Jerusalem)

mezza, hors d'oeuvres

mihrab, a niche in a mosque that indicates the direction of Mecca

milleem, a penny

muezzin, the person at a mosque who leads the call to prayer

mukhtar, the head of a village

musakhan, a Palestinian dish made of chicken, sumac, pine nuts, and bread

Nabulsi, an olive oil-based soap made in Nablus

nakbeh, cataclysm or catastrophe (the loss of Palestine)

nidr, a contractual prayer in which the petitioner couples a request with a conditional promise

Nush-kur Allah, Thank God

'oud, a pear-shaped, stringed musical instrument

pantalones, pants

piaster, a unit of currency (coins)

Rose el Yusuf, an Egyptian magazine

Sabah el-khair, Good morning

sadaka, alms given to the needy

salaam, peace

sambusik, stuffed pastries

samideen, those who choose to remain, despite hardships

saru, evergreen trees

say-wa-do, a number in backgammon (colloquial)

Sayyid, Mister

Sayyidna, Our master

service, a communal taxi

sfeeha, a meat pie

Shabuoth, a Jewish feast that commemorates the revelation of the Law on Mount Sinai, also called Shavu'ot

shaish baish, backgammon (colloquial)

shawarma, a wrap containing meat grilled on a spit

sheikh, an elder of a tribe, a revered wise man, or an Islamic scholar

shukran, thank you

Sitt (or *Sitti*), My lady (a title of respect for a woman), or My grandmother

smeed, semolina

snober, pine nuts

souk, a marketplace

sumac, ground dried berries from a flowering plant, used as a spice

sura, a chapter in the Koran

tabak, a round straw mat

tabbouleh, a salad made with bulgur, tomato, cucumber, parsley, and mint

taboon, a clay oven

tahini, a paste of ground sesame seeds used in cooking and as a sauce with *falafil*

takka wigri, a baseball-like game played with sticks

tawla, a backgammon table

tcharawyeh, an Iraqi head-dress (a turban), usually worn over a cap

thobe, an ankle-length women's garment, usually with long sleeves, similar to a robe

turmus, lupini beans

Um, Mother, or "the mother of"

wadi, a valley

wlad sharameet, children of prostitutes

Yu hibbuni, God loves me

za'atar, a spice mixture made from dried thyme and oregano, toasted sesame seeds, and salt

zaghareet, a ululation, performed to honor someone or in celebration of a wedding, for example

zbune, an ankle-length striped Baghdadi garment worn with a sash or belt with gilded fringes and gold stripes over satin or silk

z'ut, snuff

Acknowledgments

My thanks go out to all who have shared my journey especially my writers' group. My sincere thanks go to my daughter, Ellen, with whom I've exchanged both ideas and editorial suggestions, and whose perseverance is my inspiration. Also my unwavering graditude goes to my son, Jeff, who has touched my life with his talents, humor, and creativity. And to my husband, Albert, whose faith in my work has given me the courage to create fiction so I can better understand truth.

Heartfelt gratitude and blessings also go to my dear friends: to Ann Walton Sieber, who co-founded our writers' group with me, and to Karen Müller, who tirelessly edited, advised, and encouraged me. I couldn't have done it without you.

About the Author

May Mansoor Munn was born in Jerusalem to Palestinian-Quaker parents. May's native language is Arabic, but she fell in love with the English language when she attended the Friends Girls' School in Ramallah, the West Bank. At 15, She left for college in the United States, receiving, at 19, a BA in both English and Religion from Earlham College in Richmond, Indiana. She later minored in history at the University of Houston.

She taught at the Friends Girls' School in Ramallah, where her mother had taught before her. She married and moved back to the States, settling in Houston, where she taught world history. But her real passion has always been writing.

She continued to visit family and friends in Jerusalem, and in Ramallah and the West Bank. She did considerable research on the political background of *Ladies of the Dance*, but she says her most authentic source was her mother, Ellen Audi Mansur.

Over the years, May has written and published essays, articles, poems, and short stories. Her work has appeared in the *Christian Science Monitor*, *Ms* magazine, and in several book collections of writings from the Middle East. This is her first published novel.

May lives in Houston with her husband, Albert, and Bisseh, their friendly Quaker cat.